DARK SNOW

DARK SNOW

Mike Lawrence

ISBN: 0692615423

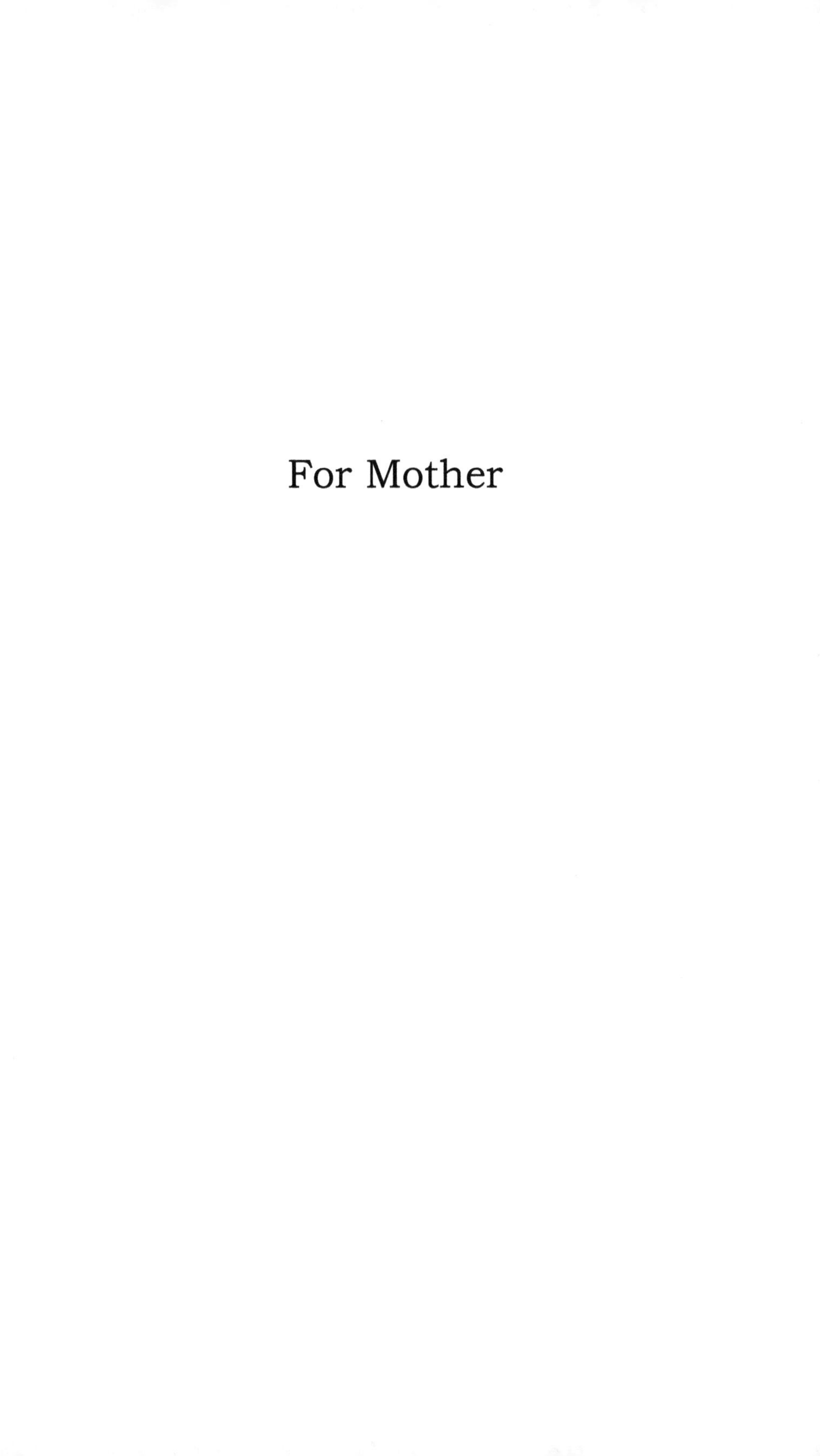

For Mother

1 Coins

Bill Shultz had handed me eighty cents for ten hours of cutting firewood, and I was euphoric. The sun was gone, it was another cold night, and I was walking home to my sixteenth birthday dinner, January 6, 1886. I could not have been happier even if Shultz had paid me the full man's wage of a dollar. I had bested my father.

Everyone called me a big boy, and, indeed, I was at five-ten, but it was mostly because I had matured before any of the other nine boys I knew my age. Some men had said, "Remmy, you look like a man." Still, I was all arms and legs, not built for brute strength. Bulldog Shultz liked to hire me because I could go all day without a break, something even he couldn't do.

I was a good worker, and I had to admit that Father had trained me that way. I liked my father. No, that's not true. At that time, I loved my father, but I did not like him. We could not seem to agree on very much, and I was often mad at him. That night was no exception. Just the thought of beating him at something upset me—not the winning, that was great, but because it was Father.

Let me explain. Father upset me, win, lose, or draw. Anything that reminded me of him was upsetting. He did not want me to work for Shultz, but I did, which made me the winner. Still, thinking about it also reminded me of Father, making me still a loser.

So, as I was walking along the narrow country lane covered with nearly a foot of mud-spattered snow, with deep wagon ruts and frozen mush, I saw a nice roundish ball of slush and kicked it to the side, thinking, *Take that, Father.* The poorly aimed kick shocked my toes and reminded me that haste makes waste, a stitch in time saves nine, he that seeks trouble never misses, and several other non-helpful maxims. I did not assault any more ice.

I was walking on home territory, so the millions of stars and the sliver of a waxing moon dispensed adequate light. I certainly wasn't afraid; Eastern Kansas was far from the frontier and about the only danger was the possibility a bobcat might mistake me for a mouse.

Mother had demanded—no, that's not the right word, she never demanded. She had urged me to wear two pair of woolies, her special quilted pants, a pair of denims, two shirts, and a substantial winter coat. I'd had the coat off all day and unbuttoned as I walked home. She'd seemed convinced that some freak storm was going to blast me into a block of ice without all that protection. I could have walked across Canada and not felt the cold.

I walked a zigzag path along the lanes heading east to section four of Mission Township and home. It was an easy walk, except for the ice, which I mostly avoided by walking through the untouched snow on the edges of the lanes.

At the corner of the timber our family rented for our hogs, I left the lane, climbed the massive corner post, and jumped into the pen. The winter had been so bad that Father had sold most of the porkers before they froze to death, keeping three in a shed.

I had no difficulty threading my way through the trees in the faint light because I had been following the same path for as long as I could remember; I could walk it in my sleep if it came to that. Still, as I ventured forward, I began to shorten my stride. Mother would have my favorite cherry pie for the meal, but even that image could not hold the anxiety at bay.

To this day, I do not understand that dread. It was hardly the first time I had experienced it either. It had to do with Father, but I have never quite put my finger on the cause, though I know some of it.

As I neared the edge of the woods, I could see moonlight between the trees. By then I was fairly dragging my feet along the path. I stopped just inside the tree line. I looked at the familiar south side of our small house—cabin, really, with its meager shed roof over the back door and the full porch along the east side. The two side windows shared the inviting warmth of the fireplace and kerosene lanterns.

There was a patch of the warm light on the snow in front of the house.

My eye caught some movement to the right at the tree line just north of the house. It was some distance away, but I could clearly see a saddled horse tied to a tree.

It seemed no more than an instant later that a shot shattered the calm of the night—and my dull life with it. I jerked my head back to the house in time to see a yellow flash at the windows followed by another report, then three more.

2 Run

Perhaps Mother should have given me a burly hat as well as the coat, because my brain froze. I could not think. Someone fired in my house five times, but I could not have spoken it; I was not even thinking it. My thoughts, if I had any, were moving at a glacier's pace.

That changed when a man opened our front door and stepped onto our porch. As he looked away to the north, I realized two things nearly at once: the man was holding a six-shooter, and I had to run. That pistol took my thoughts from ice to lightning in a flash.

Even as I turned to run, I saw the man look my way. That one instant still haunts me sometimes. In the span of time so short it could not be measured, I understood that all of my family had been murdered and that the man had killed them. I did not know the man, but I knew he intended to kill me too. I knew he saw me, or at least my movement. It is bewildering that so much went through my mind in that blip of time. I don't remember having another thought of any kind for perhaps a half-mile of running.

If you have never worn heavy boots and thirty pounds of wool to sprint through snow halfway to your knees, then you may not have an idea of what I experienced. I crashed through our trees, glancing off more than one, and vaulted over the corner post without breaking stride.

I crossed the lane and entered our neighbors' partially cleared stand of trees. There was light, enough to allow me to see the dark trunks against the slightly less dark openness. Even so, I barely dodged several big trees and hit some small ones. All that wool gave me enough protection to keep going.

Out of the timber, I began to cross an open field, still with no constructive thought other than to keep moving. On the verge of collapse, I slipped on some ice, plunging chest-first into the snow, plowing the stinging powder into my face and down my neck. I lay there, unable to do anything but gasp for air. Finally pushing myself to my knees, I shook myself like a dog and glanced behind me; I saw no man with a big pistol.

I began to chew over what I might do to get away. I looked back again and this time the line of my footprints was so glaring in the smidgen of light, it looked like a dagger pointing at my heart. Then a horse whinnied in the distance.

My legs suddenly took on new life, and I sprinted again, though with more control so that I could continue to puzzle out a way to stay alive. In those days, houses were sparse in the county. The nearest neighbor was another two miles. With more instinct than thought, I got myself oriented; I was on the Jensen farm at least a mile from home. I am still not sure how my body, after a day of heavy labor, survived the punishment of that run. Still, it was not over.

As my brain dealt with the task of finding safety and ignoring all the pain messages my body was sending to it, the image of the cave rose above all else. My legs had changed direction before I was fully aware of the possibilities of refuge.

When I made it to the edge of a narrow, brush-covered gully, I looked back again, no longer worried about the tracks, only the man who was still not in sight. I plunged into the thicket, recklessly fighting my way through, getting hit in the shoulder when a whip-like sapling slipped from my hand, and then having a long tendril of a wild rose bush rake my face. At least the man's horse would have to take the long way around.

On the other side, I faced another flat, snow-covered field, but it was the one I wanted. I ran again, my lungs desperate for air, but I ignored the pain because safety was so close.

I began to see other tracks in the snow, more with every step. Jensen and his sons had been cutting firewood there for a week. The place was nonstop footprints, stacked one on another. Wood chips and sawdust were everywhere. Not even Big Jim could track me through the mess.

For the first time in my run, I had more than desperate hope.

I passed the small storage shed on sledge rails that held all the axes and saws. I wanted to grab an ax, but I knew Jensen kept it locked tight, so I ran straight to the creek. The challenge of finding one stunted cedar tree while running through the snow at night threatened to defeat me, but the memory of my former playground sent me unerringly to it. I jumped headfirst past the gnarled tree, down the creek bank, thumping into the dense brush at the entrance before rolling back into the opening.

How long I lay there, sucking in chunks of icy air, I cannot say; it seemed interminable, but my brain had nearly shut down, so I was not keeping track of time or anything else. As my breathing was catching up with my needs, I realized the cave smelled of skunk. Swiping my arms around, I established I was alone.

It was only a washed-out hole on the creek bank a couple of feet high, four feet to the back, and long enough to lie in. Not much, but with the screen of brush, I had a chance.

Three of us had found it when I was about six and accidentally fell in. It had become our secret hideout until it would no longer hold all of us.

With my breathing close to normal, I began to try to sort out what was happening to me, something I would continue to do for months to come. My long escape with its load of fear left no room for considering the philosophical niceties of my plight. In the cave, my first serious thought was: *What the hell is going on*? Why would a stranger want to kill us? I was so exhausted and confused that I could not think much beyond that.

Nevertheless, my logical bent helped me deal with how to avoid being murdered. I knew a man was chasing me, and I knew he wanted me dead. I knew I was in a good hiding spot and that trying to outrun a man on horseback was insane. Also, I knew if he found me in the cave, I had no chance.

I can't say I relaxed exactly, but I did ease up a bit on the tension. For the first time (and if you think I'm a degenerate for saying this, too bad) I began to think of my family. Instead of seeing only the muzzle flashes, I visualized my family as they died. I didn't want to; they simply appeared in all their gore. With tears rolling down my cheeks, the first shot echoed in my mind, and I saw Father fall. Then Mother, Lyle, Wilber, Doris. All dead. My stomach flipped; I dry heaved.

That's when a horse snorted, rousing me from the anguish. I pushed emotions to the side, quickly checking to see if all was ready to receive the killer without him spotting me. My clothes were dark enough, but I was jolted with the realization that my face must shine like a lantern in the gloom. With my jackknife, I jabbed at the frozen dirt and rubbed a chunk of it over my face and neck, with the stench of animal feces filling my nose. It went well enough until I pushed some in my left eye causing a burn that brought a flood of tears, adding to the icicles on my cheek.

I forced myself to finish the job with one eye shut tight. Then I lay still, waiting for the man's next move while trying to blink my eye clean. I concentrated on catching the sounds of the man or his horse.

Minutes passed with no dangerous harbinger. In fact, in the stillness of the snow-covered winter's night in the farmlands of Kansas, I began to wonder if I had gone deaf.

The whinny of the nearby horse answered that question. Soon I could hear the muffled click of iron horseshoes striking the snow-blanketed ice of the creek. I should explain that it was not really a creek—we boys always thought of it as a creek, but it was what we farmers call a slough, a narrow depression in an open field that carries water to the river and sometimes has standing water a few inches deep, or standing ice as it did that night. Brush and trees covered the slough, as they did in most others in those days.

With the man approaching, I concentrated on breathing noiselessly and listened to the clacking of the horseshoes, with the occasional soft scrunch of a slip. The sounds slowly faded to nothing, giving me reason to hope. Nevertheless, it was short-lived, as the distant click-click returned.

My heart began to thump louder, even as I subdued my breathing again. I pulled my coat collar over my mouth to hide the vapor. I was as ready as I could be.

Just as the first flicker of movement appeared through the inky brush, my right leg convulsed in a full-force, hip-to-knee hamstring charley horse that shot pain in all directions. Teeth clenched tight, I fought off the screech. Tears blurred my sight of the man leading his horse past the brush.

Almost as suddenly as it came, the cramp loosened. It was all I could do to hold in a sharp sigh of relief. When the faint clop-clop of the hoofs faded, I took the chance of moving around to stretch and loosen my overworked legs.

The horse sound dwindled to nothing. The blanket of white fluff absorbed most of the sounds of nature, and I returned to the land of the deafened.

My penchant for logic returned as I considered the incredulity of the man leading his horse onto the unfamiliar ice in the middle of the night. I knew then he was no outdoorsman, let alone a tracker. He should never have brought his horse along to make such a ruckus.

The horse snickered, close again. Peering through the brush, I caught glimpses of movement through the trees. The man was walking along the opposite edge of the draw, no doubt to see if any tracks led into that part of the open field.

With no prints leaving the creek or work area, the man would know I had to be somewhere inside that circle. What would he do about it? I tried to think of a way to get away, but I believed if I left the cave, the man would find me, so I stayed put.

My right leg locked in another spasm that I worked out while reliving the horror of the night. When the shooting had begun, I'd frozen, locked up, grown roots. If I had not seen the pistol, no telling how long I would have stood there, trying to make sense of the irrational.

My mind has revisited those five flashes of the gun, sleeping and waking, nearly every day since then. Who I am today is partly, sadly, the result of the murder of most of the Bevans family.

That night, my mind and body finally slid past the limits of endurance into a struggling sleep, one to prepare me for the next formidable day.

3 Hide

I jerked awake to the steady thwack thwack of trees under attack by the axe men, and I was glad for it. It brought me from a nightmare in which I walked toward Father, pumping round after round into him with my .22 rifle. Almost as bad, the image changed to Bill Shultz shooting at me. The idea of me killing Father made my stomach queasy. Father could be a pain, but I would never hurt him.

Looking through the shrubs, I could see the day was well along, sunny but frozen. I, on the other hand, was frozen but not so sunny. I'd woken many times through the night and pumped my legs and arms to warm up. That, and Mother's insistence on wool, probably saved my life.

I shuddered from the cold, and my jaw throbbed from chattering all night. My legs felt as though I actually had run through Canada. I could barely feel my toes.

Squirming around, thumping my arms and legs helped. I began to feel needles of pain in my toes. Needing to pee, I turned on my side but dribbled on my pants.

Buttoned up, I rolled on my stomach and quickly fell asleep, burdened with images of Father, Mother, Lyle, Wilber, and Doris, all chasing me, all bloody, all dead.

I woke in an instant with tears already blotting my vision. For the first time since leaving Shultz, I spoke aloud, "They are really dead." The sounds tumbled through a knotted throat, but I repeated the fact three more times. My tears turned to sobs, sobs to whimpers, whimpers to silence.

It was some time before I returned to the cave and the chopping and the cutting and the man lurking somewhere, waiting for me to make a mistake. I rolled to my back and tried to focus my thoughts again. I closed my eyes and tried to picture the man. There was little for me to go on with one brief glance and a walk by in the dark with my eyes flooded. Besides his gun, which seemed to get larger with every remembrance, the hat was unusual, with a short brim and a high crown, with maybe a touch of red on it.

I gave up on the man and concentrated on the horse. I clearly remembered a saddle, with a rifle in a scabbard and saddlebags behind. The horse was dark, with a white patch on its left rump. My image of the horse was firm, probably because life was still normal when I'd first seen it.

With no more memories to go on, I then wasted a great deal of time considering a host of harebrained ideas about getting away. There is no reason to list them now, even if one might have been a serious option. I also dreamed of food and warm fires, which yielded pretty much the same result. I was insistent on one thing, though: the killer was nearby, in the cold, and not sitting by a fire in town. My new motto was: If I have to suffer, he'd better be out here too.

At about midday, the work noises stopped, and I heard Jensen's oxen bawling as he gave them the bullwhip crack of encouragement to pull the heavy sledge loaded with wood. I tried to check the time, but low clouds blocked the sun. I envisioned the men eating lunch in the warm Jensen house with their two big fireplaces and new wood cook stove.

My stomach growled, and my nose bragged it could smell the fried chicken. A chunk of year-old salt-pork would have been tasty about then. I had never gone twenty-four hours without food before. Even so, I fell asleep.

The sounds of woodcutting once again pulled me from my sleep. I worked my arms and legs enough to warm up as I listened to the men work. Melancholy began to come over me. My logical preference dozed off while emotions played over me, an orphan alone in a hole in the ground, starving, every muscle aching, pitiful and feeling worse by the minute: I nearly lost hope then.

After wallowing in misery for a time, I thought about the coming night, and logic returned. Again, I spoke aloud: "I refuse to spend another night in this hole." With that declaration, I rehashed escape plans. My best idea was to wait for dark, hoping the cloud cover remained, and crawl along the slough to the Neosho River. I imagined the river would have enough ice for me to cross to the other side, as cold as it had been this year. From there—I would work something out. The man might shoot me, but I would not freeze or starve in a hole.

I found I could not concentrate long enough to fill in any details on my plan. I looked outside again and saw a few flakes of snow falling. We had had snow nearly every week since November, but to me it was always beautiful. An additional benefit was that a pleasant snow would provide some cover for my escape. As I watched, I began to relax. I felt warm for the first time all day. The lazy path of the flakes to earth sent me back to my dreams.

Loud shouts roused me brusquely. It was nearly as dark as night, and I could not see the covering brush. All I could make out was the snow coming down by the wagonloads. I could hear it striking the ground in an unending crinkling of compaction. From the men's excitement and the clanging of metal on metal, I could tell they were hurling tools in the shed and rushing home. In this mess, they would probably have to trust the oxen to find the way.

I struggled to get out of the cave to go after them but quickly realized they were already sledding along. I made it past my protective screen when the sounds began to diminish, and I stopped, still on all fours.

As quiet reclaimed the streambed, I shivered, but not from the cold. The snow had turned against me. I crept back into the hated hole.

I considered crawling to the river right then, but once there, how could I navigate in the blackout? People who walked in blinding snow always ended up going in circles until they froze to death. Besides, I had never been across the river. There were too many soft spots in the ice to consider walking on it very far.

I banged my fists against the wall of the cave, more than once.

As nightfall took away the last memory of light, I curled into a tight ball. I had to fight the panic that threatened to send me scuttling insanely through the dark snow. Yet, even that thought seemed pleasant compared to another night in the cave.

4 Coyote

Trapped in another bizarre nightmare, this time about Wilber, I heard growling, but it was not Wilber. I fought my way out of the dream, only to face a very real coyote and wish for the dream back. My heart instantly jumped to double beats as I attempted to push myself through the back wall of the cave, slapping wildly for my jackknife, which had wandered off somewhere.

In that second of thrashing, the fangs disappeared, the critter no doubt frightened by my display of weapon dexterity. Once I found the knife, I closed it and put it in my coat pocket where I was less likely to hurt myself. When I looked out, the snowfall was still generous, but I could see trees across the waterway. The wind was still double-quick, yet the clouds were less ominous. I decided I might be able to travel.

As I warmed up my arms and legs, I mused about why the coyote had come so close; I guessed the skunk smell covered my own. More importantly, he wouldn't be roaming the area if the man were nearby. I decided it was time to risk it all.

Decision made, I rolled onto all fours, scraping the ceiling, every muscle carping, and crawled from the cave. But, crawling was nothing compared to standing. Struggling to get my legs under me and keep my balance, I thought of old Mr. Kyser on his porch. For the first time, I understood why the man groaned so much when he got out of the rocker.

I studied the tracks, seeing that the beast had come from the river and left me to continue east. In my mind, the killer should be in that direction, because the tree line in the center of the field would have given him the best cover to watch the whole area. However, trusting the coyote, I pushed east.

After a couple of hundred yards, I came to the headwaters of the slough. It became a solid wall of undergrowth that even the coyote did not want to push through. He had turned to the left to enter the plowed field surrounding the creek, so I followed.

In the open, drawing on every skill I had learned about tracking animals, I scrutinized every bump and dimple in the snow for any hint of the man. I walked in the animal tracks until I reached the point at which the clear farmland circled around the brush. The paw prints continued in a straight line to the middle of the section, right where I thought the man should be waiting.

I stood and slowly turned, searching every quadrant, counting the odds. I wanted a glimpse of the tree line, but no amount of straining my eyes helped. I muttered to the wind, "The coyote says the man is gone. Of course, he mistook me for a skunk, but I'm going to follow anyway."

The wind was the worst I had ever experienced, even in our most violent thunderstorms. It formed snow eddies around me as I walked. I sketched a rough map of the area in my mind. I knew the Missouri-Kansas-Texas rails angled northeast from Osage Mission to Fort Scott, even though I had never been that far east. I thought all I had to do was walk straight for roughly five miles. I could then follow the line to Fort Scott. I had already decided that going to Erie was out. The killer was probably waiting there; besides, Father had never trusted that sheriff. Mission was closer, but I did not want to endanger all those kids.

As I walked, I did my best imitation of an owl by swinging my head side-to-side, looking for any hint of the man. The tree line appeared right where my mental map placed it, and the coyote tracks went straight in; I followed. Once in the trees, I actually had to mop sweat from my face. I took deep breaths to calm myself again. The snarl of the wind and the creaking of branches under its attack kept me poor company, but I was out of the hole, safe and on the move. I think I smiled, at least inside.

To keep myself on a straight line in the storm, I wanted to be near the middle of the row, so I carefully worked my way north, watching for the one tree I knew was near the middle. In ten yards, the massive cedar began to materialize.

The tree's lower branches were so thick that I could have crawled under them and been protected fully from the wind. The thought was so tempting I separated some branches to look. I froze, heart thudding yet again.

Empty food cans. New.

I held the branch, not even moving my eyes for fear of attracting attention, of the man shooting me. The man had eaten a meal here.

The strain finally forced me to blink, but the movement did not bring shots. My wheezing lungs did not lure any bullets. Back in control, I kneeled close and studied the cans. The food had at least a day's crust on it. The coyote was right, after all.

I crossed the next open field with no more jolts to my already jangled nerves. I passed through the hedgerow and rested at the edge of a narrow lane, ready to duck for cover if a shadow appeared. The snow was piling up quickly, so I crossed the lane and squeezed through the next hedgerow. I stared at all the snow ahead of me—so much snow.

A different kind of jolt hit me—my family, dead. I don't know why it hit me so hard just then. It was hardly news, but it flipped my stomach as if I had never known they were gone. I forced myself to push them from my thoughts; I had too far to go.

The snow was now knee-deep between higher drifts. Every step was a struggle. Eventually, the center hedgerow of the section came into view. I grabbed a small tree to keep from dropping to my knees. The desire to lie down was becoming painful. There was little shelter there, so reluctantly I stepped into the next half of the section of snow-blanketed farmland.

If someone had thrashed me with a stick for half an hour instead, I would have felt better. I crawled over downed trees, bumping into stumps hidden in the snow, all while pushing through three- and four-foot drifts. It was a playground for the demons of anguish.

I made it but reckoned I had at least another two miles before reaching the rails. There was no question: shelter now, forget straight lines.

Staggering on, I searched for some place to hide from the wind. The next half-mile ate what little reserve I had left. My muscles seized every few steps; I spent more time waiting for my body to function than I did moving; but, without cover, I would die.

Finally, I saw through the snow a thicket of cedars. I crawled under the low branches where the ground was dry, and nothing but the noise of the wind could reach me. I think I was asleep before I stopped moving. I know my legs continued to quiver and spasm long after.

5 Cedars

Muscle cramps woke me several times in the night. I felt for the cave wall two times before remembering I had traded it for a new hole. I had no way of knowing if it was worth the trade, but I did know it came at a considerable price.

When I finally opened my eyes to shades of dark gray instead of tar, I pushed myself to one elbow and looked around at my new hellhole. I was alive, though not sure I wanted to be.

Lying back, I pulled my right foot toward my butt, expecting howling pain, but getting only low-level screeching. I worked both legs and arms before crawling to a small pile of snow that had filtered through the trees. There I ate as much as possible, dulling my hunger even as the shivers set in.

Crawling under the interlocking limbs to the edge of the grove, I tunneled through snow at least four feet deep before seeing daylight. Using a tree about three inches thick as a support, I managed to pull myself upright. I held on, waiting for my head to stop spinning and my eyes to focus. The wind was blowing so much snow around that I could not tell if any was actually falling. A few minutes later, still holding onto the tree, I realized there was a white oak tree nearly two feet thick that I could use for a bit of shelter.

I knew my legs would never make it through the snow piled up to my belly, so I stretched out on top and used my arms to sort of swim to the tree. Then I started digging down to the ground with only my hands. It was tough going, but in time, I had a hole that sheltered me from the wind, even as snow blew in from the top.

Propping myself against the tree trunk, I waited for my body to stop shaking. I watched the clouds scudding overhead at an alarming rate and was able to catch enough flashes of the sun to tell me my bearings and the time of day.

It hardly mattered. I had nothing left to give. Without food, there was no way I could make it to the M-K-T. I was not sure I could even stand again. Digging the snow out could have been my last work ever.

My eyes closed, and I could feel my whole body shutting down. Numbness spread from my toes and fingers to my legs and arms. The noise of the wind seemed to fade away. With my eyes closed, the light gradually went away. I was conscious only of breathing.

"Remmy, that you?"

The sound was inside me; I wanted to brush it away like a fly. “Remmy.” I thought I should open my eyes to see the fly, but they refused to open. Then the fly seemed to be shaking me. Somehow, I lifted my left eyelid and saw not a fly but a hand.

The man!

I tried to strike at the man, but my arms would not move. Then my brain jumped to what passed for full alert, and my right eye also opened. *He has me. How do I get away? Wait. Not the man. Familiar.*

"Jim Bighorse. Remember?"

The stupor faded and I could see the man I knew well. Big Jim. I croaked, "Jim. Sorry. Thought you were someone else."

"You a mess. What happened?" Jim used a snowshoe to dig out more snow so he could step into the hole beside me. He began to rub my arms and legs.

I tried several times to speak, but my throat was too froggy to get much out. Jim wrapped me in a waterproof cloth, and gave me some of his water. He also had a small amount of honey with him, which soothed my throat. As I warmed, it became easier to talk. The story dripped out at first, through a thick rasp, but gaining speed, it tumbled. Jim handed me more water between bursts of the tale. I ended with, "I tried to use all the things you taught me about tracking to avoid him following me. I think I've done it."

I should say here that Jim was an Osage who had chosen to stay in the area when the government had ordered his people to a different reservation in the Indian Territory some fifteen years earlier. He had learned the ways of whites, owned his own land and intended to die on it. No one felt a need to dispute the issue with a man a foot taller and a hundred pounds heavier than the next largest man around.

Jim answered, "Couldn't track you in this snow. You safe now, but what you do?"

"I was heading for the railroad. I thought I would try to make my way to Fort Scott for the sheriff. I guess you found me first."

"Got traps set round here. Need find 'em under this snow."

"I don't know what to do now. I don't think he's a tracker. I know he can't follow me now, but what'll he do next? I saw him. He can't just leave me."

"I check traps and look for man. I see man, he not bother you."

Knowing what Jim meant lifted my spirits better than a hot meal, almost. "If you don't find him, should I go to Fort Scott?"

"You know why he want you?"

"I have no idea why he wanted to kill us."

"You remember seeing him?"

"He walked right past the cave, leading his horse," I added, disgusted.

"While trying find you?" Jim shook his head in disbelief.

"I know. That's when I knew he was no tracker. The only thing I saw for sure was a strange hat, and the horse had one white spot on the left flank."

Jim asked, "You have food?"

"Nothing in two days."

"We fix," he said as he fished out jerky and cornbread. While I ate, Jim extended the shelter area, then collected some dry wood and soon had a small fire sending much-needed warmth my way.

Jim set up a tripod of branches and started a small pot of snow melting over the fire. He threw some coffee beans in the pot, the aroma setting off a new round of hunger pangs. "You need someth'n hot drink. We warm up can beans. Don't fill on jerky."

"Thanks, Jim. I'm feeling some better. The cornbread was great. Did Red Swan make it?" She was Jim's wife.

"Course. Wouldn't want my cornbread." He worked the fire, adding just the right amount of wood to melt the snow without wasting wood.

Jim once told me his name in Osage, but I've forgotten it except that it means *Bighorse.* Jim was the white name given to him when he attended school at the Mission. He was a man when he was in school, but again, no one argued with him. Some whites just called him *Big,* but not to his face. In addition to his height, he had a chest like a cracker barrel and hands twice the size of mine. Yet, his face always looked soft, like a small child's; not small, just tender looking.

I learned from him that most of the Osage were big, though few were as tall as Jim. They had been the biggest men of the plains in their day. The other tribes feared them, but they were a small tribe and had to have allies to survive. Even so, they seldom lost battles.

When Jim handed me the steaming cup of coffee, it seemed to loosen my thoughts. "I should go home to bury my family."

"No. I go see if man near. You stay night."

"It should be safe with this snow."

"Safe for me, not you. If man gone, I take you home. It is settled."

I knew there was no argument now. While I finished my coffee, Jim began cutting cedar branches, slicing the small branches with the green leaves into a large pile. Then he placed leafed branches against the snow walls to provide protection from the cold. Long cedar branches were stacked across the opening to form a solid roof.

Finished with my coffee, I fell asleep. When I woke, Jim had a cedar-lined cave facing the fire for me.

"Jim, this is great. It's better than my bed at home. Is there room for both of us?"

"Have waterproof, sleep here." He indicated a spot near the stack of firewood, so I knew he would be keeping the fire going all night.

"You didn't have to do all this for me. I can wrap in a waterproof and sleep on the snow."

"Later. Now you need get well." I did not argue.

6 Jim

Sleeping in the dugout with a full stomach put a generous smile on my face when I woke. Jim had kept the fire going all night but left at first light. That meant my first morning chore was adding wood to the fire and setting a pan of snow over it before going in search of firewood. I was up to the task, but just. I gathered only a couple of hours' worth of dry wood.

I drank the first pan of water as hot as I could stand, warming me from the inside out. Oats went in the next batch, which yielded an unsweetened mush. I added jerky to the third pan to soften it up, which made it more like eating fresh meat.

It was easy to follow Jim's advice to work slowly, because I had the strength of a baby and the stamina of a twenty-year-old dog. I managed to collect enough wood by taking numerous breaks and one nap. Yet, rest time was no fun. Constant images of my family, the shootings, and the chase would not allow me to relax. Living through it once was nasty, but over and over was torture.

By sunset, I was sitting by the fire, poking at it with a long stick, eyes glazed over, stomach in knots from worry and frustration. Jim was nearly beside me when I finally heard him. "Jim! I'm glad to see you! What'd you find?"

He undid his snowshoes and removed an extra pair from his pack for me. He handed me more cornbread and jerky before sitting on a pile of wood. All that without a word—I knew there was trouble. "Still not safe. Sheriff there now. Think you shot them."

"What? Me? How could anyone think that?" I was shouting. "Why would I kill my own family?" I would have jumped up, but the squat roof stopped me.

"Sheriff not know about man."

On my knees and ready to run, I said, "I have to go tell him."

"Sheriff arrest you. Can't go."

I rocked back onto my haunches, mouth open, eyes wide, head shaking.

Jim said, "Sit. Tell again all you know that night."

I talked; Jim questioned. Darkness enveloped us. We tended the fire and we ate jerky.

Jim concluded the session: "Stay here day, two. I check what sheriff doing. We decide soon what you do."

In frustration, I threw a stick into the fire, causing hot coals to fly. One landed close to Jim. I looked away, pretending I had not noticed. "Don't know if I can stand it here alone."

I could see Jim on the edge of my vision, watching the red coal sizzle its way through the icy ground, sending up a small geyser of steam. I picked up another stick and poked the frozen ground in front of me. When the heat of the coal was gone, Jim said, "Can't be Osage if can't be alone one day."

I put a little heat in my voice, "I like being alone, but not now. I just, well, I have too much time to think." I still could not look at Jim. I was upset with myself about striking out at the fire, a childish move that embarrassed me in front of Big Jim.

He stood and undid a string from his pack. "Brought traps. Tomorrow, you set these. Show you mine. Skin and clean catch. Want hide and meat from my traps."

That stirred up some interest for me, and I started to comment when Jim went on, "Sheriff maybe watch me. Know we friends."

A touch of fear prickled my neck. I nearly squeaked, "You can't come back?"

Jim twisted his mouth into what I knew passed for a smile. "No one follow me."

I relaxed a little. Having Jim on my side was good, but it did not dampen all the fear.

That night, as I tried to find sleep, I thought about Jim and Father. Jim had helped me survive the past few days because of all he had taught me since I'd met him. Once I'd mastered the skills of trapping, skinning, and scraping animal pelts, I'd been able to sell enough to help the family income and buy shells for the .22 rifle. That in turn had brought more meat to the dinner table. Yet, it all irritated Father no end. The thing between Father and Jim was hard for me to fathom.

7 Traps

I opened my eyes to see Jim's hand on my shoulder. This time, it was reassuring. "It can't be morning already."

He smiled and handed me the extra snowshoes. "Put these on. Show you traps." My time of recovery was over. For the next hour, we walked Jim's trap line and talked about hunting, fishing, anything except the shooting. Jim did more talking in that hour than in a typical month.

Returning to camp with three frozen rabbits, Jim said, "Skin these, and scrape the pelts. Slice off what meat you can. Set own traps. I return two days."

"Two days! I'll be nuts by then."

"You have work. Have idea, tell you when back."

Jim was right. The days passed in a blur of work. I struggled to remove the frozen pelts. Jim had shown me how to use the fire to thaw just the pelts without damage, but it took time. In between hauling firewood, with the help of Jim's hatchet, I built a simple rack to stand over the fire for drying meat. I also gathered green hickory to smoke the meat. With all of that, I only managed to set two new traps the first day. All the running around on snowshoes was killing my legs.

The best news was that I had a restful and nightmare—free sleep both nights.

Jim approached late Tuesday afternoon as I was drying more meat. He brought food, clothes, and a thick wool blanket. The food included dried fruit.

With a mouth full of apple slices, I garbled, "This is great!"

Jim, as usual, got down to business. "Sheriff still want you. Best way go big city north, get lost with people." I stopped chewing. "Work until safe come home."

I shifted the apple around before swallowing it as a lump. I could feel my eyebrows scrunched together.

Despondency dropped on me like a wagonload of sleet. "It's that bad?"

Jim went on. "Father Joseph at St. Catherine send letter to church close stockyards, Holy Name Church. You go there, tell him where you living. He tell you when safe."

Fear edged my voice. "I have to run? What'll I do in the city?"

"Get job. Stockyard good. You know work."

I slumped with the thought. Jim meant Kansas City. How could I survive in a city full of people? Where would I live? How could I ever get a job? No one had trained me to live in a city.

"It not easy, but you can do. I become like white man. You become like city man."

The image buoyed me only a little. I considered taking off for the wilds of the west and living as a trapper, but I knew that was just a dream. I knew a couple of older boys who had gone off to KC; if they could, I could. "I'll do it. I guess city people are just like us." I hoped my words showed strength and resolve, but to me they sounded as hollow as a dead elm tree. "Do you have to go back tonight?"

"Yes. Dry more rabbit to take with you. May not be back next day. Bring some money next time." Brushing my thanks aside, Jim was gone.

I spent another day searching for firewood, running traps, drying rabbit, and trying to ignore the memories of the gunshots, the fear, the horrible loss. That day, Wednesday the 13th, was the one-week anniversary of losing my family, a day filled with too many memories. Tears came at odd moments. I tried to keep busy, but the images and pain bored through the zeal. That night, the wicked dreams came in droves.

I had to drag myself through the next day, but at least it had one pleasant difference. I had set one trap with breadcrumbs, and a young turkey fell for it. I roasted a big chunk of the breast wrapped in the skin and ate it almost too hot to hold. After all the jerky, it nearly made me cry. I dried the remainder to split with Jim.

The next morning, Jim brought some good news. "Told sheriff I take care of family. Sheriff glad."

The idea hit me hard. I tried to hold myself steady but sagged and sat. I put my hands over my eyes. Jim waited. Knowing I would never see them again, not even at a funeral, stabbed me deeper than anything else so far. I tried to speak, cleared my throat, and managed a gravelly, “Where will you bury them?”

Jim asked, “Mission?”

I thought for a couple of minutes before nodding. “With good people and away from where they....”

I had to compose myself before Jim went on. "They about finished clearing train tracks. They's rumors in Mission you dead. Some think you died in blizzard. Hope man think that."

I added, with little emotion, “Sheriff, too.”

"Walk Walnut, get on when train stop for water and coal."

"How will I manage on my own in a big city? I've never been anywhere larger than Erie."

Jim reached out his hand and touched my shoulder with the gentleness of a mother. "Won't be easy, but you do it. Have no choice.” Removing his hand, he reached into his bag. “Here eleven dollar. You get job you get city. Try stockyard. It big."

I appreciated the tenderness but felt queasy. "What if they won't take me on?"

Now Jim locked both my shoulders in a solid grip. His words came hard. "You keep look'n. You do it. You brave." He looked into my eyes for a long time.

Nodding my head, I said, "Yes, I can do it." I was well short of shouting to the world, but I did believe it.

Turning aside, all business again, Jim said, "We go'n sit here or run traps?"

I could not help but smile as I stood. "I'll get some more wood and run the traps I set. Do you want me to bring them in?"

"Yes. I set 'em new area," and he was off.

I spent the rest of the day going through the same motions as before, but with new thoughts and worries.

Knowing Jim would bury my family eased my sadness a bit. I knew I could not have done it myself, anyway. I tried not to be fearful of Kansas City, but thinking about it gave me the wobbles. It was the largest city west of Saint Louis.

In the late afternoon, the sky began to drop sleet on us. It grew in intensity, leaving nearly an inch before finally changing to snow. Jim and I skinned the animals and cut up the meat, but we did not dry it. There would not be enough time.

The next morning, with no snow in the air, Jim sliced thick chunks of bacon and let them crackle in the pan before adding potato slices. The smell had my mouth ready, but the knots in my stomach made it difficult to enjoy.

After cleaning the pan with snow, Jim said, "Time to go."

I tried to swallow what felt like a whole potato in my throat as I fought back tears. Jim encircled me with one arm and led me to the snowshoes. We shoed up and slung on our packs, Jim having brought one to me. It was so heavy I wasn't sure I could walk very far with it. I gave a nod to Jim and turned east. The brave face could not hide my fears from myself.

8 Walnut

I decided not to walk the fields, walking north to the road and then east to the railroad on untouched snow, since no one had been on the lane. At the M-K-T tracks, I found a narrow cut through the snow with high mounds of castoff on either side. Snowplows had already cleared the overnight sleet and snow. With the mounds, the cut looked to be ten feet deep. I decided not to try to jump into the valley, opting instead to snowshoe along the right-of-way. It took me most of the day to cover less than ten miles, a hike I could have done in two hours in the summer. At least the snow had stopped falling, and the sun even popped out a few minutes at a time.

I had a good look at the station house in Walnut as I lay on top of the castoff mound. The setting sun cast a pink glow on the snow. Without wind, the columns of smoke rose like skinny tree trunks.

I could see no one around, but soon saw lantern light inside. As the pink faded to gray, a man came on the platform and lit several lamps. They pushed the gray back a bit, giving the nearby snow a sickly yellow complexion.

A shrill whistle sounded from the south, and in minutes, a short train pulled onto a sidetrack several hundred feet from the depot. Its engine sat filling the air with black, sulfurous smoke. There did not seem to be any open cars, but I was not ready to make a try anyway. I needed to be doubly sure first; jumping on freight cars was not anything I had ever considered before.

Another whistle announced a train from the north. When it arrived, the engine pulled to a stop under the wooden water tower where a man lowered a long spout to fill it up. It rolled next to the coaling station and replenished the tender. With no wind, the black, sooty smoke settled all around me as the train left Walnut. When I could see again, there was a wooden box on the platform.

As soon as the southbound train was gone, the first train returned to the main tracks and took on coal and water before stopping its cars at the depot. When the train chugged away to the north and I could breathe something besides sulfurous soot, I saw an additional wooden crate.

With the sun a memory, I had no desire to climb into a dark freight car. Having seen what I needed, I shuffled into the woods on my snowshoes to look for a safe spot to sleep. It would be a colder night than the past few, because I could not risk a fire this close to town.

Well into the dark timber, I found two large trees that had grown side by side until the trunks had merged, creating a wall of wood at least four feet wide. I laid the large waterproof cloth Jim had given me on the downwind side and the smaller cloth and blanket on top. I intended to roll up in them.

Sitting on the blanket, I enjoyed the meal of cold rabbit jerky washed down with snow. I kept the full water skin under my coat for my morning drink. The day had gone well. I had a good idea how things worked at the station and figured an open car was in my near future. Thinking of it reminded me that I was heading for a major city, which in turn resulted in tension. I did my best to relax.

Snug in the wrap, waiting for sleep to creep in, my mind filled with images of Mother busy cooking at the fireplace. Tears formed at losing her, but a smile came as well, as I watched with closed eyes. I could smell the sizzling bacon in the skillet as I watched her cut the onions, sniffed them as they hit the grease. She turned and said something. I thought it strange I couldn't hear her words when I could hear the fire popping and the bacon crisping, but it didn't matter. She gave me her big, warm smile, the one that always made me feel like a prince, loved and protected.

I wanted to see more, but instead, my mind gave me the cave, the noises of cutting and chopping, it even gave me the smell of the skunk. My last image before sleep that night was of the deluge of snow, rekindling the sense of despair.

9 Paint

Like a squirrel anticipating spring, I stuck my face through the opening of the waterproofs to make sure the sun was rising and no one was around with a gun. Satisfied, I sat against the tree to eat chilly rabbit and stale bread, washed down with tepid water. I grinned because this was the day I would get a step closer to my goal. Getting lost in the city should keep me safe until the sheriff came to his senses.

I waddled on the snowshoes to the station and crawled up the snow bank again to watch what little went on at the depot. There was a horse and wagon tethered to the loading dock. The telegrapher was at his station, mostly listening to the clacking key. I could imagine men sitting close to the potbellied stove, but I could only see the smoke from its chimney. I looked south and saw a thin wisp of something that looked to be engine smoke.

Turning back to the depot, my eyes instantly locked on a rider approaching on a bay horse. Blood rushed to my head, and fear forced me to scrunch an inch lower before logic stopped me. There was only one thing in my vision, a rider on a bay with a prominent, white, heart-shaped spot on its left rump. The life that I had slowly been rebuilding shattered like a falling icicle.

The distinctive marking absorbed me for the first few seconds before I focused on the man astride the horse. A red beard covered his face; an unusual, short-brimmed, high-crowned hat covered his head. A cloth to protect his ears from the cold now held the hat securely on his head.

Everything fit my memory. As the rider stopped his mount at the depot, the horse shied, turning a complete circle. There was no mistake, just the one white mark on it. The odds of two horses having that identical heart-shaped mark were beyond calculation.

Even though the pistol had hogged my memory of the man, everything seemed to fit. I was sure of the horse, and the man fit what little I could remember. This was my first good look at the killer, the man I never wanted to see again but would have loved to shoot.

My legs began to twinge in memory of the desperate race through the snowy night. My mind filled with a whirlpool of possibilities, none of them to my liking. As that mental struggle continued, the logical me absorbed every detail of the man walking into the building. The beard, short, scraggly, red. The chin, though covered, too large for his face. The eyes hidden under a cliff of a brow. His clothes a cross between city and country. I would know him the next time we met.

Hearing a train whistle, I looked back south at the freight train coming toward me. Back at the depot, the man and a couple of others were walking on the platform, watching the train roll in. I still had to fight the urge to duck back, knowing the movement could give me away. The three men talked but did not seem to have spotted me. I relaxed a dab as I realized I blended into the soot-covered snow.

I kept my eyes on the men as the engine took on coal and water. Then the train pulled down the track and blocked my view. When it pulled away, all the men were gone, but the horse was still at the hitching rail. I searched frantically for the man but saw no one.

I lay there a long time watching the building, because I couldn't think of anything else to do. When my numbness subsided, I slid down to get back into the trees. I stood for more than an hour near the edge of the trees, watching and worrying over my tracks with no wind to cover them. When another train had come and gone, I turned into the woods.

My overriding question was: *How does he know I'm here*?

10 Camp

My mind was in two camps, one a swirl of confusion, the other crisply issuing orders to save my life. The second mind noted everything around me until the first slowed to a rational level. When my thoughts had again smoothed out, I decided to give the man another day to leave the area before I started poking my head over the snow bank again.

It was becoming clear to me the killer did not know I was there, so I decided to spend the night where I could build a fire. For extra protection, I confused my trail by wandering around, crossing my own tracks and even backtracking several times. Having possibly overdone the job, I stepped onto a thicket of wild roses still a foot above the snow. With all the snow packed around the canes and me wearing snowshoes, they supported me readily. An expert tracker would spot it, but most people would think they had lost me.

I chose that rose bush because a large tree had fallen across it, the top edge blown clear of snow. The limbs held it above the snow level. I climbed on top, took off the shoes, and walked to where the trunk disappeared into the whiteness. From there, shoes on, I followed a narrow draw to the east, away from the trains and the killer.

After plodding almost half an hour, the draw curved hard to the right. There I saw what I needed. A tree had fallen across the draw and left a good gap between it and the bottom of the waterway. Using a snowshoe as a shovel, I filled in the gap with snow. On the south side, I dug down to the frozen ground and built an acceptable lean-to with the tree trunk as the back wall, the large waterproof as the roof, and the outside corners supported by two tree limbs. I could even stand up at the back of the shelter.

I spent much of the afternoon pretending to pick up firewood while I watched my trail for any sign of the man. Each time I returned to the shelter with some wood, my hands began to shake. The thought of the man spotting my tracks had me stirred up again. I struggled with what to do. I finally decided: *This is ridiculous, just light a fire.* Nevertheless, my hands shook too much to cut shavings and my throat began to constrict. Therefore, I put the shoes on and walked back along the trail, throat relaxed again. I stood by a tree for another hour, just looking in the direction of the depot, the stench of fear keeping me company.

The sun slowly faded behind high cirrus clouds that thickened into lower cumulus, which, near dusk, began to share a gentle snow. I ate dried rabbit and the last of the cornbread where I stood.

With wind and snow on the increase, I returned to the camp and dropped the outer corners of the waterproof so that the front half lay on ground. I crawled under the cloth and gathered it around and under me. A fire seemed like too much of an invitation to the killer. The shakes finally stopped.

11 Peaches

Morning came without me noticing, I was well hidden and well protected. I had slept soundly once sleep had arrived, which was long after reliving every detail of the past days. The blackness when my eyes opened caused a brief panic, until I remembered being rolled up like a sausage. I had to push a good bit of blown snow away from the cloth to get out.

I surveyed the new world, this one all white as opposed to the world yesterday that was all white with snowshoe tracks. The killer had not found me. The snow was again my friend.

I reset the limbs to hold up the large waterproof and cleared away most of the snow from under it. Next, I uncovered the wood I had gathered and built the fire, finally, and without shaking. Melting snow for a hot drink was first on the agenda.

Sitting in the dark gray of morning with snow piling up at an alarming rate, I tried to shake my gloom and concoct a new plan. Seeing the man had turned my brain to slush. Still, even in this state of confusion, I was starting to guess the overnight snow might have blocked the lines again. At this rate, it might be faster to walk to Kansas City.

As I listened for the sound of trains, I stirred oats into boiling water, added molasses, and began eating. That brought to mind Lyle, Wilber, and Doris, all of us sitting at the table eating our winter staple. It was a pleasing memory, even mixed with the anguish of loss.

Wilber. I never understood him. Reading books was all he ever wanted to do. I liked to read, but I liked other things too. He would not see his tenth birthday. Damn. Being ten was great; I wished he could have made it. I had to wipe away tears. I didn't ever remember Wilber starting a conversation with anyone but Mother. Of course, I never talked to him either.

Lyle started all kinds of things, pushy little brat. Always in everyone else's business. He always wanted to be around me. Why would I want a twelve-year-old hanging on me? He really was a good worker, though. Mother never had to remind him to do a chore, and he did them pretty well. I don't miss him pestering me, but I do miss him.

Doris. She was just starting to live a healthy life. Six years of being sick before being able to run and play, she deserved more. Why did he have to shoot Doris? How was a seven-year-old girl a threat to anybody?

I watched her in my mind, climbing trees and swinging on a rope, chasing the rest of us around the yard and helping with the chores. Knowing it could never happen was the most depressing thought of all. I could not finish the mush. Setting it down, I stared at the fire for minutes, misery for company.

Enough. I stood and put myself right to search for more wood. Walking toward the southeast took me to a simple shed roughly four feet square, with nothing else around it, half-buried in a snowdrift and leaning a few degrees north. Using a snowshoe to shovel the snow from the door, I struggled against the rusty hasp and hinges. I braced one foot against the wall as I pulled, and it grudgingly screeched its way open.

It was a cutting shed as I expected, better stocked than the exterior suggested: three new axes all oiled and wrapped in cloth, two solid bucksaws, also oiled, and an assortment of tinned foods, mostly beans, but some peaches and meat. The cans bulged from being frozen but were otherwise unharmed. In addition, I found a sizable bundle of matches wrapped in a waterproof, the heads dipped in wax.

I took a few of the matches, all the fruit, and several bean cans. I also found a can opener. The bucksaw was easy to sling over my shoulder, leaving both hands free to carry wood. I placed a silver dollar on a can of meat as payment.

Returning to camp with my bounty, I actually smiled while lining up all the cans just to admire them. A bulging can of peaches went on a rock near the fire and the rest against the back of the lean-to.

While the peaches thawed, I returned to a fallen tree I had worked over on an early trip. I was able to cut large chunks of wood from it and drag them back to camp. Within an hour, I had almost as much wood as I had gathered all yesterday.

Taking out the opener, an old Warner sickle, I cut the top of the peach can, leaving that distinctive ragged edge. Then with my knife, I dug out the top peach, biting into a taste of heaven. I ate them all and carefully drank the juice without cutting my tongue.

Basking in the glow of peaches and the fire, the ragged night caught up with me. I stretched out for a nap and was asleep in seconds.

Father and I were in a field of tall grass, each swinging the long, two-handed grass scythes, cutting hay for the milk cows. The sky was bright blue with little, puffy, white clouds floating over. Swinging the scythe was effortless. Each slice released the essence of freshly cut grass and flowers.

Smiling at the ease of the work, I looked but could no longer see Father. Instead, I spotted a wall of smoke, black and menacing.

"Father," I yelled with no response. I tried to run, but my legs became dead weights. With agony, I placed one foot in front of the other. I looked over my shoulder to see flames now. Straining every muscle, my legs refused to move. The flames became a wall of angry red, bearing down on me at speed.

I woke, sweat soaking my shirt, the echo of my scream still in the air.

Most dreams are nonsense; they tell me nothing of the real world. Nevertheless, some dreams seem to contain a message. My nightmare described my current predicament a little too graphically. Father was gone, and I was struggling to get away from the red-bearded man. If I took the dream literally, I would not be able to get away; I would be stuck when the red flames of the man overtook me.

If I believed that to be true, then it would be time to give up, but I would not give up. Red Beard would have to find me before he could kill me. *Ah, Red Beard, that's a good name for him.*

At least I woke from the nap somewhat rested. With little else to do and half the day gone, I picked up the saw and went for more wood. I slept that night secure in the presence of a large stack of wood.

12 North

Two more days of feeling sorry for myself, two more days of snow, two more days without train whistles. My big accomplishment was deciding to call the killer Red Beard. I wished Jim could come to visit; I was not keeping myself decent company.

Tuesday morning changed all that. The day was bright and sunny. As I crawled out of my comfy bed, I could tell it was warmer, maybe upper twenties. While eating a piece of heated jerky, I heard a train whistle. It was far to the north but a joyous sound nonetheless.

Not knowing how the railroaders cleaned snow from the tracks, I decided to walk back to the depot to wait. First, I took the bow saw and can opener back to the cutting shed and then hiked back to the tree line, burning up at least an hour.

I could see there was nothing to see, except one man slowly clearing a path along the loading dock of the depot. He had not even started the fire in the depot stove, so I had more time to kill. I did that at a safer distance by digging and fashioning a chair out of snow, over which I draped the waterproof and blanket.

I was too antsy to stay put for long and walked around on the snowshoes from time to time. My mind was a jumble of thoughts, none meaningful, all time-fillers.

Whistles sounded both north and south, keeping me posted on progress. The sound to the north seemed to be closer, and indeed that train was the first to arrive.

I left my chair and went to see the action. It turned out that the train had three engines with a plow on the lead engine. I was able to see them when they were close. They stopped, backed up, and charged the snow again, making it to within a hundred feet of the depot. The next try put them past the station. That time they stopped, and men streamed out of the way cars with shovels.

I crawled up to a perch on the fresh snowbank to watch a small army of men clearing the snow from the depot and the coal pile. There was a muted rumble from the shovels and the workers. I checked for the painted horse or Red Beard but saw neither. That, I hoped, was good news.

I observed for perhaps an hour as the crew worked. When they cleared all the snow, the men climbed aboard the way cars, and the engines again hurled themselves at the snow. They left Walnut to its own entertainment.

The entertainment for me was standing in the timber, waiting for my ride to arrive. Less than an hour later, the engines returned to the north, running backward toward Fort Scott. For the next few hours, nothing moved except a few animals. No noises came from the depot; no signs of life appeared except the column of smoke from the now-burning potbelly. I continued my clumsy snowshoe walk back and forth to stay warm and kill time in between spells of sitting on the chair.

A whistle sounded from the south, and I climbed to my post. I could see freight cars and three passenger cars just ahead of the way car. I looked the length of the boxcars, and none were open. Even so, there were those passenger cars.

Looking, thinking, looking again, I slid down the trackside slope, ran to the first car, and entered to find it full. I made my way down the aisle, every eye in the car on me. I asked the colored porter at the back of the car, "Is there room for me somewhere?"

"Yes, sir. The third car has seats open."

I walked the full length of the second car, again picked apart by dozens of eyes. In the third car, I found the conductor, who was helping some people settle in. He was a short, round man with a ready smile.

I asked, "Could I buy a ticket for Fort Scott? I didn't have time to get to the depot."

"No problem, son. Sit right down, and I'll come by when we get rolling."

As the train pulled out of Walnut, I turned away from the depot, left my hat on and kept my face down. Once we were away, I peeled my coat and hat off in the unbearably hot car. I wanted to strip off more but could not risk calling any more attention to myself.

Twenty minutes later, the conductor was back.

"How much is the ticket to Fort Scott?"

"The K-T desperately needs your 47¢."

I pulled out a greenback. The conductor punched a ticket and handed it to me with the change. "Will you need to change to another train once we get there?" I shook a *no,* and the conductor walked away with, "Enjoy your trip." Truthfully, I had no idea if I needed another train at Fort Scott or not. I would just have to get there and see what was next.

Nervous and overdressed, I could feel my long johns becoming soggy. Being on a moving train was intimidating. I looked back and forth from the passing-snow covered scenes to the people in the car. I decided to risk taking off my outer shirt, making sure no one was watching. That helped, and the sweating slowed.

The train gave a long whistle. The conductor came in and announced, "Next stop, Hepler," as I felt the train begin to slow. In a few minutes, we came to a stop with my car in front of a tiny depot.

One person climbed on, and the train was again on its way. Another seven or eight miles and we slowed again; this time the conductor announced, "Next stop, Hiattville." After a few more miles, he declared a stop in Walker. I was glad he announced the stops. I couldn't afford to end up in the middle of Missouri.

After the stop at Walker, the conductor announced, "Last stop for this train is coming up. Everyone must detrain at Fort Scott."

I asked the conductor if there was a train going to Kansas City.

"There is, but it's not K-T. That line's the KC, Ft. Scott, Gulf. Their depot is on the east edge of town. Anything else?" He looked pleased in his helpfulness.

"Thank you. This is my first time on a train."

"Well, I hope you enjoyed it. It's a great way to travel. We even have Pullman cars on some of the lines."

Not knowing what a Pullman was, I said, "Oh, nice."

"I'd better get ready to detrain. You have a pleasant day, now."

"Thanks." How could it be pleasant? I was going to have to make my way in a new town, the largest I had ever seen, and avoid running into Red Beard.

13 Woodshed

I could see a crowd in the depot, so I bypassed it. Instead, I began to search for a warm place to sleep before dark, in town if possible, but more likely in the woods again. The street and its sidewalks to the south were clear of snow, and there seemed to be a lot of traffic on the spacious street, including horse-drawn trolleys. I inspected every man I saw until I became distracted watching a gang of men shoveling snow into wagons to finish clearing a side street. I remember thinking; *With the winter we're having, that must be a full-time job.*

When I nearly tripped, I looked down and realized I was on a concrete sidewalk. Looking up again, I saw a man cranking a great canvas awning over the store windows to keep the sunshine out. Then I noticed the beautiful gas street lamps every thirty feet or so. *Wow*, I thought, *so this is the city?*

What little I knew of rooming houses and hotels came by word of mouth. I saw a sign advertising *Rooms*, but a notice on the door reading, *Full*, so I moved on.

A second set of *Rooms* and *Full* signs seemed to be setting a trend, so I went in anyway. A pleasant-looking older woman about the age of Mother met me, saying, "I'm sorry, but we are full."

"Yes, ma'am, but I was wondering if I could get a meal here?"

She looked at me for a moment, seeming to consider. Neatly dressed in what I took to be current fashion for older women, she seemed kind enough, even as she said, "We only feed our guests. Do you plan to stay long?"

“No, ma'am. I'm on my way to Kansas City."

"I might be able to help, if you are interested. I see you're dressed for the outdoors. We have a first-rate woodshed you could stay in, and you could pay for your meals by bringing in wood and helping in the kitchen. The boy who does that is sick. Would you be interested?"

"Yes, ma'am," I gave her what I hoped was a champion's smile.

She did not return it. "Very well. Follow me." She led me into the kitchen. "This is Maude, our cook. She will tell you what to do. Maude, this young man will be staying in the woodshed and will help you in exchange for meals." Without waiting for a reply, she left.

Maude was busy at the stove and said nothing as she stirred one pot, put something into another, and generally did the things Mother did. The difference was the two large black cook stoves and pots big enough to boil a whole pig, at least a small one.

When everything was to her satisfaction, Maude turned to look at me for the first time. She was not as old as I'd first imagined. She was not attractive, not ugly, just plain; no neck, hands large and red, a little thick in the middle, but not fat.

As she pushed some dark hair back with her wrist, she asked, "So, what's your name?"

"I'm Remmy, ma'am." I flirted with adding something but could not think what.

"Remmy's an unusual name. Is it a nickname?" She stirred something in a pot.

"My real name's Remiel, but no one calls me that."

"And, do you have a last name?"

"Yes, ma'am, I'm sorry. I'm Remmy, Remiel Bevans."

"Well, Remmy Remiel," she said with a smile, "I need more wood. These monsters really eat it up."

"Yes, ma'am." I scampered out back.

Finding my new bedroom, I could see the owner was spot-on; it was solid as a new barn. No snow had filtered in, in spite of all the wind. I gathered up a good armload and returned to the kitchen. Maude pointed with a spoon. "Put it there and bring in three more loads." She went back to stirring.

Once the wood was stacked and my coat was off, Maude said, "Throw a good chunk in each firebox now."

Finishing that, she said, "Now, take these towels, and grab this pot. We need to dump the water off the potatoes."

There must have been twenty pounds of potatoes in the huge pot, plus all the water. I pulled it off the stove, straining every muscle to keep the steaming water from sloshing. Following her to the colander in the washbasin, I disappeared in the cloud of steam as I dumped the load.

Maude said, "Now we'll let it cool a bit." She opened one of the ovens and checked the contents. "Meat's ready. Help me get it out." Still holding the towels, I took the pan and placed it on the worktable. The lush aroma of pork roast made my stomach growl.

We loaded up bowls and platters with the food and carried them to the dining room nearly filled with two long tables. The lodgers started coming in as we made a second trip with more food. Soon, people permeated the room with talk, clattering cutlery, and a fair amount of lip smacking.

Returning to the kitchen, Maude sat in a chair with a groan. "I've been on my feet for four hours. We can rest now, but don't get too comfortable. In fifteen minutes, we'll clear the tables and start washing the dishes. In fact, you need to put more wood under those two pots. It's our dishwater."

As I put the wood in, I said, "I need to take off a few of these heavy clothes." She waved me away, and I pulled off my outer clothes in the woodshed.

Returning, I asked, "So, what about the boy who usually helps you?"

"Daniel. He's a good kid. He had a fever this morning but wanted to work anyway. His mother made him stay in bed. I think he's fourteen, but he's a little on the scrawny side. I lift the heavier pots because I'm afraid he'll drop one."

I noticed with some surprise Maude's slender ankles. I asked, "How long have you been working here?"

"Six years now. As I said, they're easy people to work for. I cooked in a couple of places before this but couldn't stand the people."

"Where do you live?"

"I have a room here, part of my salary." She grinned and added, "My room's nicer than yours."

I laughed. "Actually, my room's nicer than what I've had lately."

Maude took a casual tone. "So, I take it you're on the move?"

"I need to get to Kansas City."

She let that settle awhile. "It must be important, if you're out in this weather."

I focused on the floor, unable to respond.

Maude said, "I'm not trying to be nosy. Young men go to the city all the time, looking for work. I hope you have success."

"Thanks."

"Speaking of work, time to get back to it. Help me clear the tables."

After wiping the tables clean, we sat in the kitchen to eat from what the tenants had left. As excellent as the pork smelled, I filled up with potatoes and bread, thick slabs of butter on both. I added some beans for balance. As I piled butter on my third slice of bread, Maude asked, "Been awhile since you had bread?"

I smiled as I chewed and nodded my head. After swallowing, I said, "I've been eating jerky for several days. This tastes great."

"I guess it would. And that explains why you didn't polish off the pork."

I smiled again and kept on eating.

When she was finished eating, Maude started working on cleanup. She put the last of the bread in the breadbox, the butter in the butter crock, and the leftover meat in another crock, setting them in the cold room. Everything else she dumped into a large pan to feed to the chickens later.

I soon finished eating and helped Maude stack the dishes and pump some water into the basin. She instructed me to carry a pot of boiling water to the basin, and she used a pan to dip some of it into the wash water. Maude washed; I dried.

I liked her almost at once and thought it was time to start the conversation. "Are you married?" I nearly dropped a plate. *Did I just say that*?

She continued to wash for a few moments before smiling and saying, "No, I'm not. Are you?"

I started to say, *I'm sorry*, but stopped myself in time. "I'm just sixteen."

"Oh, really? I guessed eighteen. You must be a farm boy."

My voice quivered just a little. "Yes."

She gave me a hard stare before saying, "Something happened, didn't it? You don't have to tell me. In fact, you shouldn't tell me. At first, I thought you were just another farm boy going to the city, but that's not it. Something serious happened." She took the just washed-dish and handed it to me as she studied my face. She turned away, shook her head, and scrubbed the life out of a plate.

"I...."

"No, I don't want to know. I can see it in your eyes now, and I don't need any more pain. We need to talk about something else."

I was at a loss. We worked in silence for a few minutes.

Maude said, "I'm sorry. It's not on you. For some reason, I'm able to sense when people have had bad experiences. When I sense it, I feel as bad as they do. I try to avoid it as much as I can."

My mind was blank. I mumbled, "It's not too serious. I'll be fine in KC."

She brightened. "Yes, you will."

14 Cook

The grass fire was my dream, a wall of red coming at me, when I heard several gunshots before a voice said, "Remmy Remiel, time to get the fires going." I popped my eyes open to see a smiling Maude with a lantern.

I unrolled myself from the waterproof and mumbled, "What time is it?"

"Past 4:30. Thought you said you were a farm boy."

"I didn't have to do morning chores."

"Well, you do now." She hung the lantern on a nail and picked up a couple of pieces of wood. "Bring in five or six loads. We have to get the other fires in the house going, too."

She had shown me the heating stoves before bedtime as we had banked the fires with large chunks of coal to burn all night. It produced enough heat to keep the rooms from getting too cold overnight. Maude said, “On the cold and windy nights, we take turns staying up with the fires. It would be bad for business if a guest froze.”

After shaking down the cinders, I placed several small sticks of wood on the remaining hot lumps and opened the flues to get the wood burning. Once they were blazing, I added larger chunks of wood.

In the kitchen, I filled a large pot with water to boil for coffee and began slicing a slab of bacon with the two-foot butcher knife. Maude said, “When you finish, cut across the slices to make them the width of your hand. Put it all in this big pan, and we'll pop it in the oven." There was a rack in each pan to hold the bacon out of the grease.

When I went to put the meat in the oven, she said, "Add more wood to all the cook stoves and then stoke the heaters again."

Finishing that, I went to help slice the bread. She said, "I'll toast some of it at the last minute, and the rest goes plain. We'll also put out the preserves."

I asked her, "How do you ever get enough sleep? We worked until eight last night."

"I guess I'm used to it. It's worse now because the trains stranded travelers. Most days we feed half as many people, and I get a short nap in the afternoon. There are just six people for lunch, including us, and it's either soup or cold meats.

"Well, I think we're ready for the eggs. Get three dozen out of the pantry." The two of us cracked and dropped the eggs in a bowl before Maude added some cream, salt, pepper, and a little cinnamon; I whipped them.

"Is cinnamon your secret ingredient?"

"Cinnamon? What cinnamon?"

Maude took down a cast-iron skillet so cumbersome she used both hands to hold it. She opened the oven and ladled out a generous amount of bacon grease for the skillet. Once it was bubbling, I poured in the eggs.

"All right, throw ten or twelve slices of bread on the stovetop. Keep a close eye on them. No one wants burned toast."

When the eggs were ready, she asked me to lift the skillet to the table, and she scooped out the golden crumbles to fill several bowls. I hoisted the pan of bacon out of the oven, and we put the slices on platters. I took dishes into the dining room while Maude dished up the bread and toast.

Fifteen minutes later, we carried everything back to the kitchen, ate our meal, and started washing the dishes.

As we washed, I had to ask, incredulously, "You do this every day?"

With just a smile, she replied, "Oh, yes, every day, with a day off every two weeks. But, think about it: your mother does it every day without any days off."

I turned away with instant tears. When I peeked back, I saw Maude was crying. I tried to speak, but my voice cracked. I cleared my throat and rasped out, "What's wrong?"

She waved it away and continued to wash as tears continued to flow. After a few minutes she managed, "I didn't want to hurt you. I didn’t know you lost your mother." She stopped washing and looked at me. "I tried to ignore what I sensed with you, but I can't. Can you tell me the rest? I don't want to hurt you again. That hurts me even more."

I was bewildered. She seemed to know more than anyone could know. I mulled that over for a moment, not daring to look away from her sympathetic eyes. "My whole family was murdered."

Maude closed her eyes and began to tremble. I wanted to hug and comfort her, but I was too young to know how and when to share such emotional moments. At length, she opened her tearful eyes and reached out to hug me.

She pulled back and grabbed a clean towel, handing it to me as she took up the washing again. We worked in silence until most of the dishes were clean. I cleared my throat several times, thinking I might say something astute, but everything I came up with was naïve drivel. Then Maude said, "Don't be afraid to share with people you come to trust. You'll always live with the memory of their lives and of their bitter ends, but it will be easier if you share."

"I don't know if I can upset people the way I've upset you."

She waved her hand. "I doubt you'll meet anyone who reacts the way I do. Besides, you've taught me it's easier to know what has happened than not to know. I was sensing strong emotions without knowing why. Now I can deal with them. Other people won't know why you act the way you sometimes do, why you're sad for no reason. You need to tell them—I mean your friends. They'll help you, and you'll become stronger with their help."

She rinsed her hands, "I'm finished with the dishes. Will you throw this dirty water outside?" I did and tended the fires, grateful for her understanding. At the same time, her unusual ability made me nervous, and I decided to move on.

Returning, I said, "I need to get back on the road."

Her eyes opened wide. "Oh, no. I mean... I thought you would stay until Daniel returned."

"That could be days."

“His mother said he was better already and should be back in a day or two. Please, stay and help me until then.”

I flushed, never having experienced a woman pleading with me. Confusion stepped in. “I...well...I could stay a little longer.”

A grateful smile claimed her face. "I understand you want to get moving, but whatever is waiting for you will still be there in a few days.”

As we got back to work, I asked, “Doesn’t Daniel go to school?”

“No, he had to start work last year to help support the family. They have eleven kids, and his father had a leg crushed in an accident.”

All I could manage was, “Oh.”

More businesslike, she added, “You're finished for a couple of hours if you have something else to do." She placed her red hand on my arm, gave me a penetrating look, and then waved me out.

I had nothing to do, nor did I want to risk the streets, so I sat in the woodshed to think. I should have known better. I was asleep in no time.

My dream: *A man stood some distance away, too far to tell who he was. He was dressed for hard work, and his gray plainsman hat covered his head, shielding his eyes. He waved at me to come to him. He seemed familiar but a stranger at the same time. I wondered: Is he a friend, or is he dangerous?*

15 Clean

That peculiar dream repeated twice later at night, yet my doubt about the man continued. I did not think he was Red Beard, but he could have been another man who wanted to kill me. Probably, I just had murder on my mind.

The last of the stranded travelers had all left, and Daniel was back. Maude teased him. She was right; he was a good boy, though he did seem extra shy around me. His voice was loud for such a frail boy, and it carried well, so I heard him joking with Maude.

The morning cleanup was finished early, and Maude said she would take a nap while Daniel and I tended the fires. She slept an hour and then sent me away. "Go for a walk or something. Take a nap in the sitting room. Do something besides hang around here. Daniel and I have to catch up."

I decided to risk it and walked south on that nifty sidewalk, but not without checking the men in all directions. My body tensed with every rider on a horse, causing me to "study" items in store windows. It took ten minutes to walk a block.

I gave up and went into a general store just to look, first checking the two men inside for beards. Relaxing a bit, I began to see items I might like to buy someday, when I had a little money. I wanted to buy a razor and soap, but it was too expensive. My own beard was not very thick, but I had been shaving every few days for the past three years. It least beards were still fashionable, so I fit in.

If not for Maude, I would have gone directly to a train. How enjoyable it would be to get on the first open car I saw and get off whenever I felt like it. Why Kansas City? Why not Joplin or De Moines, or maybe Canada? Red Beard would never find me there, and I did like snow. My sense of adventure was kicking in.

That gave me a new sense of abandon as I walked the street, daring Red Beard to appear, even as I studied every man I saw; I had not lost my senses. Having proven my bravery, if only to myself, I returned to the kitchen.

I joined Maude and Daniel peeling potatoes; we made short work of the job, only needing five pounds. I then brought in more wood from outside, because Maude wanted Daniel to stay inside. He then took the wood to the several stoves.

Maude said, "Let's get ready for tonight. Mrs. Kallstrom decided to splurge and bought round steak for our dinner. How does steak and potatoes sound, or are you still off meat?"

My silly grin said it all.

We went through the routine of preparing food and getting it on the table at the proper time. Half an hour later, Maude and I were starting the cleanup as Daniel returned home.

As we worked, Maude said, "Tell me where you grew up."

"Our farm...." My throat tightened, and I had to wait a moment. "Our farm was halfway between Erie and Osage Mission. I was born west of St. Louis, because my folks were headed for homesteading."

"Ah, we've got something in common. I'm a bushwhacker, born and raised. I came here from Nevada, Missouri, to find work. But, I suppose you don't consider yourself a Missourian."

"No, just an accident of birth. My parents came here from somewhere in Pennsylvania, but they never said where. I'm pretty sure my father, at least, was a farmer there."

"I grew up on a farm, too. At least, that's what we called it. It was just trees and hills. We raised hogs because they could live on acorns and almost anything else they could run down in the woods."

I said, "We had a boar, so there were new litters every spring. We sold some as soon as they were weaned. Father didn't want to mess with too many. In the fall, we'd butcher one and then one more in the spring."

"I suppose you worked in the fields with your father most of the time?"

"Sure." I was puzzled at such an obvious question.

"My farm life was a little different. We spent all day, every day, in or near the house, cooking, cleaning, washing, sewing, cooking some more. I might be a farmer today if I could actually be in the fields tending crops."

"I guess I hadn't thought about it. I just assumed all girls wanted to do those things."

Maude snorted. "Believe me, I'd walk away from this job today if I had a chance to do almost anything else. Don't get me wrong, I've got a much better position than most single women my age, but I don't want to spend my life doing this."

When we finished, I asked, "Would it be all right if I wash my clothes tonight and let them dry in the kitchen?"

"That'll be fine. Go ahead and heat some more water; and you can sleep in the cold room tonight if you want. I'll see you in the morning."

As I worked, I thought of my life on the farm, with its hard work and long days. In the summer, we worked up to eighteen hours every day except Sunday. Even on Sunday, there were chores to do.

I knew what it was like for me, but what had it been like for Mother? No matter how late I came in from the field, dinner was ready and Mother had the dirty dishes washed before she went to bed. I tried to remember when I was younger, before I started working all the time, what Mother did all day. In my every memory, she was working on something.

Thinking of Mother gave me an impression of fear, which made no sense because there was nothing about Mother to fear. A faded dream of the chase to the cave flashed through my mind, carrying little emotion with it. *Did Mother have something to do with the chase? Not possible.* I never feared her, yet fear is what I felt.

With my clothes hanging all over the kitchen, I gave myself a quick wash before putting on the first dry things available. Clean for the first time in nearly three weeks, I rolled into my blanket and hoped for pleasant dreams.

Instead, I spent an hour wrestling with the new conundrum. Why did Mother cause the fear?

16 Jump

I woke before Maude, packed my clothes, and started the fires.

"Well, aren't you the early bird?" She teased me some more as we went through the business of starting breakfast. I'm sure she knew I would be leaving.

"Thanks for letting me sleep inside. I liked it, but I kept waking up because I was hot." I did not mention the nightmares.

That made her laugh. "You are an outdoor fellow. Hang around here long enough, and we'll turn you into a city slicker."

"That'll get me ready for KC."

Daniel came in to find the stoves all filled and a nice stack of wood. "What should I do?"

Maude smiled. "Bring in the flour box, and I'll make biscuits. Then get a string of sausage links from the cold room. We'll heat it in the oven. Remmy, you slice some of the ham from the cold room to put in with the sausage. We have just the regulars today, so I think two pounds of each will be enough."

We all worked, chattering casually. Daniel was warming up to me by then. I went out to bring in more wood, but otherwise Daniel took care of the stoves. That left little for me to do except to think of leaving. I liked Maude and would have liked to stay if I hadn't been on the "Wanted for Murder" list.

As the guests consumed the meal, I told her, "I'll be heading out now. I need to catch the train to KC."

Maude looked surprised for just an instant before saying, "I guess I knew you'd be going today. You've been a great help with Daniel being sick. I hope KC is bully for you. But, don't leave until you've eaten."

Meal eaten, I put on my extra shirt and coat. I had my long johns and extra pants on. "I'll bring in some more wood before I leave."

Putting the wood down, I turned to say goodbye, but Maude hugged me first. She also whispered, "Go to the first corner north. That's Wall Street. It's five or six blocks to the tracks. Walk along the far side of the tracks, and jump into a car as the train leaves town. It'll be going slow enough." She then pushed me back and smiled. I started to speak, but she waved me away and turned to her work, her red hands seeming to do three things at once. It was the perfect last image of her.

I had forgotten that the K-T had its own station house, so I was glad Maude had told me how to get to it, or I might have ended up in St. Louis. It was a frigid morning, almost as cold as during the blizzard, even with partial sunshine. Approaching the depot, I knew I would have to time things carefully. I went back to a place where I could loiter without arousing too much interest from the railroaders and still observe the depot.

After a freight train had stopped, I walked down to the tracks and crossed in front of the engine, giving the impression I was going to walk east along the road out of town. As the engine started its chug-chugging past the road, I turned back and peered down the line for an open car. One came right away, and I jumped in with little trouble.

Once I righted myself, I found two men watching me, one an Indian. I greeted them, but the Indian did not respond. I felt a prickling along my neck as I looked at him. The man who did speak motioned for me to sit near him. "Name's Brit Iseminger. What's your'n?"

It took no powerful intuition to tell Brit was a talker, and with a thick Southern accent. He piled a new question on the tail of an answer as he flitted from topic to topic. Before long, the Indian moved a little farther away as though all the conversation was getting on his nerves. Brit took no notice. "That's Bear. He thinks I talk too much. Anyway...."

As Brit droned on, I found it harder and harder to pay attention. The swaying motion of the train lulled me to sleep. Something smacked my leg a hard blow. I sat up in a start. In the semidarkness, I could see the two men fighting as the train hurtled through the snow. A knife blade flashed.

I shouted, "What's going on? Stop it!"

Brit yelled, "Jump. He means ta kill ya."

For a second, I considered helping Brit, until the blade flashed again. Grabbing my pack, I jumped.

If there had been time to plan my exit, I would have chosen a better spot, filled as it was with large chunks of ice. Once my head stopped spinning and I could focus again, I checked myself for serious damage. My forehead had taken a good whack, but it seemed to be the lone source of blood. Still, pain was clouding my brain from all quarters, so I sat still for a long time, holding my hankie over the cut.

Satisfied I would live, I struggled to stand. I stood still and held myself as steady as I could until I was sure I was ready to try walking. There was a goose egg over my right eye already, the eye partially closed. At least the cut had almost stopped bleeding.

Searching for my pack became an ordeal. I found it a hundred feet away, wedged into the snow and ice, the snowshoes mangled beyond hope. The cloud cover left no hint as to my location or the time of day. Snow began to fall.

With no other options, I started walking, slowly, painfully, along the tracks, hopefully headed north.

17 Remorse

I ignored the pain while taking cautious, shuffling steps to allow the bumps and bruises to work themselves out; my mind lurched from notion to nonsense. Could Bear be working with Red Beard? How could he know I would be on this train, in this car? It did not seem likely. He'd have needed a man on every open car on every train for a hundred miles. So, if he wasn't with Red Beard, why had Bear attacked?

Almost being killed a second time left my head spinning, quite apart from the physical blow. Splinters of thought swirled around a few times before I sat down with a thud. Even my vision was reeling. My forehead thumped with each pulsing of my heart. A few minutes rest seemed in order as I tried to put my brain on idle.

The physical dizzy spell passed, but the pain and mental fuzz stuck around. I tried to think of pleasant memories as I remained on the chunk of ice, but an unbidden image of Father took over.

The resinous scent of cut wood seemed to fill my nose as the remembered image played through my mind of Father swinging his double-bit ax into the trunk of a standing tree, sending chips flying with each well-aimed strike. In a steady rhythm, the notch in the tree increased on both sides until gravity's force overcame the remaining timber in that distinctive shredding-popping-screech of a tree pulling apart, followed by the muted crash of branches and trunk slamming into the snow-covered ground at high speed.

I always marveled at Father's steady ability to do any job with few wasted motions. I had dropped a ton of trees, but I could never do it with the mix of grace and control Father always exhibited.

Wonder at his skill, yes, but what else had I felt that day? Anger? Envy?

Why this memory now? I tried to resist, but my mind insisted on opening totally to the fight. And to my own frustration. Yes, frustration rather than anger.

I remembered renewing my reasonable request as Father readied himself to trim the branches. “I’ve already told Mr. Shultz I’ll be there to help him tomorrow, and you always tell me not to go back on my word.”

Father did not look at me as he drank some water from the burlap-wrapped jug. Just as I was ready to press my case, Father said, “You agreed to help bring in this wood, and we aren’t finished. You’d be going back on your word to me.” He replaced the jug.

I frowned at my own mistake and changed the direction of the argument. “I need to buy more shells for my rifle so I can bring in more squirrels and rabbits.”

“We’ve food enough. The squirrels will wait.” With one swing, a branch separated from the trunk.

Now boiling over, I snarled, “I can’t believe you won’t let me do this.” Another branch chopped off. “I’ve been working for you for a week now.” A third branch. “He needs me a couple of days, and then I’ll be back.”

As the recollection continued, I picked up some snow to cool my face. I was furious just remembering the fight. It had been only, what, two weeks before, two and a half? As the scene replayed behind my eyes, I remembered how angry I had been at that moment. I picked up more snow for my face, as if it could cool my memories.

Why was Father so stubborn? Why could he not listen to reason? I remembered grabbing the bow saw in a fury, accidentally hitting the back of my other hand with the long teeth. I felt the surge of violent anger anew. Looking at my wrist, I could still see the fresh scarring.

There was something missing, though, some connection between my hand and Father. The anger was still in me, the scene strong in my mind, but I could not make the connection. Thumbing through my memories again, I looked for what I had missed. Nothing.

Yielding to defeat, I stood and took a few steps along the track before it struck me: Mother. She had cleaned the wound and spoken kindly of how dangerous anger could be. “It’s like this cut,” she said. “If you don’t clean it out, it will fester and become deadly. I know you’re upset, but you can’t let that feeling control you.”

Even as she said those words, I was considering how to get even. *Was that why I felt fear the other day when I thought of Mother? Fear that Mother might know I was plotting against Father?*

That was a new notion to me, an abhorrent one. *Was I actually planning against Father*? That question hung in front of me for many minutes as I swept through my emotional memories of Father. I concluded that I was not actually plotting to hurt Father, only to get to work for Shultz. But, I remembered walking home thinking, *I beat father.* I had to accept that I had been ruthless and callous, not to mention self-centered.

Mother mediated between us that night, as she often did. She had finally gotten Father to agree that I could work for Shultz for two days and no more. Mother was like that. She always tried to help everyone get along with each other.

I found another chunk of ice to sit on, the unvisited memory now fresh. The fight with Father had taken place the day before my birthday. Had I in truth felt all that frustration, anger and self-pity? And guilt? Why guilt? What was I guilty of? Sure, I’d a fight with Father. Again.

Father, murdered the next day.

The dream of the wall of fire and the disappearance of Father sailed through me.

We had fought before, the worst being when I’d brought the .22 rifle home. Father had blown up then. Remembering it, a sense of shame crept in. I had long ago accepted my own foolishness in the incident, if not blame. I had saved money for some time and when I had enough, I had taken off for town without telling anyone where I was going. I knew Father would try to stop me. However, leaving without permission was a big mistake, especially since I was supposed to be cleaning out a waterway choked with weeds. The discomfort I felt was in never apologizing for sneaking off.

That was my guilt. There was nothing wrong with buying a rifle. Nothing wrong with working for Shultz. My blame was failing to tell Father I was sorry for the way I'd done those things.

Did I love Father before he died? I searched my memories for my actual feelings about him at different times, good and bad. There were more good than bad. The conflicts were rather recent, since meeting Big Jim.

As though bumping my head knocked it loose, the dangerous memory returned, the one I worked at forgetting. Just over two years ago, Jim had come to our house. I had only seen him from a distance before then. I'd been splitting wood when the giant had approached and asked, "Can set traps in slough?" pointing to the wooded stretch to the south.

I'd been thirteen. "Father is not here, but Mother is inside. Why don't you ask her?"

I'd gone to the door and called Mother even as Big Jim said, "I come back."

Mother had been at the door and said, "Mr. Bighorse, you are welcome. Come in out of the cold," as she had waved him in.

"Have question for husband. Can come back." He had not moved.

"R.O. went to town, but should be back any minute. Why don't you come in for a cup of coffee while you wait?"

Jim had stood for another moment, but then said, "Coffee good, thank you," and ducked through the door of the house, taking a seat at the table, where I'd sat beside him. Wilber and Doris had been in the loft, peeking over the railing, and Lyle had crept halfway down the stairs to sit and gawk. Silence had been the rule for all, including me; my mind was blank as I stared in amazement.

Mother had been carrying the coffee pot to the table when Father had entered the room, and looked at Jim. "What are you doing in this house?" He'd spoken too loudly.

Mother had said, "Mr. Bighorse has a question to ask you," and she set the pot on the table.

"I don't care why you're here. You should not be in this house with my wife. Get out!" I had never heard Father shout like that in my life.

Jim had left quickly without a word. Father had glared at Mother but said nothing. Mother had held her head high, frowned, but said nothing in return.

Father had said, again too loudly, “Remmy, get back to the wood pile. Lyle, go carry some wood inside.” Lyle had jumped down the steps in record time and slipped into his coat before I was through the door. Wilber and Doris had scurried under the covers when the shouting began.

Silence had filled the cabin through dinner and well after. In bed, I’d refused to talk with Lyle about what had happened, mainly because I had no idea what had happened, or why. Long after I should have been asleep, I’d heard our parents whispering to each other in their bed near the fireplace, but I could not make out any words.

Looking back on the incident from the mature age of sixteen, I knew it was improper for a woman to invite a man into the house, but Father’s reaction seemed out of proportion. After all, everyone knew Big Jim, and I’d been there as well. I wondered if it was because Jim was Indian.

Shortly after that, I’d decided to find out more about the man who’d caused such a dust-up with our parents. I’d walked to Mission to find him and had been surprised when Jim at first had told me I should not have come. “You Father not like it.”

“You said you wanted to set some traps. Could you show me how to set them?”

“No.”

“But, everyone says you are the best, and I want to learn. I want to be able to survive on my own if need be. I don’t want to farm all my life.”

Jim had refused that day, but I had gone back the next week. Jim had refused then as well. I had started following him, at first not close enough for him to see me, and I’d lost his tracks right away. So, I’d begun staying within sight. Even then, I’d always lost Jim. I’d kept trying day after day. After a few months, I got getting better at finding Jim’s trail once I had lost it.

One gray day in February, with no snow but plenty of damp leaves to soften my footfalls, I had been so intent on following the faint signs of Jim’s passing that I’d failed to notice I had also been following my own footsteps. Stunned when the unmistakable sank in, I had stopped and turned around. Jim had been fifteen feet behind.

That was the day I learned that Jim had been teaching me to track a person through all kinds of conditions. From then on, we developed an unusual friendship as I began to take in the skills initially refused me.

18 Tales

My body was not convinced that walking was a good idea, but I forced the issue. A mile or so along the track, I heard moaning. Approaching with care, I could see a man propped against the snow pile. Pulling out my jackknife, I called, "Who's there?"

Brit yelled, "That sombitch cut me!" After swearing at the man named Bear for a full minute, Brit said, "Help me up."

I held out both arms for Brit to pull on, but Brit kept his left hand on his chest. "Is that where you're cut?" Brit pulled his hand away, exposing a nasty gash through his coat and into muscle. I said, "I don't think it's too deep. Let's pack some snow on it to stop the bleeding?"

Brit said, "Good idee."

We had nothing to hold it in place, so Brit said, "I jist hold my hand over it. The glove's soaked in blood anyhow."

"Why don't you sit on this clump of ice until the bleeding stops?"

"'Another good idee."

I asked, "What was going on in the car? Why did he come at me?"

"Don't rightly know. I's jist startin' to nod off when Bear come 'cross the car with that stickin' knife. I jumped up 'n he says, 'Out o' my way, I wants the kid.' That's when the wrestlin' got intense."

I was back to thinking Bear might be working with Red Beard. "Why'd he want to kill me?"

"Well, I didn't git round to askin'. We 'rastled some after you jumped. I pushed him away and he slashed me. That's when I jumped. I think I hit the only rock fur a mile."

"Did Bear say he was working with anyone else?"

"Naw, said he were goin' to Potawatomi Res by Lawrence, but he weren't no Pot. He were Quapaw if I ever seed one."

I tried to think if I knew anything about the Quapaws, but nothing came to mind. I asked, “How’d he get away from his reservation?”

“They don’t guard ‘em. Those boys always workin’ some scheme. He were maybe goin’ to buy a load o’ whiskey or somethin’.”

"Well, anyway, thanks for saving my life. I feel sorry you got hurt on account of me."

"Don't worry none about that. I'd done it fur anyone. Now, tell me, what's a nice kid like you doin' jumpin’ freights?"

I was ready with what I would say if anyone asked. "I have to get to Kansas City to find someone, and I don't have much money." Most of it was true. I hoped no one would ask who I was looking for, or why.

"Puts us in the same fix. I ain't got no money, 'n’ I gots to git to KC. Maybe we can git there together."

I put on a polite if reluctant smile. "I guess we could travel together for a while, but I don't think you're going to hop any freights soon."

"Oh, That's nothin'. Why, in the war, I got hit so many times I couldn't walk no more for all the lead in me. They had to take some out so's I could fight again."

After listening to a couple of other stories, I asked, "Can you stand?"

Brit’s voice changed back from his storytelling tone to a more honest sound. "Don't know."

"Why don't you give it a try, and we'll see if you can walk without bleeding?"

After several attempts, Brit made it to his feet and hobbled along the track. I kept the same slow pace while trying to figure out Bear’s place in my troubles. I gave up and went back to listening to Brit with one ear. I had not missed anything of importance.

We struggled to make half a mile when a train roared by, going north. The cut in the snow was narrow, but we found a small depression in the wall for him, and I scampered to the top. I saw a few car doors open, but I could not have jumped on because of the speed, and I could not leave Brit. I had been struggling with that desire, because I wanted to move quickly. Nonetheless, it was hard to go against sixteen years of training to help people.

After the train noise died down and the smoke cleared, we started again. I said, "Tell me some true stories."

Brit laughed. "You don't like my tall tales, eh? okay, here's a true'n. I growed up in Arkansas, down in cotton country. Before the war started, this plantation owner gives a speech sayin' the Southern way of life would come to a end if Lincoln be 'lected. I figured that were a good enough reason to 'lect him, seein' the Southern way weren't doin' me no good. Made my way north, and ended up in the 7th Indiana Cavalry in '63.

"Three months later, we was in a forced march in freezing weather to cut off General Forrest. We had our first taste of battle at Paris, Tennessee, but the Rebs was jist a few companies, and they fell back pretty fast. We chased Forrest and his Butternuts around 'til February. When we caught him, he proceeded ta whip us to hell 'n back. I gotta give our Colonel Shanks credit, though. He got us in the thick of fightin', but he tooken good care of us. Most the other regiments cut 'n' run, but we covered 'em and didn't take too bad a beaten for it."

"What was it like being shot at?" I now had an intense personal reason for asking.

"Hell, it's like a beehive. You hear the buzzin' those mini balls make, and ain't nothin' you can do. You git stung, you jist git stung. Otherwise, you keep goin'. Ain't no secret to war. You kill 'til one side quits."

"You did that for two years?"

"Na, that's the other thing most people don't know. I figured up we spent six days fightin' in a year 'n a half. Most the time we was guardin' or scoutin'. That means we was either sittin' watchin' grass grow or gittin' saddle sores and breathin' dirt all day. After a few weeks a that, we was glad to fight.

"Our mounts were wild mustangs broke hard 'n shipped right to us. They didn't take much to carryin' 200 pounds all day. Soon as you'd look cross-eyed, they'd commence to buckin'. We had to chase a bunch of 'em', 'n' some got clean away."

"I guess war's not so much fun."

"Oh, we all joined up thinkin' it'd be excitin', 'n' maybe the women would swoon over us. Hell, most days we was covered in dirt 'n' smelled so bad even skunks stayed away."

I smiled at the image. Still, I was impressed with Brit. He was a real war hero. "I heard in school that Forrest was one of the best cavalry commanders in the war. What do you think?"

"He was good, no doubt. Course, a lot of us Southern boys growed up ridin' 'n' shootin'. That helped him some. Not me, though. We was too poor to own a horse—not much of a house, neither. But, I learned fast, 'n' so did plenty those Indy boys. We caught Forrest nappin' at Vernon, Mississip, and took him prisoner right before the end of '64."

"So, were you really wounded?"

"Not so's it counted. Reb saber cut my arm once, but I wrapped a cloth around it. The closest I came were in a full runnin' charge, when a mini hit my horse in the heart. Dropped like a ton a coal. Flew a good ten foot 'n' rolled another twenty, but came up saber at the ready."

I was impressed. "You were good."

"Pure-D lucky, that's all. Bein' good helps some, but it's mostly luck." Brit stopped walking, clutching his chest. "I gots to sit."

I helped him down on another chunk of ice set back in an opening in the wall of snow. "Let me look at it." As Brit pulled his glove away, I could see fresh bleeding. The walking was not doing him any good. "Let's pack some more snow on it." When that was in place, I went through my bag and pulled out the smaller waterproof to tie around Brit's chest to hold the snow in. "I don't know why I didn't think of this sooner."

"That's a good idee. Cinch her up tight."

I pulled hard on the two ends and Brit groaned. "Is it too tight?"

Through clenched teeth, he said, "Ease up jist a mite."

"Okay now?"

"Yeah." Brit leaned back against the snow bank and closed his eyes. "I needs a little rest. This is worse 'n' chasin' General Forrest. I'm tuckered."

There was a good spot to lie down on the other side of the tracks from which I could also see Brit. Neither of us moved for half an hour. I gave up trying to figure out what Bear had wanted to do and thought some more on life with Father.

When a train blasted its way by us, Brit did not even open his eyes.

I returned to my troubles with Father. What had it been about him that always seemed to set me on edge? He had always been a good man; everyone said so. He had never mistreated anyone that I knew of. All the same, he had been demanding with me. He did not seem to consider that I might not have wanted to be a farmer. I wanted to get out and see the world, do something else, not be Father's slave.

Brit stood and said, "I can go awhile now."

We started, slowly, along the tracks once more. Brit wasn't as talkative as before. It was clear he was too weak to go much longer, so I watched for an easy place to get away from the tracks. Brit needed a better place to lie down. Any notion of moving with speed was gone. Maybe it would be for the best; it would give Bear more time to outrun us.

When we came to a sloping break in the snow bank, I led the agreeable Brit to a small stand of trees close to the tracks. I struggled to break a trail for him through the chest-high snow. At the trees, I packed snow into a shelf and placed the large waterproof on it so Brit could lie down. The small cloth and blanket covered him as protection from the new snow that was beginning to fall.

"You rest here. I'll get a fire started and we can drink some hot coffee and have a bite to eat. Then you'll feel like walking again." Brit just nodded.

19 Mine

I dug a pit in the deep snow and built the fire. Brit slept, and trains passed, each a missed opportunity. Helping Brit was costing time. I had no idea how far from KC we were, and I hated to be stuck along the way, I wanted to get there and be settled. Yet, leaving a bleeding man was not an option.

As darkness began its steady invasion, Brit asked, "Got any coffee?"

"Will in a few minutes." I had kept the water level high by adding snow as it boiled away. I had a sock filled with coffee grounds ready to drop in the water. When the brew was black enough to walk on, I gave Brit a cup after helping him sit up. "You want molasses in it?"

"No, son. I needs more hair on my chest. That's the way I like it."

I had to pour quite a bit in mine, adding snow besides.

Brit asked, "You got anythin' to eat? I sorta had to leave my knap on the car."

I had not thought of Brit's losing everything. As I rummaged in my bag, I asked, "Did you lose much?"

"Clothes, mostly. Had some jerky 'n' bean cans."

"Did you lose any money?"

"Don't never put money in your nap."

"I'll remember," I said as I thought of the money in my own pack.

Brit ate and took his time finishing the coffee before announcing, "Think I can walk again."

"How's your cut?"

"Holdin' good. The cloth were the right thin'."

Darkness reigned when I kicked snow on the fire and helped Brit to his feet. We made it back to the rails and headed north again through the steadily falling snow.

Brit was revived for a time and talked some more about the war, mostly of the men he knew and how they acted, who was brave, who was not. George Hammon upset him in particular. “He deserted one night, without no warning. Him and me was close. He betrayed me. He could've told me why. He owed me that much."

He lapsed into silence, not saying anything for at least an hour. One train approached from the north, and we scrambled to cover.

Walking on, I considered what loyalty meant. I thought at once of our family motto, *semper virtuti constans.* Mother told us often of the Welsh motto and the importance of virtue in our lives. She said we should be honest, responsible, and righteous, but what did that mean in these modern days?

Was I virtuous by helping Brit? It was obvious he needed help, but did I have to hold his hand forever? Once he was in a safe place, would I be free to move on?

If I did leave him, would I be deserting him the way George Hammon had?

The noise of Brit's breathing was getting louder, so I suggested, "Let's rest a spell." Brit dropped on the first chunk of ice he saw while I searched out a safer pocket. When I helped him move to a better opening, I dug out some soot-free snow for us to eat.

Half an hour later, we started out again. Every train that passed carried a plow that tossed an inch or two of snow on us. I learned to hold my hands on the back of my neck to keep the snow off. The pattern of walking and resting went on most of the night, until we limped past the railroad sign reading, *Pleasanton,* just as I imagined the sky was starting to lighten in the east.

With a big grin, Brit said, "Now I know where the hell I is. I was in a big battle south of here. We walked right past it."

"I didn't know there was a battle in this area."

"It was second biggest cavalry fight of the whole war. The biggest were at Gettysburg, and General Pleasanton commanded both of them. Let me fill you in on your own history.

"Five companies of the Seventh Cav joined the Fourth Iowa Cav with some infantry and went into Missouri chasin' General Price. He had such a head start we took riverboats up the Mississip to St. Louis and then up the Missouri to Jeff City. When we finally caught Price in October at Westport, where Kansas City is now, we thumped him pretty good, and he started jumpin' the river to Kansas. Then all the Iowa boys left—guess they's ordered back—but the Seventh was loaned to General Pleasanton.

"Then the day of the big fight, our company, led by Lieutenant Crane, hit them in the morning at Independence, in Missouri, but it were jist a rear guard. We chased them south 'til we caught them crossing the Marais des Cygnes. Most days, that river be easy crossin', but we was havin' heavy rains, and those Butternuts had no choice but to stay 'n' fight. I suspect they was feelin' good because they outnumbered us four to one. What they didn't know was we had them new seven-shot Spencer rifles. We cut through them like a plague of grasshoppers in a grain field.

"Somehow they made the crossin', 'n' we went at them again. Caught them at Mine Creek jist south of here, when they was jist starten' to git the wagon train across the river. We set up artillery and started blowin' up wagons. They lost all five hundred of them wagons.

"Then it were cav against cav. We charged, and they met us, thousands of sabers flashin'. I were a slashin' right and left. Then we wheeled and went at 'em again. They broke and run. It didn't last long, but it were one hell of a fight while it lasted. I heard later we wiped out a whole division of Rebs, and us jist two regiments.

"Problem was, Price had another division across the river, and that one was headin' to the supply depot at Ft. Scott. We chased him again and had our third fight that day at Marmiton River. When that were done, we had to rest. Our horses was plumb wore out, and our arms was hurtin' from swingin' the saber.

"We kept up the chase into Indian Territory, but Price never slowed down enough to catch him again."

I said, "And all that happened around here. I had no idea. Is that why you're back here?"

"I've lived round here since the war ended. Me and some others decided to settle here. There weren't many people livin' here then. I kind of bummed around, job to job. Jist couldn't settle down."

All I could think was: *A real war hero. Not like Father. I can learn from this man.*

20 Gargling

The snow had finally stopped, and daylight was forcing its way through the clouds to announce another cold day. Brit knew his way around the tiny settlement of Pleasanton. "I stops at David's, time to time." He soon found the house of the man he knew from the war. "Let's go around back. It'll be less fuss."

Approaching the back of the house, we surprised a child returning from the privy. She shrieked as she ran into the house. In seconds, a man appeared at the back door with a shotgun, his wife right behind. "Your name or die!"

As soon as he saw the gun, Brit raised both his hands as high as his wound would allow; mine were already up. "It's me, Brit. Don't shoot."

"Advance, and be recognized!"

With the gun pointed right at him, Brit walked close to the door. I kept my hands high but did not move.

"Brit, you worthless dirtbag. What's the idea, scaring my little girl like that?"

"Sorry, I thought the back door would be less fuss. Didn't know you'd shoot guests."

David put his gun down. "You ain't a guest yet. What do you need this time?"

"This young feller and me got into a scrape. I'm cut some."

David softened. "All right, get on in here." He waved to me to come in. As I passed him, David asked, "What's your name, son?"

"Remmy, sir, Remmy Bevans."

"I'm David Swelgart, and this is my wife, Becca, and this girl Brit scared to death is Sarah."

I said, "Glad to meet all of you, and thank you for letting us in." My words began to tumble too fast. "Brit's cut has been bleeding all night. He stopped a man from killing me, and we both had to jump from the train."

Becca said, "It's all right now, we'll take care of your wounds. David, take a look at Brit, and I'll tend to Remmy." I jumped as she touched my forehead. "This will be okay once the swelling goes down. Take off your heavy things, and we'll see what else happened to you."

"I think I'm okay, just bruises from jumping from a moving train."

David said, "I should have known it involved hopping a freight. Becca, look at this cut. Do you think we can wrap it tight enough to stop the bleeding?"

"It's long, but not too deep. I've got just what he needs. I'll be back in a minute."

David asked, "So, Brit, how did you come to get in a knife fight in a boxcar?"

"That's the funny thing. I don't rightly know. I got on the car down at Girard. Another feller was already on. He didn't talk much. Said he were called *Bear*. I told him some stories...."

"No wonder he cut you. He couldn't stand any more of your stories."

"Anyway, I commenced to sleepin'. Woke up when we stopped at Ft. Scott. Young Remmy here jumped on as we was pullin' out. Him and me talked some before Remmy fell to sleep."

"Bored by your tall tales, no doubt."

Becca had returned. "Now, David, let the man tell his story."

"Thanky, ma'am. Soon, I fell to sleepin', too, but before I's there, this Bear went fur Remmy with a knife. I grabbed him and shouted to Remmy to jump. He did, and I got cut and jumped too."

David looked at me and asked, "Any idea why he'd want to kill you?"

"It was like Brit said. He just came at me. I spoke to him when I got on, but he didn't answer. He just scowled at me."

Brit said, "I think it might be your knapsack. What tribe did you git it from?"

"Big Jim's an Osage. Why would it be a problem?"

"I'm thinkin' Bear might've been unfriendly to the Osage, and he thought you was one."

Becca said, "Oh, my! That's horrible."

I was standing with my mouth open. Why would anyone want to kill someone like Jim? I said, "I can't believe it."

David said, "It makes sense. Of course, he might have just thought you had money in there. It's a first-rate bag."

Becca added, "We're glad Brit was able to stop him, aren't we, David?" as she gave him a stern look.

David took the hint. "You did good, Holbert."

I looked at David, then Brit. "Holbert?"

David took that one with a grin. "Some of us from the company learned his whole name and used it on the few occasions he did something decent."

I asked, "So, how do you get 'Brit' out of that?"

Brit shrugged. "Far as I know, you join the army. Which sergeant was that, David? Lando?"

"No, the Quartermaster, Jimmy Barnes."

"That's right. He was callin' names to pick up sabers, and it come out *Brit Iseminger*. Been that ever since."

David added, "I heard even General Grant had it happen. He went to the Point as Hiram Ulysses, and they wrote down Ulysses Simpson. I guess he figured the army never made mistakes, so he left it."

"I never knowed 'em to make a mistake."

Becca jumped in, "Now, that's enough you two. David, you need to get ready for work, and these boys need some sleep. You can trade war stories tonight."

David grinned as he left the room.

Becca had brought in a long strip of cloth and had been wrapping it around Brit's chest. After tying it off, she asked, "How's it feel, Brit?"

"Mighty good, ma'am."

"All right, I have a bottle for each of you. Have you heard of Merchant's Gargling Oil?"

We both said, "No, ma'am."

"You rub it on to relieve the soreness and the bruises. And, Brit, no matter what it's called, you don't drink it." She gave him a stern look.

"Yes, ma'am. I be good."

I took the cork out and sniffed. If overpowering smell could heal, I was as good as cured.

After we had eaten some bread and sausage, with hot coffee, Becca showed us to a room next to the kitchen. "We use this for storage. You boys can bed down here. I'm sure you're tired from all the walking."

"Thank you, ma'am."

"Thanky, ma'am."

I slept in fits and spurts. I seemed to dream the whole time. The dreams had Indians, trains, fires, shootings, snow, and even some unpleasant events. Every time I woke, Brit was in the same position. He slept deeply and loudly.

I got up mid-afternoon and went out to the privy. Returning, Becca asked, "Are you hungry?"

My stomach had been telling me the answer for some time. "I could eat." She sliced some more bread and set it out with more sausage. "Very nice of you, ma'am. Thank you."

She walked over and closed the door to the storage room where Brit was still sleeping. Sitting, she quietly said, "Brit's a nice enough man, but you should know the war left him, well, a little strange. For one thing, he goes on drinking benders. He never causes anyone any real trouble. He just can't be around people for very long. We'll help him for a few days, but it would be best if you could go soon."

I thought I understood what she meant, and I had no problem with leaving at the first opportunity. "I need to get to KC soon, and I thought I'd leave him here, but he'll need help on the train, and I could use his help in KC, so I guess I'll stay."

She nodded and said, "Just don't expect too much from him. And don't be surprised when he disappears. Anyway, how are you feeling?"

"Better. I didn't sleep very well. I kept having dreams."

"It'll be better tonight."

"Could I chop some firewood or anything like that? I'd like to help out."

She smiled. "You can bring some wood in. That would be nice."

I kept the stoves hot the rest of the day and brought in enough wood to last until tomorrow. That evening, we all sat down to big platters of sliced ham, biscuits, and fried eggs. Listening to the family talk about the day seemed very familiar. It was good to hear, even tinged with my loss.

Finished eating, I helped clear the table. Becca told me not to, but I did anyway. David and Brit talked about some of the men in the company, about what they were doing twenty years after the war.

When I joined them, David said, "Brit, you're in no shape to hop a freight. Why don't you stay a couple of days, until you're healed up enough to jump?" I wished Brit would decline, even as I knew he should not. At least Red Beard would never think to look for me in Pleasanton, Kansas.

21 Volunteer

For two days, I battled my urge to move. There was little to take my mind off my problems. I would decide to leave Brit, and then decided to stay with him. Resolution came when Brit announced, "Don't want to overstay my welcome."

David said, "You've already done that, you old buzzard."

As David and the kids prepared for their day, Brit and I put on all our winter clothes and made ready to travel. Becca gave each of us some biscuits and ham for the road.

David had told us the night before that a train only stopped here twice a week, but there was a sharp bend in the road just out of town, and all the trains had to slow to make it. It was not too hard to jump on there. "I've done it a few times myself to get to La Cygne for business, but don't tell Becca."

At the curve, I made a dugout in the wall of snow and ice, and we settled in to wait. To kill time, I asked, "Brit, you said you went north before the war started, right?"

"Yep, left afore Lincoln took office, afore Kansas were a state, even."

"So, that was 1860, but you didn't join until '63. I've been thinking you might have joined right away."

"Tried to, but couldn't prove I's eighteen. Left home at fifteen, so's I looked kinda young. Besides, they jist taken infantry, and I didn't want to walk through the war."

"That makes sense. You said you didn't ride as a kid. Was it hard to learn?"

"Naw, the hard part was learnin' the saber. Had to slash down both right and left sides. Lot'ta boys cut their horses learnin'. Shootin' from the horse weren't easy, neither. We carried a short-barreled rifle called a carbine.

Weren't much good past a hundred yards, but better than muskets."

"I had a neighbor who still hunts with a muzzleloader. He said it was more accurate than most rifles."

"That weren't no musket. Musket were a smoothbore, and the shot might hit anywheres in a two-foot target from fifty feet."

"Then, why were they used in the war?"

"Well, son, that's what we had. The rifles you see today was still bein' invented. Besides, ten thousand men fires muskets all at once, somebody gits hurt."

"So, why did everybody line up and stand up?"

"We was shoulder to shoulder to 'concentrate fire.' That's what the officers called it. You had to stand to load a muzzleloader. So, both sides shot and reloaded every fifteen seconds 'til one side gived up."

"So, you just had to stand there and hope not to get hit?"

"Another reason I stayed away from the infantry. Man on a runnin' horse harder to hit."

"That kind of war doesn't sound like much fun."

"War's only fun 'til the killin' starts."

We sat in silence for a while before I heard a train approaching and stood to see which direction it was traveling. When I sat back down Brit said, "Goin' south, huh?"

"Wrong. Get ready to jump."

Once the engine had passed, we stood and watched the cars coming at us. Even though the train had slowed, it still looked too fast to jump on. Brit said, "Cup your hands, and let me put my foot on them. When the car comes, you throw me on."

It worked well for Brit, but I barely caught the door to drag myself in. Once we settled, I noticed Brit holding his chest and grimacing. "You hurt again?"

He croaked through clenched teeth. "Bit."

Pulling Brit's hand back and unbuttoning his mended coat and shirt, I saw some blood on the inner shirt. "Wound's open again." Taking out a thick cloth Becca had given me, I placed it over the wound. "Now, button up, and keep pressure on it. Becca said that's the best way to stop the bleeding."

Once his coat was re-buttoned, I helped Brit lie down, and I put my hand over the wound and pressed down. "We'll take turns." I did not relax until Brit's eyes started to lose their tight squint and his mouth lost its grimace. "Pain better?" All I got was a positive nod of the head.

After a time, Brit said, "Hurts more now than it did the first time. Kinda reminds me of the time my horse fell on me."

By now, I had heard enough of David's responses to Brit's tall tales to know what to say. "I feel sorry for the horse."

"Should've never let you hang around Swelgart. He a bad influence."

"You do tend to talk a lot."

"That's what happens when you start pickin' cotton at five."

I retorted derisively, "You weren't five."

"Don't need to tell no tales about that. Ten of us chillen's, all pickin' in the hot sun, sunrise to sunset. Why you think I left?"

I was not sure if I believed him, but Brit seemed sincere. "Here, you put some pressure on your wound. What did you do when there was no cotton?"

"We hoed cotton, and all the other crops. Pappy hated weeds."

"Did you raise any animals?"

"You mean, besides chillen's? Sure, hogs and chickens mostly. I picked my share of chicken feathers."

"Me, too. That's a nasty job."

"You got that right. Really tough in the winter. Them feathers freeze right on your hands."

I was starting to believe him now. "Did you hunt in the winter?"

"Of course. Ate jist about anythin', coons, possums, turkey, razorbacks—."

"What's a razorback?"

"Jist the meanest mass of gristle on four legs. It be a wild hog with tusks that'll rip you apart afore you can blink."

"Another tall tale."

Brit raised his hand. "On my honor as a Seventh Cav Trooper."

I was learning such an oath was not frivolous. "I believe you. Sorry."

Brit waved his hand. "That's okay. I does invent things."

"How's your wound feel?"

"Think it stopped bleedin'."

"You better stay down a while longer. Don't want to break it open again."

Brit did not argue and was snoring in minutes. I leaned against the wall of the rocking rail car and allowed by thoughts to return to Father. I never remembered him doing anything but work. He was nothing like either Mr. Swelgart or Brit, war heroes both. If only Father could have been more like them.

22 Stockyards

The train rattled on through the day, stopping occasionally to take on water and coal. I continued to think of Father, wondering why we argued so much. In some ways, Brit was no R.O. Bevans, a commanding presence from my earliest memories who always seemed in control of every situation. He had been neither well-muscled nor large, yet bigger and stronger men deferred to him.

What had been the source of his confidence? I never knew. He always acted as though he knew what to do, no matter what came up, but he never forced others to agree with him. They just did, and he was usually right.

Father—what a pain. Did I hate Father or hate his command? I wanted to be my own man, and Father did not seem to like that. Maybe that was the problem.

As the boxcar darkened, I made my way to the open door to look at the passing landscape. The clouds were showing signs of more snow, but I could tell the sun was setting. Looking through the gritty smoke ahead, I could see no sign of where we were. I settled again near the still-snoring Brit.

Not long after darkness was total, I began to see lights flash past the car opening. I stood again and looked ahead. It turned out to be my first glimpse of the city, a glimpse through another snowfall.

Waking Brit, I helped him stand so he could look. "You're right, Rem, that's it. But, don't get excited. It'll be awhile before we hit the stockyards." I helped Brit sit against the wall next to the door where he could look out. I was too excited to sit. I could not believe how many buildings and lights there were.

Nearing the stockyards, I became aware of a peculiar odor, a mix of slaughtered animals and rotting carcasses. Brit took away the mystery. "That, my boy, that's the smell of meat-packin' plants. You don't want to live downwind of them." Once we passed them, the odor became the more familiar barnyard smell of thousands of animals.

We rolled into the stockyards, and I noticed they had gaslights everywhere and some electric lights near the buildings. There were men working the livestock. Working at night—it did not seem possible. I could now believe it was the second-largest yard in the world.

The train came to a halt in a maze of tracks along the edge of the stockyard. I helped Brit down from the car, and we quickly moved away from the train, to avoid arrest.

Trying to look like we belonged there, we walked next to stock pens for a quarter mile until we came to a spacious lane leading up to two massive buildings. Again, Brit filled in the details. "That first buildin', that's the central office fur the yards. That's where you go to beg fur work. The one next to it's the sale barn, where they hold the auctions."

The size of the buildings thrilled me, as did all the lights in and around them. Once we were next to the office building, Brit stopped a couple of men and asked, "You know where there's a open roomin' house nearby?"

"Sure. Go out the main gate, cross the street and go west two blocks. Place called Everts. They ain't bad. Tell 'em Seth sent you."

"Much obliged."

The snow continued to fall as we did the winter waddle along the snow-packed sidewalks. The walks in and near the yards had been scraped clear, but not the rest of the city walks. Not enough businesses in the area cared for such niceties to go the expense.

Arriving safely at Everts, we did find a room, but we had to pay a week in advance. Rather, I did, because Brit did not seem to remember where he had hidden his money. That nearly emptied my pockets.

In the room, I said, "Let's see your wound." When we peeled everything off, the lesion was still bleeding, and the skin was an angry red around the opening.

Brit said, "See if they has any whiskey downstairs to pour on the wound." The owner did have small, unlabeled bottles for sale at two bits apiece.

Returning to the room, I poured a good portion of the whiskey over the wound. I started to re-cork the bottle when Brit grabbed it and drank the rest like a man stranded in the desert. Becca's words flashed through my mind.

After putting a fresh bandage on Brit and wrapping him again, we both lay on the bed to sleep. With my body still rocking from being on the train, sleep was slow to come.

23 Bread

Not long into the night, I gave up trying to sleep next to Brit and set myself up on the floor with my coat for a pillow. I slept better but still woke before sunrise, watching it through the grimy window and ashen clouds.

Because we were paying for room only, I was getting ready to leave to find something to eat when Brit woke up and said I should get some bread, sausage, and whiskey.

I stupidly asked, "Are you sure you need the whiskey?"

"Now, you ain't my ma. Here's a quarter eagle. You can keep the change for what you already bought. You might git all three at the saloon across the street."

I took the gold piece, the first I had ever handled, and headed for the saloon while thinking that Brit's hero status was tarnished.

When I opened the door to the saloon, I saw a room no more than twelve feet wide but fifty feet long. It had mud and slush around the door, overwhelming the sawdust on the floor. Only a few gaslights were quivering, and there were no windows at either end of the narrow chamber.

I could see men sitting, drinking, smoking. A few talked. One ate while another sprawled, head on the table with a half-full mug in front of him. The air was a caustic mix of body odor, urine, stale beer, tobacco, and stockyard dung, with a hint of puke.

I approached the barkeep and asked if I could buy the three items to take to the room. "Loaf of bread's five cents, five links of sausage fifteen cents, and the bottle of whiskey's a dollar."

I pulled out my last greenback and some coins to pay. I didn't feel safe flashing gold in this place.

"I'll get you the bread, unless you want to get some already sliced."

"The loaf's fine." I knew I could use the hunting knife Jim had given me.

"You're paying for the big sausages at the back of the table."

I pulled out the small waterproof and took five sausages. They went in my pocket. Back at the bar, I put the bottle in my other coat pocket and kept the bread in my hand. As I turned to leave I said, "Thank you."

The barkeep gave a little laugh of surprise and said, "Eat in health."

At the door, I heard him say, "Lloyd, sit. You leave the boy alone." A man was giving me a hungry stare. I closed the door and hurried across the street.

Once in the room, I was able to eat in peace, because Brit was asleep again. I rolled a sausage link in a hefty slab of bread and went to work on it. It was good, and the bread was fresh. I washed it down with a couple of shots of whiskey, my first store-bought. Bill Shultz made his own, and we had some with lunch, 'to keep the cold away' any time I worked for him, even in the summer.

I was halfway through a second sausage when Brit woke. He mumbled and fussed at the bed for a couple of minutes before making it to the table. His breakfast started with a shot of whiskey, "For the pain."

He ate slowly at first, pausing for drinks along the way. His eating became sincere, and he stopped drinking. We split the fifth sausage. Brit did not interrupt with talk, which I took to mean he was unusually hungry.

Finished, Brit said, "That were good," and he rubbed his belly, as best he could.

I said, "I think you've been to that saloon before." Brit smiled. I went on, "Have you worked the yards here?"

"You bet. Been in and out of here dozen times," he said with pride. "But, I ain't stayed in this house before."

"So, how do I get a job in the yards?"

"I expect you want a yard job. They have office jobs, too. You go to the gate we went out. Inside, signs will direct you. Problem is, lots of cowboys spend the winter in the yards if they don't got a line job."

I frowned, and Brit saw it.

"Course, by this time of year most are too drunk to work."

I thought of the men in the saloon. With a shrug, I said, "I guess I'll just have to go see."

24 Job

I stood on the opposite side of the street to admire the main gates to the Kansas City Stockyards Horse and Mule Barn with its elaborate carvings covering the entire set of openings. There were four entrances massive enough to drive three wagons through at a time and one immense roof covering them all. Buildings extended at least two hundred feet both south and east from the corner entrance.

I walked east past the main entrance to the smaller, but still ornate, yard gate. Inside the yards, I followed the signs to an office in the east wing of buildings. I gawked at the people working inside. There must have been more people in that one wing than in all of Erie.

The office I entered had an accumulation of snow and mush near the door. I added to the collection by stomping my boots clean. At the counter, I asked the lady if I could work in the yards.

"You'll have to talk to Frank. He should be back in a few minutes. Have a seat."

I peeled off my coat and waited in one of the several empty chairs lined up along the outside wall. Ten minutes later, a man entered, stomped his boots, and walked past the counter. In a couple of minutes, he returned and asked, "You looking for work?"

I stood, "Yes, sir."

"Follow me." I soon found myself in a small room with a large roll top desk piled so high with papers it would be impossible to close the top. The man looked out of place in any office. He had the look of a dime novel cowboy. All that was missing were chaps and most of his hair.

"I'm Frank. And you are?"

"Remiel Bevans, but I'm called Remmy."

"You ever worked a yard before?"

"No."

"How old are you?"

"Sixteen, sir."

"Farm boy, I take it. Ever work cattle?"

"We always kept fifty head, besides milkers."

"Can you ride?"

"Yes, sir." I had been on a horse once.

Frank fiddled with his mustache as he studied me. It was making me nervous. "This is hard and dangerous work. We had a guy killed here last month. Lose nearly one a year. You get tired after twelve hours, and you get sloppy. That's when a thousand pounds of steer decides to use you for a pincushion. There ain't no glamor here." He paused and studied some more. "You sure you want to give it a try?"

I was not the least bit discouraged by the speech. "Yes, sir!"

Frank fiddled a bit longer before asking, "You run away from home?"

Surprised and confused, I blurted, "A man killed my family, and I had to run because he wants to kill me, too." That stopped the fiddling.

"On the level?" He could already see the tears coming in my eyes and said, "Never mind. Course it is." He stammered a bit before saying, "Don't tell anyone. Some of these boys would sell you out for a bottle of whiskey. Tell you what. I'll put you on the feeding crew if you can start right now."

I didn't bother to wipe the tears. "Now is great!"

Frank leaned forward and said, "I'm a farm boy myself. Hated it, and ran away at fifteen. One thing I learned poking cows is farmers work harder. I think you'll fit in just fine."

Then he leaned back, all businesslike. "Go back to Margaret, and she'll get the papers filled out for you. We can't do anything without papers around here, as you can see." He waved an arm in the direction of the desk. "And, if you have any trouble from some of those rougher boys, you just let me know. Us farmers got to stick together." He winked.

As I stood up, Frank said, "Wait, I just thought of something." He motioned for me to sit again. "Maybe we should list you under a fake name, in case someone comes looking for you." I nodded my agreement. "How about Bailey? That's close to Bevans."

"I think I can remember that. Thanks." Frank waved me out.

Margaret was sitting at her neat desk, pounding on a contraption I had heard of in school called a typewriter. I watched Margaret type and could see she was probably only twenty or so and pleasant-looking, with a trim figure, though I could not see her lower half. Pulling a paper out of the machine, she asked, "Are you hired?"

"Yes, ma'am. He said I needed to get some papers."

She smiled and removed a clean sheet of paper from her desk drawer, put it in the machine, rolled it into position, and asked, "What's your last name?"

She went through several other questions and typed in the answers. When she asked for the name of next of kin, I started to say, “R.O.,” but stopped myself. I was not sure how to answer and finally said, "No one."

She glanced at me before pounding out the answer.

Finished, she pulled the paper from the machine and inserted another. On it she typed for just a minute before pulling it out and saying, "You need to sign your name right here," as she pointed to a box beside the number 27. As I was signing, she said, "Frank will show you around."

Frank was pulling on his coat, a nice sheepskin. "I'll show you the most important office first." He picked up the paper I had just signed, and led me out and down the walk to a door with a small sign reading, *Paymaster*. "Every Saturday, you come here for your pay. But, you won't get paid unless you sign in and out." He led me inside.

The office was large, with many desks and people. There was a long counter between me and the workers, and I could see boxes on it with every letter of the alphabet and some besides. Frank led me to the box marked, Ba-Bl.

Inserting the paper, he explained, "You report here every day to sign in. You just signed in for today, January 27. Tonight at six, you and everyone else will come in here and sign again for January 27. On Saturday, these fine people will take all the papers and figure up how many hours you worked, so when you come in Saturday night, they will pay you for the week, Saturday through Friday. You'll see how it goes. You get eight and a half cents an hour. You'll be docked an hour if you haven't signed in by five 'til six in the morning, and you can't sign out until after six at night.

"Let's go put you to work." He led me back outside and toward a huge barn. "You'll report here every morning. The crew's out now, but I'll show you around 'til they get back." There was more hay filling the barn than I had ever imagined could exist in one place. Frank said, "We get shipments of hay in every week by rail car. One of your jobs will be to offload hay to this barn."

We went to a smaller barn, where there was an open space on one side with several wagons standing empty. There were empty horse stalls on the other side of the barn.

Frank said, "We'll go back to the hay barn. Wagons will be there soon. The crew I want you to work with is short-handed because of an accident."

We watched as several wagons loading hay; large grapples dropped down on the hay and then closed around it to lift the loads to the wagons. The grapples slid along iron rails to the right position and then back to the wagon with the hay. Our barn had a much smaller one, so I knew how they worked. There were at least twenty of them in the barn so that several wagons could work at the same time to reach the enormous mounds of grass.

When the right wagon came in, Frank did the introductions. "This is Truman Selee, but he's called Lee. He's the wagon boss, so you do what he says. And this is Sam Hostetter. The two of you will pitch while Lee drives." All the while, the two men loaded hay with a big grapple and merely nodded when introduced.

Frank handed me a pitchfork and said, "Have fun."

I gave Lee a quick look. He was at least as old as Father. I turned to Sam who had red hair sticking out from under his winter hat. He was of average height but broad in the shoulders. There were deep creases from his nose to just below his mouth, looking like parentheses.

I climbed on the wagon once they had finished loading, and Sam said, "Glad to have you. I'm plum wore out. Charlie Matthews fell and broke his leg yesterday. You done this before?"

"I haven't worked a big yard, but we fed cows at home."

"Not much different here, except we do it all day. You look about my age. How old are you?"

"Sixteen. You?"

"Seventeen. I've been here since September. My older brothers took over the farm and didn't need me, so here I am. It's not bad."

The wagon stopped at a pen, and Lee said, "Ten forks," and we each forked five loads of hay into the pen. We moved along the aisles, with Lee reading the amount each pen received. Once I got into the rhythm, the wagon did not have to slow. Sam said, "Sure is a lot easier with help."

For me, the work was a welcome relief. My body was used to running a pitchfork, and talking with Sam kept me from thinking of my troubles. As we were riding back for another load, Sam said, "We'll be doing this most of the time, but we also help move stock when they need us. A load of pigs comes in two or three times a day, and sometimes we'll get sheep. Actually, Lee said things are slower this year because of all this snow.

"When a load comes in, we just stand on the fence and yell at the cows to get them into the pens. You'll notice the gates are just long enough to reach across the aisles. There's a stop on the other side, so they can't push past it. When they're all in, we close the gate. Like at home, really, just bigger."

"How do they keep track of all this livestock?"

Sam laughed. "I have no idea. I guess that's why they have all those people and all that paper. Every stock pen has a number, and the stock from one seller goes in the same pen. After that, I don't know."

25 Whiskey

I had no difficulty with the new job. The biggest problem was money. I was down to a few pennies and I had no idea how much Brit carried. When I asked, he just said, "Got enough," and he did have food ready when I made it back each evening.

However, payday was a big day. At 6 pm, I found myself at the back of the line, everyone eager for some money. Even so, the wait was not long. After I had signed my name, a clerk handed me an envelope containing $2.72, two greenbacks, three quarters and two pennies for two days and part of another. Not bad. A great day all around with the thermometer on the barn reading *21°*. I had my coat off most of the day.

I tucked the bills into my shirt pocket and buttoned my coat like a vault. The coins went into my pants' pocket. I knew it would be dangerous to be alone on the streets on Saturday night. Thieves knew when all the paydays came and they waited for an easy mark. I ran to catch up with three men I knew who lived in the house. I only knew them by sight, so didn't walk beside them, just close enough for protection. We made it without incident. I wasn't used to having money to worry about.

I gave Brit one dollar, hoping I could hang on to the other to put it in the money pocket on the inside back of my coat. Mother had sown it in when she made the coat. She did it so expertly a person had to do a close inspection to see it. The quarter eagle was there, wrapped in a cloth with the coins Shultz had paid me. Those six dimes and four new liberty head nickels were a reminder of my family. Spending them would be like spending blood money.

Brit's wound was improving every day, but he was still sleeping a lot and couldn't walk very far without wearing out. Still, he managed to buy food and we ate well, though heavy on bread and sausage.

The next morning, I walked to work in falling snow with two inches already on the ground, the third snow in the five days I had been in the city. In the yard, I saw the night crew shoveling the walks, and horses pulled several big blades to clear the aisles between pens. Snow was beginning to get old.

The three of us had a smooth routine for harnessing the horses to the wagon, and we were usually the first away with a load of hay. It snowed all day, and the three of us spent the last hour shoveling snow around the office buildings. Apparently, the bosses did not want their indoor people to get their shoes wet.

Tuesday evening, I arrived back in the room to find Brit asleep on the bed. There was no new food, nothing but the leftover bread from yesterday. I made several loud noises to wake him, but he did not budge. I leaned over to try to shake him awake but stopped short. He was whiskey-pickled.

I shouted, "Brit, wake up," and shook him hard. "Wake up, you old goat. Wasting all my money like that. Wake up, so I can put you to sleep the way you deserve." Yet, my shouting did no good. I found the empty bottle and threw it against the wall; luckily, it didn't break. I found six cents when I searched his pockets and then threw the coat at Brit as hard as I could. It landed on the old man's head.

I went in search of food, but to let my anger cool, I walked a few blocks to the north before entering a store that had foods I had never seen before. It had some fresh foods like turnips and carrots. That brought me around. Even Maude had not had anything fresh while I'd been there, not counting meat and potatoes.

I bought two carrots to eat raw as well as a loaf of bread, a one-pound block of butter, a can of tomatoes, and two onions to eat with the bread and butter. I picked up some boiled eggs and biscuits for breakfast and lunch.

Starting back to the room, I saw a boy selling the evening edition of the *Kansas City Star* newspaper. I had not read anything in a month, so I paid the 2¢ and imagined with pleasure reading while eating.

Brit was still unconscious. I did not look at him as I set everything out; I pretended to be alone. I sliced a generous block of bread and spread butter on as thick as a steak, added a couple of slices of onion, and then forked out some tomatoes. It was as good as I had imagined. It could only have been better if the tomatoes had been fresh. I ate four slices before taking up the paper.

Reading the first paragraph or two of each article, I found little of interest, but it didn't matter. I was reading. On the third page, I saw an article describing a new baseball team in Kansas City. *The National League has announced the Kansas City Cowboys will join the league for the upcoming season. They plan to play 125 games, about half of them at Association Park in Kansas City. The schedule will be announced at a later date. The manager of the team will be Dave Rowe, who will also be an outfielder. In addition to the Cowboys, the National League is adding the Washington Nationals. The two teams will replace the Buffalo Bisons and the Providence Grays, both of which closed for financial reasons.*

My friends and I, in scouring the Montgomery Ward Catalog, had become familiar with the equipment of the game, if not how to play it, and Willy had actually carved his own bat. We'd hit rocks with it because no one had a ball. I thought I might like to see a game if I was still in the city and could find a way to get off work one day, which was not likely.

Finished with the paper, I pulled the coat back and checked Brit. My anger returned, but I resisted the urge to hit the drunk. I did give up the last vestige of hero worship.

26 Change

The next few days were sunny and back in the twenties, even melting some of the snow. I shopped for food after work each day and had no chance to talk with Brit the whole time. I was down to my last pennies, trying to hold onto the bill in my coat. I saw Brit twice—dead drunk both times—but I needed some money from him, so I did a more thorough search of his clothes and coat, coming up with another 35¢.

I talked to Sam about what to do. "Why don't you stay at our place? One of the fellows just left, and we could use another renter."

"How many of you live there?"

"There are two guys who work nights and now just me working days. With four of us, the rent's 75¢ each for the week. Sound good?"

"Sounds great. I can't afford to live alone. When can I move in?"

"Tonight too soon?"

"I'll be there as soon as I can pick up my bag. Where do you live?"

"I'll just walk with you. We can pick up something to eat, too."

I left a note on the table. *I'm moving in with a friend from work. Thanks for saving my life. Remmy.* Picking up my bag, I followed Sam to my new home. It was Friday, February 5. I felt a twinge of guilt for leaving Brit that way, but it was his fault.

The room was not much different from the one I'd left, except it had two beds instead of one. Sam said, "We put the dirty sheets out before we leave on Saturday mornings, and Josh and Al put the clean ones on. They also have a bath available any day if you arrange for it a day ahead. Costs a dime."

I asked, "Which bed do I get?"

"I always sleep in the one by the window. Okay?"

"Sure. I've been sleeping on the floor. Brit was too hard to sleep with."

We spent a little extra on food that night, tinned peaches and fresh vegetables to go with some potted meat. We also bought some sausages and bread for the next day.

It was a pleasure to talk to someone my own age again. Even though we worked together all day, it was not the same. We talked and laughed over nothing and everything well into that first night.

It was a sleepy Saturday morning, but we managed to check in on time. Lee seemed happier all day, perhaps because we scarcely talked at all.

With a full week's pay of $7.14 that night, the two of us walked happily behind several men from the same rooming house. We spent some time marveling over the new silver certificates, the ones with the picture of Martha Washington on the front and back that filled our pay packets. How to hide my money was still a problem. I gave Sam a dollar for the rent and put three dollars in my hidden pocket while Sam was downstairs paying. The rest had to stay in my pants pocket.

When Sam returned, I asked him if he knew of a safe way to hide money. "I don't know of any. I know a couple of guys who have secret pockets on the insides of their boots, but I've heard thieves always look in boots. I just keep mine on me and hope for the best. Most of the men don't have to worry about it, 'cause they just drink and gamble it away."

"Always seemed like a waste to me. I like a drink now and then, but I don't see much point in getting drunk."

"I'm with you, but I do like to play cards, except when those boys in the saloons start throwing a whole dollar down for one card. I can't play for that kind of money."

The more we talked, the more I realized Sam needed to know my story. I did not want to tell it again, with all the emotion wrapped up with it, but Maude was right. I just hoped Sam wouldn't feel sorry for me.

Once we had started eating in the room, I said, "I don't want you getting the wrong idea about me. I'm going to tell you something no one else here knows, but I don't want it to change anything between us. Agreed?"

Sam stopped eating and stared at me. Then with a questioning tone, he said, "Sure. You can tell me anything."

At first, it seemed strange to describe murder while eating, but it actually made it easier for me. I didn't hold anything back. Sam heard the uncensored version, even more than Jim: five shots, running through the snow, Maude, Brit, the sheriff, even my anger at Father. Sam listened, barely looking at the food he was shoving into his mouth. When I finished, Sam looked thoughtful for awhile, then said, "So, you ready to play some poker?" I laughed and felt a bit of my heavy load lifted away.

Neither of us ever mentioned it again, and I could see no difference in Sam's attitude.

I began to relax. I had a good job, a good friend, some money, and only a few bad dreams. I knew I could lose it all at any moment, but I never gave much thought to the police arresting me. My fear was having Red Beard find me.

27 Shock

We awoke to a late-winter blizzard colder and windier than it had any right to be. The extra clothing did little to keep the cold wind from bristling and prickling our hides. We struggled all day, fighting to keep the hay on the cart long enough to fork it into the pens, fighting to shovel snow drifts from walks, fighting just to stay warm. For the most part, we lost the fight.

As the shift ended, the wind, as though to mock us, died away. We walked to our room in a gentle snow falling from a quiet sky. Neither of us had the strength to buy food, satisfied with stale bread before collapsing into sleep.

Tuesday morning was sunny with no wind, but still arctic. We made it out of bed early enough to buy some bread and sausage to eat as we walked to work. Otherwise, the day proved normal. After the skirmish of the previous day, it was a pleasure to pitch hay all day in the sunshine. We even felt warm, though the thermometer read 2 degrees.

The brief cold snap reminded us of the killing blizzard of January 7, one in which at least 100 Kansans had frozen to death, as had 100,000 head of cattle and countless other animals. When I first read the numbers in the paper, I got the shakes, realizing that I'd come perilously close to being one of the frozen. I gave Mother a special *thank you* for making me overdress. I'd barely made it, even with all the clothes.

I was adjusting to my new life as a city boy, though working with livestock all day was barely city living. I now marveled at why I had been so afraid. I still had dreams, still missed my family, but life was going well. Even so, being happy gave me a sense of guilt.

I had been to Holy Name Church a few times to check for a message, but there was no good news—rather, no news, good or bad. As far as I knew, the sheriff was still hunting me as a murderer. I considered moving farther away, but I did not have enough money to go very far, and I had a good friend here. Still, the possibility that the local police might have my wanted poster made me nervous when I thought of it. On the other hand, I had yet to see a copper in our part of the city.

Two days later, warm air blew in from the south, and the streets became rivers by nightfall. As the ground of the aisles in the yard thawed, an inch or more of mud formed on top of the still-frozen dirt, making movement treacherous for men and beasts.

That same night, walking past an intersection on the way home, I glanced down the side street to my right. A man on a horse. High bowler. Red on the hat. Brown horse. Flash of white on the left rump. Raw instinct kept me frozen instead of diving to the ground and crawling under a fast melting snowdrift. Blood rushed to my eyes as I strained to see more. I could not hear my own thudding heart. Was it Red Beard? A mere whisper of the image of a man and horse remained.

Sam told me later that he tugged on my arm and asked, "What's wrong?" Then he shook my arm and asked more loudly, "What's wrong?" Finally, he turned me to him and shouted the words a third time.

The horse and rider were long gone when I realized I was facing Sam. "Did you see him?"

"Who? What's wrong?" Only half-aware of Sam's questions, I turned my head to peer again through the empty penumbra of the single gaslight. Sam poked my ribs. "What's happening?"

I broke from my near trance. "I think I saw him. Did you see a man on a horse down there?" I pointed.

"No. Who did you see?"

I started to speak, dropped my head, and finally said, "Maybe the killer, I don't know. I just saw his back for a second." I lifted my head and looked into Sam's eyes. "It looked like him. Same hat for sure."

"What do you want to do?"

"Run like hell."

Sam pulled me out of the street and pushed me back to the apartment. "We could go to the police."

"No. I don't even know if it was Red Beard, and if it was, I have no idea where he went. Besides, I'm the one accused. They'd just arrest me."

"Yeah, I forgot I'm living with a murderer."

"We'll just have to be extra careful."

"Careful? Come on, he's a killer, and he'll probably shoot both of us. I know you're used to being chased by a lunatic, but I'm new at this."

"Don't cry, you big baby." I gave him a quick jab to the arm, with meaning.

"Hey, what's that for?"

"Sorry, seeing him makes me want to hit someone, and you're it."

Sam could now see that I was serious. "Okay, but next time you see Red Beard, hit him, or at least my other arm." He rubbed the sore spot.

For the next few days, I walked to work and back with my hat pulled low and without making any stops. Sam did all the shopping. It was not that different; we seldom went anywhere anyway.

28 Flowers

March lived up to its notoriety; days of cold wind proceeded days of warm wind. There was a brief snow flurry in the first week and several rain showers throughout the month. By the end of the month, the first flowers were in full bloom, though we saw few of them in our neighborhood.

There were no additional sightings of any man looking like the killer. Neither of us ever left the safety of the room without a careful study of every man and horse we saw. Even at the yard, we kept our eyes open. We often talked about what to do if we saw him but developed no plan. We never studied, "how to deal with a killer," in school.

I became a little fixated on going to the far west and getting a job on a ranch. As the weeks slid by and the pennies were saved, I puzzled out a plan to go to Cheyenne, thinking, *How hard can it be to find work there? It should be far enough away from Red Beard.* Sam's response put a damper on the plan. "You'll have to go alone. I'm not going to ride a horse all day."

My retort? "You'd rather look at a mule's butt all day."

Sam was from near Chillicothe, Missouri, and had lived in a luxury I could only imagine. Instead of hoeing for sixteen hours, Sam sat on a cultivator and kept a couple of mules in line. His father had all the latest farm equipment and plenty of horses and mules trained for each piece. No one I knew in all of Neosho County had that kind of money.

"Even with the equipment, there was more than enough work for everyone," Sam said. "I was flabbergasted when Bob told me I needed to find work. I always thought I would join them in running the place. I don't know why, but Dad left the whole place to Bob and Bill, and I guess they decided they didn't want to share."

"How much older are they?"

"Bob's thirty-two, and Bill's thirty. Their mother died trying to birth twins when the boys were little. My mother had three girls before I was born. I never knew her. She died birthing me."

"That's bad. Did your dad remarry?"

"No, I think having three wives die put him off marriage. Besides, he was getting old. He was never close to me and treated me more like a hired hand."

"Did he...hurt you?"

"Oh, no. He mostly ignored me. He hired a lady from town to take care of me until I could work some." Sam shrugged. "It was all right. Anyway, I ended up here, and I'm saving money to get my own place in a few years."

"You really like to farm?"

"Sure. Don't you?"

"It's okay, but I'd like to do something more exciting."

I went back to my newspaper as we relaxed before sleep. I read that Congress had set aside half a million dollars to build a monument to President Lincoln in the nation's capital. The author hoped the monument would not take forty years to complete like the one for President Washington. I said, "It's about time."

Sam said, "It's a waste of money. I could buy half of Missouri for that." I started to retaliate but remembered I was living with a Border Ruffian.

In another story, I read of the new Hudson River League of professional baseball, with teams in Albany, Troy, Kingston, Newburg, Hudson, Poughkeepsie, Yonkers, and Peekskill. I had heard of Albany and the Hudson, but not the others. I asked, "Where do people get money to pay just to watch a ballgame?"

"And when would they have time to watch? All the games are during working hours. We'll never see one."

A more serious news story caught my attention. "Hay, Sam, listen to this. 'The Knights of Labor called for a strike against the Union Pacific; Missouri Pacific; and the Missouri, Kansas, and Texas rail lines, all of which run through Kansas City. They are demanding more pay and fewer hours.'"

"Why didn't we think of that?"

I added, "I can see us telling Frank we want two dollars a day or we'll quit!"

"Then where would we work?"

"Right. According to this, there are 200,000 workers on strike. That could hurt the railroads."

"I've heard of people going on strike, but I never understood it. I'm just happy to have a job."

"It would be nice for workers to be able to have a say in the business. After all, they do all the hard work and know what goes on. I've got some ideas about how the yard could be improved."

Sam said, "You know the only reason we are here is to make the owner of the yard rich. If he gave us more money, he might not be able to afford all his household servants."

"I wonder what the workers do when they go on strike. How can they afford not to work?" The Knights of Labor and their strike intrigued me, and I later learned of Jay Gould's role in it. He controlled the three rail lines and was ruthless in how he treated the workers. My sympathy went to them.

I grew up on a farm, and farmers are an independent bunch. They learn to wrestle with nature, with very little help from anyone else. Farmers assume everyone should be willing to work all day every day for little reward. The work is the reward. I, however, was beginning to understand that I was not a farmer. I rather liked the notion that the Knights of Labor were trying to have some control over their working conditions. Another nickel a day wouldn't hurt my disposition, either.

29 Longhorns

As the weather turned warmer at the end of March, several cowboys, in frantic need of open prairie, left to find work on the western range. Frank approached the two of us and said, "I need a couple of good hands on the loading crew, and you're two of my best. I hate to take you away from Lee, but I'd really like to have you. You want to switch?"

We looked at each other before saying, "Sure."

"Great. I've got a couple of new boys in the office now. I'll give them to Lee in an hour. Then I'll take you to your new spots. Lee, I know you'll break them in right. Thanks."

Lee gave a little wave as Frank left, then said, "I'll deny ever saying this, so don't bother repeating it. You're the best crew I've worked with in the fifteen years I've been here. Now, show those lazy loaders how real men work." With that, he snapped the reins, and we headed for the pens with a load of hay.

The new job started easily enough. The foreman told us to stand on the gate that opened the pen and blocked the aisle, forcing the cattle into the pen. As we watched, twenty cows ran down the aisle, straight for us. Every muscle tensing, I shouted, “Sam, they’re going to kill us!”

For his part, Sam screamed and waved his hat like a crazed man. The cows turned in with hardly a glance at the two of us. By the time the third carload reached us, we were able to wave them in without visions of being trampled to death.

The hardest part of the job turned out to be all the walking. The next pen was often located in the next aisle or two over, but we had to walk a half-mile to get to it. Most of the pens had 2x8’s along the top for us to walk on, but even that shortcut was a long-cut. By day’s end, our legs, trained to stand all day on a moving wagon, were turning to pulp.

We were envious of the older men who rode horses to drive the herds.

After a week of being the target of the stock runs, the foreman rotated us to the sides, where it was somewhat safer. The second week gave us a nasty view of what could go wrong. A load of longhorns from Texas came off with a full head of steam. They coursed past me like water from a burst dam; I did not have to do anything to keep them moving. I watched as the two men standing on the gate waving and shouting realized they were in trouble. The steers hit the gate with heads down and horns out. Their combined mass snapped the heavy lumber into kindling.

I saw one of the men jump to a side fence just as the herd hit the gate, but the other man rode it until it hit the side. In an instant, everyone was running to the scene. Some chased the steers as several of us helped the injured. The jumper broke his leg in a bad landing, but the horns missed him. The other man sailed into a pen where several heifers, dehorned but spooked by the stampede, attacked him. Still, it was much better than ending up in the aisle where dying was a sure thing. He had cuts and bruises all over but no broken bones. The worst of it was one of the longhorns was killed in the mad dash.

Everyone was extra careful for a week or so. I started to wonder if we had made a wise choice to switch.

30 Special

By late April, I was getting tired of doing the same thing every day. I couldn't stop thinking of all the different kinds of work we did on the farm in the spring. Everything happened at once, and the days never ended at sunset, but it was interesting. I hated to admit it, but I missed farm work.

When we finished offloading the last of the cattle from one train, Frank called the two of us over and introduced us to Zac Sanders. I had noticed him earlier looking at the stock. He was the type of man who could disappear in any group, as average as a head of cabbage.

"Boys, Zac here needs a couple of good hands to travel with him and take care of his livestock. I'll let him tell you the details. I'll say it would be a great opportunity for you, so give him some attention."

Zac said, "You're Remmy, and you're Sam, right?"

Together, we replied, "Yes, sir."

"I'm Zac to those who know me. Three years ago, I went to work on a little circus called Buffalo Bill's Wild West. We travel around the country showing people what the West is really like. There are a couple of hundred people with the show and even more animals. We could use some more good hands this season to help with the animals. I've known Frank a long time, and he told me you boys are good workers and aren't tied down. Do you think you would be interested in traveling with us?"

Sam snapped, "Yes, sir!"

I followed with, "Sounds good, sir." I didn't know much about either Buffalo Bill or the circus, but it seemed to solve my problem of how to get farther away from Red Beard and have a little adventure besides.

"One thing: you'll have to stop calling me *sir*. I was a private in the army. Tomorrow, you'll be on the payroll. I'll go settle things with the office, and you can pick up your pay tonight. You won't need to report here until noon tomorrow. That'll give you time to take care of any last business. Meet me at Frank's office. Now, go give them a good last day of work."

"Yes, sir, I mean, Zac."

As we worked, we saw him a few more times looking at stock and wondered what all he was buying. We did help cut two longhorns and run them into his loading pen, where there were already several other steers and heifers of all breeds.

We each picked up an envelope that night containing three days' pay, $3.06 each. I added the 6¢ to the coins in a sock in my pants pocket to keep them from rattling. I put one dollar in the other pocket and two dollars in my boot. Sam did much the same before we headed for our room for the last time.

On the way, Sam said, "Let's celebrate! We'll eat at the saloon next to the house. For a nickel beer, we can eat all we want, and I'm thinking I might have two beers."

"Do they have anything besides boiled eggs and sausage?"

"Not much, but we can eat all we want. Come on."

My stomach tensed at the thought of more sausage, but I agreed.

We found a quiet corner so others could not eavesdrop. We also needed to keep an eye out for Red Beard. Sam filled me in on Buffalo Bill. "He was a scout, both in the War and in some of the Indian wars. He rode for the Pony Express and hunted Buffalo in Kansas for the railroad workers to eat. That's how he got his name. He's one of the most famous men in the country. I can't believe you haven't heard of him."

"Sorry, we had to work on our farm. But, I did learn some of that in school."

Sam ignored the dig. "Anyway, it should be fun to travel all over and get paid for it."

"How much?"

"How much what?"

"How much is he paying us?"

Sam looked surprised. "I don't know. He never did say, did he? But, I'm sure it'll be at least what we get now."

"I hope so. You're right, though. It'll be fun at least, even if we don't make much. You can always buy your farm later."

"Sure. A chance like this doesn't come along often."

I talked Sam out of having a third beer, and we went up to the room to pack and talk. Sleep came late.

The next morning we told Josh, Al, and the house owner we were leaving. Everyone wished us well. Al said, "If he needs any more help, don't forget us."

Before noon, we were watching Margaret beat on the machine and add paper after paper to the growing pile on her desk. No one seemed to look at the great stacks of paper Margaret and others created. I tried to imagine what could be so important to pay someone a day's wage for what seemed a waste.

At about 12:30, Frank and Zac erupted into the office, bringing their laughter with them. I detected the beer fumes at once and guessed they had eaten their lunch at a nearby saloon. We were used to eating out of our pockets as we worked.

Zac said, "Ready to get to work, boys?"

"Yes." I had to bite off the *sir.*

"Some of my boys are getting set to load the stock I bought here as well as some I got out in Hays City. I stopped there on my way in from Denver. Anyway, let's go see how they're coming along, and you boys can start earning your pay. I've already paid you half a day just to sit here and watch this beautiful young lady pound those keys." Margaret blushed but kept typing.

We arrived at a meager train of six cattle cars plus two coach cars. Zac introduced us to the others before saying, "I'll start you out easy. Within a few weeks, you should know just about every aspect of this job. We have at least one of almost every kind of animal that people back east are willing to pay money to see.

"You'll take care of the stock, help train them, load them, run them in and out of the show, and do anything else you're told to do. You'll help set up tents, signs, stages, music stands, stadium seats, ticket booths, and vendor stalls. In your free time, you'll help cook, clean, sew, and generally make yourselves useful. If you took this job because it sounded easy, you might want to reconsider now." He gave each of us a long look.

"Another thing Cody never mentions—there are two classes of people in this outfit: those of us who do all the work and those who go on stage and pretend to be cowboys and Indians. Oh, yes. There are lots of Indians in the crew, and Mexicans, Canadians, and some I don't know what. They don't all speak English. The Mexicans on our crew are all right; they do good work, so don't give them any trouble. You'll find fighting almost always leads to unemployment with Cody. He expects us to get along with everyone. Any questions?"

All we heard, so we just shook our heads no, dazed us both.

"Good. Your first job will be to help load all this stock. You're experts now, so I shouldn't have to tell you too much. You know your way around the yards, so you open and close the gates and make sure we don't do any damage to their fine facility."

We helped with the cattle, horses, hogs, sheep, and goats. The sheep and goats went in a small pen inside a car, and a couple of hogs went into another pen. Cody had specially ordered two wild razorback hogs from Arkansas, so the crew had already built a stronger pen inside the car just for them. Not looking much like pigs, they were tall, thin, and black, with tusks sticking several inches out of their mouths. One of the older men commented, “I saw one of the brutes tear a fifty-pound hunting dog into scraps. Give ‘em plenty of room.”

The cattle and horses were loaded so they were facing the sides of the cars. Pushers forced each animal into position. It was the hardest of the loading jobs. Once they were in place, the animals could not, move and they held each other up as the train rocked and swayed along the tracks.

As we worked, my eagerness to get out of the city grew. I had not realized how living for weeks with the thought of Red Beard sharing the city had depressed me. I experienced a kind of new birth, a freedom. Alternatively, maybe I just needed a change.

31 Omaha

Our new abode turned out to be one of the coach cars we had seen earlier. Specially outfitted for members of the crew to live in, it had fifteen bunk beds, three high, along one wall and an open area at one end with a coal stove and some chairs. The space on the other side was where we stored our personal items. Zac told us to take the top bunks, because the old hands got the lower ones.

He filled us in on the show itself. "Most of our hands and actors will be in St. Louis waiting for us. We'll pick up some in Omaha and Chicago, along with more stock. This season won't involve as much travel as the first three did. We'll do six weeks of shows as we make our way to New York, but once we're there, we'll stay until fall.

"Cody started the Wild West in Omaha back in '83. I signed on almost the first day. We spent our first three summers in cars like these and the tents you'll see later. We traveled all over the country, sometimes doing six towns in a week."

Sam asked, "What did you do in the winters?"

"We used to have to find our own jobs, but Cody is trying to put together a winter show this year. Still, a lot of people will come and go, even in one season.

"This car will be for single boys like you. Many of them were with us last year, but there are plenty of new boys as well. You'll find yourselves spending most of your time with them. Cody tells the press we're one big happy family, but a lot of the actors don't like to mix with us workers. I'm just telling you, so you don't get into trouble. Don't try being friends with them. If they approach you, that's fine."

Sam asked, "Should we call him Mr. Cody?"

"No, call him Cody. I'm not sure he'd answer to anything else."

We were grinning like idiots. There were five others in the car, three of them playing poker and the other two watching. They talked with the ease of friendship. Sam and I were the lone new hands so far.

I asked, "What is our pay?"

Zac gave a sad smile. "Nate Salsbury runs the business end of the show, and he has set the starting salary at $25 a month, plus room and board. I know what the yard paid you, but you didn't get room and board. If I like your work, and you stay a year, you can expect to see some increase.

"The two boys over there watching the poker are making $30, and the others are getting $28. The two watching the play save most of their money. They don't waste it on drink, either. I'd suggest you do the same."

I had already done the math. "That's great pay." I could see myself saving $20 a month instead of $2.

Zac added, "I'll let you in on a little secret. Nate and Cody are willing to pay good money, but they expect good work for the money. Cody's all smiles with the public, but he can be a bit of a slave driver, so don't expect to get calluses on your butts unless it's from him kicking you."

The trip to Omaha didn't take long. We waited for a time in Atchison for a southbound train, but from there it was all clear, and we learned the train was going fifty miles an hour at times.

When I was thinking of going to sleep, the train stopped. Zac and the old hands were up and leaving the car when Zac said, "Come on boys, time to earn your keep." We soon had their first view of the Omaha Stockyards, good-sized, but no contest to KC. It took more than an hour to offload, feed, and water the stock.

The engine was decoupled, and I noticed another, longer train on the siding next to us. Zac said, "Get some sleep. We load at dawn."

One of the older men was asleep within minutes, his snoring in tune with the mooing cattle. I was too excited to sleep, so I slipped outside to check our new home. I saw someone step down from the other train. We eyed each other a moment before I approached, and I was soon talking with JR Grice. He was maybe my age, shorter by several inches, with a roundish head and deep-set eyes. His eyes drew me in. They were large and dark, seeming to see right into my soul.

"So, where are you headed?"

JR hesitated before saying, "I'm going into town to look around. You want to go?"

I wasn't sure Zac would allow us to leave. "What if we get caught?"

JR laughed. "Are we prisoners?"

My face flushed. I said, "You're right." We started walking. "How long will you be gone?"

"Not more than a couple of hours. We'll be up early, but we can sleep once we're underway."

Prowling the dark streets cued my memory of heading to the room in KC after work. Except for the sporadic drunk, the streets were deserted. Life, such as it was, appeared to exist only in the open saloons.

I said, "Not much to see at night, huh?"

"No, but it's a city, however small. Let's see what the locals are drinking." He opened the door to one of the bigger saloons.

We had no more than sat down with our beers when a redheaded man faltered his way toward us, muttering something in a strange language.

My memory of the event is a bit suspect. JR gave me the details later. I jumped up and shouted, "Get away!" The man kept coming. I dove at him, catching him at the belt with my shoulder and taking him to the sawdust floor.

I raised my right fist to smash the man's face, but a muscular hand grabbed me and jerked me to my feet. The barman said with no emotion, "This dumb Ruski wants you to buy him a drink. I think you should do that before you leave."

My attention left the man on the floor and took in the substantial barkeep gripping my arm while holding a solid club in the other hand. I gave a nod of agreement, but JR had a quarter out before I could get my hand free.

I looked again at the man on the floor. He didn't even have a beard.

32 Chicago

Sleep that night was ragged. Nothing in my life had prepared me for the animal fear that had taken and shaken me in the saloon. In my mind, I could still see Red Beard coming at me. Yet, the image of the real man on the floor was just as clear. How could I mistake a beardless drunk for the killer? JR had been square with it. He never said a word as we made our way back. We talked about it weeks later, when we came to know each other well enough.

The promise of sunlight was in the east, and the bouquet of horses and cattle relaxed me for the job of loading. As we worked, I wondered why JR had not asked any questions the night before. After all, we had just met, yet he'd taken care of everything, even leading me like a lost child. It was strange that I trusted him almost on sight. However, for a few days, suspicions of his motives grew like weeds.

All such thoughts vanished when the buffalo rumbled by. As I stood on the fence, my first close look at the brutes gave me my first smile of the day. The nearer they came, the more my heart raced. Even as my instincts demanded a run for cover, I managed to hold my post and even relished the last of the half-ton monarchs as they skidded past, their massive low-slung heads barely clearing the ground.

I didn't even notice they were all cows. Nate explained on the train later that summer was mating season, and they left the bulls home to avoid the constant fighting that would certainly disrupt the show. It was incredible to learn the bulls were nearly twice as large.

Later, actually touching living deer, antelope, and elk sent prickles through my body and put a goofy grin on my face. Still, because of their fear of closed spaces, they were difficult to lead into the cars.

Jerry the Moose was a delight. He was so tame he needed little prodding to enter his car. The mountain goats were another story. Stubborn, swift, and nimble, they had to be roped and dragged into the cars.

By the time I slammed the last door cleat into place, I had forgotten my troubles for the day. As the train headed east on the Chicago and Rock Island RR, the crew sat in a dining car that everyone called the pie car. It contained one long table with chairs on either side. Servers brought our breakfast.

A man came in with long brown hair and an elaborate goatee. Several of the older men greeted him with the ease of familiarity. Sam poked me, saying, "That's Cody." The star of the show made his way around the table, talking to each man in turn, commenting on my Kansas roots.

There was little to do for most of the trip. At every stop through the day, part of the crew would check the livestock and then go back to drink hot coffee, play poker, and tell tall tales. We stopped before sundown and let all the animals out for feed and water, only to reload them for an all-night ride. I learned that would be the procedure for all longer trips.

I had little trouble falling asleep after that workout, but I woke several times when the train had to stop to take on coal and water or to wait for a train to pass. Once, someone woke me with two others to check the animals. Others did the checking at other stops.

A beautiful sunrise greeted us a few miles short of Iowa City, but I didn't have time to enjoy the sunset or the city as we set to work offloading and feeding the animals.

Back on the road, I sat down next to JR at breakfast as we crossed the Mississippi River at Rock Island, Illinois. Having no idea how to start, I settled on, "Hi."

JR gave me a big grin. "Hit any drunks lately?"

That stung. I stammered, "I...don't...I.... What do you think of me?"

JR lost his smile. Putting his fork on the table, he said, "Forget it. I know you had your reasons and you don't have to tell me. But, it was the best entertainment I've had in months." Just the hint of a grin.

I studied JR's face, trying to interpret his meaning. "It didn't seem that funny to me."

JR's grin dropped at once. "No, I'm sure it wasn't. Look, this isn't the place to talk, but I think we have something in common. You thought that drunk was a danger to you. I've got dangerous people to watch for, too. Maybe we can help each other."

My head twitched back just an inch. *Now what?* Still studying JR's face, I asked, "Have you tackled any drunks?""

Now JR did laugh, aloud. "You're all right. Let's forget it for now. We'll talk later."

With little else to do, I spent much of the day rehashing the conversation with JR. I wished I knew what he was up to. What did he mean he had people chasing him?

The sun was setting as the train pulled up to another small stockyard and the process of feeding and watering began. We worked in a light rain without bothering with rain gear. Lanterns were set up long before the work was finished, but at least the rain moved on. We were too soon back on the swaying train, where I ate ham and beans with cornbread and was asleep an hour later.

At some point in the night, I woke when the train bumped to a halt. I had just closed my eyes to get back to sleep when Zac yelled, "Up and at 'em!"

Following the others outside, I saw a yard complex that disappeared into the gloom. There could be no doubt that it was the Chicago Union Stockyard. Zac was standing on a loading ramp, roaring, "We have to get all the stock off the cars and settled in tonight. Get with your group leader, and let's get going. We start with the horses."

Offloading stock in daylight could be dangerous; at night, it was doubly so. I worked with one of the yardmen opening and closing gates. When the first carload of horses streamed down the corridor, I was standing atop the blocking gate, waving my hat. All went well with the cattle, but when the buffalo thundered toward me, I clutched the gate in a good imitation of eagle's talons.

The work finished, a few of the men opted to go right to bed, but most headed to the pie car for food. Our reward was sausage and scrambled eggs. One man quipped, "I think we just offloaded this pig."

As we ate, the train jiggled and jarred around the yards, ending on the far side of the rail lines but still in sight of the pens we had just filled.

Zac came through and said, "I'll be calling you by groups to tend to the animals through the day and night. Otherwise, you're free, but no one leaves this part of the yards without my permission. I can tell you more tomorrow."

Some of the younger men went outside to look around our new home. Most, including Sam and me, headed for our bunks. We'd slept no more than an hour when we were the first to receive the call.

One of the razorbacks had managed to get out of the pen. While a dozen men risked losing body parts to recapture the elusive beasts, I had to poke my hand through the fence to position new lumber over the hole made by the escapee. The remaining hog, offended by my actions, charged every time he saw my hand. When the errant beast returned, the two animals became more interested in each other than in me, and we finished the patching job.

When the other men trudged back to their bunks, Sam and I, now reasonably awake, decided to explore a little. After all, we'd had a good hour's nap. We crawled on top of a car, which gave us a panorama of the Union Stock Yards. Straight ahead to the north, there were pens as far as we could see, and to the right were thousands of rail cars on dozens of rail lines. To the left were enormous buildings spewing smoke to add to the city's defiled air.

Sam pointed at the buildings. "Look at those packing houses! They make the ones in Kansas City look like anthills. I never imagined this place would be this big."

"Whenever anyone asks me what Hell looks like, I'll tell them I've seen it and it's the packing plants."

After a long nap and lunch, Sam joined a poker game in one car while I watched. I sat near a couple of older men who were talking quietly, one of them nursing a pipe, filling the air with its fruity bouquet. Sam was losing almost every hand—never more than a few pennies, but losing.

My attention drifted from the game as I listened to the men beside me. The one with the pipe was saying, "I imagine Cody took himself downtown to a fancy hotel while we sit in this manure pile."

The other man, some years younger than the first, said, "I've heard we're waiting on some Frenchies from Canada."

The first waved his pipe. "Yeah, supposed to make us more international."

Sam gave up on the game, and the two of us headed to the pie car for some coffee. One of the great things about working for Cody was the coffee. There were several large urns full during the day and one at night. There was also sugar and cream for the faint of heart.

As we drank, I asked, "So, how much did you lose?"

"More than I should have. I kept thinking the cards would get better. I'll get 'em next time."

"Who was the big winner while you were there?"

"No one. Everyone took hands except me."

"I guess that's good."

"Why?"

"My father said a real gambler would win most of the hands in a game like that."

Sam gave him a quizzical look. "Your father a gambler?"

I laughed. "Sure, he was a farmer. He always said playing poker was for sissies. Putting all your money into a crop and waiting for the weather to ruin it was real gambling."

Sam smiled. "You got it. We did well most of the time, but we had some crummy years, too. One year we lived on rabbits and squirrels, because two crops failed and our bull died."

We went on talking of our farm experiences and found we had more in common than just farming. Sam had a brother who had been ill most of his life before dying of phenomena. Tears formed in our eyes as we remembered the dead in each of our families.

33 Easter

The short wait turned into a long one when Zac informed us we could expect to be in the yards for at least a week. Storms in Canada had delayed the trains with some of the show's actors and crew.

Then he added, "Tomorrow is Easter, and some of you may want to go to church. Check with me before you leave, so I can be sure we have enough to work the stock. Everybody will get a day or two off, so don't worry about it. Whenever you go, you must be back before dark. I don't need anyone crawling back here with a knot on his head."

I was close to JR and asked, "You going?"

"Oh, yeah. Want to come along?"

"Sure. Sam, you want to walk around Chicago for a while?"

"No, I've seen enough of cities for now. You guys go on."

I was eager to talk with JR and was glad Sam stayed behind. Once we were on our way, I asked, "How bad did I look in Omaha?"

JR gave a soft snigger. "You could have just told him to buy his own drinks."

That broke the tension. "I really thought he was someone else; I ... just overreacted. Hope I didn't embarrass you too much."

"Don't worry, half the guys in there didn't even look up. That goes on all the time, especially with begging drunks."

"Thanks. Anyway, I'll stand you a few beers."

"You don't owe me anything."

"You pulled me out of a tight spot."

"You would have done the same for me."

"I'd like to think so."

"Besides, if you call that a tight spot, you lead a dull life."

I wondered what he meant, but asked instead, "What did you mean when you said you had enemies?"

JR did not answer at first. We walked the noisy streets of the rowdy city, catching a dozen different languages before JR's answer came. "I don't know you well enough yet to tell you everything, and I doubt you want to tell me everything. But, since you gave me a peek at your danger, I'll tell you that I've lived in Nebraska for just two years. Before that...well...my life was different."

I waited. "That's it? Different? No enemies?"

"We can talk about them later. Let's enjoy our walk."

JR seemed to enjoy it, but I had to spend some time rehashing the conversation before I could return my full attention to the street. When I did, I realized we had entered an area with mostly English signs, one of which advertised books and newspapers. "Let's go in. I'd like to get a paper." I picked up a copy of the *Chicago Mail.* As I was getting ready to check out, Mark Twain's newest, *The Adventures of Huckleberry Finn,* caught my eye.

I struggled over the dollar price tag when JR said, "If you don't get it. I will." I bought it.

Back near the car, we situated ourselves in the shade and began to read the paper, splitting it between us. I found a long article that described socialists, suggesting the city was loaded with them, but I couldn't make out what they were. That they were bad seemed clear enough.

"JR, do you know anything about these socialists?"

"They in the paper?"

"There's a big article that says they want better pay and working conditions."

"I think most of them are foreigners, Germans especially."

"When I was in KC, I read about the rail workers who were on strike, and it said they were socialists, too. This article seems to say socialists are more than just strikers. It also says some are 'anarchists'. What's that?"

"I know they don't like governments, but then, that means were all anarchist."

On Monday, I went to a shop closer to the yards. Inside, I found an eclectic mix of languages, spoken and printed. I almost turned to leave, but after standing a minute to take it in, I gave the room a more serious look. No one seemed to pay me any attention. No one looked like an anarchist.

The shop itself was unusual, with furnishings and interior walls covered in shades of gray, highlighted with patches of white newsprint. It smelled of stale body odor, stale tobacco, and stale beer, much like most saloons but without the puke. Its salvation was the scent of new paper and ink. As my eyes adjusted to the dimness at the back of the shop, I could see men huddled in tight groups, talking in languages I had no hope of grasping. Most of them were dressed in work clothes, yet it was evident they weren't working.

I later realized I had entered one of the many gathering spots for the city's socialists and I suspect now that they were speaking German. At the time, I just wondered why they were not working.

Walking to the racks of newspapers, I found just two in English. With a copy of each, I gave a nickel to the lady, who gave me 2¢ saying, "Danke." Before I left, I noticed books on shelves on the other side of the shop. They were in many languages, but none in English.

Back at the yard, I found an empty stool next to our car. The day was warm and sunny, so the shade felt good after my walk of three or four miles. As I cooled down, I closed my eyes and allowed the memory of the bookshop to play through a few times, savoring anew the realization that there were people and things in this world I'd never imagined before.

I picked up a paper calling itself the *Voice of the Workers!* On the front page were articles quoting large sections of speeches made by Albert Parsons and August Spies. The only thing that made much sense to me was a call for the workers to go on strike for shorter workdays and more money. If this was socialism, I was a socialist.

An editorial inside denounced someone in Europe named Karl Marx for insisting on legal strikes only. The writer disagreed, saying nothing would change without violent action. He cited a book called *Revolutionary War*

Science by Johann Most, who advocated throwing bombs into police stations and shooting police at every opportunity. If this was socialism, then I was no socialist.

Laying the paper aside, I thought about what I had read and tried to piece it together. It seemed workers, some of whom worked as long as eighteen hours a day, wanted to have a time limit on the work. That seemed reasonable to me. As a farmer, we often worked eighteen hours in the summer. Still, a set time limit seemed a good thing if it was possible.

I knew most of the strikers were asking for an eight-hour workday, with two or even three groups of people working in the same twenty-four-hour period. They called it working in shifts. Two shifts would be perfect for farming in the summer when long days were routine, but it would not work in the winter.

The other thing they wanted was more money. I was uncertain what the socialists meant by that demand; from what I had read, they were all over the map on the issue. Most workers I knew seemed to accept a dollar a day as typical pay. Counting room and board, I was getting a little more. What if I worked just eight hours and still earned a dollar? I would have sixteen hours to do other things, but I could think of nothing I would want to spend so much time doing, except maybe reading. Besides, I wouldn't have enough money to do much with the extra eight hours.

No, working twelve hours seemed right, and a day off every week was significant, especially after my experience at the stockyards. The fact that Zac was paying me to sit in the shade and read the paper was even better.

Picking up the second paper, I at once saw an article describing the coming May Day. As I read, though, I realized it was not the May Day I was expecting. It spoke of the day as *victory for the workers.* Nationally, companies large and small would implement the eight-hour workday. The workers should take the day to celebrate their victory. I wondered if Cody knew about the victory.

34 Workers

JR and I walked to the gray bookshop and bought copies of the two papers again. We took them into a saloon, ordered beers, and began to comb the papers for more information on the May Day events.

I finished my paper, learning nothing new. JR was still looking at page two of his edition. I asked, "Did you find something?" JR shushed me. Then I realized he wasn't even looking at the paper; his eyes were closed.

Now totally confused, I waited a minute before asking, "What are you doing?"

"I'm listening." He nodded his head toward a nearby table.

I looked at the table, seeing two men sitting close together and speaking quietly. I realized they were speaking English, though the accents threw me.

"Krempfer can't be there, but the rest will make it."

"We need everybody there. The bigger the crowd the more they have to listen to us."

"I can't force men to come." They went back and forth, but I didn't catch much more, given their accents.

The two men left and I asked JR, "What were they saying?"

"Some kind of meeting. I think they're part of the socialist movement we've been reading about. There is a parade tomorrow, but there is also a big speech the next day. They need to get a big crowd at the speech."

"I heard the part about the crowd. What are they up to?"

"I don't know, but it sounds interesting. I think I'll try to find it. Want to come along?"

I half-joked. "What, and get arrested for being a socialist?"

"You can't get arrested for being a socialist. Besides, we're not socialists and we won't be very close to the action.

I just want to be across the street and see what's happening."

"I'm in."

On May Day, Zac told everyone to stay in the yards, because there might be trouble. "Today's a good day to play poker." That was all right with me. We planned to go the next day.

Sam, David, and JR were sitting in a shady spot when I came along. "Mind if I join you?"

Sam asked, "No paper today? I thought maybe Zac would let you get one."

"No. I guess he thinks the socialists are going to take over the city."

David said, "I've overheard some of the yard workers talking about today. They think they're getting an eight-hour workday and more money. I think they're crazy."

I added, "They've been striking for months, trying to get it."

David said, "That's the foreigners for you. They come here, take our jobs, and then complain about it. Why don't they just go back home?"

Sam said, "They're not leaving here. They make too much money ever to leave."

"So, now they should get paid more to do less? That proves how lazy they really are."

I tried to mediate. "Actually, they're asking for a pay cut."

"Pay cut? How do you figure that?"

"Let's just say, to make the math easy, I'm working sixteen hours for 10¢. That's $1.60 a day, right?" They all nodded. "I work eight hours and get paid for ten, that's just a dollar."

David was quick on that: "It's still an increase. It should be 80¢."

I changed the subject. "What do you think it's like in one of those packing plants?"

Sam said, "It's just like when we butcher at home, except more of it."

I said, "When we finish one hog, I'm covered in blood. I can't imagine doing thousands in one day. There must be a river of blood in those buildings."

We were quiet a minute before I said, "I wouldn't work there, even if they got an eight-hour day and fifty cents an hour."

The next day, Sunday, was the day of the speech JR had overheard the men discussing. Finding the location of the event proved easier than I imagined. We knew the McCormick factory was the hot spot, so we rode the streetcars close to the area and started following rough-looking men in overalls. As more men joined, JR became convinced we were following the right crowd.

The gigantic event turned out to be a rally in support of the workers' demands for better conditions and shorter hours—no mention of increasing pay. Speeches in several languages left us ignorant, though JR was able to tell me what most of the languages were. "I've been lucky enough to hear a lot of accents, so I can recognize the languages."

After listening a while longer, we became bored and left. Three wagons rushed past with uniformed coppers in them. JR said, "It's a good thing we left. I think things might get nasty now."

On Monday, I was able to return to the shop for papers. I eagerly read about the May Day events of Saturday. Albert Parsons and his Negro wife, Lucy, had led 30,000 workers in a march up Michigan Avenue, in the heart of the city. Many thousands more had roamed the city, celebrating what they thought was success.

However, I also read that many of the largest businesses, including most of the meat packers, had not yet agreed to any of the demands. Cyrus McCormick had announced he would replace all striking workers with non-union workers, and the police would protect the replacements.

As a farm boy, I knew the McCormick name. My family had not been prosperous enough to buy many of the McCormick farm implements, but I saw them in use by neighbors. I found I had mixed feelings about the replacement workers. I wanted McCormick to succeed because he was so important for farmers, but I also hated to see men shut out of a job.

JR said in a near whisper, “I said there would be trouble. I’m glad we got out of there when we did. This paper says the police killed five men and wounded many others.”

I had just come across a similar article, after I’d stopped crying for poor Mr. McCormick. “This paper says just two killed. They also say the police attacked the strikers without reason. I sure didn’t see anything that would cause the coppers to start shooting.”

After reading some more, JR said, “Ah, the shooting took place at the McCormick gates. We weren’t anywhere near there. Something else must have been going on. Yeah, here it is. ‘A crowd of blacklegs was exiting the plant and was being heckled by the strikers, when the police arrived and began firing.’ I’d bet they were doing more than shouting at the blacklegs.”

“What’s a blackleg?”

“They get hired to work in place of the strikers. Some call them scabs.”

“Oh, strikebreakers. You’re probably right. It could have gotten rough.”

JR and I talked through the day about what we had read and heard, and neither of us was satisfied. We wanted to know more.

35 Haymarket

That morning, I asked Zac if I could get a paper. "I'll let you go with guards. I want to find out what's going on, too, so I'm going to send two men with you for protection. Come back to me with the papers, and we'll read them together. How many can you get?"

"I've seen just two in English, unless we go another mile or so."

"Figures. Just get the two. Here's a quarter. Get several copies if you can, and I'll put them in the cars for others to read. I've been getting a lot of questions. People are getting worried. Oh, and see if they have Spanish and French papers."

The normally bustling streets were boiling with men walking and running in all directions. At times, even the trolleys stopped to avoid running into large groups of men. At the shop, I pushed my way through the jam of men to the papers. Most had sold out, but the two English ones were still available. I picked up all seven copies and asked the lady, nearly shouting, if she had Spanish and French. She produced one paper. I could not tell which it was.

Back on the train, Zac thought the one paper was French and sent it to the kitchen for the French Canadians to read. I dropped the others in each of the men's cars, keeping one each for JR and myself.

We read updates on the shootings with conflicting information and outrageous quotes. Whatever had happened, it was clear the coppers had shot more than one person. Had someone shot at them? Were they even provoked? We could not tell from what we were reading. Neither of us was content with what we read.

Late that night, had anyone looked at the right spot in the immenseness of the yards, he would have seen JR and me walking along the poorly lit fringes. Once on the streets, we rubbed shoulders with and bumped into hundreds of men until we returned to the English-speaking area, where we could ask men what was happening.

The stories ranged from excited to delirious. Most were preposterous, but several men did say a protest rally was underway at the Haymarket, so JR and I started walking. It was a long hike with no trolleys running.

By the time we arrived, the crowd was small, maybe three hundred men. There was a Negro woman and two children on the flatbed wagon serving as a stage. JR said, "That must be Albert Parsons doing the talking, because that has to be his wife."

Edging along a building to get as close as possible while staying away from possible trouble, we did all we could to assure a quick getaway. Both of us had stepped in horse manure several times. The air was stiff with the fragrance. The square was an extra wide area of the street two or three blocks long. Every day, hundreds of delivery wagons used it as a central point for loading and transferring goods, the thousands of horses leaving a thick blanket of waste thoroughly compacted by wagon wheels, boots, and hoofs. It was the street's paving.

We didn't have to listen long to know the speech was fiery enough to blister paint, and we couldn't even hear half of what he said. Parsons was urging the men to retaliate against the police for the shootings on Sunday.

At the same time, we could hear thunder and see lightning as nature sent a different storm our way. I said, "Let's get out of here." JR didn't hesitate, but we had walked only a few paces when wagons loaded with police passed by. They jumped out and took up positions close to what remained of the crowd.

We, perhaps unwisely, turned to watch. There was an exchange between a copper and the speaker we could not hear. I saw something fly through the air just before a monstrous explosion lifted several coppers into the air. The concussion hammered my chest as the screams bombarded my ears. Almost at once, the coppers started shooting, but we were already running. The screams fought for attention over the unrelenting roar of a hundred pistols. A bullet zinged my shoulder and splattered brick on both of us. Glass exploded along our path.

Only when the gunfire stopped and the screams were memory did we slow to a walk. Struggling to catch our breaths, unable to talk, we walked the dark streets, hoping we were not lost. Then the thunderstorm hit full force, soaking us in an instant. Cold wind blew rain against us with conviction. We took to a slow run just to warm up.

By the time we knocked on the door of our car, the storm had passed. Still, when Sam looked through the window, he jumped back. "Sam, it's me, Remmy. Let us in." Once in, we stood shivering like wet puppies.

Sam asked the obvious: “What happened to you two?”

JR managed to chatter out, “We decided to check out the packing houses. Got lost in the aisles of the yards.” I was too numb to notice how stupid it sounded.

Just then, two men burst through the still-unlocked car door. In their broken English, they begged, "Hide us! Coppers shot hundreds. They killing foreigners." That was all we learned before Zac's man came in and dragged the two away.

The car was buzzing with speculation about what had happened. I dried off and crawled into my bunk, turning my back to the others. Only then did I allow the tears to flow.

The tears stopped. The talking died. Others hit the bunks. Lights went out. Snoring took over.

I could feel the burn of the bullet-scorched path on my right shoulder. I could smell the burned flesh and even taste the powder I knew had sent the lead my way. The tears had come first, from the fear I supposed, but as men began the routine of bed, the fear left. It was gone—no reason.

As the lights went out and the last man rolled into his bunk, I saw a flash followed by gunfire—not the roar of Haymarket, not the bomb, but single gunshots: one, then two, three, four, five, and then silence in the dark snow.

I tried not to breathe too loudly, not out of fear but better to hear the shots, five shots. A flash came with each shot, yellow as it wafted over the snow. I did not attempt to understand: I just let it happen. Each time the shots came, a new small detail came as well. The horse reared its head. Snow fell from a tree branch. My stomach lurched. One by one, as the night slipped along, the bits came to me.

Closer to sunrise than sunset, all the bits and pieces were in place. Coins clinking in my pocket, the horse tied to a tree, the heart-shaped white spot, the rifle in its scabbard, the first flash of a gun out of the corner of my eye, and the bang as I turned my head. Two. Three. Four. Five. I did not have to see what happened inside the cabin to have it gouge a hole in my heart.

36 Guilt

Reliving every minute of that snow-covered night, smelling every residue, hearing every footfall, and feeling every thud of my heart, I could taste my cowardliness. Why had I done nothing to help them? I had run, and I was still running.

Men in the car began to get up and dress. Talk increased. They left for the dining car. Minutes later, Sam returned. “Remmy, you okay?”

I gave a sharp, “No.”

“Do you need anything?”

I put a muzzle on my anger. “I need rest, Sam. I’ll be all right.”

Sam left, and I could once again wallow in my guilt.

It did not last as the crew returned, and several of them asked me if I was sick. I finally gave up, got up, and went for coffee alone. There were men still in the pie car having their own coffee, so I looked for a corner. I wanted to go outside, but we were on strict lockdown until the troubles melted away.

I was able to sit by myself, near exhaustion, mind refusing to function, but alone, or nearly so. I needed to figure out what to do. I had the feeling I should return to KC and hunt...the man...what was his name? Red... something. Resting my eyes seemed a good idea. I put my head down for a few seconds.

Noise woke me as the dining car filled for lunch. Sam and JR were on either side of me, looking at my drool-stained arm. “You sure you’re not sick?”

I had no idea where I was. Oh, yes, the train, the Wild West. “I’m all right. I didn’t sleep last night.”

JR said, “Getting shot will do that to you.”

Sam nearly shouted, “What? Shot? What happened?”

JR groaned. “Sorry, that slipped out. He wasn’t really shot. I’ll tell you later. Too many men here. Rem, you need a decent meal and a long nap. I need one, too. I woke up a dozen times last night."

"I'm not hungry."

"I don't care. You're going to eat." He went to get coffee and made sure I had a decent plate of food.

Sam looked as though he might explode if he didn't find out soon what was going on. I took pity on him and said in a near whisper, "We saw the bombing. Tell you more later." That did not relieve the pained expression on Sam's face, but he kept quiet.

A three-hour nap did wonders. The lock-down had ended, though we had to stay close to the cars. I sat outside, away from everyone, and considered my new situation. *I can give a better description of Red Beard to the police. If I go back now, I might be able to convince them to look for the man.*

On the other hand, the sheriff might arrest me. I needed to get a letter sent through the church to Big Jim and find out what is happening. When was the last time I checked? Two months? First chance, that letter goes out.

Even if I am on the wanted list, maybe I can go back to the stockyards and spend nights looking in all the saloons. If I could point to Red Beard, the police would have to look at him for the crime. Or would they? Maybe, maybe not. That might not be worth the chance. I'd better stay with the show until Big Jim gives me the all clear.

I began to think of Big Jim. Father had warned me not to hang out with the Indian: "He's a bad influence. I don't trust him." Mother had cried when she'd heard Father's comments. *Why was he so worried? Was it just because he's Indian? I wish I knew. Jim had been great to me. I'd probably be dead now if it weren't for him. He's a better man than Father was.*

37 St. Louis

A huge engine with eight drive wheels pulled up with the rest of the train and coupled on. We all cheered and left our cars to see who had arrived. They were all performers, but it was an opportunity to relax after the tension of the past few days.

I was surprised when I overheard someone introduce a man as Chief American Horse. The chief was dressed in denim and a checkered shirt, like most of the crew. I had thought he was one of the Mexican workers. I was equally surprised to hear him speak. His English was passable, at least good enough not to stand out in Chicago, where more than half the population spoke no English.

Cody stood on a car platform and called everyone to gather round. It was the first time I experienced Cody's show voice. Even with all the noise of the livestock in the yards and the fact there were nearly a hundred people in front of him, no one had to strain to hear. He was not shouting: he just had a big voice.

"It's good to have part of the family together. We'll meet the rest soon. We have already had to fight some bad spring snows in Canada and, as all of you know, some frightening events in Chicago. We will still arrive in St. Louis with time to rehearse and get the show right before we let the customers in.

"We have plenty of work to do in the next few days and weeks. We have to learn how to work together. Everyone here has a given job. Once that job is finished, you need to help with other work as needed. We all have to pull together like an excellent eight-horse team.

"For now, we have to load the stock, and then we'll leave this fair city to its own troubles."

Zac took over and directed the loading of stock as the rest of the Wild West crew milled around or returned to their cars.

Loading animals into rail cars is always harder than offloading them. Even normally docile cows do not want to go into dark boxes. Loading in Chicago took some patience and a mountain of yelling and waving. It went smoothly enough, no one was hurt, and all cars were loaded by 4 PM.

Buffalo Bill's Wild West Special left the yards and the city as the crew and cast sat down to their evening meals in their own pie cars.

After eating, Sam and I stood on the open platform between cars and watched the dark countryside glide by. I asked, "Do you think we made the right choice, coming on this trip?"

"Sure, it'll be a great adventure. Someday we'll tell our grandkids what Buffalo Bill was really like. Besides, if you had stayed home, you might never have been shot."

"If I'd stayed home, I would have been shot dead."

“Sorry, I shouldn’t have said that. I guess I’m just jealous I wasn’t along for the excitement.”

I let it drop. St. Louis and adventure were down the road—hopefully not as much adventure as yesterday. I decided to stay with the show. After all, I had agreed to work for Zac, and a promise was a promise.

We returned to our car and watched the others play poker. When Sam finally gave in and joined them, I took out my copy of *Huck Finn* and began to read.

Near 10:30, I went to the pie car for a steaming cup of coffee: half coffee, half cream, half sugar, and all delicious. I went back and read for another hour before settling in. It took some time, but I was eventually lulled to sleep by the rocking of the train.

The whole crew was up before dawn to offload, feed, water, and reload the livestock. I skipped breakfast and went back to sleep. When I woke, I went to the pie car and helped myself to another cup of the coffee-cream mix with a slice of apple pie. Then a second cup of coffee. And a third.

I got my first look at St. Louis near midday Friday as the train threaded its way into the city. We finally stopped next to another train that consisted mostly of empty flatcars. I could see that the show was mostly set up, just needing some animals. Zac got us working as soon as the train stopped moving.

Once the stock had food and water, the fence needed painting, signs needed posting, and cinders needed spreading. The show was a muddle of action, with men and women by the hundreds carrying, pushing, pulling, and riding the bits and pieces into place.

The show used the field of the St. Louis Brown Stockings Baseball Team. The permanent grandstands formed one side of the show arena, what Cody called the Red Section for the big spenders, and traveling benches on two longer sides formed the Blue Sections. I learned later that the show carried seats for the Red Section as well. A tent roof covered all the seats, and canvas hung on the backsides of all seating to discourage peepers.

The end opposite the Red Seats had a canvas wall with an opening in the center where the acts would enter and exit. Ten feet behind it was a short canvas wall blocking the customers' view through the opening of our staging area.

That evening, the kitchen staff proved their worth. The entire Wild West team sat down in the dining tent for the first time. Each table had a waiter to bring the food and keep the glasses and cups filled. I had never experienced such opulence. Even better, the meal was a feast of steak, beans, potatoes, boiled cabbage, fresh green beans, fresh lettuce, radishes, and something called burritos.

I noticed the Mexicans had their own mix of something green they poured on their beans and burritos. When I asked Will what it was, he just said, "Fire. Don't eat it."

In my bunk that night, I smiled as I thought about the day. It had been hard work, but the adventure was here. Now that I had met all my work mates, I thought we would get along. I had been too busy all day to think on my personal problems, and that was good.

38 Rehearsal

Nate Salsbury, Cody's partner, was the show's director, pushing everyone to perfect the show in just two days. The new animals required the most time and attention. Alone and with the experienced animals, we walked them through every part of the many acts. Gunshots became familiar background noise for people and animals alike.

The farrier had to check the show horses, so I spent Friday leading one after another to the blacksmith's tent. I helped with each animal while the farrier worked on the hooves and the smithy made new shoes for those needing them.

While I was leading a horse, one of the cowboys said, "Hey, kid, why don't you stick to mules and let real cowboys handle the horses?"

I responded, "Okay, you go tell Zac." I watched his swaggering retreat, thinking, *I need to find out who this bad hat is.*

The farrier had seen the exchange and told me, "That walking puss pocket's Carl Segebart. Stay well away from him. I don't know how he ever got hired, him and his buddy, Vix Pivonka. Double snake eyes for sure."

On Saturday, I practiced what would be my usual show duties, herding the cattle and buffalo to the entrance in time for the cue. The only difficulty was remembering, even with the printed sheets, which group entered for which scene. The actors had the dangerous jobs. Once the animals were loose in the arena, they could charge right into the seating, so the actors had to herd the animals without appearing to do so.

The show had nearly four hundred horses, including baggage horses—what we farmers knew as draft horses. Just over a hundred show horses were available to ride in various acts. One crew tended all the riding stock and another the baggage horses. A few of the actors preferred to manage their own horses, but most let us do the job. Another crew maintained all the saddles and tack for the horses. Yet another crew harnessed and tended the wagons. The show had its own harness maker. They even had an old sailor who had been the sail maker on several ships. His job now was to keep the show's canvas in shape. There was a special crew for every aspect of the show.

A full cast walk-through came Saturday before lunch. Everyone for every act was in proper position and rode, drove a wagon, or walked the entire scene without music, costumes, or very much action; it was what the theater and circus people called 'blocking' the show.

During the blocking, I realized I had not seen Cody since arriving in the city. I asked around, but no one else had seen him, either.

Nate was barking directions nonstop. There were several mistakes and timing issues. Some scenes had to start over. The whole thing took over two hours.

After lunch, we did a complete walk-through with the band and all other noisemakers. After a short rest, the entire show ran with all action, shooting, music, and specialty acts sprinkled between scenes. Cody made his appearance, with no explanation of his absence. He appeared in several scenes, including his own shooting exhibition.

It was also the first time I saw Annie Oakley. I only saw her for a minute before she went into the arena. I guessed she was five feet tall and in her twenties. She was young, attractive, and athletic. Time would prove me right on those guesses and much more besides.

After the rehearsal, Cody called everyone into the arena for congratulations on putting the show together in such a short time. "I'm sure there will be some problems on Monday when the stands are filled with people. Just keep going. That's how we run a show. Remember, the audience doesn't know the script, so most of the time they'll think we intended the mistake. Relax tonight, and tomorrow afternoon we'll run the stock through once more. Everyone else, enjoy a relaxing day off."

After all the animals had their feed and water, Sam and I walked around the tented area to check out the menagerie. We had helped offload a number of small animals kept in cages, such as snakes and bobcats, and were glad someone else took care of them. Feeding a live mouse to a rattlesnake did not sound like much fun.

There were a number of sections of the menagerie where workers demonstrated crafts, such as making lye soap, quilting, or churning butter. The butter found its way to the dining tent later. The crew used some items, the rest were sold or given to charity.

I had to ask why people were willing to pay money to watch someone churn butter. The answer surprised me a little. People in the cities never did those things. They bought many things readymade. It was still hard to imagine living that way.

Saturday evening, Zac asked me to follow him. Approaching Cody's car, I started to worry about what trouble had found me. Inside, both Zac and Cody seemed unusually solemn, and there was a third man there. Cody said, "Remmy, we've got a touchy situation involving you. Zac, why don't you read the letter?"

Zac said, "I got this letter from Frank Tarbitt. This is what he says: *You need to know young Remmy Bailey has trouble on his trail. A man killed his family, but he can tell you all about that. Remmy's real name is Bevans. We changed it here to try to protect him. It was not enough.*

"I have just heard from some of my men that someone is looking for him. Somehow, he learned or guessed that Remmy worked here. I cannot say how much he knows, but I would bet he would figure Remmy is with you. I cannot tell you anything about the man, because he seems to have hired several others to ask the questions. I'll let you know if I learn anything more."

Cody said, "I guess it means you have some decisions to make. I don't want you to leave the show unless you really think it's best. Before you decide, Tom here has some ideas protecting you. He's a former Pinkerton man who's in charge of our security. Tom."

"I have friends from here to Boston, and I can get them to keep their ears open for any hint of trouble. Also, I have a couple of excellent men who can follow you when you leave the grounds. You just need to let us know when you're leaving and where you're going. You won't even know they're around. I think you would be better off staying with the show, because we can give you better protection than you could have anywhere else."

Cody took over again. "Now, Remmy, tell us your story so we can help you." I was trembling as I told them the basics, with Tom Gibson asking for more detail.

I was still shaking when I returned to the car, so I sat outside for a while, trying to come to grips with the news. I'd thought all I had to do was get away from Kansas City. Now that plan was in doubt. It shot a hole in my confidence.

As I sat trying to puzzle it out, I noticed movement under the donniker, the portable toilet used by the customers. Still distracted, I only half-watched as someone rolled out, stood, brushed himself off, and skulked away. *Somebody must be doing some late night cleaning.*

I went to bed no closer to satisfaction, my sleep erratic.

39 Show

Zac assigned a Sunday rotation to take care of the essential work. Sam, David, and JR drew the first Sunday, so they were up early making sure the stock was hale, hearty, fed, and watered.

After a lunch of soup and make-your-own sandwiches, Will and I decided to take a walk around the complex to meet more people. It was a good day for it, because most of the crew was outside enjoying the sun and pleasant May weather.

We saw a Mexican who was practicing rope tricks. He twirled the lasso over his head, then to his sides, and jumped through the lasso as it was spinning in front of him. After a few minutes, during which the rope never stopped moving, Will, from New Mexico territory, asked, "Habla Inglés?"

With just a hint of an accent, he replied, "Don Viscente Oropeza, at your service. Are you boys enjoying your new jobs?"

We felt silly at our mistaken assumptions. I said, "We really liked your rope work. Is that your act?"

"It's one of my specialties. I'm also chief of the Vaqueros, so I go on with the whole crew several times in the show."

Will said, "I thought I heard Joe Esquivel was the head Vaquero."

"He's the chief of all the cowboys, which includes the Vaqueros, so he's my boss."

After watching Don some more, we went into the arena and sat on the bleachers. Several people were going through their routines. As we watched and talked, several men and two women rode in on horses. Will said, "I'll bet one of those women is the one Cody brought in yesterday."

"What? I didn't hear about that."

Will gave us a salacious grin. "Seems he went to the St. James Hotel on Friday to get her but didn't make it back until just before the big run through yesterday."

"Are you saying he spent the night with her?"

"That's what I hear, and he seems to do that with a lot of women. They say that's why his wife stays in Denver."

I wasn't sure what to make of it and decided to ignore it as a rumor. After all, Cody was my protector.

As we were ready to leave, several people with rifles entered. We stayed to watch Cody, three other men, and Annie Oakley practice shooting. They hit several different types of targets, including some thrown into the air. I noticed Cody missed a couple.

I asked Will, "Do you know who the others are?"

"I don't know his name, but the man with the beard is a Frenchie who came with Cody. The woman, of course, is Annie Oakley. I don't know the others."

"They're all good, but Miss Oakley never seems to miss."

Walking back to the car, we heard, "Hey, plow boy." It was Segebart and his shadow Pivonka. Segebart said, "Why don't you go back to your pig farm, where you belong?"

I said nothing but took a long step toward Segebart. I had already decided the man was a bully, and forcing him to make the next move might be enough to get him to back off.

Segebart said with a grin, "So, the little boy wants a fight." We stood eye to eye, though Segebart had at least twenty-five pounds over me. He switched to a mock snivel. "What should I do? I'm too scared to face him. Vix, will you help me?" He and Pivonka both roared at the witticism.

I tried hard to keep my face smooth, to show no anger. It was all I could do not to curl my fingers into fists. Segebart and I exchanged visual daggers for a minute before the bully moved on.

Will said, "That was fun. You think you can take him?"

I kept my eyes on Segebart. "Maybe not, but I can get in some good licks if Pivonka stays out of it."

"Have you ever been in a fight before?"

I gave him a grin. "No."

After spending Monday morning with a paintbrush in my hand, Zac sent me to the pens to help get the horses and mules ready for the parade. I had heard of the parade, how it was supposed to let people see the actors and be encouraged to attend the shows. I still wasn't sure how walking down the street would do that, but I assumed it must have worked.

The actors dressed in their show clothes, and went to the dining tent for an early lunch so they could leave at 12:15 to get in position for the parade. The crew would eat while the actors were gone.

At 2:30, the gates opened to allow the first customers to wander through the grounds, to buy tickets, popcorn, and drinks, and to view the menageries. At 3:00, the band started to play in the arena and ushers helped the customers find their seats. At 3:30, Nate signaled the Grand Parade to charge into the arena. Indian braves rode their horses at a run the full length of the arena, stopping in a cloud of dust in front of the Red Seats. As they moved to the side, the chiefs followed, as did all the other riding groups until Buffalo Bill Cody charged in, dazzling in his buckskins and oversized white hat.

I saw none of it, because I was busy getting the animals lined up for each entrance. For the crew I was in, the only major problem was getting the buffalo into the arena. The lead animal balked at the gate, and moving the half-ton beauty proved impossible for the crew. Cody himself had to lead her gently to the opening. There were a few other minor mishaps, but the show seemed to go well. It lasted three hours, and people were shouting for more.

By the time the last customer was gone and the gates were locked, the sun was a memory. Dinner was starting to smell better than ever.

Before we went in to eat, Cody called everyone together in the stands to thank us for a job well done. "This has been a great first show, the best in my time doing this. A week from now, we'll have all those little glitches worked out, and we'll be running as smooth as a railroad watch.

Let's have two good shows tomorrow and the rest of the week, and we'll leave these good people of St. Louis with the sure knowledge they have seen the true Wild West."

40 Doc

Two shows a day, 1:00 and 5:30, rain, sleet, hail, or snow became our pulse of the summer. On Wednesday, we suffered our first injury. One of the Indians had his horse gored by a buffalo, with horse and rider rolling over each other. The bruised brave was able to lead his limping horse from the arena without help, though several actors stopped to check on him. The crowd applauded as he left.

The show's veterinarian, Doc to all, patched the horse before checking the Indian. Bruised but not broken, the brave rode the next day, though on a different mount. By Saturday, there had been seven other minor injuries of the actors, and I understood why they earned more money.

On Thursday night, JR asked me if I wanted to go into town. “You sure you want to be seen with me?”

“No problem. I’m not going to claim to know you.” He winked one of his brooding eyes.

“After last time, I don’t blame you.”

“I need you to come because you’re buying the beer.”

“I guess I do owe you. But, I don't want to be out very late."

JR said, "Don't worry, there's a crowd every night. We'll probably be the first ones back. I don't spend the night drinking like some of them."

We walked with several others until we reached the first saloon. JR and I went farther south on a busy street, just enjoying the sights, sounds, and smells. The city was starting to grow on me. Foods dominated the odors, but the undercurrent of horse apples still registered.

In a saloon, we sipped our beers and talked with some of the others in the show, crew, actors, and stars alike. I met some of the workers I did not know yet. JR was right; some of them could really put it away.

We were in our bunks by midnight.

As the first Indians rode into the arena for the second show on Saturday, teardown began. When I was not working animals in the show, I helped with whatever chore I had time for, breaking down unneeded fencing, folding canvas, carrying this and that. By the time the audience came out of the arena three hours later, we were already rolling many of the show wagons on flat cars and stuffing the show stock into boxcars.

The Wild West had arrived in St. Louis in drips, dribbles, and two disorganized trains. The cast and crew came from all over the US and added their personal items to the traveling circus. The show left St. Louis after dark, in two well-organized trains. The lead train consisted of a powerful engine (what they called a 4-8-0), flatcars loaded with the wagons, the actors' cars, dining cars, and stars' cars, in that order. The second train had a matching engine, stock cars full of animals, men's crew car, dining cars, and women's crew cars, in that order. We were headed east on the Terre Haute and Indianapolis Railroad for Terre Haute, Indiana.

I slept undisturbed through the night, but by the time a slice of orange formed on the eastern horizon, I was busy offloading my part of the show. It was a beautiful Sunday morning, except for the grinding work of setting up the Wild West.

Unlike St. Louis, where the show had been set up next to the rail siding, the show ground in Terre Haute was nearly a half-mile away. It took longer to pull all the wagons so far and then walk the horse teams back. I helped drive the stock down a temporary barbed wire aisle from the siding to the show grounds. Animals complained, men swore, tempers flared, and sweat dropped, but by noon, the circus was in town.

Since breakfast had been a sausage sandwich eaten while herding longhorns, the hot lunch in the dining tent was an extravagance dampened only by being dirty and tired. Eat, bathe, sleep, possibly not in that order.

I awoke near three in the afternoon and sought out a quiet, shady spot with no company. Dreams had come in my sleep, dreams that required straight thinking. A red wall of fire, a snowstorm, the fire held back by the snow, Father waving for me to come, walking along the tracks in the summer, arguing with Father, Father hugging me, Father dying, Father shot, me shooting Father. Shooting Father. Shooting.

That image would not go away. It was like one of those stereoscopic cards I had seen once: so real, but only a photograph. I let the dreams and thoughts slide through my mind until each settled where it would. Dreams are not real, but they can sometimes tell me what's on my mind. Because I dreamed of Father, I knew I needed to look again at my feelings for him.

In the shooting dream, I held my own .22 rifle as I shot Father. *Why would I be shooting him? All I ever wanted was for him to respect me for who I am. I never wanted him dead.*

What was the look on Father's face in the dream? Not hatred—that was not Father. Anger, yes; disappointment, yes; not hatred.

I concluded that I'd had the dream because I was getting my wish of traveling, doing something besides farming. With Father out of the way, it was happening. I did not kill Father, and I didn't want him dead. I kept telling myself that.

41 Rain

Cheerless clouds blotted the morning sky, the overture of coming rain. As the crew ate lunch and the actors headed out for the parade, a gentle rain came in from the south. The parade went on, and I heard that people stood to watch in surprising numbers.

As the first Indians were sweeping into the show arena, the sun came out, and the day quickly went from warm to a hot soup of air, difficult to breathe and impossible to avoid. Most of the cowboys and crew came from the arid west and suffered in the heaviness of the Indiana humidity. I did not find it much different from home.

The show continued, unimpeded by two more short rain showers and the continued heat. The customers were high and dry, thanks to all the canvas, but they were sweating just the same.

Between shows, I saw Segebart and Pivonka walking among the pens. I readied myself for conflict, but they bypassed me. Before I turned back to my work, I realized they were walking directly for Will, who had his back to them. I shouted, grabbed George, and ran over to help, but it was all for nothing as Segebart bumped Will in the back and sent him face-first into the mud. The cowboys walked on as though nothing had happened.

I was able to catch Will just as he started after them. "Don't do it! You'll get fired for fighting. It's what he wants."

It took a while, but George and I calmed him down and cleaned him up. George said, "We'll catch them away from here sometime. We can't do anything here. Cody would probably side with the cowboys."

The heat was down to a tolerable level only by show's end, with several short rain showers adding to the discomfort of the actors and crew. The cold drink concessions did a land office business. They had to send out for more ice and beer between shows. The soda stands nearly sold out.

The heat continued into Tuesday, but without the rain. As soon as the second show began, so did the teardown. The kitchen crew—as sweat-drenched as everyone else—had buckets of ice water ready to drink, though some ladled it over their heads.

By dark, the train was on its way to Dayton, Ohio, and the crew was seeking relief from the heat. Several men opened car windows but quickly closed them because the engine smoke was hanging over the rails like a vindictive spirit. Many of the experienced hands found spots on the platforms between the cars, covering their faces with kerchiefs.

The Wednesday weather was much like Tuesday but with more rain, though it missed the parade this time. The mud in the arena sent the danger level up a few notches. All the actors came out spattered with mud, and one cowboy, thrown from a bucking horse, managed to hit the biggest mud hole in the arena.

The heat finally broke overnight, and the shows on Thursday were more pleasant, if still muddy. The actors had their worst injury of the trip so far in the first show. Bridle Bill, one of the many cowboys who seemed to have only nicknames, broke his left arm in a fall from a bucking horse.

Teardown went smoothly, but the train sat on the siding a long time before finally leaving for Newark, Ohio, for a one-day stand. A rumor swept through the train that Cody had been out drinking and needed help into his car. Everybody in the car had an opinion, but no one seemed to have any facts.

I did not know what to believe. I really didn't know Cody at that time. One of the older men said, "Cody doesn't care if you're drunk, as long as you do the work. I've heard Cody even gets too drunk to do the show sometimes." That kind of talk hurt me a little. I respected Cody and was not willing to accept any unproven rumor about him.

Sam and Charlie went to play poker in the next car. George went to find anything other than sitting around to do. JR asked me if he could read one of my newspapers. Everyone else just sat around talking.

An hour later, James said, "I'm heading to the pie car for some coffee. Anybody want to go?"

Tired of reading, JR and I went with him. On the way, we stopped to check on the poker game and saw Sam was winning some money for a change.

In the pie car, we settled at a table with our coffee. The man called “Frenchie”, was talking, so we sat near enough to listen. I had learned his real name was Gabriel Dumont. I wondered why a star of the show was in the workers’ pie car.

Dumont was drinking blistering coffee in large gulps, and it only enlivened his storytelling. He often referred to himself as a Métis, and I had to listen to several stories before deciding the Métis must be Indians. It was a little confusing, because Dumont looked white. He had a thick beard, piercing eyes, an ample body, and hands too large for his arms. He was dressed more like a worker than a star of the show.

He was in the middle of describing the effort of the Métis to set up their own government in Canada. "Louis Riel was our real leader and as such was our chief, what the Canadian government insisted was our Prime Minister. I acted as the war chief, or as they liked it, the adjutant general.

"We first met the government forces at Fish Creek and gave them a good lickin', but then General Middleton brought in some 800 men to engage us at the ferry crossing I own near Batoche. Batoche was our capital city, so we had to defend it. We held them off for several days, until their numbers overwhelmed us."

Someone asked, "How did you end up in the states?"

"A bunch of us made our way into Montana Territory and surrendered to your army. They quickly decided they didn't want us, so here I am."

Another man asked, "How did you end up with the show?"

Dumont laughed and said, "Bill Cody knows a lot of people in the West. He heard I was in Montana and sent me a telegram. We met at Fort Laramie in Wyoming Territory and he offered me a job. Since I didn't want to go back home just yet, I took his offer."

One of the Cowboys from Montana asked, "I know something about the Indians in the West, but I don't know any Métis Indians. Who are you?"

Dumont laughed again, got up, and filled his cup before saying, "The word Métis is French for *half-blood* or *mixed-race*. We are part Indian and part white. My grandfather, Jean-Baptiste Dumont, married a Sarcee-Crow woman, and my father, Isidore, married Louise Laframboise, so I look white to most of you. I was raised both French and Crow, but you can be sure that Indians see me as Crow. We judge people by their dress, speech, and customs, not by their skin or hair."

One of the men worked up his courage and asked, "We heard you and Cody were out drinking today. Is it true?"

"Why do you think I'm drinking all this coffee?" He laughed and added, "Actually, I was drinking with Johnny. That little kid can really put it away. I didn't want Cody to find out, so I decided to hide here for a while." He raised his cup in salute.

Someone asked him about his shooting skills. "I learned to shoot from the time I could hold up the old muzzle-loader. Being able to shoot has always paid off for me. I can defend myself, and I can always put food on the table. I always tell men they should know how to shoot."

I began to think about whether I should know how to shoot to defend myself. Jim had taught me how to survive in the open and live off the land. Now, with a killer to catch, I needed to learn how to take on that job. I needed to be able to shoot Red Beard.

42 Frogs

Halfway through the afternoon show, the police dumped two of the crew from another car next to our train, neither able to walk. I watched as Gibson's security men dragged them to their bunks with considerable lack of attention to their well-being.

That night, after the show was loaded and rolling toward Zanesville, several of us went to track down the story. We knew we were in the right car when we saw a man sucking on a cup of coffee and telling the story. The car was crowded.

"We was in our second saloon, drinkin' whiskey with beer chasers. The place weren't too crowded, and we was mindin' our own business. Of a sudden, this guy jerks me off the stool and shoves Bart away. 'This's my spot,' says he.

"So, course, Bart 'n me jump him. We bust him up a little, and we leave. We find another saloon and, well, that's the last thing I 'member."

Just then, Cody came in with two of his men. In a voice just below a shout, "On your feet, Jack." The story-telling drunk struggled to stand. "Where's Bart?"

Someone said, "He's still in his bunk."

Still booming, "Drag his worthless butt out here. I need to chew it off." While two men ran to the next car, Cody asked, "Jack, what the hell were you two thinking, or were you thinking at all?"

With the train moving, Jack had to hold onto a chair. He mumbled, "I don't know."

"My guess is you don't know much at all." Bart, half-carried into the car, seemed to sober up a bit when he spotted Cody. The men placed Bart beside the wavering Jack.

Cody started again as the two men held each other up, this time with a little less edge in his voice. "The police tell me you two beat a man, broke his arm, and strolled merrily down the street to another saloon. They found you passed out drunk. Does any of that ring a bell with you?"

Jack and Bart look at each other, and Jack said, "The guy started...."

"No!" Everyone in the car jumped, except Jack and Bart, who were lucky to be standing. "You will not tell me it was the other man's fault. He's five feet tall and weighs 130 pounds! You will not put the blame on him. I don't care if he is the son of a copper. In fact, you're lucky he's a copper who cares about his job. He could have broken your arms and your knees as well, and no one would have blamed him. Are you getting the point yet?" Cody's volume increased with each word.

"Yes, sir." Their heads were hanging so low they were in danger of rolling off their shoulders.

After a pause, Cody said in a calm voice, "Your fine is paid. The doctor bill for the broken arm is paid. Do you know who paid them?"

Jack and Bart looked puzzled. "No?"

"You did." It came out softly.

Now their puzzlement intensified, and their heads were back on their shoulders. "We did? How?"

"That should interest you. Piled on my doorstep, you had 38¢ between you. I'm letting you keep it. The fine and expenses will come from your next two months' wages, which means for June and July, you are my slaves. And, if you even think of running away, be sure I'll track you down, and you'll go to prison for theft." Cody then stepped to within six inches of their faces and quietly asked, "Any questions?"

They shook their heads but did not speak.

Cody stomped out, and the two men crumpled to the floor. The car buzzed with talk.

The dreaded call, "Up and at 'em," came at 5 AM. "Boys, we've got a mess. It's raining bullfrogs, and we have a show to set up. Don't even try to put on waterproofs today. You're going to get soaked, no matter what you do."

Everyone was dressed and ready to get to work before the train came to a stop, in... I couldn't remember where. Storm lanterns were the first items up. Tents were next. By the time they were all in place and staked down, the rain slowed, and the clouds lightened. An hour later, the sun broke through. We still had extra work because the tents were covering sodden ground, so wood floors had to go down before installing the exhibits. Somewhere in the midst of work, I remembered we were in Zanesville, and it was Saturday.

Once again, Zac ordered the livestock kept in the cars until later. Some wag muttered that the cows got better treatment than the people did.

By 8:30, we were finally setting up the pens, and an hour later, we offloaded the first livestock. By 11 AM, the animals, penned and fed, were ready to perform. I was glad I didn't have to perform. I wasn't even sure I could get the animals to the entrance on time. Show business was getting to be a lot less fun.

All morning, local men hauled in wagonloads of cinders to spread in the pathways for the paying customers. The stars would again have to wade through the muddy arena. The Chinese laundrymen were making good money this week.

The kitchen crew spent much of the morning delivering biscuits, sausages, and hot coffee to the crew as we labored. Most of the stars and actors had pitched in to help with the setup. As each group finished its assigned tasks, we did a quick change into dry clothes and headed for lunch in the pie car as the actors left for the parade. I was sure we would end up eating cold sandwiches for lunch, but the cooks managed to put together a decent hot meal.

Clouds reclaimed the sky, with a gentle rain beginning just after the first customers started through the menagerie. Most customers had waterproofs or umbrellas, and the rain didn't seem to discourage them, though we were short of a full house for the first time. I was starting to wonder what it would take to close the show.

The rain continued into the night, and the work of packing during the second show gave me a dizzy moment when I could not remember if we were packing or unpacking. Conditions would have to improve to be miserable. The good news was that we finished close to on time.

When the train pulled away, my friends and I sat in the rocking car, too tired to go visiting. In fact, some of us were thinking of skipping dinner. George said, "Remmy, why don't you get a box and load it up with some food to bring back here, so I don't have to get up?"

I thought for a moment before saying, "I will if you get the box. There's one in the dining car."

We all found the energy to go eat, but everyone was asleep in his bunk well before ten.

Sunday morning, the show set up in Wheeling, West Virginia, giving everyone a much-needed afternoon off. The week had been brutal on us. Even JR had not ventured into town for days.

I was too tired to have any nightmares, and I had not thought of my family or hunting Red Beard in days.

43 Oakley

After Sunday lunch, I was thinking a nap might be in order when a man approached and said Cody would like to visit with me. I expected the worst as I walked to Cody's car. The great man was sitting under the large awning next to his train car. I also recognized Annie Oakley and her husband, plus the boy I knew as the famous drinker, Johnny.

Cody said, "Come on, come on. I thought it was time we got to talk a bit. Sit here." He pointed to a chair near him. "Would you like some lemonade?"

"Yes, thank you, sir."

"You've forgotten already. I'm just Cody."

Miss Oakley spoke. "Now, Colonel, he's just being polite."

"Yes, Missy, he is, and more polite than I by far. Forgive me for not introducing you sooner. Remmy, this here's Mrs. Annie Butler, her husband Mr. Frank Butler, and my friend from North Platte, Johnny Baker. And, this admirable lad, everyone, is Remmy Bailey from Kansas."

I had almost forgotten my false name. "Pleased to meet you, ma'am, sir." They both nodded with smiles.

Mrs. Butler said, "Remmy is an unusual name. Is it a nickname?"

"Yes, ma'am. My real name is Remiel."

She responded, "Oh my, an archangel. A beautiful name, but difficult to live up to. Were your parents churchgoers?"

I stammered a bit. "Ah... no. I guess not." She just nodded.

Cody was not one to be left out of a conversation for long. "Tell me just where you're from again. As you may know, I lived and worked in Kansas for many years." He seemed to be trying to make sure the others did not need to know about my problems.

"Yes, sir, I mean, Cody. I grew up on a farm in Neosho County, halfway between the county seat of Erie and the old Osage Mission."

"I know the Mission, and I know the Osage. They were strapping fighters, and I was lucky I never faced them. I was fifteen and left Leavenworth to seek fame and fortune. Osage still lived in the area then. I have to admit, I've been lucky. I've gotten to do some exciting things over the years."

I found the courage to ask, "What did you most enjoy?"

Cody gave me a puzzled look, then said, "Enjoy, eh? I still think of myself as an army scout. I can't think of anything I'd rather be doing. I just got too old for it, and they stopped hiring civilian scouts anyway. But, it was great while it lasted."

Mrs. Butler said, "Colonel, we really need to do some practicing. We'll talk again soon." Everyone stood, and Mrs. Butler said to me, "It was nice to meet you, Remiel." Mr. Butler shook my hand, and they left.

Cody said, "They have become good friends. Last year, when Captain Bogardus left the show, I was finally able to hire the Butlers. You know she is known as Miss Annie Oakley, of course?"

I nearly barked, "I've heard a lot about how great she is. Is her husband a good shooter, too?"

"He's as good as she is, but he decided to let her be the star because the crowds love her. She's become quite the little actress. Just so you know, she prefers *Mrs. Butler*, unless the public is around. She and Frank met at a shooting contest, and she won the shootout and Frank's heart. They used to travel on their own, both of them putting on exhibitions, and then they did a year with the Sells Circus. I was very fortunate to hire them. They make quite a team." I noticed Johnny seemed less than impressed.

"But, I thought we could talk about our home state. I was born in Iowa, but we didn't stay there long. Spent most of my young life at Leavenworth, where I learned the army way of life. How about you. Are you Kansas born?"

"My folks were on their way there in '70, and I was born in the wagon just west of St. Louis. But, I never think of myself as anything but a free stater."

"Good for you. We have to watch out for those bushwhackers." He gave a big grin.

I ventured, "I know you did a lot of hunting for the railroad. Did you ever do any of the hide hunting?"

"Lord, no! Those boys shot hundreds of buffalo and left the carcasses to rot. They couldn't pay me enough to do that."

"I do some hunting myself, but I would hate that. Even when we trap animals for fur, we generally eat at least some of the meat."

"That's the way of the real West. Still, some big businesses pay for that kind of slaughter. Money's more important, I guess. We try to show the real West, if you haven't figured that out yet. You may have noticed we even have some displays of farm tools."

We talked a little longer, and I finally learned Johnny Baker was also sixteen and that he'd learned to shoot from both Cody and Mrs. Butler. When Cody announced he had to get back to work, Johnny and I left. Johnny never seemed to want to have anything to do with me; he was only interested in being with men, and I was not yet man enough for him. That was fine by me. I didn't like him anyway.

Having Cody introduce the Butlers to me was a great privilege, but meeting them set me to wondering if they could help me prepare for Red Beard. Of course, they could shoot, but what did that mean? Could they take on a killer? That was the constant question for me in those early weeks of the summer.

I spent Sunday evening telling my friends about the visit with the Butlers and Cody. I knew I was showing off, but I couldn't help it.

44 Kendall

Monday morning brought more rain, but it cleared quickly. The previous week had soaked the site, so we spent a couple of hours spreading cinders along the main paths to keep the customers out of the mud. In some places, we had to lay down long boards to keep shoes out of the standing water.

As far as I could tell, the two shows went well. The animals had calmed down considerably after two weeks of routine, and the rain and mud had become a part of life in the Wild West, even as they caused more slips and falls with bruised riders limping back to the dressing tents, not to mention a dozen horses out for recovery and one having to be put down. I'd come for an adventure, and I was getting it, but I also saw behind the glamor, behind the curtain, as it were. Circus life was hard work, in some ways more strenuous than farming.

I was able to catch parts of the show through a large gap in the canvas wall, courtesy of the stakes moving in the mud. I shared it with workers and actors alike. The opening entrance was the most incredible scene. Not only did each group charge into the arena, but at Cody's command they left the arena at a full gallop through a byzantine jumble, appearing to run right into one another, mud flying in all directions.

I never saw any of the shooting exhibitions during a show because they were aiming most of the shots at the canvas wall. Even though they used birdshot, at that distance it could put out an eye. I still don't know how they were always able to shoot toward the tall canvas at the open end and not hit any of the customers. I guess that was why the shooters made the most money

Tuesday was cloudless and pleasant, and after the second show began, the crew was hard at work packing and loading. We worked quietly because no one needed orders, and all the items on our long list of complaints and all the mud jokes were stale from overuse.

Wednesday was a repeat of the weather of the day before, this time in Cumberland, Maryland. Men jumped from the cars before the train came to a stop. The trip from Wheeling had taken longer than usual because of the mountains and a long wait for a passenger train to pass, the hazards of being a special train. We again had to make up time.

While we were offloading the horses, one slipped on the ramp and fell over the edge. She landed on her feet, but Zac called Doc. As he was looking her over, Segebart ran up. "What the hell happened to my horse?" When Zac told him, he really exploded. "What idiot led my horse off the ramp?"

I said, "I did."

JR at once said, "No, I did."

Will joined in, "No, I did."

George, the only other one there, said the same.

Segebart looked at each of us with hate in his eyes. Doc stepped in front of him and calmly said, "Your horse is fine. Let her rest today if you're worried."

Zac told him, "I saw your horse slip on the muddy ramp. It happens sometimes. Forget it." Somewhat cooled, Segebart left, but not without a menacing glare at me.

Like the other one-day stops, we did not put up the dining tent, the stars' tents, or most of the tepees. Their absence did not dampen the crowd's enthusiasm. The stands were full, and they bought popcorn as if they had never seen it before.

Thursday morning was again cloudless and sunny. After another overnight trip, we were in the nation's capital, where we would spend the next week and a half. I heard at least a dozen jokes suggesting the hot air from Congress would keep all the clouds away.

The show was set up just north of the city in a place called Kendall Green, right next to the Baltimore and Ohio Railroad. Cody announced he had arranged for cars to pick up those interested in riding the rails to Union Station on Cody's dime Sunday morning.

The beauty of Sunday morning almost made up for all the recent dreary days. After quietly telling Zac what we were doing, I went with Sam, David, JR, and George toward the downtown area of Washington. We wanted an earlier start, so we walked along the rail line to the depot, ate breakfast at the Harvey House, and walked the few blocks to the Capitol Building. From there we walked to all the government buildings, including the Washington Monument.

By mid-afternoon, we were starting to wear out, so we crossed the Sixth Street rail line, walked past the Botanic Garden Building just west of the Capitol Building, and returned to the Harvey House for another meal.

We took our time eating and then drinking two more beers, all the while talking excitedly about what we had seen. Someone told us no American city could compare with the great European ones, but we boys of Middle America could not believe any city could outshine our own capital.

Back at the show grounds, I realized I had never noticed the two men who'd trailed after us all day. Gibson's men were good.

I thought, *How much danger could I be in? Nothing had happened and I don't think I have to worry about anyone except Segebart. Having two men tailing me is probably a waste of time.* I thought I would go off some night with JR again without telling my minders. I was really feeling safe and secure. My dreams had been mostly the usual type, and the recurring ones seemed less threatening. Joining the Wild West was the right thing to do. I began to think I would be ready to go look for Red Beard soon.

45 Surprise

Some of the patrons came in on free tickets for the first afternoon show at Kendall Green. They were from the Columbia Institution housed on the Green. Some were blind, but most were deaf. The stars always went out of their way to entertain special groups of kids, and this time was no exception.

After six weeks of working with the animals, the chores almost did themselves. I knew all the animals by name and which were likely to cause trouble, and I knew how to prevent most of it. The shows were a blur; almost nothing stood out as unique or memorable. It was good but monotonous.

Life on the train was just as predictable. Only the occasional news story gave us any material that had not already been picked apart and rebuilt dozens of times. A couple of the older men always had a good story to engage us, and I think one of them actually told true accounts.

I was surprised at how JR was keeping up. He was again out walking the city most nights, rarely tucked in before midnight, but he did come back sober. For all my bluster about being in no danger, I did not go with him. Besides, all JR wanted to do was walk the dark streets; it made no sense to me. Cities were busy, noisy, ugly, sooty, and full of manure. The average city street carried more horse pucks than all of our Wild West holding pens.

The crew continued to impress me with how well we managed to work and live together. Some who had been sworn enemies a few months ago were becoming close friends now. They often found they had much in common. There were Mexicans, Indians, Chinese, and a few Negroes, who never left the camp, but they had friends in the camp, and none of us gave them any trouble.

My own group of friends was changing subtly. I avoided James because everything he did, had, saw, or knew, was better, bigger, more beautiful, or not worth knowing. One day in the car, James was wearing a hat Eddie said was his. They argued a couple of minutes, neither giving ground. Then, with no warning, James punched Eddie in the stomach, folding him like a piece of canvas. Everyone else jumped on James' case, and he apologized later, but the two were never friendly again.

Sam often played poker while JR read papers with me, so JR became my new best friend without me realizing it for some time. One day as we were both reading, I had a sudden inspiration. I asked JR, "How long did you live in New York?"

JR casually looked around to see who was close before saying, "Fourteen years."

I was incredulous. "You were born there?"

"Yeah."

"So, how did you end up in Nebraska?"

"I'll tell you sometime. It worked out all right for me, but I wasn't too happy at the time. I thought I'd gone to the end of the world."

"I'll bet. Since I've seen some big cities, I can guess how you might have felt. Of course, I kind of think cities are the end of the world."

JR smiled at his own memory. "When I saw Omaha on this trip, I knew I was home. They actually have paved streets more than two blocks long. Chicago was almost heaven. Once I got away from the stockyards, the smells alone were fantastic, a real city. I'm not sure I'll even survive seeing New York again."

"That's why you sneak out at night. What do you find so interesting about dark, smelly streets and locked buildings?"

"It's what's behind the locked doors and the smells. Thousands of people going about their lives—cooking meals, throwing their garbage in the streets, putting the kids to bed, sleeping, hoping tomorrow will be a better day."

"You get all that slinking through the dark?"

"I can almost see them."

"Will you take me around New York when we get there, preferably in the daylight?"

"Sure! I'll even show you where I lived, if it's still there."

"Why haven't you mentioned all this before?"

JR shrugged before saying, "At first I didn't want Cody to know, because he might not have hired me if he thought I was a city boy. Then I just thought it would be easier not to have to explain to anyone. Don't tell, okay?"

I was a little puzzled by that, but I agreed. I should have realized it sooner; all the signs were there. JR was a city boy.

That evening after the show, I was taking the last of the feed grain to the longhorns when I heard a gunshot. Looking around to see who was practicing this late, I began to feel pain in my right thigh; a spot of red was growing on my blue denim. At the same instant, something splintered the fencing beside me as I heard another shot. This time my brain put it together, and I hit the ground, hard.

I missed the blur of action after that, because I was too busy hugging the ground and trying to guess how bad my leg was. Another shot hit the ground inches from my head, kicking mud and manure over me. I stopped worrying about my leg and tried to press myself into the ground.

More shots and much shouting occurred before JR rolled me over and shouted, “Are you all right?”

“Get down! He’s shooting at me!”

“It’s okay. They just got him. Sit up. Are you hit?” Others came running.

I pointed out the mud-covered hole that was still bleeding. “That stings.”

JR laughed. “I bet it does. Getting shot’ll do that. I’ve got to stay away from you. You attract bullets like flies.”

Two men lifted me and carried me to Doc’s tent. After a thorough exam, the wound turned out to be two holes, as the bullet had passed through a small portion of my muscle, missing the bone by a half-inch. Doc said, “If it had hit the femur, you would be in a world of hurt. I’ll use this whiskey to clean the wound, so hang on tight.”

With orders not to walk for a couple of days, I was resting on a cot so I didn’t have to climb to the third bunk. That night, Zac, Cody, and Tom came in, asking how I was doing before Tom delivered the good news. “We caught the thug who shot you. He crawled in under the fencing and waited for a clear shot. It took some persuasion, but he said he walked around before the show until he heard someone call you by name. He was hired to kill you, and after I gave him a few love taps, he said he was contacted by a friend of a friend and expected $50 when he returned."

Cody jumped in, "All he’s going to get is a lot of jail time. The police are hunting his friend. With luck, we'll know who set this all up."

Tom added, "Don't expect too much. If we find this "friend," chances are he won't know who hired him. This kind of scum don't have friends. Someone offers them money, they don't ask questions."

Zac said, "In a way, this is good, because we know for sure someone is still trying for you, and we know he has money to spread around. We'll tighten our guard."

Tom said, "For sure."

Their assurances helped my sleep like crawling into the bunk with a porcupine would, but I did enjoy the next couple of days of pampering. I sat outside the car both days and nearly everyone in the show came by; even those who did not speak English shook my hand and smiled. The visitor I enjoyed the most was Ruth, the dark-haired girl from St. Louis I had noticed working in the dining tent. She brought my meals with a ray of sunshine, but she could not stay long to talk because of her duties. I made some personal plans regarding Ruth.

American Horse came to greet me as an old friend, even though we had never spoken before. I tried to stand for him, but the chief would not let me. “You need rest. You have been shot by a white man.” That came with a big grin.

I did no serious work for the next week, though I helped where I could. My leg felt as if Doc had left a stick in it, but I could walk and carry light items. I found it hurt less if I kept working it, gently. I was little help when they moved the show, mostly sitting with the two cowboys with broken bones, listening to the warmhearted insults of our friends.

46 Dinner

I finished my morning chores, or rather, chore. My only job was to limp around, feeding some grain to each horse—the very job I had been doing when the bullets flew. It was Sunday. We were in Philadelphia, and many of the cast and crew headed for the Liberty Bell. I could not take the trip, so Sam and I took on the feeding chores. A man approached with a folded note. "I'm to get your reply," he said.

I set the bucket down and read. *Remmy, Mr. Butler and I would like to invite you to dine with us tonight in our rail car. Would 7 p.m. be acceptable? Mrs. Butler.*

The expression that popped onto my face put a grin on the messenger's face as I said emphatically, "Yes." The man nodded and left. I read the note again and put it in my pocket.

Sam asked, "What's that all about? Is Cody going to fire you because that longhorn charged into the stands the other day?"

Still amazed, I said, "I've been invited to dine with the Butlers tonight."

"You're kidding!"

"No kidding."

"Wow! Annie Oakley. Can you bring a friend?"

I playfully tried to swing an empty bucket at him. "You know her name is Mrs. Butler."

"You have a lovely time. Don't worry about the rest of us. I'm sure we'll survive on cabbage soup." He gave me a bump with his shoulder. It hurt my leg but lifted my spirits. The two of us had not spoken much lately.

I took a bath that evening, listening to the catcalls of my friends. "Two baths in one week. He thinks he's a dandy boy." I put on my best clothes: the denim pants with no patches and a shirt I had only worn five or six times.

I flushed with embarrassment as I limped back through the car where the others were sitting. As I reached for the door, JR said, "Hey, enjoy, and tell us all about it when you get back. And stop limping—you're not really hurt."

I looked at each of them, and they were all smiles. I waved and left, failing to avoid a limp.

Mr. Butler greeted me at the door of their private car. "Come on in, Remmy. It's good of you to come." He motioned to a cushioned chair. "Have a seat. Mrs. Butler will be out shortly."

We talked for a few minutes about the mostly uneventful move from Washington. We both stood as Mrs. Butler entered the room. He greeted her with a kiss on the cheek.

She greeted me with, "I'm so glad you could make it on such short notice. We do try to have people in occasionally. It makes this seem more like home. We thought you might like to eat a meal without all the dining tent noise."

"Thank you very much for the invitation, ma'am. I'm sure you could have found more interesting guests, though."

"Now, don't put yourself down. How's your leg doing?"

"Good, thank you."

"Let's sit at the table and talk as we eat."

The man who served our food was dressed in black pants and a white shirt. He didn't smell of sweat like those who served in the dining car. The food was basic but well prepared and we had a superb dessert as well.

As we ate, Mrs. Butler asked, "What crops did you grow on your farm?"

"Corn mostly, with oats, rye, wheat, and barley. We let some hogs run in the timber, and we generally had fifty head of cattle as cash crops."

"I suppose you had the usual run of animals, like milk cows and chickens."

"Oh, yes, ducks and geese, too."

"You mentioned timber. Is the county forested? I always thought Kansas was all prairie."

"They tell me it is not too far west of us, but our area is like most of Missouri, except not as hilly. We spent a lot of time every year clearing stumps for new fields. Lyle and I took picks and shovels to spend the whole day uncovering tree roots. Of course, we had to dig down deep to kill the taproots of the oaks and hickories. Last summer Wilbur joined us." I stopped at the sudden realization that I was talking about my dead brothers.

We ate in silence for a few minutes, or rather, the Butlers ate; I sat fighting back tears.

Mrs. Butler quietly said, "When I was nine, my mother sent me to live at the County Infirmary because my father had died, and she could not support all of us. I lived with the superintendent's family. They forced me to do the dirtiest work, yelling at me and beating me while I was doing it. I called them 'the Wolves'. I had to live with them for four long years."

No one was eating. Mrs. Butler spoke again, "I did receive an education I could not have gotten at home, and She Wolf taught me to sew. It was not pleasant, but I survived. I think you are surviving, too." She let the words hang in the stillness of the room.

I did not dare look up. I could not see what was on my plate. I tried to speak, but my throat was too tight to make any sound. I cleared my throat and drank some water. The Butlers waited patiently.

Working my throat some more, I was able to say, "My family is dead."

No one moved for a moment, and then Mr. Butler gently touched my shoulder and said, "I'm sorry. How did it happen?"

Taking a deep breath and wiping my eyes, I said, slowly and deliberately, "They were shot in our cabin while I was outside. I stood there and watched a man kill my parents, my brothers, and my sister. I did nothing to save them." The last I nearly spat out, saying what had been lurking in my hidden thoughts for months.

Mrs. Butler waited for a full minute before asking, "What could you have done?"

The question surprised me. I had only told the story to others four times, but this was the first time I'd heard the question; I'd certainly never thought it. "I could have run to the cabin and attacked the man." My voice filled with something like desperation.

"How far would you have had to run?"

That was a jolt. All the times I had dreamed and thought of the shootings and running to the cabin, I had never considered the distance. Now I pictured the cabin that night in my mind. It was, I remembered, eighty yards to the edge of the timber where I had stood. Facts replaced emotions for the first time. If had I started the moment of the first shot, I would have been no closer than halfway when the man stepped outside.

"There was snow on the ground." Then I looked up, realizing I had said it out loud. "Eighty yards over deep snow; I had no chance, did I?"

Now Mr. Butler said, "No, you had no chance to save your family. He would have killed you, too." He put his hand on my shoulder.

I shook my head, wanting to believe it, but my heart still said I should have at least tried.

Mrs. Butler said what I could never have expected. "You are alive, so you have already beaten the killer. And if you are alive, your family is alive."

"I haven't beaten him. He killed my family."

"You think about it. It's not an easy concept. It took several years for me to work it out. I felt so much self-pity when the Wolves were abusing me, but the more they abused me, the harder I worked. By the time I left, they had no reason to yell at me. I beat them at their own game." She paused for a long moment. "I beat them, and it made me determined to be the best at whatever I tried. Think on all this, and in time you'll realize that you are the real winner."

Mr. Butler said, "Obviously, the killer is still trying to get you."

I just nodded.

"You have good protection here for now. I hope we have seen the last attempt, even though we know he was not the real killer. Still, you're not ready to face him yourself."

Mrs. Butler added, “By the way, now that we have told each other our deep secrets, you should call us Frank and Annie, all right?"

"Yes, ma'am."

Annie smiled but did not correct me.

It was dark by the time I left the Butlers to make my way along the train to our car. I was deep in memories of the evening, but did notice Segebart in time to stop in the shadows. My nemesis moved directly to the donniker and disappeared behind it.

With the way clear, I continued to savor the evening and was hardly aware of my bunkmates when I entered the car. James said, "Out with it. What was it like eating with Annie Oakley?"

The others added, "Yeah, tell us!"

I walked on, saying, "I need to get to bed," and meaning it.

"Oh no, you don't. You sit right here and talk."

I wanted to make a run for it but decided they would not leave me alone. With a big sigh, I sat. After trying to think of what to say, I blurted out, "She likes to be called by her real name, Mrs. Annie Butler."

"We know that. Tell us what you ate, what you talked about."

I had a sudden inspiration. "You have to promise never to tell anyone. Promise?"

They all agreed.

"We had quail eggs and duck liver. She actually shot the duck this morning and found the eggs nearby." No one seemed to notice quail eggs would have hatched out long ago, assuming there were any in Philadelphia.

"They had a staff of people to take care of them. There were three people just to carry the plates in and out." I went on with a Brit-sized tall tale until they had had enough.

Sam said, "I'm going to hit you on the leg if you don't tell us." I had to smile.

George said, "Come on, tell us something true."

I talked about everything except the dark secrets and answered most of their questions. I found the tension leaving me as I talked and relaxed with my friends. I was beginning to understand the importance of friends. Friends can talk and have fun together, but friends are more importantly helpers and healers. Without all of the wonderful people who helped me, I could never have recovered from my grief. I might never have been ready for the confrontations to come.

47 Family

Finished with my lightweight morning chores, I needed to rest my throbbing leg. Hearing the sounds of practice in the arena, I made my way to the stands to watch with my leg stretched on the bench. The Butlers were standing there with several rifles and shotguns as others took their practice shots. After a warm greeting, Annie said, "We're just ready for our session. We need to work on several new shots we may put in the show soon."

"Mind if I watch?"

"Of course not. Find a comfortable seat."

The act had me spellbound. It led me to spend the day thinking about learning to shoot. If Red Beard still wanted me dead, why shouldn't I take the fight to him? But with what? I could shoot a .22 okay, but I couldn't shoot like Annie or Frank, and I would need something bigger than that peashooter.

That night, in my bunk, waiting for sleep to find me, my mind struggled with dozens of unanswered questions. Watching how easily the Butlers handled their guns got me thinking I should be able to avenge my parents' murders with a gun.

I remembered the talk at dinner on Sunday, and Frank saying, *You're not ready to face him.* My own mind was saying, *Yes, I am.* Did Frank say that just because I was sixteen, or was there more to it?

They said I should take the police with me. Why? They would just arrest him, and I wanted him dead. Besides, I didn't have proof he was the killer. A man with a red beard and spotted horse? The police would probably laugh at me. It would only mean Red Beard would know where to find me.

No, I had to find the man and shoot him. It was the only option I could see. I was living with people who used rifles and pistols every day. The gun was the real law, at least in the West.

Yet, Annie's words kept coming back: *I beat them at their own game. You have already beaten the killer.* I wondered, *Have I actually bested Red Beard? True, I'm still alive, but that was just dumb luck. What did Annie mean? Sure, she had spent time with the Wolves, but how could that have been like watching my family massacred? She was beaten and abused, but her family was safe.*

Annie's others words burned the most. *What could you have done?* I should have run to the house and attacked the man as he came out. I should have run to the man's horse and gotten his rifle to shoot him. I should have run back to Bill Shultz and gotten him to help. I should have at least run to Jenson's cutting crew the next day. The possibilities shamed me.

Instead, I ran like a scared little boy. The thought brought tears to my eyes yet again.

What could you have done? The repeated question finally receded enough for sleep to overtake me, but it was another restless sleep.

48 Bruised

The show closed in Philadelphia with two more actors out with broken bones and most of the others groaning with wounded and exhausted bodies. Because we had a week to prepare for the opening in Erastina on June 28, Cody and Nate ordered everyone to spend Sunday in complete rest, except for essential staff.

By bedtime, the dining tent was nearly the only thing left standing. Everyone went to sleep early. I was especially tired, because I had put in my first full day of work.

A now-familiar dream woke me deep in the night. Red Beard centered in the sights of a rifle at the railroad depot in Walnut. I was just a spectator in the dream, watching myself on the snow bank. I could see Red Beard on the platform with the other men, but I could also see down the barrel. I could feel the trigger on my finger, even as I sat somewhere in the distance. I always woke before I pulled the trigger.

I woke again late in the morning and drank enough coffee to wake the dead. In the middle of the afternoon, Sam and I went for more coffee in the dining tent, and I saw Ruth sitting with some girlfriends. I poked Sam and whispered, "There she is."

Sam took a more direct approach. Coffee in hand, he led me to the girls' table and said, "Mind if we join you?" They did not. Sam pulled out a chair next to Ruth and then sat two seats over. I blushed as I sat in the offered chair.

Not knowing what to say, I just listened to the conversation. After a few minutes, Ruth spoke to me as the others were talking, "So, where are you from?"

I looked at those eyes, trying successfully to ignore what the others were saying. "I'm from Kansas. Where are you from?"

"St. Louis. I signed on the day the train came from Chicago."

"I was on that train."

"I know."

She knew. A little flustered, I asked, "What do you do in the kitchen?"

"They call it food prep. I peel potatoes, cut up veggies and fruit, fetch and carry, or whatever the cooks need me to do. It takes time to peel three hundred pounds of potatoes."

"Wow, by yourself?"

She smiled that great smile. "There are several of us."

After talking about our respective duties and lives in the show, I realized the others had left. "Could I walk you to your car?" It was a short walk that took a long time. As we walked and talked, I took the full measure of Ruth. She was as tall as Annie, but just a little on the side of stocky, in an appealing way. She was pretty, if not a beauty. She kept her brown hair piled on top of her head in whatever style women called it, though I know it was not a true bun. Her face was narrow but not so much that it was at first noticeable. When she smiled, which was often, her teeth were mostly straight. Still, her eyes were like those of a puppy, soft and inviting, eyes to get lost in and thrill at the experience. I had to force myself not to stare into those desirable eyes.

When I returned to my car, I carried a smile and her Sunday work schedule.

On Monday morning, we packed what was left of the show, and the trains left for Erastina. Actually, we went to New Jersey where the cars were transferred to railcar-ferryboats for the ride to the island. We did not watch the loading, though I would have liked to. I could see that there were rails on the boats, so it seemed they just lined the boats up with the ends of the rails on land and pushed the cars on. Anyway, we took a regular ferry.

That ride was beyond any possible dreams. Hundreds of boats and ships spread out over more water than I ever believed could exist. The ride was rough, because of a hurricane creating big waves as it pushed its way north. For me, it was like riding the hay wagon at the stockyards with its constant roll and sway. The ferry even went right past Bedloe Island, where construction was underway for the Statue of Liberty. Arriving at the new town of St. George, two engines pulled the Wild West cars the four miles to Mariners Harbor.

Erastus Wiman offered the show an idyllic setting, five hundred feet from water's edge on the island that was rapidly becoming a second home to the rich and famous of New York society. As an extra incentive for Cody, Wiman built a solid grandstand as well as high protective fences, concessions, and the crowning touch: electric arc lamps for the arena and electric lighting for the rest of the area. It was like working in a wonderland.

At the show grounds, the day's work was abnormal in the extreme. The carpenters had a tremendous pile of lumber to use for new construction of a variety of platforms, displays, and walkways. We had a great deal of work to do before we could offload the wagons. The actors did not get the day off, either. They set to work at once, changing details in the show to fit the new grounds. Those details changed our routine for lining up all the show stock, but the changes were minor.

My crew at least had a normal morning offloading the animals. Stockyard-quality pens waited based on plans sent by Cody. In addition, a pasture enclosed by a high six-strand barbed wire fence was available, but mostly for the horses.

The electric experts were stringing wires and lighting to every tent. They also attached lines to all the rooming cars. The arena had floodlights installed. I attempted to watch as I worked, trying to figure out how it all went together, but, it was in vain; the electric thing made no sense to me.

Everyone was tired after the long day, but the dinner was nonetheless festive. We all understood that Staten Island was going to be almost restful after doing so many short stands. The hard work was over for a few months. As a special treat, cold beers were available with the meal, but only one each.

49 Storm

Deep into Tuesday night—properly Wednesday—a violent thunderstorm rolled over the encampment like an evil demon. Nearly everyone in the show awoke the instant a bolt of lightning struck inside the camp, splitting a tall tree and blasting bark a hundred feet like shotgun pellets. The men in our car hurriedly put on clothes and rain gear. We were already leaving the car when Zac's man came to get us.

Lightning jumped cloud-to-cloud every few seconds and struck the ground occasionally. The constant roar of thunder and wind spooked the stock. The electricians turned on what lights they could, though many blew from being wet. The crew dug out storm lanterns and carried them to the fences. I held a lantern to my face as I spoke to let them see who was talking. I think I was more afraid of the storm than the animals were, and they were plenty scared.

Within ten minutes, the light and noise muted as the storm moved on, though the rain continued to drench us. Back in the car, no one was ready for sleep. We talked about the scare and then our thoughts on the island. Still, in an hour all was quiet.

The morning was partly cloudy, and the electricians were hard at work to repair the damage and make the system rainproof. I spent the morning caressing a paintbrush. After lunch, I spent the afternoon helping with the canvas rigging before returning to the painting. By dinnertime, we had nearly finished the painting, and the electrical work was close. They had streetlights positioned throughout the show grounds, and every tent and tepee had its own light, with most of the pens strung out ready for the final installations.

After dinner, most of the crew returned to their favorite forms of entertainment. There were the usual gossip groups, card games, and secret imbibings, but I sought out the quiet of the stock pens. There was enough light in the pens for me to see the animals and hear their contented munching, grazing, and browsing. I worked with these animals every day, but I was now seeing them almost in a natural state, not as pieces on display. The scene made me feel at home, which made me cry.

I had been just as happy as everyone else at dinner. I had even planned to join in one of the evening activities, but a sudden urge to be alone had overtaken me. So, I was leaning against a wooden fence with tears on my cheeks, not knowing why.

A vision of my parents came to mind, as happened often. I realized I had not seriously thought of them for several days. It had been even longer since I had dreamed of the shootings. Why? My thoughts were too muddled to make much sense. The pain of losing my family had not diminished. I had not forgotten.

I struggled again with ideas about what I should do if I saw Red Beard. I had watched the cowboys and Indians closely, trying to pick up any hints on what they might do in such a case. I was sure the Indians would immediately track and kill Red Beard, probably barehanded, but the cowboys were not that dependable. The show represented them as rough, tough, honest, and brave, but I had the feeling many of them would rather go to a saloon than concern themselves with the killer. No honor among thieves, but not much more among cowboys.

I respected the advice of the Butlers more than any others, even of Cody, yet I was still not sure I wanted the police to do my job. It was my duty to avenge my family's deaths.

Singing began to filter into my thoughts, and I realized it was coming from one of the tepees behind me. As I listened, other voices joined in from other tepees. Neither the song nor the language was familiar to me, but it seemed sad and suited my mood entirely. I imagined they remembered their own families, and it gave me comfort. When the song ended and a chant began, sounding more war-like, I went back to my own car.

50 Parade

During the week of preparation, no one went on strike for an eight-hour workday, nor did we get one. We did finish the last touches while the actors were parading so that when we sat down to our dinner, we knew we could stay and enjoy coffee and conversation as long as we wanted; there were no shows this Saturday.

The camp and show grounds were ready, but few of the show's people were; everyone wanted and needed more rest. Nonetheless, the biggest parade of the season did take place, ready or not. With show wagons repainted, the tack cleaned and polished, and the horses groomed, all were loaded for the train ride back to St. George and the ferry to New York, followed by the two-mile march through the heart of the city.

However, the train left without Annie. An insect had dug a hole in her ear, causing her so much pain, she no longer maintained her constant smile. By Saturday morning, parade day, she admitted defeat and went to a doctor. He cleaned it out and told her she had blood poisoning and needed complete bed rest.

Instead, being Annie Oakley, I saw her rush into camp, where she changed clothes and raced her horse to St. George in time to board the ferry. I heard later she made it through the long parade, but was so exhausted afterward that two men had to lift her from her horse. Frank told me she slept twelve hours straight. She was so sick she did not leave her car until Wednesday and was shaking like an aspen after her first performance on Thursday; even so, she hit all her shots.

It was unusual to have a parade, then not have a show for two days, but we were in New York. Sunday was a much-needed day of rest. I heard the rumor that even Johnny stayed in camp. Almost no one left to find a cafe, satisfied instead with cold sandwiches until the vegetable beef soup in the evening.

Ruth was on duty, and I spent most of the day in the dining tent, along with half the camp. My friends and her friends sat around talking. She had to get up a number of times to make more coffee, get more ice, and add more soda and syrup to the dispensing machines. We were able to ignore the others at the table a few times and pretend we were by ourselves.

Monday, June 28, was the first normal day of the island schedule that ran to September 30. A train arrived at 10:45 and another at 11. The customers bought food from the vendors and wandered through the menageries before the band began to play. At 12:30, the Grand Review stormed into the arena as the last of the customers hurried into the stands. The show ended at 3:30, and the trains carried all the customers back to the ferry by 4:30.

At 5:00, the next trains arrived, and the whole process began again. Kicking Bear's horse stumbled and somersaulted over him in the evening show. He lay unconscious for a few minutes while cowboys and Indians tended him. He was able to walk out to applause but missed the rest of the show. By 10:45, the camp was empty of customers.

That became the rhythm of the rest of the summer, every day but Sunday.

The rhythm hit a not-so-small bump Tuesday night of the second week. I took a walk through the pens to put my thoughts in order before going to bed. When the dreams were bad or my thinking was tangled up again, a walk among the animals had a calming effect.

Segebart was within ten feet of me before I saw him. “If it ain’t the pig farmer. What are you doing out here, besides stinking up the place?”

“What are you doing here? I figured you’d be busy beating up the town drunk.”

“That’s no way to talk to your betters. I’m a cowboy, and you’re just a pig farmer. I guess I’ll have to teach you some manners.”

I squared off, clenched my fists, and readied for the assault. Instead, someone grabbed my arms from behind. Pivonka. I should have known. The first blow hit my left eye. I swung a boot at his leg, but was too busy taking another fist to my face to know the results. One more shot to my face and a solid punch in the stomach crumpled me. As I struggled for air, Segebart could not resist a final kick to the ribs. I hardly felt that one as night descended just for me.

I woke in pain, with no idea how long I had been eating dirt. I found my right eye closed and blood dripping into my left. Each breath brought pain to my ribs. Slowly righting myself, I held my kerchief to my left eye so I could see. I pushed myself to a standing position, and when the world started to spin, I grabbed the fence. As my head settled down, I used the fence as a crutch and struggled back to the car.

As I stumbled in, Will asked, "What happened to you?"

"I slipped."

Sam said, "That's no slip. Who did this?"

"No one."

JR said, "No one named Segebart, I'll bet."

"Forget it."

"Like hell. We'll jump him and Pivonka tonight."

"*No!*" The shout stopped everyone as it stabbed my ribs. Others came in to hear what happened. Soon, the whole crew was plotting how to catch the two thugs. I kept telling them to leave it alone.

Zac stuck his head in. "Boys, your windows are open. I heard you down the street. This is the way it is. I'll put Segebart and Pivonka on short leashes. You will go to sleep tonight. You will stay well away from those two. You are all good workers, and I don't want to lose you because of two fried eggs. If need be, I can get them fired. Are we clear here?"

Everyone agreed, but there was still some quiet grumbling after Zac left. JR went to the kitchen for some ice for my head. I should have told Zac to get them fired, but I wanted to take care of them myself. Segebart would be a warm-up for Red Beard.

51 Newsboys

I recovered quickly enough physically, with no residual issues. As to my state of mind, Segebart had done me a favor. I gave up worrying so much. As I thought of it, Red Beard had chased me, shot me, and beaten me, but I was still standing. I never considered Segebart as anything but a stand-in for Red Beard, and he had given me his worst, so I could relax. I still mourned my family, I still had bad days, but mostly I learned to live today and not try to live tomorrow.

Most of our paying customers came from the cities of New York, Harlem, Queens, and, Brooklyn, but there were a fair share from New Jersey, and almost every week brought a trainload of people from as far away as Boston.

Monday, July 19, was different. Cody personally paid to bring newsboys from New York City to the show, and Father Drumgoole brought all of his boys from the St. Vincent's Home for Homeless Newsboys as well, which had recently opened on the island. The boys had free access to the concessions, the menageries, and the show. Johnny Baker and others handed out sack lunches to all of them.

The stars seemed to go out of their way to welcome the boys. They were on *Star Street* talking with the boys and showing them some of their skills. I enjoyed showing off the animals and describing how they lived on ranches. The boys were excited to see animals besides the horses and mules that were common in the city.

Annie, now healthy again, played with the boys. She was a terrific athlete and, even being only five feet tall was a strong woman. She would “race” the younger ones, who always won, and yet she would beat the older boys. She picked up and held small boys by the hundred, telling them how wonderful they were.

Cody disappeared in a troop of older boys enraptured by his tales of life on the frontier. While Cody was never one to let the truth get in the way of a good story, he generally stayed close with these boys. He believed he was a teacher about the old times, especially that day.

The boys hooted and cheered the full three-hour show, and Cody even brought many of them into the arena to participate in parts of the show. I heard many performers remark later how much fun it had been.

Once the trainload of boys left, the crew had an hour to relax, but JR said to me, "Let's go for a walk." I could tell from his expression that it was not just a walk. We headed south past the pens and into the scrub and trees of the middle of the island. After a few inconsequential remarks, JR said, "You remember I said I was from New York?"

"Yeah."

We walked a little more while I waited for JR to continue. At length he said, "I was one of those boys. Not a newsboy, but an orphan."

He stopped talking, and I found myself at a loss. Finally, I asked, "You were an orphan?"

JR nodded agreement. After a minute of walking he added, "I think I was ten or eleven when my father died, and I was fourteen when my mother died. No one could take me in, so I ended up in an orphanage."

I numbly asked, "What was it like?"

"It wasn't too bad. I was lucky. The church ran it, and the nuns were mostly kind to us. There were a couple who whipped us, but I learned to avoid them."

"So, how did you get out?"

"Have you ever heard of the orphan trains?"

"No."

"Every few years when the orphanages get too full, they ask kids to volunteer to take a train west where people are willing to care for them. They describe the excellent homes and loving families who want children. So, I agreed to go when I was sixteen."

By this time, we had made ourselves comfortable against a fallen tree. JR went on, "If they had told us what was really going to happen, none of us would have gone. Our train started making stops in Ohio. At each stop, a dozen or so of us left the train and did not return. We all began to worry about what was really happening.

"By the time we arrived in North Platte, the train was down to one car of us, and they were pulling freight cars to help pay the expense. As it turned out, North Platte was our last stop. The remaining seventeen of us went in a church and stood in front of a room full of men and women. We were each asked to say our names, our ages, and a little about ourselves. Then people asked us questions. Based on that, a family chose each of us.

"Gordon and Elizabeth Bowman chose me. Again, I was lucky. They didn't take me in as a son, but they treated me fairly. I was never beaten and worked when not in school. They had three younger children of their own, and I came to realize they chose me to do some of the heavy work around the ranch the younger boys couldn't do.

"Gordon rarely said much to me, as long as I was doing the work, but Liz, as she wanted me to call her, nearly begged me to talk and it didn't matter what about. I think she was lonely, living so far from other people. She wanted to know all about New York and was probably disappointed I had seen so little of it.

"After a year with them, I had the choice of leaving or staying. I would have liked to go back to the city, but I had no money and no one to take me in. I was only seventeen, so I decided to stay another year. Besides, I was enjoying school. There were only ten of us in the twelve grades. Mary Chadwick was our teacher, and she was only four years older than I was."

I said, "Sounds like you had an eye on her."

He laughed. "No, not really. She was even shorter and fatter than Lillian Smith, and her face was blotched from smallpox. But, she was a great teacher and helped me more than anyone besides my own mother. She especially helped me learn to love reading. I think you would have liked her, too."

"I already like her."

"Well, you know the rest of my story. Just don't tell anyone else what you know. I know I can trust you."

"You have my word."

The following Thursday held a surprise of another kind. A big storm slowly moved into the area and eventually deposited some sixteen inches of water on the show grounds. Rain nearly washed away the afternoon show, and by the time the customers ran to their trains, the downpour was at full strength. Nate canceled the night show, but only because the ferryboats stopped running. Friday had the poorest attendance of the summer.

I didn't mind at all; it was a change in the routine. Conversation was tricky with the pounding of rain on the roof of the car, but it was easy enough to read by. I found myself reading a few minutes, then thinking about JR as an orphan. Maybe I'd liked him on sight because we orphans could sense each other. Whatever it was, I now felt even closer to him.

52 Angel

Rain was not the only thing the island had to offer. Two types of people lived on the island: fishermen and wealthy New Yorkers who wanted to get out of the city. We seldom saw either, because the fishermen were on their boats all day and the well-heeled returned to the city to work. I spent as much time as possible exploring the wilds of the island, the center of which was still mostly wild. I enjoyed walks through the woods because it was so much like being home, but walks along the shorelines became as pleasurable and enlightening.

The dining tent was a cornucopia of newness for me: fresh fish of all kinds, oysters, clams, lobsters, bananas, oranges, lemons, a hundred vegetables and fruits I had never heard of. It seemed New York had everything, at least if you could afford it, and Cody could. It was rumored the show spent $300 a day on food. Of course, it spent almost that much on ammunition.

In addition, the food was always fresh. Growing up eating salt pork and beef did not prepare me for the nearly savage pleasure of eating such delicacies. Mother had used gallons of vinegar to put cabbage, cucumbers, and other foods in winter storage. I remembered how fantastic those first dandelion leaves of the spring tasted—in fact, the taste of anything not soaked in vinegar or salt. That was one reason I hunted and trapped in the winter.

Sam and I received a note inviting us to an evening meal with Bill Cody and Buck Taylor. We looked forward to meeting the big man. Big, as in six feet, four inches, or as Buck always said, "five feet, sixteen." Big, as in three hundred pounds. Big, as in shoulders wide enough to match a Texas longhorn. Big, as in handsome, in a tough way: long nose, drooping mustache, long brown hair, and eyes like iron rivets.

We had watched him for weeks and were amazed that such a giant could be so nimble. His part in the show was trick riding, roping, and bronc riding. He was also a pickup artist. Riding at a gallop, he would lean over and snatch a small object from the ground, often a lady's hanky. The workers respected him especially, because he was the first to jump in and help with the stock whenever needed.

The meal was outside Cody's large tent, in the shade of a tree. The food was the same as in the dining tent, but the crowd was quieter.

As we approached, Cody said, "Here come the Kansas Angel and his bushwhacker friend. Good to see you both." Cody rose and shook our hands. "I want you to meet a God-honest cowboy, William Levi Taylor. I only call him that because I know he doesn't want me to. Better call him Buck."

Cody did not offer us cigars, but he and Buck continued to pull on theirs. "So, you boys sorry yet I took you away from the stockyards?"

Sam jumped right in, "No way! We love it here. This is the best place to work in the whole world."

Cody and Buck both laughed loudly. Buck said, "Bill, I don't think you're working these boys hard enough."

With another laugh, Cody said, "I know they work harder than you do."

Lemonade came with chipped ice.

Throughout the evening, Cody and Buck entertained us with stories of the glory days of the real Wild West in the '60s and '70s. Cody ended in a serious mood with, "Remmy, do you remember anything of the last Indian battle in Kansas back in '79? It was with the Cheyenne."

"We talked about it in school, but I don't really remember much."

"Well, to me, it marked the end of the West. I was here in New York, trying to learn this acting thing, so I just read about it in the papers like most folks. The Northern Cheyenne on a reservation in Indian Territory were having a terrible time of it. They were starving, because the government didn't deliver the promised food. So, they took it upon themselves to head back to their homelands in the north. Along the way, they had to cross roads, railroads, and telegraph lines, and they had to avoid towns all over the place. The army out of Fort Dodge caught up with them at a pleasant little natural spring area some 45 miles north of the fort. I've been there several times. Anyway, a firefight ensued. Colonel Lewis, leading the troops, was shot in the thigh and bled to death. That made it possible for the Cheyenne to get away. He was the only casualty on either side.

"My point is this, just three years earlier the same band of Cheyenne was part of the attack on Custer. They went, in just three years, from mighty warriors of the open plains to having to sneak past farms and railroads. The army eventually caught most of them in Nebraska, and they never made it to their homeland. Later, the soldiers killed most when they tried to escape. That's when I knew for sure the old days were over. You agree, Buck?"

"I hadn't thought about it, but I think you're right. The attack on Custer was their last great victory, for sure. There have been some fights since, but the war's over. We own the West."

Cody added, "I don't have to tell you my exaggerations. I was in some bitter fights with different Indian tribes, but I've always respected them. We were taking their homes away from them, and they tried to stop us. It's what we should have expected. I never liked some of the dirty tricks we played on them, especially giving them blankets covered with smallpox. Fight fair, I say. We were stronger, and we deserved to win."

Throughout the summer, Cody gave invitations to all the guys in our work crew to eat with him at one time or another, but I was always with them. The others began to tease me that I was Cody's pet, and I secretly took pride in it. I was also pleased with Cody's nickname for me.

On another Sunday, Cody came by our car and asked me to take a walk. That was new. We went a short way from the camp with Cody in a serious mood. As we walked, I wondered what new trouble had found me.

Once we were out of earshot, Cody said, "I've been giving your problem a lot of thought, and I want to help you every way possible. Right now, we're just sitting here waiting for another attack, and I can tell you from experience, you don't win wars by sitting around. We need to take the offensive. Can you think of anything else that might help us locate this killer?"

For the first time in two months, the whole night flashed through my mind at a dizzying speed. I even flinched with every shot. It was some moments before my mind returned to the present. As I write this, it is still that way; I never know what will trigger the memories.

For once, Cody was patient. We had stopped and were standing under some trees. Cody sat on a log. Finally, I managed, "I don't know what to do." Tears attempted to cloud my vision; I blinked them away. Still Cody waited. "I see the shooting as clearly now as I did that night, but I can't see anything new."

Cody nodded and then said, "Sit here." He patted the log. "I don't tell many people this story, because it stills pains me. My father was a staunch abolitionist, which is why we ended up in Kansas. He gave speeches against slavery at every opportunity, and he taught me to do the same.

"One day when I was eleven, I was giving what we now call a stem-winder, bringing down the wrath of God on all slave owners. We didn't realize at least half the crowd had come over from Missouri. They were real bushwhackers and looking for trouble.

"But, instead of attacking me, they went after my father. They stabbed him several times before the Free Staters pulled them away and the brawl ensued. I, naturally, went to my father and did what I could for him. He lived, but he never really recovered and died a few months later." Cody cleared his throat and studied the ground without speaking.

"Anyway," he went on, "I didn't see my parents murdered, but it was close. I left home when my father died in '57. I guess, in a way, I've been running ever since."

His story was more like mine than I would have imagined, and he'd gone on to greatness. I asked, "What should I do?"

Cody looked directly at me for the first time since starting his personal experience. "Angel, I'm not the best one to give advice on this kind of thing. I just meet things head-on. That's who I am. Like I've said before, it could get me killed and very nearly has more than once. I don't think you can do things my way, especially not these days."

I pushed. "But, what do you think you would have done if your family had been killed in front of you when you were sixteen?"

Cody paused a moment, then said, "I often wondered what I would have done if there had been no crowd there to take on the bushwhackers. I like to think I would have taken them on single-handed or tracked them down to kill them or die trying. You have to remember, Fort Leavenworth was the edge of civilization then. The only law was our own skills at survival. We live now in modern times. Here we are, doing this show under electric lights! I can hardly believe I've seen so many changes in my forty years. You have to do things differently."

"Do you think I should hunt for him and tell the sheriff when I find him?"

"The man you want to track is a killer. He knows how to do it, and you don't. I can tell you for a fact, killing a man isn't easy, especially not the first time. And I did it in war.

"I did have one up-close fight to the death. It was ugly and brutish. I make it look glamorous in the show, but it wasn't. To tell the truth, Yellow Hand missed slitting my belly wide open by a whisker. I spent a lot of sleepless nights after that fight."

"How do I live with myself?"

"That's easy, and hard. You have to be Remiel Bevans for now. No matter what else happens, be yourself. After my father died, I worked for John Willis, and then Lou Simpson, both bull-whackers leading wagon trains on into Kansas Territory. I was only eleven, twelve, and they called me a smart-aleck kid and a lot worse. I stuck it out and proved my worth. I was Willie when I left home. I became Billy, eventually Bill, then Buffalo Bill. You just keep going."

"I see what you're saying, but I still don't know what to do."

Now Cody stood abruptly and said, "Let's walk back. I think you're where you need to be for now. You have friends and a good job. We're in a position to protect you. Think on it, at least until winter. You'll know what to do when the right time comes. But, when it comes, grab it, hold on, and don't look back."

That night, I thought of the Cheyenne's attempt to go home. Big Jim had told me about life in Indian Territory, so I knew even in those modern days, the government rarely provided what they promised. I understood why starving people would be willing to risk it all to live ordinary lives. Most of them died trying, but they grabbed the chance and held on.

53 Sheep-dip

Near the end of July, I noticed Cody was not in the Grand Parade, nor did he appear in the show at all that night. In the dining tent, some of the older hands said that Cody was drunk. "He had too much of the Kansas sheep-dip again."

Sitting in front of our car that night, Cody was the talk of the night. Charlie, whose father had been a drunk, was disgusted. "I put up with that crap for too long. If Cody's going to do this all the time, I'm quitting. I hate being around drunks."

"It happened before." This was from Sam. "He and Dumont held up the train in Dayton, remember?"

I put in, "It was really Johnny, not Cody."

Charlie did not notice. "That's when I shoulda quit! Then Cody chewed Bart and Jack out for being drunk in Newark. He's two-faced, for sure."

James jumped in. "I've seen several men drunk on this trip so far. Cody was mad at Bart and Jack because he had to bail them out of jail."

The discussion went on for a while, but my experience with Brit and my loyalty to Cody left me conflicted. Cody was on time for every event after that, so most of us soon forgot about it; but the action the next night might have had more to do with forgetting.

The guards found a watchman near the pens, bleeding from a bash to his head. The reaction was swift and sure, thanks to Tom Gibson's training. The first thing I knew, my two guards grabbed my arms and nearly carried me to the gun wagon. They told me what little they knew and sat there with guns out. It was late that night before I heard the whole story.

Within minutes, every man they could spare from the show was armed. Gibson's men started a systematic search. They quickly swept through the pens, where they picked up a trail that led to the empty wagons.

The first wagon by the pens was an empty box on wheels that held canvas when it was full, but it held no men when searched. The second wagon had three partition walls for storing items from the menagerie. When the guards opened the middle section, two men stood, one holding a knife, the other holding his hands above his head. The sight of four pistols was enough to induce the man to drop the knife.

The guards took them, handcuffed, to the pens where they were out of sight of the customers. Meanwhile, the search continued through the remaining wagons and the rest of the grounds. They found no more men by the time the show ended.

Once the guards locked the gates for the night, Cody called all employees to the dining tent, including me. He gave a short version of the night's events as some security men took a careful head count while others searched the camp again to make sure there were only the two men.

Gibson told me the next day, "I questioned the two men most of the night, but all they gave me were insults. I'm convinced they're part of some gang, so I'll turn them over to the Richmond County Sheriff for prosecution. I'll also make sure he checks with the New York Police about their gang. I've got a good idea it's the Whyos."

A week later, the news came from the city that the two thugs were members of the Whyos, the largest and nastiest gang in the city. They were so powerful and well-protected that they printed flyers with their price list for whatever the customer wanted to purchase: $2 to punch an enemy, $15 to chew off an ear, $25 to stab without killing, $100 to murder.

Once Gibson knew who to talk to, he returned to the city and met with the Whyos' leaders. He had a simple business proposal for them, approved by Nate and Cody. "I will pay you $200 to forget the contract on Remmy Bevans." After some negotiation, he paid them $450. "If you can give me the name of the man who wants Remmy dead, it's worth double."

Reporting back, Tom said, “I don’t expect to hear the name. Your Red Beard has been smart to use gangs to do all the contacting. I doubt that his contact in Kansas City knows his name. But, it’s worth a try.”

By August, the days began to blend together so much I sometimes had to check the top of the newspaper to know the date. The real calendar was marked by who was injured or by the occasional storms dumping way too much rain on the camp.

One such downpour stopped the show for half an hour because the customers could not see. I stood the whole time next to the gate, ready to release the buffalo, only two of which were close enough to see through the curtain of water. It pounded on my waterproof like hail. The bombardment left my ears ringing for hours after.

There was one pleasant development in those weeks. Work permitting, Ruth and I spent time together. Mostly we sat and talked, in the dining tent and around the camp, often with others. She learned cherry pie was my favorite, so she saved slices to bring to me when we met. I offered to bring her a pie from my work, but she declined.

One night, after the chores were finished, we took a rare walk through town and along the river. We sat and watched the lighthouse on Shooter’s Island. We kissed.

It seemed so natural. We were talking, relaxed and happy to be near each other. Without giving it thought, I kissed her on the lips, sending a tingle through mine. I started to kiss her again when a jolt of another kind struck—the men following me. I jumped up, looking for them. Ruth asked, "What's wrong?"

Then I remembered I had not thought to tell anyone we were leaving camp. "Uh, I just remembered something. We need to get back to camp. I'm sorry.

Ruth asked, "Is it because of your guards?"

"You know about them?"

"The whole camp knows. You were shot; of course, we know someone wants you dead, but we don't know why. What's going on?"

We walked back to camp. I had not recovered from either the kiss or the sudden realization. I had to think for a minute how to answer Ruth. "Look, if I tell you, please don't tell anyone else."

"But, there are a lot of crazy ideas going around. Why not set them straight?"

I had no answer for that. "I only share with people I trust. Can I trust you?"

She stopped and held my arm. Looking directly into my eyes, she said, "Yes." I had no doubt.

I told Ruth the story, leaving out some gory details. I explained how Red Beard was using gangs to try to get me. In the end, she held me tightly without saying a word. As we separated at the camp, she said, "Thank you for telling me, and for trusting me."

I enjoyed being with Ruth, but I couldn't help wondering if it was a mistake to get too close to her. I might have to take off at any minute. Yet, why not be happy now? Having told her about my family, she would understand if I had to leave. Besides, it was just for the summer. Right?

54 Baseball

The day we arrived on the Island, we saw the large stadium at St. George and assumed it was our new home. Instead, Zac told us that Mr. Wiman also owned a professional baseball team called the New York Metropolitans, and the stadium was their home. The team had fireworks after every game to bring in larger crowds.

Those fireworks became a part of the background of life on Staten Island, but baseball wormed its way into the soul of the show. It was a constant source of entertainment. On Sundays, half of our show seemed to visit the impressive, roofed, double-decked grandstand used for baseball, lacrosse, concerts, and whatever else Wiman could schedule to draw a crowd. The restaurants and other activities added to the allure. Their food was not as good as ours, but it was a change.

Within weeks, pickup teams formed for a quick game in the mornings or sometimes between shows. Few of us had ever played before, and we were not very good, but it was fun. Watching the Metropolitans play, we picked up more details of the game.

By August, organized, with rules, the competition became serious. Pitching proved to give us the most trouble. The National League of professional teams had just allowed overhand pitching two years earlier, but most of the Wild West players wanted to stick to pitching underhand, partly because most of the professional pitchers still used the technique. The Pawnee named Snake Killer wanted the overhand throw because he could hurl it like a shooting star. In the end, everyone agreed to stay with the National League rules allowing both styles. Therefore, whenever Snake Killer pitched, his team generally won.

The pitcher's box was another point of contention. It was supposed to be a rectangle starting 50 feet from home plate, four feet wide, and five and a half feet back toward second base. The Metropolitans' field had the box neatly marked out with caulk, but we made due with a dragline with our toes. The pitcher was supposed to have one foot on the back line and the other foot inside the box when he released the ball.

Late in August when Snake Killer was pitching for one team and Rodriguez for the other, the brewing war bubbled over. Snake was tall, with long legs. When he threw overhand, his front foot was always in front of the box. He had been throwing that way for weeks, but no one wanted to say anything because he was as mean as his name implied.

Rodriguez was a superb underhand pitcher. His pitches were not as fast but were more accurate. As a result, the score was very low. At the end of the seventh inning, Snake Killer's team was ahead, 5 to 4. That's when the fun began.

Snake Killer had gone to a mission school and spoke English fairly well. His job was to translate for the other Pawnee. As the summer wore on, he became less and less willing to use English, in an effort to impress the various chiefs among the Indian contingent.

In the fateful game, he added to everyone's growing frustration by verbally assaulting every batter in the Pawnee language. The other Pawnee who were watching the game became upset and began to shout back at Snake. They were able to sign to a Sioux and use enough English to let the spectators know they were trying to get Snake to stop his insults. The more Snake shouted, the more others shouted back, and soon, shouting was the game. The war vets later called it dueling artillery barrages.

In addition to his verbal assaults, Snake was edging closer and closer to home base with every pitch. People were shouting at him to move back, but that only encouraged him.

Then, with two out and two strikes, Snake Killer's next pitch hit the batter in the lower leg, knocking the man down and breaking one of the bones. For a stunned moment, all was quiet except for the cries of the batter. As if on cue, everyone, including Snake Killer's teammates, charged him. I was the first to arrive. I dove for Snake's ankles, catching only one as my momentum sent Snake backward. The second man in, less than a second later, hit Snake in the stomach with a flying tackle. In seconds, Snake was under a pile of people, everyone trying to beat him. The batter was still moaning on the ground, alone.

Cody took charge by firing three rounds of his Colt Single Action Army revolver. Of course, it was loaded with blanks, probably. He ordered everyone to leave the arena and had two men help the injured batter make his way to Doc. He ordered Snake Killer to stay. No one ever learned what Cody said in the arena, but Snake was a humble man for some time.

Thus ended the baseball war.

I was on the bottom of the dog pile and landed no punches, but I was as angry as everyone else, maybe more so because of my own unanswered beating. I felt pride in actually bringing Snake to the ground.

That same night, I saw Pivonka slinking away from the donniker, brushing his clothes. This was getting too crazy. I had not recognized the man I'd first seen, but I promised myself to catch Tom Gibson tomorrow and tell him what I had seen on three occasions. There must have been something going on. By the next day, I had forgotten.

In late August, the papers had long stories about the biggest hurricane to hit the US. It struck the Indianola, Texas area with winds clocked at 155 miles per hour, destroying the town and killing at least 25 people.

Two more blew along the East Coast, close enough to carry heavy rains to the show. Attendance was only half of normal, and the rains caused havoc with the shooting acts. Those two hurricanes passed Staten Island just a day apart, August 23 and 24. They were the last to strike the New York area that year. There were ten total for the year, seven striking the US, a record year.

I was interested in hurricanes because I had never heard of them before, and I was impressed with their power. Power was important to me. I was still trying to develop my own sense of power, or rather, my awareness of the powers I had. I believed baseball served some of the same purpose for me at that time. I found that I was one of the better players, and that helped build my confidence.

Yet, I still had the recurring inner storms, much like the occasional hurricane.

55 Doubt

As the summer twisted its way through hot, dry days and wet, muggy ones, I rocked back and forth in my struggle with leaving the show. I liked being with the show: I had good friends, and the safety was great. Still, some days the guilt would sweep over me like one of those hurricanes until I wanted to hop the first train headed west. The lack of a clear picture of what I would or could do kept me rooted in the New York version of the Wild West. In addition, saving so much money gave me confidence that I could afford to hunt Red Beard when the time came.

I continued to ask the Butlers for advice, and they continued to encourage me to prepare myself. Their counsel was to build myself physically and mentally, and they believed two years would be best. Besides, they said, "No one will expect you then, and they may not even recognize you."

Cody also assured me I needed time to prepare. The second time we talked, he said, "I've sent a telegram to a friend in Leavenworth who is a US Marshal. I asked him to find out whatever he could about your family's murders. I'll do everything I can to help you."

Ruth and I continued our close relationship. We went to St. George with friends a few times. She had a knack for knowing when I was troubled, and she was like Mother in getting me to talk, in spite of my reluctance. "I don't need to depress you, too," I would say, but within an hour, I would be telling her everything.

Mostly we enjoyed talking in the shade of the camp, a kind of private tent with no walls. She was a city girl, but we had a great deal in common. She was the oldest of six children, and her father worked in the rail yard twelve hours a day, every day of the year.

Ruth had joined the show to relieve her parents of the burden of supporting her. Now, she was able to send half of her pay home to help them. I asked her if she planned to go back when the show ended in September. "Oh, no. I am going to stay on in New York and learn more cooking skills. It could turn out well for me. Do you think you'll stay?"

"Probably until next summer."

Cody received a letter from his friend with details of the murder and the investigation, but it proved a mixed bag to both of us. The most important new information was that the sheriff was searching for a lone killer with a double-action six-shooter. He believed that all five of my family died within seconds and that every shot was a killing shot. He also removed my name from the "Wanted" list.

The sheriff had found no motive for me to kill my family (big surprise), no evidence I'd ever fired a pistol (I had not before joining the show), and no evidence I had somehow purchased or stolen an expensive-double action (I still couldn't afford one). He'd also found evidence of a stranger having broken into Jensen's cutting shack that night, and when the snow had melted he'd found five of the newer brass cartridges near a mound of horse manure at the cabin. We did not own horses.

None of the news, however, gave a clue to the killer. A brief letter from Big Jim gave much the same report. I was disappointed that the sheriff still had no information on Red Beard, but at least I was in the clear. I could go back any time now.

One thing nagged me, though. Every time I considered going up against Red Beard, I felt dread. I still had dreams of shooting him, and I wanted to, but facing a man who could kill five people so expertly was a fearful prospect best kept in the distant future.

I did take one decisive step forward. I wrote a description of Red Beard as well as my encounters with him and sent it to the sheriff.

56 Sand

Not long after moving to the island, I became aware of a conflict between Annie and Lillian Smith. Cody had booked *The California Girl*, as she was billed, to take advantage of the customers' indisputable interest in Annie the previous season. He assumed they would be just as enthusiastic about another female shooter, especially since she was only fifteen.

She had joined the show at Erastina, and through most of those three months, her portion of the show had been to run on between acts and do a few trick shots to keep the crowds entertained as the crew set up for the next act. She became so good at it that the fans started asking to see more of her. That was the problem; they were becoming as enthusiastic as they had been for Annie.

I heard that Lillian was trying to take over star billing, and Annie hated her for it. Knowing Annie, I didn't think she could hate anyone, except the Wolves. I believed I could talk with her, so I asked about the rumors. Annie said, "I do not wish to talk about that girl." That was all she ever said to me or anyone else.

I talked with Lillian a couple of times and found her crude and self-centered. Neither did I think she was pretty, with her round face, small eyes, small mouth, and large body. Beside Annie's one hundred pounds and sixteen-inch waist, Lillian looked like a pumpkin.

She could shoot, no denying that. I did get to see her a few times in practice, but she had no style. Still, she boasted she was the better markswoman and the better show woman. I even heard her say, "Annie Oakley is done for."

Lillian also developed a reputation with the boys, as in many boys. Her love life became the source for a great deal of gossip.

Neither was I immune to the lure of romance. I watched the crew in their various romantic activities, even as I tried to decide how involved I should allow myself to be. I liked Ruth, but I needed to be ready to leave in a minute if some news arrived or I happened to see Red Beard. I knew Ruth wanted more from me than I was willing to give; at least, I knew it somewhere under that confused and inexperienced façade of a sixteen-year-old.

The high point, and low, of our romance came on a Sunday outing with George, Ed, Ruth, and two young women Ed had invited, Georgia and Fern who worked in the dining tent.

We took the local train to a popular beach in the south of the island. The girls packed a large basket, two jugs of water, and one of lemonade for our picnic. Wrapped in burlap, the jugs were nestled in a box of ice.

It was a perfect day for the outing. The light blue sky had numerous cloud puffs floating by. The temperature was warm, with a cooling breeze off the ocean. Many small boats and large ships sailed by.

Walking and talking on the beach was the main activity; we examined every little thing we saw. The seagulls put on a feeding exhibition, and the waves provided a soft, rhythmic background tune. The rest of the time, we sat in the shade of some nearby trees and ate, talked, and laughed.

All we boys took off our shoes and stood at the water's edge, allowing the waves to drench us as well as the bottoms of our rolled up pants. Of the girls, only Ruth was willing to pull off her shoes and wade in the water. She even managed to take off her stockings while no one was watching. The bottom of her dress was soaked, even though she held it well above her ankles. It all provided much shrieking and laughter from the whole group. It is still one of my cherished memories.

Later, Ruth and I were able to walk a little way from the others and have a more private conversation, still in sight of them of course. When we found a log to sit on, Ruth asked, "Remmy, do you like me?"

Surprised, I blurted, "Of course I do."

"I guess I didn't mean it quite that way. I know you like me. What I mean is...." She thought for a moment. "Do you want to do more than just kiss?"

Now, I was confused. I could think of more than one meaning to the question, and I was afraid to respond to any of them. "I think you're special, and I wouldn't want to hurt you."

For the first time since I had known her, Ruth looked embarrassed. "I'm not saying this very well. I guess what I mean is, do you ever think of getting married in a year or two?"

The idea of marriage never entered my head. In fact, the sudden suggestion left my mind completely blank. The best I could do was, "I don't think so."

Ruth's face revealed her pain for just a second before she forced a smile and said, "Okay. I just wanted to know what you were expecting. Let's get back to the party." I knew I had hurt her, but I did not quite know how.

I am embarrassed to report it, but when we returned to the camp, I remembered the donniker happenings and told Tom Gibson what I had seen. "I'll look into it. It sounds fishy."

Why would that come to mind after I had sabotaged my relationship with Ruth?

57 Moody

As I was busy giving the livestock some grain on the last day of August, around ten at night, when cattle shied away from the feed, horses began running in circles, and wild deer ran from the woods as fast as they could. As I puzzled on it, the ground rolled under me. It reminded me of the way the waves had felt at the beach. People all around started shouting to each other, "Do you feel that?" There was more quivering of the formerly solid earth. Someone shouted that there must have been an earthquake nearby.

Thanks to the speed of the telegraph, the news arrived the next morning; a massive earthquake had shaken Charleston, South Carolina. At first, it was conflicting and uncertain, but it was clearly big. Eventually, the facts sorted themselves out and became the only talk for days. Customers milled around, describing the destroyed buildings and the mounting death toll (sixty in all were eventually counted). Crews talked and gossiped about it as well. The New York papers filled their pages with stories and graphic drawings. Only small ripples had made it through the ground to New York, but the impact was enormous.

More than one person said things like, "God finally punished them for starting the War," a puzzling idea for me. I thought losing the war might have been punishment enough. I had to wonder what kind of god would send an earthquake twenty-five years later to punish anyone.

I brought it up one evening as most of us sat in the car. Sam must have been broke, because he was there too. None of them thought the idea was strange. Even James from Texas said, "Why not? He's God."

I put the question aside until I had a chance to talk with Annie and Frank. In the middle of September, the occasion arose. By then, I knew them well enough to ask a direct question: "Do you think God punished Charleston with the earthquake?"

Frank was quick to say, "I've heard people say things like that, and I think it's nonsense. God does not destroy a city for the sins of a few, and certainly not two decades later."

"So, why do people say things like that?"

Annie said, "Mostly, they are people who rarely think about God until something happens they can't explain. Then, to make themselves feel better, they try to turn God into a small and petty dictator. It makes them feel they have control."

Frank gave his wife a questioning look. "Small and petty?"

"I've had some experience with such people." Frank smiled. Going on, Annie said, "Remmy, many people believe God punishes sin by sending plagues, floods, drought, and even earthquakes. Some even believe God will cause a particular person to fall and break an arm because of a specific sin he committed. But, there is nothing in the Bible saying anything of the sort."

That led the Butlers to invite me to spend a day listening to Dwight L. Moody. I had never heard of him and had no idea what I was going to experience, but I was happy to spend the time with the Butlers.

Annie explained, "He's the most famous preacher in America. He started a school in Chicago years ago and has helped start others since then. He has preached all over the country and in England. He is doing a campaign in New York, and we have arranged for the three of us to hear him. We asked George to trade work Sunday with you. It's all arranged."

I found myself sitting in a chair in a hall the size of the show arena, listening to a solid-looking, middle-aged man with a commanding presence. Many of the words were peculiar to me, and I was lost more than once. Yet, I could not turn away. Moody pulled me in and gave me comfort, even as I failed to understand the words.

Moody spoke with reverence of the forgiveness of God. He said no human could ever commit any sin God would not forgive. He spoke often of Christ, and I eventually understood Christ must be the same as either God or Jesus. Somehow, through this Christ, all the forgiveness occurred. My family never attended church, and I knew almost nothing about Christianity, so his statements were mostly baffling for me.

Several hours later, as we made our way from the hall, I was exhausted from the effort of trying to understand every word Moody spoke; he was that dynamic. I was thankful the Butlers were willing to take the trolley back to the ferry pier, for I was not sure I could have walked two blocks.

Once we settled in the trolley, Annie asked, "So, Remmy, do you have any questions?"

My head was spinning with thoughts and ideas, but I could not think of one question to ask. I mumbled, "Not now, I guess."

Later, as we waited for the ferry to arrive, I asked hesitantly, "Would God forgive Red Beard?"

Frank shifted in his seat but did not say anything. After a long silence, Annie quietly said, "I have often wondered the same thing about the Wolves. I can't imagine having to live with them for eternity."

After another long silence, Frank said, "Maybe in heaven you will not know who they are and you will not even remember the sins they did."

Annie quickly said, "I hope so. I really don't want to remember."

I had much thinking to do.

As summer gave way to fall, I dug deeper into my clothes drawer, until the morning came when I needed my winter coat. I pulled it out, along with my other winter gear. I almost automatically felt the hidden pocket in the coat where I kept the dimes and nickels from Shultz and the gold piece from Brit, my link to the past.

At first, I assumed I had touched the wrong spot, and then I thought they had fallen out, but after a search left all my clothes on the floor and my heart racing, I knew. The last link to my parents was gone.

By then, I was alone in the car, the others having gone to the dining tent. I sat amid my clothes and tried to think of what might have happened. Had I moved them? No. Had I finally taken them to the bank to put them in my savings account? Never.

The unmistakable came in a flash. Only one other person knew about the coins. I wanted to jump up and run into the dining tent and grab Sam by the throat, but I did not move.

Sam. My friend.

I began to drop my clothes back into the drawer. I pulled the coat on and carefully made my way to the tent. I saw my friends eating together. They were mostly finished and ready to leave. I squeezed myself in between Charlie and Sam. Sam glanced my way, then kept his eyes fixed on his plate. Charlie said, "Hey, sorry I'm in the way!"

I ignored him and everyone else. They all went silent. Sam started to stand, but I grabbed his arm and held him down, then said, "Why don't the rest of you get to work? I have a question for Sam."

They all looked at each other, at Sam, at me, but left without a word. Sam did not look at me, nor had I looked at him. All I said was, "Why?"

To Sam's credit, he was enough of a friend not to lie. "I was sure I could win it all back."

I continued to look at the table. I wanted to punch my friend in the face. I wanted to poke a fork in his hand. I wanted to hurt Sam as much as Sam had hurt me. Maybe more.

Instead, I stood and left the tent. JR told me later that I walked right by all the guys at the tent opening, but I never saw them. He told me that half the tent had gone silent, watching my every move, but I did not notice. Ruth said she nearly came to stop me from hitting Sam because that was the look on my face; I did remember that feeling.

I went to the stock and began the familiar chores. I found excuses to throw things and bang buckets. The others gave me a wide path. Sam found work out of my sight.

By lunchtime, I'd talked myself into accepting the loss; they were just coins. Nonetheless, I waited for Sam to enter the dining tent first and chose a seat well away from him. JR joined me with, "When are you two going to shoot it out like Cody and Yellow Hand in the show?"

I could not smile, even though I saw the humor. "I'm not going to shoot Sam. Cody would charge me for the bullet."

JR didn't push. We ate for a bit in silence before he said, "Sam told us what he did. It was a low thing to do, especially to a friend. But, I think there is more to it than just stealing your money."

I had to think for a bit before realizing Sam had at least kept the secret. He may have been weak enough to steal, but he'd kept his promise.

I had not eaten breakfast, and I was only halfway through lunch, but I pushed my plate away. "I don't know, JR. I think if anyone else had taken the money, I wouldn't be so upset. But Sam knew. Why did it have to be him?"

JR shrugged and said, "Bullshit stinks."

It was weeks before I spoke to Sam again.

58 Geronimo

In the second week of September, when the earthquake news finally died down, I read an article describing the capture of Geronimo. He and his band of Apaches were the last major group of Indians still avoiding capture. According to the report, Lieutenant Gatewood of the 4th Cavalry out of Fort Huachuca was the man who actually tracked down the famous war leader and medicine man. He and his small band had been run to ground in Mexico and were too exhausted to go any farther.

I immediately began to wonder if Cody would try to get him for the show. It seemed natural. Geronimo would be an even greater attraction than Sitting Bull had been the year before.

On the other hand, he was an Apache. Few other tribes could get along with the scourge of the Southwest. He would require additional guards, and finding a translator might be a problem. The more I thought, the less likely it seemed.

I decided to seek out Chief American Horse and see what he thought of the Apache. I found the Sioux chief easy to approach, especially since he spoke English so well.

I located him alone near the stock pens, staring at the horses in the pasture. As was the plains custom, I stood at the same fence, a respectful distance away, and watched the horses. Soon, American Horse spoke; "Young Angel, are you well this night?"

"Thank you, honored Chief, I am well. It's a good night for such fine animals."

"Yes, they almost seem free."

I was not sure how to respond, so I continued to look at the horses. At length, American Horse said, "When I see them like this, I see myself riding my old pony through the tall grass of my homeland. But now, my pony is gone, and I am as caged as these fine horses." He waited only a few beats before adding with a sigh, "At least this cage is better than the one at Pine Ridge."

I saw my chance and said, "I have just read of another great leader who has been captured by the army. Geronimo was taken prisoner by General Miles."

American Horse turned toward me and asked directly for details before saying, "It is a sad day." He turned back to the horses.

I waited for what was a respectful time before asking, "What do you think of him and his Apaches?"

"My people know of the Apaches, but we never faced them in battle. We would have defeated them, but not without a great fight. Geronimo is a great warrior. He fought long and well. He should be respected."

I quickly added, "As you are respected. Do you think Cody will try to get him for the show?"

"I fear so, and then he would be put in this cage with the buffalo and other lost things, like me." I wanted to put my hand on the hand of the great man and tell him it was not so, but I knew it would be a lie.

I thought again of Big Jim and what a good man he was. Since he came from a small tribe that caused no trouble, the government left him alone to live his life in relative freedom. The Sioux and others were prisoners. Even American Horse, who had never fought against the US, could be in the show only because Cody promised to return him in the fall. Being an Indian in the US was problematic.

Months later, Cody told me he had made inquiries about the most famous Apache and learned his guard was extensive at Fort Pickens in Pensacola, Florida, and the Army would not release him for a million dollars.

That summer, I learned a great deal about American Horse and came to respect him as much as I did Big Jim, though the two Indians were very different in their personalities. American Horse told everyone behind the scenes to call him Horse. He also gave us permission, by his actions, to laugh at him and with him. He had a great sense of humor and delighted in playing jokes on the cast and crew.

On one memorable occasion, he managed to get hold of one of Cody's Stetsons and his buckskin coat. He walked around barking directions to the crew in a voice very much like Cody's. He was a terrific mimic. He sat in the dining tent with crewmembers and cast, telling and listening to stories, sometimes well into the night. I especially liked the one about scouting for a war party.

"We were as promising a party of young warriors as our tribe ever sent against any of its ancestral enemies. It was midsummer, and after going two days' journey from home, we began to send two scouts ahead daily while the main body kept a half-day behind. The scouts set out every evening and traveled all night. One night, the great war pipe was held out to me and to Young-Man-Afraid-of-His-Horses. At daybreak, having met no one, we hid our horses and climbed to the top of the nearest butte to take an observation. It was a very hot day. We lay flat on our blankets, facing the west, where the cliff fell off in a sheer descent, and with our backs toward the more gradual slope dotted with scrub pines and cedars. We stuck some tall grass on our heads and proceeded to study the landscape spread before us for any sign of man.

"The sweeping valleys were dotted with herds, both large and small, of buffalo and elk, and now and then we caught a glimpse of a coyote slinking into the gulches, returning from night hunting to sleep. While intently watching some moving bodies at a distance, we could not yet tell whether of men or animals, I heard a faint noise behind me and slowly turned my head. Behold! A grizzly bear sneaking up on all fours and almost ready to spring!

"'Run!' I yelled into the ear of my companion, and we both leaped to our feet in a second. 'Separate! Separate!' he shouted, and as we did so, the bear chose me for his meat. I ran downhill as fast as I could, but he was gaining. 'Dodge around a tree!' screamed Young-Man-Afraid. I took a deep breath and made a last spurt, desperately circling the first tree I came to. As the ground was steep just there, I turned a somersault one way and the bear the other. I picked myself up in time to climb the tree, and was fairly out of reach when he gathered himself together and came at me more furiously than ever, holding in one paw the shreds of my breechcloth, for in the fall he had just scratched my back and cut my belt in two, and carried off my only garment for a trophy!

"My friend was well up another tree and laughing heartily at my predicament, and when the bear saw that he could not get either of us he reluctantly departed, after I had politely addressed him and promised to make an offering to his spirit on my safe return. I don't think I ever had a narrower escape," he concluded.

From all I heard, mostly from Cody, it was clear Horse was neither a fool nor a coward. He'd almost single-handedly kept his band of people out of war and out of harm through most of the Indian Wars. He'd even kept them from joining Sitting Bull in 1876, thus sparing them the retaliation for Custer's loses at the Greasy Grass.

Horse was seldom bitter and never cruel, but I did hear him say once in a solemn voice, "If we can only get to your heaven by wearing golden moccasins, no Indian will make it, because you whites have the Black Hills and all its gold."

I considered American Horse to be the most honorable man in the whole show, right up there with Annie.

59 Coppers

The cowboys in the show were considered actors, even though most of them did little besides ride around the arena and shoot blanks. In spite of the exalted title, most of them thought of themselves as workingmen, so they tended to spend their time with the roustabouts and other crewmembers, especially when it involved drinking.

The exceptions among the cowboys were Segebart and Pivonka. At St. Louis, the two took their fighting ways into town. The first time they got into a bar fight, they came back too stove up to work the next day. They had their pay docked for that. Other times, when they came back beaten from head to toe, they still managed to ride. That went on all summer, but at least they didn't fight anyone on the show, except for me, and that was hardly a fight.

On Wednesday, September 22, as everyone was getting ready for the afternoon show, the end finally arrived for the would-be fighters. Saddling their horses, they noticed six blue-suited coppers coming toward them. They jumped on their horses and rode straight ahead, into the arena, where the band was already playing the pre-show concert and customers were looking for seats. It was still fifteen minutes before show time.

Since the arena was totally enclosed, they could only thunder around it full tilt. Bill Sweeney looked over his shoulder as he heard the horses fly by and stopped directing. The band played on while Sweeney tried to figure out what was happening.

Just then, the blue coats ran into the arena, waving their nightsticks. Two of them stood guard at the entrance, and the others gave chase. Sweeney quickly told the band to switch to chase music. The crowd thought it was part of the show and began to cheer loudly.

As the two riders rounded the arena a second time, they took aim for the entrance where the two coppers were standing. One of them, knowing a bit about horses, jumped and waved as the horses closed in. That caused the first horse to stop sharply, nearly throwing Segebart over its head. Pivonka steered his horse back into the arena.

The second copper stepped up to Segebart's horse and hit the horse in the rump with his stick, whereupon the horse kicked the copper ten feet into the arena. That brought a tremendous cheer from the crowd. Segebart's horse started bucking and kicking as the first copper ran to his fallen partner.

Pivonka came by at a hard gallop, and Segebart finally got his horse under control and trailed after. Once they were out of the arena, they headed for the main entrance, forgetting it had stout, narrow turnstiles.

Pivonka turned his horse and headed for the pens with Segebart close behind. By now, most everyone in the show knew the boys were wanted for some crime or other and were glad to help the men in blue. We threw things at the riders and did our best to scare the horses. The two tried to get out near the pens, but there was too much fencing.

The chase ended when Vicente Oropeza lassoed Pivonka, jerking him off his horse, and Joe Esquivel gave Segebart the same treatment. By the time the blue coats caught up, the thugs were hogtied, and the Wild West crew was cheering almost as loudly as the crowd had.

Before the Grand Parade, Cody led the entire group—police (except the one Doc was treating), Mexicans, and the two trussed-up cowboys—in front of the crowd. He explained that the police had just arrested the two for robbery in St. George and New York. He praised the police and especially his two cowboy bosses.

I learned more the next day when Tom Gibson pulled me aside. "I want to thank you in person for helping us catch those two meatheads yesterday."

"Me? I didn't have anything to do with it. I just watched."

"Oh, you watched all right. You watched those two hiding their stolen goods in a secret compartment under the donniker, the last place I would have looked."

“So, that’s what they were up to. I couldn’t figure it out.”

“I crawled under there after you told me about seeing them. Once I realized what they were doing, I kept a watch on them and the donniker and we caught them red-handed. I let the police know what we had, and they came right out. Didn’t figure on so much excitement, though. Tell you what, if you ever have need of information or maybe even a job, here are the names of a few Pinkerton men I know. Show them this note, and they’ll take good care of you. You’re good at observing what’s going on around you. That can take you a long way.”

60 Garden

Cody called a general meeting for everyone in the show. Shortly after breakfast, everyone took seats in the red section of the arena with Cody standing before us all, his show voice booming with pleasure.

"I have some big news that'll affect all of you. I think most of you will like it. For some time, we've been negotiating with The Garden near Madison Square in New York for the chance to use it for winter shows. Yesterday, we signed the agreement papers." There was some cheering, but most of us were not sure what it meant for us.

"For those of you who don't know about The Garden, it's a huge building taking a whole city block, and it's available for shows like ours. You may know that P. T. Barnum and Adam Foropaugh combined their circus shows and played The Garden all summer. I was afraid it might hurt our business, but, of course, how could it?" That brought cheers and laughter.

"Anyway, you all have some decisions to make. If you're looking for winter work, this is it. If you have to leave, just let us know. Our plan is to be in The Garden until spring, when we start getting ready for the next season on the road.

"Just to let you know, we'll do our last show here September 30. We'll stay here for some days after that, until the folks at The Garden are ready for us to start moving in. There'll be plenty of work for most of you as we build sets and generally put together an indoor show. We've never done this before, so it will be a challenge. We expect to open before Thanksgiving. You'll be given more details later."

The talk was raucous as we headed back to work. I listened as Sam and James talked excitedly about working in the city. I had enjoyed the relative quiet of Staten Island and would miss the long hikes in the woods and along the shoreline. However, I had to agree, it would be exciting in the city and a pleasant change. I had enjoyed my two trips there.

Finishing my morning chores, I went off by myself for some private thinking. The walk was over a rough trail that forced my mind to split attention between where I was stepping, and the competing notions of whether or not to go to The Garden. I still liked working for the show and I liked the people. On the other hand, home. The nightmares still came at times. My family was still dead. Red Beard was still out there. Maybe this was the time to start the search.

I spent a good hour trying to struggle through the decision before finally giving up. I stood throwing rocks into a stream, trying to let my mind relax. By the time I had to start back, I was more undecided than when I'd set out.

I hoped working the stock for the afternoon performance would take my mind off the debate, but it did not. Halfway through the show, I opened the gate for the cattle to leave the pen and amble into the arena. I was giving The Garden move too much attention instead of watching the stock. The lead steer suddenly rammed the gate on his way out, knocking me backward until I hit the fence and dropped to the ground, gasping for breath.

JR was right there and kept the gate from hitting me again while I was down. The others took care of the show while JR helped me until I could breathe again. He then helped me get back on my feet and slowly creep out of the pens.

Someone called Doc, who came running. "Where're you hurt?"

"It hurts ... to breathe."

Doc poked along my back and ribs, finding several spots that made me cry. As he poked, he asked, "How'd this happen?" JR gave the account, and I added I hadn't been watching. "I think you're lucky. I don't feel any broken bones, though there might be a small crack or two. You'll be stiff and sore for a few days. You'd better go rest and skip tonight's show. Come see me in the morning. Did you hurt the steer?"

I tried to smile. Doc was always a vet.

JR helped me struggle back to the car to lie down. Ruth came running as we started to climb the steps. "I just heard. Are you all right?"

I grunted, "Yes, just careless."

"You're sure no bones are broken?"

JR took over for me. "Doc says he's fine. He needs some sleep and a couple of days' rest. I'll drag him to dinner. You can see him then."

A few hours later, JR woke me and helped me to the dining tent. The effort of eating was painful. Ruth came out for a few minutes to fuss over me. I stopped at half a plate and waited for JR to help me back to bed.

I was once again on the cot. I slept so soundly my bunkmates did not wake me when they came to bed. The cot had been occupied much of the summer, so we had learned to be quiet when entering.

In the morning, I was able to pull myself up and take steps on my own, but not pain-free. I made my way to Doc's tent, only to find he was in the pens treating a horse with an injured hoof. Since going to the tent loosened me up, I walked to the pens and watched Doc work.

Finished with the horse, Doc said, "Next," and waved me over. That proved I could actually laugh without too much pain.

He poked around again. "How do you feel?"

"I felt better before you started poking me."

With a big smile he said, "You're okay. You should be able to do some of the lighter work today. If it gets to botherin' you too much, sit a spell. Seriously, stay away from the stock for a couple of days, because you won't be able to make quick moves."

Though still tender, I felt fine two days later. Having Ruth visit with ice cream and other treats helped. One sore spot held out for weeks.

Sometime in those pain-filled days, with no conscious effort, I knew I should stay through the winter. Supporting the decision with a list of facts would have been difficult, but I suspect I realized I was not ready. Plus, living with friends was reason enough to stay.

61 Celebration

There was a celebration in the dining tent after the last customer left the last show on Staten Island. As parties go, it was short and reasonably quiet. Some people said their goodbyes. Cody made what was for him a short speech thanking everyone. The summer season ended.

Later, I met Ruth to say goodbye. She found a job in Brooklyn. I think we were both ready for a break from each other; at least, I hoped she was. Since my blundering at the beach outing, Ruth had been increasingly distant with me. I knew I had blown it, but I didn't question how. I was willing to allow whatever it was to come between us, and she seemed resigned to it as well.

Over the next two months, I alternated between being overworked and having absolutely nothing to do. The first week of October was idyllic, my only duties being the care and feeding of the animals every third day.

With so much time, I chose to take long hikes around the island. On Monday, I joined some twenty cowboys and crew for the ferryboat to New York. Arriving in the city, we broke into smaller groups and tried to entertain ourselves on a cold and windy October day. We ended up spending most of our time and money in eating houses and saloons. By the time we regrouped for the ride back to the island, several of us needed help standing, having done a great disservice to our coordination by our choice of liquids.

I had indulged in at least one beer too many, but even so I was doing the supporting. The next morning, I skipped breakfast and went right to work. The exercise relieved my headache. When not working, I read a couple of new books purchased on the nearly wasted trip to the city.

The problem for everyone the first week was a lack of anything meaningful, besides taking care of the animals. After four months of the routine of the show, it had just stopped. Some had gone to jobs in the city and others to visit long-lost relatives in the area. Frank and Annie had a full schedule of shooting contests and exhibitions. For those of us still in camp, it was like being stuck in a ghost town. At least those of us caring for the animals were getting full pay.

In the second week, in the absence of the big bosses, Zac and the others gave instructions on how to sort and pack the show. Much of what we had used in the summer would go into storage on the island, because the new show would have scenes entirely different from any done before.

With the items sorted, the bosses decided which wagons to take to the city and which to leave behind, loaded with unneeded incidentals. A great deal of measuring was required to figure out how to store the things in wagons not built for them.

Another difficult chore for Zac was deciding which animals to keep, which to sell, and which to leave over the winter. The few cowboys left behind did help with the horses, and Zac made the decisions regarding the other animals. The baggage horses, most of the cattle, and some of the buffalo went to pasture for the winter. There was little room to display the menagerie, so Zac sold those animals, some for slaughter. Good riddance, razorbacks.

After that flurry of activity, we fed the livestock and waited.

On Monday, the eighteenth, I read about the beginning of the World Championship Series of baseball. It brought back memories of our own baseball wars. I also read that the Kansas City Cowboys, only winning thirty games, were folding. Only the Washington Nationals had a worse record.

The Chicago White Stockings won the National League title, and the American Association winner was the St. Louis Brown Stockings. They were set to play each other in the third World Championship. The National League had claimed they won the first two, so the beer and whiskey league had something to prove.

Chicago hosted the first three games, and the home team dominated game one by a score of 6-0. Game two went to St. Louis in a 12-0 romp, with Bob Caruthers pitching a one-hitter and Tip O'Neill becoming the first player to hit two home runs in a championship game. He also ended the series batting .400.

Wednesday, Chicago came back to win 11-4 when Caruthers, of the Browns, tried to pitch one more time in his hometown. The game ended in the eighth inning because of darkness.

Right after the game, both teams crawled aboard a train headed for St. Louis, where the Thursday game was a battle decided at sundown in the seventh inning, 8-5, St. Louis. In Friday's game, Chicago used their shortstop and right fielder as pitchers and still lost, 10-3.

The final game on Saturday began early to make sure they could get in all nine innings. Even then, it was close. Chicago kept St. Louis hitless for six innings and scoreless until the eighth, when they tied the game. In the tenth, Curt Welch was on third base when a wild pitch allowed him to slide in for the winning score. St. Louis became the World Champions and took the entire gate receipts of just under $14,000, meaning each of the twelve players received $580 extra for the season. Their first baseman, Charlie Comiskey, received more because he was also the manager.

We envisaged what it would be like to get so much money for a week's work. It was almost too much to imagine. I was feeling wealthy with almost $100 in my bank account. With another $580, I could buy a small farm.

The following week, those of us still on Staten Island received a day of once-in-a-lifetime excitement. On Thursday, October 28, the French government officially presented the Statue of Liberty to the United States, and President Grover Cleveland accepted the gift.

The events began with a long parade in the morning, starting at Madison Square Park, where the arm with the torch had stood for six years before workers had reattached it to the statue just months before. The parade then went all the way to Battery Park, where ferryboats lined up waiting for the crowd. I only read about the parade the next day, including an unusual event as the parade made its way past the New York Stock Exchange, the traders threw the long streams of paper known as ticker tape out the windows.

Most of us waited for the afternoon when Cody rented the *Staten Island Ferryboat* for use by the Wild West crew. There were at least a thousand ships and boats in the harbor, all trying to get a good position for their passengers to view the proceedings; our captain was able to get a great spot for us. We could hear the band music if not the speeches, and we could see most of what was happening.

We had all seen stages of the work of assembling the statue through the summer, but none of us had been so close before. A large French flag covered the head, dropping at the proper moment to unveil the new work. The papers reported that every cannon in and around the harbor fired a salute to the *Colossus of Liberty.*

62 Indoor

We moved into The Garden the next week. I found it peculiar to be herding buffalo in the streets of New York, yet there we were, and there they were. I was happy not to have to deal with any other part of the show for a time. The transition to the city was difficult for me, even after all this time. I needed the calming effect of the animals.

That was not entirely effective. Getting the show animals into the building required our crew and others to set up temporary ramps and fencing to funnel them into the building and down to the basement, where they would live for the winter. It reminded me, and perhaps the animals, of the cave that was both my salvation and the source of many of my nightmares.

The next few days made up for the previous downtime. Except for Sundays, everyone worked at least sixteen hours a day. We were building a new show; one staged in a way never before attempted by anyone in the world. It included backdrops larger than buildings. It had a fake collapsible building fitted on rollers and pushed around a stage half a city block in size. Most items in the show needed reworking for indoors, and sadly, I had to do my share.

"Indoors" was not quite the right term. The Garden had no roof except for the narrow building lining the sidewalks all around the block. The rest was open space where the stage and seating were set up. To deal with the issue of no roof and some other staging problems, Cody and Nate contracted with the Forepaugh Circus to leave their tenting in place when they went to winter quarters. The open area had rain and snow protection, though no protection from extreme temperature changes.

The animals hated their new quarters more than I did, perhaps because I at least did get to sleep in a nearby apartment. After the carpenters built the ramps and pens, there was room for the animals, but just. Without pastures, our crew handled hay and grain the way I had at the stockyards. Water was a bigger problem. A full-grown buffalo or steer can suck up twenty gallons at a time and the tanks installed were not large enough, even though the circuses had used them for their animals. We simply had too many for the system. A dozen of us did nothing for the first several days but feed and water the stock.

By the middle of the second week, there were larger water tanks that extended to all the pens, as well as a mechanized feed delivery system. The animals were adjusting, though cantankerously. They protested loudly every time we herded them through the maze of aisles and ramps to go onto the stage and back, and I did not blame them.

Zac hired a new man, John Townsend from the city, to work on our crew, and divided the ten of us into two teams for the Sunday work.

It was cold on the second Sunday when JR and I stepped outside and headed for Madison Square, our first break in two weeks. I slipped on a patch of ice and had to grab JR's arm to stay upright. The sun was shining, there was no wind, and we were out of the stinking basement. One of Gibson's men trailed along. Tom again provided protection in the home of the Whyos.

Finding a bench facing the sun, we sat in silence for a long time. At length, I said, "I don't think I like this job anymore."

JR was quiet for a few beats before saying, "At least I'm home." He leaned forward and picked up a pebble from the path, throwing it toward the street before leaning back on the bench.

On break, we were in no hurry for anything, not even conversation. I let his words and actions sink in before saying, "I hadn't even thought of it. Is your home close?"

He took a deep breath. "We lived on 5th Street, near the East River. It's a good jaunt from here. I was never up in this area, but I know some of the gangs working these parts. At least, they used to."

"I've only heard of the Whyos."

"I guess you wouldn't know much about gangs. They are groups of men who use force to control a small area of the city. They threaten to beat up shop owners unless they pay money each week. Sometimes, they just grab a man and tell his family to pay them money for his release."

"Why don't the coppers arrest them?"

"Sometimes they do, but mostly they can't be caught. Many of the coppers are former gang members, or the gangs pay them to look the other way. A couple of the biggest gangs from the old days were the Irish group calling themselves the Dead Rabbits and the anti-Irish group known as the Bowery Boys."

"Why Dead Rabbits?"

"A dead rabbit is someone feared in the gang world, usually because he has killed a man. These days, the main gang is the Whyos, and they control most of the action in the city and lord it over the smaller gangs. They're kind of the Dead Rabbits of today. Mike McGiloin used to head the gang, but I heard they hanged him for murder a while back. I don't know who runs it now, but someone does. They were too big to just disappear."

"How do you know so much about gangs?"

JR paused and then said, "Let's walk some." He led me down to Broadway and then toward Union Square. As we jostled our way through the crowds, JR gave the short answer to the question. "If you live in the city, you have to learn about the gangs to survive. The more you know, the better chance you have of avoiding trouble with them. By the way, you don't want to go very far from The Garden without your guards. They'll spot you as a stranger at first glance, and you'll wake up with a knot on your head and light pockets, if you're lucky."

"Is it dangerous on this street?"

"Madison Square is one of the safe areas in the city. They leave the public parks alone during the day, but you don't want to go in them at night—though I think Madison Square would be safe. Now, when we have a show, there'll be at least a hundred coppers all over The Garden area to protect our customers. But, we won't have to worry either way, because we'll be in the basement with all those angry buffalo."

We arrived at Union Square and looked around before heading north on Fourth Avenue. As we walked, JR told me more of the city, but nothing of his own family.

I finally said, "Tell me some more about your family. If you want to, I mean."

JR said nothing until we were near a saloon. "Let's go in here for a beer and a bite."

We entered to the usual sights and smells, though this saloon was a little cleaner than most, and no one had passed out yet. I picked up a couple of hard-boiled eggs to go with my beer. JR took some sausage, and I bought a beer for my guard.

At the table, JR opened up. "My mother died of pneumonia, like so many others. The only good news, it was quick. She was doing laundry on Monday and was dead on Thursday. I was holding her hand when she squeaked out her last breaths. My older sister was married, and my older brother was on a ship, we think. Three other kids had already died, so I was the only one at home. My sister refused to take me in."

I had my eggs peeled, but I set them aside to wait for JR to continue. A tear ran down JR's cheek, and I realized he was not going to speak. I finally said, "I'm sorry."

After a few moments, JR nodded his head. He added, "My sister found a good life. I would've just messed it up." I had a feeling he was not so sure.

JR went on, "Anyway, I became an orphan, and you know about that. The old man is another story altogether. He died before my mother. He had a job at a saloon like this one. Well, not as nice. It always had at least one drunk on the floor.

"He cleaned the place, lugged the beer and liquor, kept the food table full, and swept out around four in the morning. I rarely saw him. I don't know when he slept. Anyway, one night the Whyos come to collect their cut, and for some reason the owner decided to give them less than expected. They argued for a time with the owner, who said business had been slow, which was a lie, and the Whyos knew it. So, they shot the owner and my dad and calmly picked up what they said they were owed."

I was dumbfounded. "Why'd they shoot your dad?"

"They shot the owner in the knee because they wanted him to keep the saloon open. I guess they wanted to show him what would happen the next time, so they shot the guy with the broom." By now, JR's voice had taken a hard edge and there were no more tears.

I had not yet taken a sip or a bite. I waited, not knowing how to react. JR deliberately lifted his own mug and chugged it down. He stared at the empty mug for a time. "I need to find out who did it."

Now I was on familiar ground. "I'll help you."

JR shook his head. "It's just for me. You have your own troubles. Besides, you don't know your way around the city." He went to the bar for another mug.

When he returned, I said, "If you need any help...."

JR took a long drink and started to eat the sausage.

63 Newspapers

The first performance in The Garden was Thanksgiving eve. It was a star-studded audience, many of whom were wearing formal evening clothes. The show had purchased blankets to rent, but they were on loan for the wealthy crowd; money brings privilege. Besides, they paid $12 a seat. Many people brought their own blankets, but once 10,000 people crowded in, the tented area warmed up reasonably well.

I had been able to watch most of the show in rehearsal, and it looked grand from my offstage view. With all the practice, very little went wrong. Steele Mackaye had written the play as a four-act drama, with the standard Wild West interlude entertainment of shooting and horseplay. In the first act on the first night, Jerry the Moose decided to go off script, wandering along the front row of the audience, begging for treats. When the act ended, several Indians went out to retrieve him, but not before he kicked one into the seats. As Cody said, most of the people thought it was part of the show.

Cody insisted on adding a fifth act to Mackaye's drama, Custer's Last Stand. It had been one of the most praised acts all summer, and Cody would not go on without it. Cody gave up the role of Custer to the handsome King of the Cowboys, Buck Taylor, while Cody played himself at the very end of the scene, after the battle was over. He appeared in a single spotlight, and above him were projected the words, *Too Late.* Of course, in life, Cody had been on stage in New York at the time.

Even though we had played two shows a day for three months on Staten Island, and more than a million people had made the trip to see us, the New York area seemed unable to get enough of the Wild West. We had full houses two shows a day up to the Christmas season before the crowds started to thin. Still, when we closed the show in February, another million customers had plunked down the price of admission.

The ten of us shared an apartment two blocks from The Garden, and we quickly worked out an arrangement meeting Zac's approval. Five of us would get up early and tend the animals, and the other five would stay late to take care of them. It took all ten of us to handle the chores during the shows. At first, we planned on switching morning and evening each week, but when the time came, no one wanted to change. I was on the morning shift all winter, and I preferred it.

Many of the cowboys, Indians, and Vaqueros come in early in the day to take their own horses out for a ride around the arena or the city streets, some of them every day. On occasion, someone would ask me, or one of the others, to ride his horse outside for a little sunshine, and that always put a smile in my day. Any break from the routine was welcome, especially one involving the outdoors, even if it was just city streets.

On the walk to work before the sun was up, I could always count on finding at least one newsboy selling the first editions, and I bought a paper two or three times a week. I generally bought different papers each time: the *Daily Express, The Freeman, The Herald, The NY Journal,* the *Evening Post, The Sun, The NY Times*, the *NY Tribune,* and *The World.* I even bought the *Police Gazette* sometimes.

JR told me I had only touched the surface of what was available; there were daily papers in almost every language of the world. The more I read, the more I wanted to read. The news kept me in touch with the outside world. If it were not for the animals and the papers, working in that basement would have put me in the bin, and it very nearly did.

The second Sunday in December, JR and I, with my two guards, took a horse-drawn trolley up to Central Park and walked around the pond and the area along the southern edge of the park. There was just a little snow in shady areas, and the sun was out. It was a beautiful day. I would have been happy camping there for a few weeks, but even a couple of hours in the open was refreshing.

We wanted to tour the entire park, but the map at the entrance quashed that plan; we would need days to walk it all. After taking in a small portion, we made our way down Fifth Avenue the mile and a half to 42nd street, where the second Croton Aqueduct was located. Climbing the steps to the top of the concrete and stone retaining wall, we marveled at the two-city-block, man-made lake that provided our drinking water. The Croton House served an excellent meal before we crossed the street to Bryant Park. From there, it was straight down Fifth Avenue to Grand Central Depot.

We wandered around the rail depot for a time, until JR suddenly shouted, "Sid, Sid, over here," and waved to a boy our age. They backslapped and grinned their way through hello's and how are you's; I was introduced and quickly forgotten. Finally, I said, "I'll meet you back at the apartment," and left.

My escorts and I followed Fifth Avenue to The Garden and from there to the apartment. When JR came in late, he was not talkative. I tried to get him to tell me about Sid, but he brushed me off.

He did tell me on Monday that Sid was an old friend, but not much else. He seemed okay the rest of the week, and we worked the following Sunday morning. At lunchtime, I could not find him, so I went to eat with Will and James. On the street, I saw JR talking earnestly with Sid. I started to shout at him to join us, but the way they were talking stopped me.

I never saw JR again.

By chance, I noticed a small item on page fifteen of the *Daily Express* describing the murder of one John Robert Grice, the apparent victim of the Whyos. Through my tears, I wondered if JR had succeeded in avenging his father's murder first.

64 Sick

Zac hired another man to replace JR, and I hated him. Of course, I knew why. He was a good worker, so I tried hard not to be too gruff with him. In fact, I had to work at not biting off heads all day, every day. We did two shows on Christmas day, a Saturday. It kept me busy but did nothing for my funk.

On Sunday, the Butlers invited me to their hotel for a late Christmas feast, but I mumbled excuses. I spent the day tramping the city, head down, hands jammed in my coat pockets. I did not inform my minders. By that point, being mugged, beaten, and left for dead would have probably made me happy.

I walked through the gentle snow north on Fifth Avenue to Grand Central Depot. I sat inside for a time, remembering the last visit with JR. I began to wish I had not come, though it was in a way the last touch of my friend. I left the overcrowded depot and walked south on Park Avenue, thinking I might go to Union Square, but instead I stopped at a café to warm up and eat a bite.

I had no idea how to deal with what I was feeling. I missed JR. I even missed Sam, though I was still mad at him. I knew I was short-tempered with everyone, but I couldn't think of what to do about it.

I ordered a bowl of chicken soup, more to warm me than to satisfy my dwindling hunger. It may have been good, but I hardly tasted it. The café was not busy, so I sat at the table and continued to consider what I was now calling *my problem.*

Up to a few weeks earlier, I'd felt normal. The dreams of my family and Red Beard were just background noise. Most of my thinking centered on my work and friends with the show. Life seemed worth living. Now, deep into December with Christmas gone, the dreams became darker, and the sense of dread crept like a phantom into my conscious.

Sitting with the half-empty soup bowl, stumbling through a maze of memories, ideas, questions, and fears, it dawned on me that walking here through the snow had been unpleasant. Remmy, the snow king, lover of snow. What was so different now? It came to me like a slap in the face.

January 6.

Tears dropped unnoticed by me, but the waiter stopped short and backed away. The café disappeared. I saw only the flashes of light in the cabin window; I heard the six explosions; I felt the terror. The moonlight returned, and with it the snarl of the animal at the cave entrance and the smell of my own fear as I trembled in the frozen cave.

January 6. I told myself, *It's an illusion.*

I gradually returned to the warmth of the café, cleaned my face, paid my bill, and left a four-bit tip.

I went straight back to The Garden and meandered among the pens, soaking up the familiar smells and sounds. With that placation, I decided to stay the night. I told the guys I would not be back at the apartment.

Sometime in the night, I woke, unsettled, looking around the dimly lit basement, sniffing the familiar reek, trying to discern the problem. Detecting nothing, I lay back, but before sleep took me, a soft but unusual sound became an alarm bell in my mind. It took time to locate the source. The biggest buffalo was breathing with difficulty. I got one of the kerosene lanterns for a better look.

I watched her for a short time before going to one of the night watchmen. "Go get Doc. One of the buffalo is in trouble." Returning, I watched for half an hour. I knew she would die. Doc arrived just minutes after the last breath; he could not have cured the pneumonia. The important thing was to stop it from spreading.

With the help of two watchmen, we moved the remaining buffalo to another pen. The two mules hitched to a pulling yoke brayed loudly at working such odd hours, but with a lot of persuasion, they were able to get the dead animal out of the pen and up to the street. By then, the first of the Monday workers were arriving; dawn was not far behind. Doc left to give the grim news to Nate and Cody while I stayed with the deceased.

By week's end, five more buffalo were dead, but the pneumonia did not spread to any other animals. I slept hardly at all through the week and did not leave the basement. The deaths were personal. My funk dropped below my personal basement.

By Saturday, everyone was staying well away from me, but I hardly noticed. It was New Year's Day, and both shows had full houses for a change. Between the shows, Frank Butler found me at the buffalo pen, staring at the remaining animals, as I had been doing most of the week.

"Remmy, how are you?" I shrugged. "Would you be interested in dining with Annie and me tomorrow?"

"No."

After a few moments, Frank asked, "Are any of the Buffalo sick?"

"No."

Again, after a wait: "Then why are you staring at them?" I shrugged again. Frank laid his hand gently on my shoulder and said, "I have a message for you from Annie." He waited for the words to sink in. "I cannot leave here until you agree to eat with us tomorrow."

I turned to look at Frank for the first time. Frank was putting on a great show of personal injury, and it was not wholly lost on me. For the first time in...too long, I thought about how someone else might be feeling.

With some effort, I asked, "What time?"

"Why don't you come around three, and we'll have some tea and biscuits, as the English say, and then we'll eat a good dinner in the hotel dining hall."

"I don't have any decent clothes for the dining hall."

"It's a hotel. Just wear your best clothes. Most of the diners are from the show, anyway. Do take a bath." He added that with smile.

I nodded my agreement. The bath comment sank in much later. Frank stood looking into my eyes. Like a glacier, something moved in my mind. I only vaguely sensed the change, but it was enough. Hesitantly, I asked, "Can I ask you some questions? I mean tomorrow. The two of you?"

"Of course. You know Annie and I think of you as a son. We would be honored to talk with you. If you want to come before three, that would be great. We have no other plans for the day."

I shook my head in agreement, acceptance, willingness. I smiled, but I don't think it reached my mouth.

65 Memories

I walked alone to the apartment that night after the show. It was cloudy, bitterly cold, and windy, not unlike my mood. But, I could sense a change coming. Through the night, I thought of Frank and Annie, how they had treated me in the past months, what all they had taught me. A vague memory returned of my rude refusal to eat with them the last time they'd asked, whenever that had been.

It was my Sunday to work, so I spent the morning tending the animals, then traded the rest of the day with Eddie, who was the only one I had not completely alienated.

A little before two, cleaned up, I tried to tack a smile in place as I knocked at the hotel door. A beaming Frank opened the door and pumped my hand.

"Great to see you. Annie, look who's here." She was only a few feet behind and could see very well.

"Remmy, thank you for coming. This will brighten up a cold day. Sit, and I'll make some hot tea. Or, would you rather have coffee?"

"Tea is fine."

Frank tried to make small talk while Annie made the tea and brought it with a plate of cookies. I took a cookie and actually noticed the taste. "These are good. Thank you."

Frank said, "There is a marvelous shop just down the street, and we treat ourselves on special occasions."

All settled, Annie took a sip of tea and asked, "So, when's your birthday?"

I had to think a moment and count the days. "I guess it's Thursday."

"You haven't been thinking about it?"

"No. Well, a little."

Annie went on. "What have you been thinking these last few days?"

"Buffalo."

Annie looked at me over her steaming cup. "Why buffalo?"

I shrugged and said, "They are dying."

Frank said, "We heard what happened to JR, and we want you to know we are sorry. It's not easy to lose a good friend." Frank gave me time to respond, but I was blank. Then Frank asked, "How do you feel about his death?"

The question hung in the air, stinging and prodding to get at me. JR dead. The buffalo dead. I don't know how long they waited for me to respond, but all I could say was, "He was murdered."

"Yes, we heard. Do you know anything more?"

I slowly shook my head. For a moment, I could not think of what I knew; then the logjam of my thoughts shook loose, and I was able to describe how JR's father died, the Whyos, Sid, and JR's attempt to find the men who killed his father.

After a long pause, Annie asked, "Why do you think it is so hard for you to tell someone else about all that?"

"I don't know."

Annie served us all fresh tea. I used the pause to consider JR's murder as if I had just heard of it. Yet, when Annie returned to her chair, I said, "My brother Lyle would be thirteen this year."

Annie nodded and said, "What was Lyle like?"

"I thought of him before...well, before JR...." I let it lie and studied the floor. "Lyle was younger and always wanted to hang around, but I usually told him to go play with our sister or just ignored him. I remember how Lyle grabbed a pitchfork and tried to throw hay to the cattle the way Dad or I did. I remember when he tried to wear my hat, and it covered his eyes." I blinked away tears. "I miss him." My eyes were overflowing. "I try to see his face, and I can't quite see it. They're all fading away. I'm losing them."

Annie stood and hugged me. When my tears subsided, Annie scooted her chair up to face me, still close. Frank moved closer also.

"Remmy, think about this: JR is murdered, six buffalo die, one year ago this coming Thursday—your birthday—you witnessed someone murder your family, and you barely escaped. All of this dumped on you at Christmas time. Somehow, you have to deal with it. We want to help. Do you want us to help?"

I looked closely at each of them. "Yes, I do," I said with conviction.

"Then start by telling us all the good memories you have of Christmas. What is the first thing you remember, say, when you were three or four?"

I thought for a moment and then smiled. "I must've been six, because Wilber was a baby. We'd eaten dinner. The house was all warm with the fire going, and Mother had made an apple pie for Christmas with the last of the half-rotten apples. I sat in my chair with my pie, and Mother had Wilber over her shoulder. She stood up and turned just as Wilber threw up. He covered me and my pie. I screamed louder than Wilber did."

Frank and Annie smiled with me at the image. Frank asked the most important question: "Did you get another piece of pie?"

I laughed for the first time in weeks. I continued with some other Christmas memories, each one bringing my family into sharper focus. Wilber, excited to get a book. Doris, happy to get a piece of hard candy. Lyle, his first pair of overalls looking like Father's; what a smile it brought him. What a smile it gave me to remember it.

I become serious. "I miss them. I really miss them."

Annie said, "Of course, but you have just visited with them again, haven't you?"

I had to agree.

"Don't be afraid to remember them, even the bad times. No one can take them away from you. It'll be hard sometimes to keep the good memories, especially at this time of year. Nevertheless, it will get easier. Someday you'll be sitting in your rocking chair, too old to get down the steps, but your family will be forever young inside you."

We went to the dining room and continued to talk through dinner. I actually ate most of my meal. We talked of the show, of the coming year, and what I intended to do next.

"I think I need to head back to Kansas. I'll look for some way to work my way there. I'll have to find out what's happening before I ride up to the front door, but I think I'm ready to get started."

Frank said, "Good. We have a couple of ideas of how you might get there slowly. I still think it's best for you to wait another year. I know you've grown up more than a year's worth, but another year will have you ready."

Annie added, "Besides, you still need to work out what you're feeling." While she was talking, I saw Frank wave his hand to the waiter. "Frank and I have been talking and we think you need to have your birthday on a day other than January 6. How about today?"

I saw the waiter bringing a cake to our table. Several of the show people were at other tables and started applauding. Soon, the whole dining room was celebrating my new birthday.

66 Beecher

Changing my birthday was not that easy, of course. The next few days were ragged for me, but Annie and Frank made sure to talk with me every day. “Remmy, it’s a beautiful day today, isn’t it?”

“Remmy, what new memories have you had about your brothers?”

“Tell me again how good your mother’s chicken pies are.”

It was hard not to feel happy when I was around Annie.

Frank was a help in other ways. On Monday morning, the third, he gave me lessons in how to shoot glass balls thrown in the air. I was surprised it was easier than I imagined. Of course, I missed half of them. Tuesday, the two of us went for a long ride on two of the Butlers’ horses. Each day they made sure that I had something to do; they even brought me a newspaper every day. I hadn’t realized I had stopped buying them.

I began to talk with friends again, though not mentioning my troubles. I was uncomfortable at first, but once I stopped growling at them, they accepted me so readily that I soon relaxed. I even talked with Sam, though he remained more like a stranger.

The sixth was an rotten day. I took on extra chores to stay busy, talked and joked with friends, but nothing kept me from drifting to home and the murders. I wanted to get away from everyone, their jokes and smiling faces. Except for the promise to Annie, I would have spent the day watching the buffalo.

The night was worse, filled with dreams, all the old ones and some new ones as well. The one that left me immersed in sweat was being in the cave, this time with the opening sealed shut. Panic overtook me as I tried to claw my way out gasping for air. The panic remained well after I woke.

I worked in a sleepy stupor on Friday and made so many mistakes the others told me to take a nap. An hour on a stack of hay helped, and I was able to finish the day without killing myself or anyone else. That night, I fell asleep while reading in a chair, fully dressed, and woke near 3 a.m. By morning, in spite of several vivid dreams, I felt much better.

On Sunday, I was closer to whatever normal was for me those days. I had to work the afternoon because of the switch the week before, but in the morning, I bought three papers. My interest in reading was returning.

I became engrossed in a story from the fabled Sandwich Islands, now named Hawaii. It seemed King Kalakaua was spending too much money and refused to allow the US Navy to build a naval base at a place called Pearl Harbor. A group of mostly American businessmen and missionaries staged a quiet revolution and forced the king to accept a new constitution, taking away most of his powers. I was disgusted when I read how the missionaries set up businesses and forced the natives to work for them for little money.

The group taking over the government also changed the voting laws to exclude all Asian residents. Henry Ward Beecher, the famous preacher in Brooklyn, said it was another attempt to segregate people based on race only. "All people are children of God and should be treated equally." Beecher had opposed slavery before the war as well as the more recent Chinese Exclusion Act, both for the same reasons.

In the afternoon, Annie and Frank came into the pen area and asked me to help hitch Jerry to a sleigh, the same Jerry that had delighted the crowd on opening night. Annie drove down the snow-packed street with a sleigh full of show people, all laughing and having a great time.

The ride ended abruptly when Jerry turned a corner and spied an apple cart. The vendor was doing a brisk business until Jerry stopped to enjoy lunch. His lunch cost Annie $5.

Two days later, a big snowstorm closed the show. The weight of the wet snow caused considerable strain on the tent canvas, so most of the crew went to the roof of the building to drag snow off the canvas. The carpenters rigged up some long-handled pulls that worked fairly well. We spent most of the day dragging snow down the canvas and then shoveling it over the side of the building into waiting wagons.

It was such a change from the routine, it turned into playtime. There were several snowball fights and more than one fort constructed. By nightfall, everyone was ready for a hot meal and a good night's sleep.

The next day, the show remained closed. It snowed most of the night, and the tent ripped open in three places. The carpenters rigged some scaffolding, and the sailmaker was busy patching the holes while the crew cleared the roof and the mess inside.

I spent the day tending the stock, raking snow from the roof, and then clearing the sidewalks around The Garden. All of the snow was bringing sensations of that horrible night and the next day trying to avoid a killer, both man and storm. Still, it was a change, and I was glad for it.

January was a slow month for the show. I had heard during the summer it cost $7,000 a week to keep the show running. I doubted the show was bringing in anywhere near that much in the second week of January and not much more the other weeks.

Rumors of the show closing in a day or two floated around all month. Even the people who repeated them laughed when they said it. Even so, everyone was nervous. The other rumors had to do with plans for the next season. No one seemed to know what was going to happen. One day we were going back to Staten Island; the next we would open in New Orleans. So, the rumors flew.

If the show was planning a trip anywhere near Kansas City, I wanted to stay with it until then. At one point, I asked Zac, but his answer was, "I know Cody has the advance team out, but I don't know where they are or what they're working on."

67 Dawes

By the end of January, ten more buffalo had died. No one could explain why the disease affected only the buffalo. Cody shipped in more from his ranch, but I felt each death personally, as though I had caused it. I insisted on being the one to tie the ropes to pull the bodies away. It was my ritual, my way to deal with death. Annie told me later it was my way to bury my family.

Oddly, dealing with the dead buffalo seemed to help me recover, though I'm sure my conscious effort to force myself to talk with my friends helped. By the end of January, the whole staff was becoming giddy. Silly jokes brought peals of laughter. I was not immune, either, and laughed right along. We needed something to relieve the boredom of doing the show twice a day, six days a week, week after week while being stuck in a small box.

On February 8, the Dawes Act became law, and I read several news articles describing it. The more I read, the more upset I become. On first reading, the law looked innocuous enough. The Bureau of Indian Affairs of The Department of the Interior could divide the reservation land into plots, each owned by individual Indians.

As I read, I began to see some of the intent behind the law. First, the plots were small. Then, when the landowner died, the law required the land to be equally divided among the descendants, meaning as men died, many of the plots would become too small for farming. Within a few generations, the plots would not even be large enough for a house, and the descendants would be forced to sell.

To make it worse, after the initial distribution, most of the remaining millions of acres would be sold to the highest bidders, with the money going to the government. All of it land that had been granted to the Indians forever.

That section of the law made it clear to me that the law was a *legal* way for whites to take even more land from the Indians. I remembered Big Jim's emotions when he'd told me about his tribe's forced move away from the land in Kansas, land also given to them forever.

Congressman Dawes explained why he believed the law would be good for the Indians. "This Act will give the red men their freedom, freedom from the tribe, freedom from the reservation, freedom to become true Americans. This is the Magna Carta of the red men."

I threw the paper across the room with that comment. It was the next day before I could pick it up and continue. "I believe in the civilizing power of private property. Being civilized means wearing civilized clothes, cultivating the ground, living in houses, riding in Studebaker wagons, sending children to school, drinking whiskey, and owning property."

That was the last I could stand to read on the Dawes Act. I wished I could talk with Jim about the whole business, but at least I could talk to one of the Indians in the show, Jack Red Cloud. American Horse had had to return to the reservation in the fall and I'd made friends with his replacement.

I asked, "Have you heard of the Dawes Act?"

Jack always wore his feelings and emotions on his face. Generally, his face held a smile, but not in response to my question. "This is a dark day. I was in school at Fort Robinson when my people gave themselves up in '77, and I believed I would never see a worse day, but this may be it."

We discussed the details, and Jack added, "I can tell you for sure very few of my people want this to happen. Dawes can say it is what we want, and he can even believe it, but he is wrong."

"Do you think it's just another way to get more of your land?"

"That's only part of it. They also want to destroy our tribes. They don't want us to be Indians anymore."

"Why not?"

"Because we Indians are savages, little more than wolves. They think they can turn us into real people. Our tribe lived in large groups, everyone contributing to the good of the group. The men hunted game and protected the camp, and the women hunted fruits and vegetables and managed the camp. Everyone shared equally, even if it was in the suffering.

"Now, we are supposed to own property and not share any of it with our own people. In fact, they are no longer our people. With the land divided, we are to become American citizens. We are to give up being Sioux."

I only thought for a moment. "I think you will always be Sioux."

Jack smiled. "I'm educated in your schools. I'm a practicing Roman Catholic. I own property, I drink whiskey, I wear your clothes. I have even ridden in a Studebaker. But, I'm still Sioux."

68 Closed

Cody called the Wild West together between performances of the show January 31. “I have exciting news. The advance team has completed plans for the show to go to London to be a part of the American Exposition currently setting up there. This is a chance for me to pay you to go to Europe. But, I warn you, we might be gone two or three years.”

The news gave me a personal dilemma. I needed the show to go in the opposite direction. However, being paid to go to Europe was an opportunity I would not likely have again. I struggled for some time with what to do. I talked with Frank and Annie, who advised me stay with the show. Cody did as well, but in the end, I knew I had to go home and finish my business.

I had enough money saved to buy a ticket all the way to Mission and feed myself along the way, but that would leave me nearly broke. I needed someone to pay my way so I could spend time searching for Red Beard. I also needed to be mobile for the hunt.

I planned to begin my search in Kansas City, because I had seen him there and because he’d contacted people there in his pursuit of me. In all the months of anticipation, I had not developed my plan beyond that level. Now, with a definite date to leave, the whole scheme looked quixotic. How could I find one man in a city of fifty-five thousand?

Frank and Annie advised me to take my time, to be sure before I jumped into anything. Frank said, "We have until the end of March. We need you to help get the show loaded on the ship. Give us a little more time. We have contacted several people we know who travel the country and have need of help when they do. There's a good chance one of them will want you to work for them and will be able to drop you in Kansas City or somewhere close. Most of them, like us, are still making their plans."

One of the people they contacted was Dwight Moody, who responded just a week later, saying he would be happy to hire me. His preaching tour would stop in Kansas City, and he could arrange for someone to replace me there. I gratefully accepted, though the prospect of working for a preacher made me nervous. Annie assured me Moody was less dangerous than a buffalo.

Light attendance continued until the last show on Tuesday, February 22. Our celebration was a few smiles; we were all so worn out it no longer matter to us.

Everyone, except the animal crews, received two weeks off. We who stayed received a $10 bonus above our regular pay to care for the animals. The actors had a full month off. Cody went to Nebraska; Annie and Frank arranged shooting opportunities; and several others landed some work in the New York area. While most of the non-Indian actors planned to go to Europe, half the crew left the show for all kinds of reasons. As far as I know, I was the only one planning to search for a murderer.

Without a show, our work was part-time, so we were able to be out of the building much of the day. Mostly, we rode the show horses on the streets, or at least walked them around the block a few times.

A few crewmembers not working the animals stayed in their apartments at Cody's expense, resting or enjoying the offerings of the city. A few picked up odd jobs until March 7. On that day, we began the sorting and repacking, just as we had done to enter The Garden.

The show was returning to the summer program with changes, so most of The Garden sets and backdrops went into storage. Once all the wagons were in The Garden, it was a simple task to load them for the ship.

There was more time than work, so we had plenty of rest. I read newspapers every day, and the death of Henry Ward Beecher left me as shocked as if I had actually known him. *The Times* praised him as a forward-thinking man of compassion. He'd fought long and hard against slavery and the maltreatment of people as diverse as Indians and criminals. I had known nothing about him before the incident with Hawaii, so I was impressed to read of his contribution to the nation.

One article mentioned that Beecher was involved in sending rifles to the Kansas Territory during the fight over whether the territory would enter the Union as a free or slave state. When John Brown and other abolitionists ordered rifles, Reverend Beecher had the newest Sharps rifles shipped in boxes labeled, *Bibles.* As a result, the rifles carry the nickname, *Beecher Bibles.* I thought I should have learned that in school. Maybe I did and just forgot.

I asked Cody about it when he returned from Nebraska. "Oh, yes. He armed us abolitionists in the fight against the bushwhackers. Without him, Kansas might have been a slave state. I was in and out of the state by then, but I knew all about 'em. Even carried one for a while."

The last week of March gave us a busy few days. Our part in loading the ship was to get the wagons and stock to the pier, where we removed the wagon wheels and tongues and lashed them to the wagons. The stevedores took it from there, packing them tightly in the cargo holds. We stayed to watch, along with many New Yorkers, as the stevedores lifted the wagons one after another over the side of the ship and into the holds.

I helped drive the animals up a long ramp to the deck, then down other ramps where they were to spend the sea voyage crowded in small steel boxes. I felt sorry for them.

On April 1, the cast and crew loaded the last of their personal luggage in their berths. I helped as much as I could, and then I had the sad duty of saying goodbye. I may have slobbered on Annie as we hugged. I even hugged Sam. I was the last to leave the ship, appropriately named the *State of Nebraska.* I don't know how Cody arranged that.

I wanted to stay overnight and watch the ship steam away in the early morning, but it was not practical. I headed for my new temporary home, riding the trolley to the St. George ferry and on to an apartment in Mariners Harbor on Staten Island. Cody provided the apartment for me at his expense, "To a fellow Free Stater." I almost felt I was home.

I knew the generous gift was typical of Cody. He liked to please people and often gave money or other gifts to people in the show, friends, and sometimes, even strangers. Cody also gave me a set of signed photographs of all the stars of the show for the 1886 season. I knew I could sell them for enough to buy my train ticket home, but mere money could not replace them.

69 Wrestling

Saturday was lonely for me. I had spent just three weeks shy of a year with the circus. It had become my waking and my sleeping. The people had become my family. Tears crept unexpectedly into my eyes through the day. I wished I could have stayed to see the ship leave but was gratified I had not, or New Yorkers would have witnessed me blubbering on the pier. On that bittersweet day, the only thing that helped was a long hike along the shoreline.

It took time, but I settled into a routine of walking, reading, and eating in the few restaurants on the island. I grew accustomed to eating fresh fish, but never oysters.

I read the lengthy description of the arrival of the Wild West in London. Large crowds greeted the cast and crew as they disembarked and followed them through the day of offloading. Cody had the dining tent set up without the walls so the crowd could watch as they ate their evening meal. I could almost taste the food even as my tears returned.

I had purchased a Bible in the city after deciding to travel with Moody, just for research. I had never seen one before. For some reason, my parents had never spoken of religion. I knew most of the people in Neosho County attended church, and I had seen the outsides of several but never the insides.

I quickly gave up on the Old Testament and concentrated on the New Testament, finding Matthew an engaging read, though too often like reading a foreign language.

I had a great deal of time to think, too much really. My family and the shootings were familiar thoughts and dreams, but my new family began to take as much time. In my mind, JR became my older brother, and I mourned him as much as I mourned anyone— except Mother, and maybe Doris.

On May 9, the show opened in London. It was astounding to read a description of an event halfway around the world the next day, almost as it happened, thanks to the trans-Atlantic cable. It was delicious to read the glowing portrayals of my friends, even though I had read it all many times before in the past year. I could almost see myself peeking under the canvas to watch the show, as I had done many times in the summer.

Two days later, Moody arrived in New York and sent word to me to join them for packing supplies and other items for the trip. I was more relieved than I expected; having nothing to do was starting to wear on me.

It turned out not to be what I was used to calling work. I had no idea what to expect, but packing a handful of boxes was not it. I also had no idea what to expect from Moody, since I'd only sought the job as a way to travel home at someone else's expense.

We would be a group of five: Moody, John Redding (Moody's secretary), Ira Sankey (singer), and Molly Malone (Ira's accompanist). Moody was as full of life and energy as Cody, yet he was contained and non-demonstrative. He could be brusque, and he shunned the spotlight.

Redding was a young man, probably no more than three or four years older than I was. He was well educated and followed Moody like a puppy, apparently enthralled with the dynamo that was Dwight Lyman Moody.

There was no question that Sankey's voice was great. I'd heard him when the Butlers had taken me to Moody's appearance in New York. At first, the singer seemed cheerful and of a good heart, but he was susceptible to the bane of great musicians, believing he was of a higher station in life than most mortals were. I was not offended, since most everyone I knew was of a higher station than I was.

I liked Molly Malone at once. In spite of her name, she was hardly Irish. "A great-great-grandfather is from the island, but no one else we know. I'm a real American, being Irish, English, German, French, and Jewish." She had a truly wicked sense of humor she unleashed only out of earshot of both Moody and Sankey. She was also one of the most lamentable of women, being over thirty and unwed. She reminded me of Maude.

We spent two days running around the city, acquiring last-minute items and making the necessary travel arrangements. I also made my way to the Chatham National Bank to withdraw my savings of $191.32. Of that, $1.76 was interest, nearly two days' pay for doing nothing. I considered taking it in double eagles, but more than a half a pound of gold would have been difficult, so I accepted a $100 Gold Certificate (gold-back) with its portrait of Thomas H. Benton; a $50 gold-back with Silas Wright, whoever he was; two twenties; and some coins. The two big bills and a twenty I hid in my coat lining. Putting them there reminded me of Sam's betrayal. It also reminded me I'd never made up with him—except for the goodbye hug—and that gave me a twinge of guilt.

The first stop on the speaking tour was Philadelphia. Our entrance into town was very different from that of the Wild West. As Cody's train had pulled in the previous June, there'd been crowds of people waving and watching the offloading. This time, the five of us stepped off the passenger car and were greeted by three men who helped carry our luggage and other items to a waiting carriage while the rest of the throng milled around, not knowing and little caring who was in their midst.

I learned Moody designed his trips that way. He avoided the limelight unless he was preaching or teaching. He even rudely turned away from people who tried to praise him. It was Redding's job to placate the offended. Moody would accept no praise for himself.

I also learned that Moody always lined up a series of evangelists for each stop, some speaking before he arrived and some after. Their job was to stay in the city and help the new Christians get properly started.

I could not have had a greater contrast than the one between Cody and Moody. As we traveled, Moody's modesty intrigued me. It seemed unnatural for a man to shy away from accolades as much as Moody did. I gave it a lot of thought. I knew he did it for religious reasons, but it still did not make much sense to me. If someone told me I did a great job, I thanked him.

As we worked our way west, I began to sense myself getting closer to Red Beard. He began to dominate my thoughts and dreams, this time in a more constructive way. The previous spring had been a time of healing for me when I'd learned to live with a great loss. I used those lessons to control the inevitable emotional flare-ups.

I was not healed, not entirely, but I don't think anyone ever is. We all live with loss, fear, turmoil, and disappointments. If I could walk away from watching my family's murders, and never give it another thought, I would not be human. Suffering is a human condition.

There were days when the darkness of hate threatened to overtake me, days when I did not want to kill Red Beard—I wanted to dismember him and set fire to his parts. I did not like myself on those days, but I had learned how to get through such low periods. The darkness of hate was so crippling that I feared it more than Red Beard.

I heard dozens of sermons by Moody, and I read most of the New Testament. Yes, those teachings helped me. No, I was not a Christian, even though Moody had tried his best with me. He always insisted I make a decision right now, but I could not.

We were in Wheeling when I finally had the courage to approach Moody with my questions regarding Red Beard. Finding the right time was not easy, because Moody followed a tight schedule. I approached just after breakfast, when he was the most relaxed. The others had left the hotel dining room, and Moody was taking another cup of coffee while reading the morning paper.

"Dwight." I never got used to using the great man's first name, but he insisted. "Would you mind if I ask a question?"

He quickly put down his paper and leaned toward me. "Of course not. What is it?"

"Well, I'm afraid there's a long story with it. Do you have time?"

Moody did not look at the wall clock, check his pocket watch, or give any other sign of being pressed for time. "We have as much time as you need, unless it takes more than ten hours."

I smiled at the joke, getting used to his subtle sense of humor. I gave a brief account of my family's murders, of Red Beard, and of my escape. Moody seemed to feel my emotions at every step of the story, tears coming to his eyes.

His first words were, "You must want to kill the man."

Shocked, I stuttered, "How did you know?"

"Most men would feel thus. The man did a terrible thing to you and your family. You want to respond in kind. I cannot imagine watching someone kill my wife and children. The pain would be too great to bear. You, young man, are very strong indeed."

"I don't feel strong. I wish I knew what I should do. I talked with Cody, Annie, and Frank about what to do, and they believe I have the right to seek justice, though Cody would hunt the man down and shoot him and Annie would turn it all over to the law. What do you think I should do?"

Moody leaned back a little. "Ah, you have heard from the frontiersman and the gun experts. Now you want to hear from a man of God." He leaned forward at my frown and shook his hands to emphasize his words: "No, no, I'm not criticizing you. It is right to seek help in many places. God certainly has much to offer on the subject, and you shall hear my thoughts. Have you read much of the Old Testament?"

"I tried it once and found it too confusing."

"Don't tell anyone, but I find it confusing, too. There is a section in there about an eye for an eye and a tooth for a tooth."

"I think I read it in one of the Gospels."

"Right, the Sermon on the Mount. Jesus quotes the passage but then turns it on its head and says that to hate a man is the same as killing him. Wanting him dead is the same as killing him. Some would tell you, therefore, to go ahead and kill the man because you have already committed the act in your mind. But, that misses the point.

The point is that both hating and killing are sins, and we should strive to do neither."

"So, I should not hate Red Beard?"

"No, you should not, but you do, and you will. Love is difficult. Love has no room for hate. If I choose to hate, then I cannot love, and if I choose to love, I cannot hate. Still, hate is a natural reaction of humans. God is asking us to give up something that is natural for us. I work at it every day, and I get better at it, but it still sneaks in."

"Should I just let the man go?"

"Oh, no! He needs to be punished. Don't misunderstand me: the police must catch him and give him the full punishment under the law, and you can do what part may be given to you. What you need to do is try each day to give up at least a little of the hatred. Don't allow it to take over your life. You don't need to concern yourself with Red Beard's punishment. You need to concentrate on keeping yourself from allowing hate to overcome you.

"As to finding the killer and helping bring him to judgment, which is in some ways less difficult. I know you plan to leave us in Kansas City to search for this man, and I wish you all the best in that endeavor, but you must be prepared to live with the consequences. What you propose to undertake is fraught with danger, not the least of which is that he might kill you, or worse, that you might kill him.

"During our recent terrible war, I worked with many men who were overwhelmed with the responsibility of killing other humans. Some of those men have not been able to return to what we would call normal lives. A few have even killed themselves. Most learn to live with it, but it never goes away, and it is never easy. You must prepare yourself."

70 Congregational

Naturally, Moody believed everyone should become a follower of Jesus. I dodged him as much as I could and begged off often. I had too many unanswered questions; and my biggest question was, why did my parents try to keep their children from being Christians?

After a week of preaching in Terre Haute, we moved to St. Louis for another weeklong series. That stop was a bit more difficult for me, because the local people had not fully prepared the hall, and that forced me to help set up chairs in addition to my regular duties.

From Moody's perspective, the meetings went well. There were the usual large, receptive crowds, and many people came forward each evening. Ira was unhappy with how the sound carried in the hall, and I was able to get a makeshift soundboard set up to help project his voice to the back of the hall. I think the real problem was he had been sick, and his voice was not as strong. Normally, he could rattle the windows and make the deaf hear.

Moody ended the week by preaching three times on Sunday: morning, afternoon, and evening in the huge hall. He was exhausted and slept until nearly nine the next morning. We had Monday and most of Tuesday to relax before getting on the train for an evening trip to Kansas City.

In contrast to St. Louis, there was a crew waiting for us at Union Station in KC who would not let any of us carry a bag. An impressive carriage whisked us to the Coates House Hotel with our personal luggage, while a wagon carried the supplies to the Coates Opera House across the street. With nothing to do, I was asleep by ten.

At the Opera House on Wednesday, everything was in place except for the few personal touches. I grinned at being a man of leisure. For lunch, a group of local pastors and church leaders meet with all of us at the hotel in a reserved dining room. I usually avoided those meetings but wanted to meet some of the people there, since I would be staying in KC. I took a seat in the far corner and watched most of the pastors vie for the seats closest to Moody, or at least Ira.

My replacement was also there to meet me and learn his duties. Ransel Cogley was a high school graduate and eighteen, so I failed to mention my own educational background.

Actually, I was able to bask in a little idol worship because someone who had worked for Buffalo Bill intimidated him. I did not follow Moody's aversion tactics. I was starting to see how my time with the show could reward me in the future. With little work to do, I entertained Ransel with stories of the Wild West, most of them true.

On my last day of employment, pay in hand, I stood on the platform and waved to the Moody group as the engine tugged the train away from the station.

I took a trolley and then walked directly to the stockyards and hired on the night shift. I found a small place nearby that I could afford without sharing the room. I put my money in the bank, including $34 from the Moody job. I had made $48.50 but had spent more on things I did not need just because I had so much time to waste on the trip. Idle hands and all that.

Before leaving town, Moody arranged for Rev. Henry Hopkins, D. Div, minister of the Congregational Church, to help me as needed.

71 Follow

On my first night back in the yards, I felt I had been gone only a few days. The routine was comforting. Jim Smith was thrilled to have me. "If you can load buffalo and elk, you can load anything." I never confessed how easy the buffalo had been.

My boarding house had two other rooms, and each had two men, all of whom worked days in the yards. The landlady was crabby, but, she did not have to feed me, so she unloaded on the others most of the time.

Eating in saloons was a hardship I tolerated so I could watch for Red Beard. I visited all the saloons for two miles around the yards over the next weeks. I do not recommend the sausage-boiled-egg-beer diet. I was so sleepy at work that my crew chief chewed me out, and rightly so. After that, I slept until two or three in the afternoon, which gave me a couple of hours to walk the streets before reporting for work. I was up earlier on Fridays and Saturdays, catching up on my sleep Sundays. The killer was not likely to be going to church.

I was so busy searching for my nemesis that it was nearly September before I got around to sending a letter to Jim through the Holy Name Church. The reply did not come for several weeks. When it did, it was typical Jim.

Remmy,

No news killer. Family living cabin. Say father brother. Not like.

Jim.

I'd never heard either of my parents mention relatives. I always assumed they had none, maybe lost in the war. The telegram told me I had an uncle to deal with, but that would have to wait. At least the people living there were not strangers. Okay, they were strangers, but the strangers were my relatives. I was curious as to why they'd come to live in our cabin.

September slid into October, and I kept to my schedule, except for one Sunday when I went to church to speak with Dr. Hopkins before the service. I just wanted him to know that I was doing well. I had not told him about my search for Red Beard, but I think he suspected I was up to something besides working cattle. Perhaps Moody had clued him in.

As October disappeared, my resolve began to fade, and I wondered if I should give up the hunt. I had been all over the city on both sides of the river; I was running out of places to look. I considered going to North Platte to see if I could use my influence to get a job at Scout's Rest, Cody's place. If that happened, I could wait until Cody returned from Europe and probably get back on with the show. It was an idea.

I dithered, continuing to cruise the streets and visit the saloons until November, by which time I decided I might as well work the winter in KC and make my move in the spring. I cut back on my saloon visits and ate in my room more often. There was no sausage on my menu.

The *Evening News* had a lengthy piece on the hanging of the men arrested after the Haymarket incident. Only six of the seven were hanged. Louis Lingg managed to kill himself with dynamite the day before. No one seemed to know how a stick of the explosive had made it into his cell. *Albert Parsons, Adolph Fisher, August Spies, George Engel, Michael Schwab, & Samuel Fielden are hanged for inciting riot and murder in the Haymarket.*

It was no surprise, but I was disappointed. The prosecution never presented any evidence that any of the men threw the bomb or even had any knowledge of it. In a nation priding itself on the rule of law, I thought hanging seemed extreme for whatever crimes they might have committed. I still did not understand socialism, but I doubted it was a hanging offense.

A week before Thanksgiving, I was stepping with purpose down yet another often-traveled street in the area of the yards. I had done my fruitless search and turned for work. By then, I could scan everyone on a street without being conscious of it. I also found that I could remember hundreds of people on sight, which made my search that much easier; I was looking for a new face in the familiar crowd.

A man on horseback nearly a block away broke my reverie. The hat was wrong, a simple plainsman, but the horse looked right, and the man was the right shape; he looked right on the horse. It was not easy to see clearly through the evening crowds. I stepped into a store entryway to give the man time to get closer.

The nightmare returned: a red beard, a heart-shaped spot on the horse. I forced myself to turn completely away for fear Red Beard might recognize me. Once he passed, I took a deep breath and followed.

72 Arrest

With people heading home from work, I pushed my way through the jam on the sidewalks, keeping the killer in sight. Red Beard stood out most of the time. When he entered a livery stable, I stepped into a shop, pretending to look at something.

Red Beard left the stable and walked two more blocks to a rooming house, with me close behind. I hid outside for an hour as the traffic thinned and the smells of dinner drifted my way, but nothing else happened. With dark settling in, I was convinced he had to live there.

With the location of the building memorized, I went directly to the yards and reported to Jim Smith. "I'm sorry for not showing up. Let me tell you why." He was inclined to listen because of my exemplary work record. I told him a simple story of seeing my family's killer on the street, with a promise to tell him more later.

Jim asked, "Is he on the Kansas or Missouri side?"

"Kansas, straight north of here."

"Good. I know a couple of coppers who are good men. I'll go with you to find them, and you can lead them to the room. We'll have the scum locked up before midnight."

"Do you think my word will be enough?"

"To lock him up, no question. We'll worry about putting him on trial later. Come with me." Jim checked with the office, borrowed a couple of horses from the work crews, and we began the search for the men in blue.

We found Billy right away, and as he listened to my story, his eyes danced. He said, "We'll get him, sure enough. Jim, you ride over to Hazel's place. Adam should be around there. Take him to the station, and he'll round up a couple of more men. I'll ride with the boy to watch the house 'til you get there with help. You know where it is, right?" I had described the house well.

Billy and I tied the horse on the street, and I checked that Red Beard's horse was still at the livery. We stayed on the same side of the street as the rooming house, a block away. "We'll wait here until help comes. I don't want to risk spooking him with just the two of us. You say he's good with a gun?"

"Very fast."

"So, we need to overpower him before he even knows we're here." Billy kept talking, and my heart was beating so fast I never considered the copper might be just as excited and scared as I was.

The wait was no more than a quarter of an hour, but it seemed forever. Five more coppers arrived with Jim. He and I held the horses as the coppers split into two groups to surround the house.

Sitting on our horses, ready to run the man down if needed, Jim and I waited. In just a few minutes, the coppers led Red Beard outside in handcuffs and marched him to the police station. Jim and I rode behind, dark thoughts threatening my equanimity.

At the station, I learned the man's name was Josh Wallwork. I told Billy every detail I could remember of the night of January 6, as well as the encounter at the Walnut rail depot. When he had it all written down, Billy said, "You can go now. We'll have to send out some telegrams and go through all our wanted posters to see what else we can learn about this character. It'll probably be at least a week before we know anything, but check in Monday. In fact, you can check at the sergeant's desk every day if you want to."

Jim had gone to the yard while I'd told my story, but I was too jigged to work. I went anyway, only because I never go back on a promise. Jim wisely gave me small cleanup chores. I think I went through every emotion in the book: anger, hatred, frustration, elation, satisfaction, happiness, sadness, and a touch of fear. What should I feel after nearly two years? I wanted to be happy, but I felt loss most of all.

Before I left work, Jim told me, "You should come to work to help keep your mind off what happened. If you need to take a day with this business, just let me know.

You're a good worker, and I want to help you as much as I can."

I knew I should not push goodwill too far. Taking a day or two would be acceptable, but only for a good reason. I vowed to concentrate on working at night and getting my rest during the day. That rest included a daily talk with my favorite police officers.

Just after Thanksgiving, I received an early Christmas present. News came that Kirkwood, MO, near St. Louis, wanted Wallwork for murder. A few days later, a second notice came for the killing of a US Marshal near Picher, Indian Territory. Wallwork was becoming popular. The Neosho County Sheriff decided not to get into the tug-of-war for lack of physical evidence. Billy had to talk me down when I heard that Wallwork would never stand trial for murdering my family. He reminded me that I never had a good look at the man that night. The evidence was stronger with the other cases. He was going to hang, just not in my county.

I understood, but it was a bitter pill to swallow. I could already feel a bit of emptiness creeping into my heart, with a definite overtone of hate.

I went to Dr. Hopkins, seeking his advice. I gave him all the details. "And I want a trial in Erie, where I can point to the man and say, 'He shot my family.'"

Dr. Hopkins nodded in agreement. "It would be very satisfying. But, haven't you already donc that?" The comment stopped me. Of course I had, just not in the courtroom. "Besides, you got a man arrested who has eluded the US Marshals and the police in at least two states. You were the one to point right at him. You have served your family very well, I would say." That eased some of my pain.

73 Hopkins

That empty feeling faded as I began to accept that the trial I wanted was not going to happen; still, I had unfinished business with Wallwork. I continued to visit the station every day for information, but also to ask permission to visit him. The police had no problem with a visit, but Wallwork always refused.

I talked with Dr. Hopkins about it a couple of times. "I just want to understand why he did it."

Again, he let me talk and did not heap up platitudes. He helped me work my way through my confused state. Later, Hopkins said, "I'm not sure it is possible to understand the mind of someone who would kill five people he does not even know."

My counter was, "As Mr. Moody said, he chose to sin against me and my family. I want to know why he made the choice."

"Ah, I see. He freely chose to kill, but why? Still, I think you will only get a minor reason. Making such a choice is rooted so deep in the man, I doubt Wallwork would know."

"My friend Jim thinks he may have done it for hire."

"So, Wallwork's reason to sin would be money. But, why would he kill someone for money? There is still a much deeper reason to explain that. More to the point, what of the person who paid to have your family killed?"

I had focused so long on Red Beard I had never considered that aspect. After thinking for a time, I asked, "What are the usual reasons people give for murder?"

Hopkins gave a small smile. "Murder is a little out of my line of work. I generally deal with less serious sins. Still, the reasons would be much the same as for any of the other sins: revenge, hatred, jealousy, lust, greed, or just pleasure of watching someone suffer, which I suspect may be part of Wallwork's reason. There are others, but you get the idea."

"We had a small farm. Why would anyone want it enough to kill for it?"

"How small?"

"We owned a quarter section and rented another quarter."

"Good land, I presume." I nodded agreement. "Any troubles with neighbors?" I shook my head. "It is possible someone found something of sgnificant value on the land, but I shouldn't think it's very likely. I would think hatred or revenge is more likely. Don't forget, he may have done it on his own. You don't know he was paid."

"If he just rode by and decided to kill my family, how would he know about me?"

"True. It seems more likely he knew there would be six of you. Still, you should not jump to conclusions without all the facts. Continue to visit and try to see him. He may give in and allow it someday. In the meantime, try not to let it overwhelm you."

Hard advice, but I managed to stay on a reasonably even keel. Two days later, the police told me of another charge against Wallwork, this in Omaha. So, one more state was in the hanging contest.

I threw myself into work at the yards and forced myself to read more, but Wallwork continued to lurk in my thoughts as I struggled to avoid the darkness of last December.

Dr. Hopkins invited me to spend Christmas with his family. Because of work, I could only spend part of the afternoon, which worked out, since Christmas was on Sunday and the family was in church all morning.

The family did nothing special while I was there. The oldest daughter was married, and she and her husband brought their baby for a couple of hours. The other four children were still at home, the youngest being thirteen. Mostly I enjoyed watching them interact as a family. The joy of that was worth more than gold. My contribution was describing the Wild West to the teenage boy.

I left at 5:15, my pockets stuffed with food and candy, and a smile on my face.

74 Why?

Perhaps because it was Christmas, Wallwork agreed to talk with me. More likely, he was sick of my asking. I had thought of how to question him but had never settled on anything I felt comfortable with; I'd never talked to a murderer before.

I followed the jailer through the steel door to the prisoner section. It consisted of a long row of cells on each side of an aisle. A chair was set in front of a cell and the jailer told me to sit in the chair and to stay in it. "Don't approach the cell. He could grab you. I'll be down at the door watching. You can't trust anyone in here."

As I walked down the aisle, the place became as quiet as a funeral home. I glanced from side to side and saw men standing at every door, ready for the show to begin. I sat and looked into the only empty cell I had seen. I glanced back at the guard, who was there as promised. I don't know how long I waited; I know it was long enough to doubt seriously that Wallwork was going to talk. Then a voice came from the cell: "So, it's young Bevans at last. You don't seem to be dead."

My instinct was to respond, polite conversationalist I had become; but I realized the long wait was supposed to intimidate me. Having watched masters of the mind game in the Cody show, I leaned back in my chair, stretched my legs full in front of me, and crossed them at the ankles. I waited with my fingers interlocked over my stomach the way Buck Taylor did so effectively. Of course, Buck was nearly a foot taller and twice as wide, a more imposing figure, but the attitude was the same. I studied my boots. I looked up and down the cells. I exhibited intense curiosity with the ceiling.

I was determined not to talk to an empty cell. I wanted the man to show himself. The fact that he'd spoken first convinced me I had the edge. I was still blank on what to say when the chance came.

Minutes passed, and I was starting to doubt the play. I was searching for a surefire starter when I saw a stirring on the bottom bunk. Josh Wallwork sat up and looked at me from under that heavy brow. "So, that's what you look like. I'd imagined something less like a scared rabbit."

I did not respond for a few beats. Then I carefully uncrossed my legs and sat up before leaning on my knees. "I'm not here to trade insults with you. I just want to know why."

Those words and that posture were the most difficult I have ever produced. I was sitting a few feet from my family's killer, and every instinct shouted for me to rush the cell and claw the man's eyes. Wallwork walked to the cell bars but said nothing. I dropped my head and closed my eyes; I focused on calming my heart and my thoughts. When I looked up, Wallwork was staring at me. I sat up and returned the look with what I hoped was determination, despite a slight tremor in my lower lip.

Wallwork looked at the guard, considered, made a decision. He motioned for me to come closer. I stared at him, then gave a thin smile and shook my head. Wallwork shrugged and spoke in a whisper the guard could not understand: "I'll only tell you if you tell me something first."

It was my turn to consider, but we were talking, so I could see nothing to lose. "What?"

Wallwork took his time; I leaned back and looked down the bullpen. I gave a big smile at all the hands cupped over ears sticking out to catch every word. We were the best entertainment the men had seen in some time.

As I looked at the guard, I heard, "How did I lose you at the creek?"

Wallwork had spoken normally, so I did as well. "As far as I know, only three of us know about the hiding place. I was just able to fit into a small cave washed out of the creek bank and covered by thick brush. We used to play in there when we were much smaller."

Wallwork nodded his head in approval. "That was some good thinkin'. I figured it musta been some kinda hole. I went to the river, then backtracked up the creek 'til I reached the open field at the other end. I made sure you hadn't crossed the creek before I went to the cutting area and searched for your trail again. Then I crossed the open field to the hedge line and hid my horse. Figured he'd raise a fuss if you was to sneak up on him. I waited all night at the cutter's shed. Before they arrived in the morning, I went back to my horse to wait and sleep, figurin' to search the next night. When I saw the blizzard, I knew I'd lost you."

It was mostly as I had figured, so I decided to surprise him. "You were at Walnut. It's where I hopped on the train." Wallwork just shook his head.

After a couple of minutes, I asked again: "Why?"

"You ain't gonna like it."

With some grit, I said, "I didn't like watching you shoot my family. Your reason can't be any worse."

Wallwork rubbed his scraggly beard. "I had 600 reasons, a hundred for each of you. 'Course, only got 500 'cause you got away, but he paid me to track you down. We paid for your death in New York. Guess I need to get a refund."

The news shook me, in spite of all my preparation. I had to clear my head and think it through. Six hundred dollars to kill my family. "Our whole farm isn't worth that much. Who could possibly come up with so much money?"

"Well, the farm weren't the reason, and the money was no issue, least that's what he told me. He said he would take the farm 'cause R.O. owed him."

"Who hates Father so much he would pay to have him killed? What's his name?"

"Now we're agin' it, ain't we? I got something you really want. Problem is, you ain't got nothin' I want, unless you can get me out o' here."

I realized I had overplayed my hand. I should have held something back. I had nothing left. Except...I had watched Sam lose at poker for a year, and I'd become good at spotting a bluff even though he never had. Perhaps....

I waited a long time, stretching and crossing my legs again. After another minute, I could see Wallwork's face crease into just the hint of doubt. I continued to sit, then let a smile sneak onto my face—not a big one: I did not want to overplay it.

Wallwork turned away and slapped the mattress. He sat on the bunk, not looking at me. It took another five minutes to set the hook fully. Wallwork stepped to the bars again. "I ain't tellen' you no name, but I know where to find him. Tell me what you got."

"I went first last time. Where do I find him?"

Wallwork turned away for a minute but stayed close to the cell door. Turning back with a big grin, he said, "The man who paid me and then paid gangs all the way to New York to kill you...." He stopped to lick his lips. "You'll find him at your farm, of course."

75 Plan

The words hung midway between the cell and me. I could not process them. They finally struck me like a sledge. My uncle had killed my family; my uncle killed had his own brother.

I staggered toward the door, unaware of Wallwork screaming for an answer, unaware of the shouts of the other inmates, who also felt cheated. The jailer made me sit in a chair in the office and gave me a shot of whiskey. I hardly felt the burn.

My thoughts slowly came together. Eventually, I told the jailer I was ready to leave and stepped into the December cold. In one of those strange contradictions, the icy air warmed my brain. I stood on the sidewalk for a few minutes, letting the cold clear away the cobwebs. Then, with a sense of resolve, I headed back to my room.

I had five hours before work but could not sleep; instead, I concocted one plan after another. With the setting sun, I considered skipping work, but I went, only because it was better than creating plan number 301.

I threw myself at the work to stay focused, all the while letting the new facts brew in the background toward resolution. When I timed out at six and walked home, I was more numb than tired. I ate some leftover bread, washed my face, and fell asleep as soon as my head was on the bed.

I woke late but refreshed, clocked in at 6:33, put in another solid twelve hours—well, eleven and a half—and walked some distance to eat a fifty-five-cent steak and egg breakfast. I had settled my mind, except for the key element of how to approach my uncle. I decided to pretend to be someone else, since he had not seen me; but how to get him to talk would be tricky.

I was on the same search, just a step closer. My killer was still out there, and this time I knew where to look—no more stumbling down streets and skulking in saloons.

I mulled over all the options I could think of and weighed each carefully. I knew I had time to consider my plan, since my uncle thought I was dead. I needed to work out every detail.

Wallwork was the only connection to the man who'd hired him. Arresting him was only possible if Wallwork would tell the police what he'd told me, and I did not expect him to do that. Besides, I was determined to get some answers from the man who'd killed his brother, even if I could not tell anyone else.

I thought of sending a telegraph to Jim to keep an eye on the farm until I arrived, but telegraphers would talk, so I did not.

A letter was a good idea, and I knew I could trust Jim. It would also be nice to have him there to back me up. I kept that idea close while I developed my plan.

What I wanted to do was kick in the door of the cabin and hold my uncle at gunpoint until he explained why he did it. Nevertheless, one of the things I'd learned in my two years on the run was if I did not control my emotions, someone else would control me. I needed a plan to control my uncle, to force him to talk.

With a rough plan pieced together, I worked at the yards through January 6. I would celebrate my birthday at my home later. I spent the next week getting the things I needed for the trip, including a ticket for the train to Mission. I mailed a letter to Jim—late, but I still hoped it might arrive in time. I visited an old outfitter's store, a holdover from the frontier days, to supplement the few items I still had from Big Jim. I bought some of the best winter clothing and boots they had. Also, snowshoes, jerky, dried fruit, and some canned foods, as well as a backpack to hold it all. I added a good-sized waterproof with metal eyelets to fashion a tent. I hoped never to have to use all that, but after my experience two years ago, I planned to be better prepared.

I looked at several rifles and settled on a Winchester thirty-eight instead of the forty-four. It would not bring down a charging buffalo, but it would kill any game I was likely to see, or a man if need be.

Fully outfitted, I took Shank's mare the two miles to Union Station, even though my train did not leave until early the next morning. I decided to sleep in the depot waiting area. I treated myself to a big meal at the Harvey House and settled in on a nice, soft, wooden bench. I was relaxed and confident. I knew I could live with my decision, even if it turned out badly for me.

76 Stranded

It felt good to be back on the train. I was rested and calm. I left the train at Fort Scott and walked to the K-T station to find I had a couple of hours to wait. I considered going to visit Maude, but I was too close to my goal and did not want to risk any delays. Besides, I knew she would sense what I was about to do.

A small shop sold sandwiches and coffee next to the depot, and I took advantage. Back outside, the weather was warm, atypical for January. There was perhaps half a foot of melting snow on the ground, about right for the time of year. After my life as a city boy, it felt good to be close to the earth again. I could smell the difference.

I walked the length of the platform to help maintain my calm. I noticed several men, including a couple of train conductors, huddled with the telegrapher.

After everyone boarded, instead of waving the engine on, the conductor entered our car. "I need to tell you that we have received word by telegraph that a powerful winter storm has crossed into Kansas. It may or may not reach this far south. If anyone wants to stay in Fort Scott, please take your things now. You can make arraignments for a later train inside the depot." He then moved to the next car to make the same announcement.

No one in my car chose to leave, but an older couple and a family with three young children left the other one.

After watching the familiar countryside for a few miles, I dozed. I dreamed I was home, eating rabbit stew and teasing Doris. Mother smiled at me. I was warm and comfortable.

A shriek knifed me awake. Everyone was staring out the windows on the west side of the car, staring at a blanked of horizontal white fluff. The sound was like a wild animal tearing at the car, puffing snow through the cracks of the windows and even the walls of the car.

It did not seem possible the storm could have crossed most of Kansas in so short a time. The sky was getting darker every minute. The only thing to see outside the car was the darkening snow.

The conductor came in from the front car. "Is everyone all right?" We were. He spoke to the porter: "John, keep the fire at maximum." To everyone he said, "We just took on more coal and water at Walnut and should be able to make it to Osage Mission all right. Get out all your winter clothes and blankets if you have them. It will be hard to heat this car while the wind is so strong, so move near the stove, and don't be afraid to crowd together for warmth. The wind will probably let up soon."

It did not; neither did the snow. The train slowed as the drifting snow quickly built walls across the tracks; then we stopped altogether. My best guess was that we were halfway between Walnut and Mission.

Ten minutes later, the conductor came back with more bad news. "The engineer has to shut down the engine and drain all the water. If not, it will freeze and rupture the tank."

Someone asked, "Why not keep feeding it coal?"

"Because we may need it to survive this storm. There is enough coal to keep one car warm for a week, if need be. We should not need that much before the storm dies out and a rescue train comes. Meanwhile, I ask everyone, take only the things you must have, and go forward to the next car. We will shut down this stove now."

When we were ready, the conductor said, "The wind is stronger than any I've ever experienced. You'll need to hold on at all times, or it can easily blow you off the platform. Ladies, please allow men to help you get across the opening." Then he opened the door.

Cries and screams evaporated in the wind's ferocity. Wearing all the best cold weather clothing I could buy, I volunteered to stay on the platform to help people cross. In seconds, I might as well have been naked. The wind tore at my eyes and did its best to fill my nose with snow and ice.

I entered the other car, followed by the porter carrying the lantern and a scuttle of hot coals, and then the conductor. People from both cars were crying, shivering, and stamping their feet. The porter of the first car grabbed the coalscuttle and threw the hot coals in the fire. It took at least fifteen minutes before most of us reached any level of comfort.

The conductor spoke again. "Ladies and gentlemen, I'll not insult you by saying we have nothing to worry about. If we were on a ship, I'd say, 'take to the lifeboats'. Well, this is our lifeboat. I've been stranded before, and I know how to get through it. All of you need to listen and do your parts. If we stick together, we'll be fine. We'll not be as warm as we might want, but we won't freeze. Trust me.

"Now, there are some things to tend to. No one should go outside to relieve himself. I doubt anyone would want to, anyway. Ladies, I'm sorry, but we will have to take care of business in this car. We have several scuttles, and we can tack up a small partition, but that's it, and there's nothing to be done about it.

"Second, I need a couple of strong men, who have enough winter clothing, to carry coal from the tender to this car so we can keep the heat going through the night. We won't have to go right away, but in an hour or so. I think by then we can make our way along the east side of the cars and be enough shielded to make the trip."

I opened my pack and handed out extra clothing, as did several others. I gave Big Jim's thick wool blanket to two young kids in the car. We tied my waterproof over the front door near the stove, because the wind blew a lot of cold air in around the door.

We packed together on the benches, most with our feet on the facing bench, stuck between people or even on their laps. Ice formed on the floor of the car. No one wanted the last bench away from the fire, so I stretched out; I was warm enough fully dressed.

The rear door next to me burst open, and four apparitions blew in with a heap of snow. Each carried a mound of supplies. The two brakemen, the fireman, and the engineer were introduced. They brought just enough blankets for the women.

Since brakemen needed to climb on the train cars in all kinds of weather, they had the best clothing for this storm. Their gear came from Massachusetts, intended for the whaling ships: thick knitted wool caps, sweaters, and wool pants so heavy it must have taken ten sheep to make them. The most practical things they had were the famous foul-weather coats, pants, and hats of heavy canvas, all waterproofed. Not only would they repel water, but they would hold off the wind. And there were two extra sets.

David Hoban and I suited up to join the fireman and brakemen for the trips to the tender car with the coal scuttles. We formed a chain, holding buckets between us to avoid getting lost. The five of us carried coal back and piled it in the corner of the car, returning several times to make sure we would survive the night.

Gradually, exhaustion took its toll, and most of us managed to find sleep. Several men volunteered to stay awake in shifts to help the railroaders tend the fire. I was on the first watch. John Nigh—the colored porter—and I spent two hours talking quietly and feeding the fire. We woke a brakeman and the other porter for the next shift.

The next morning, the five of us fought our way to the tender. Once there, we had to rake off the blanket of snow until we hit the solid chunks of frozen coal. We made too many trips to keep track. By the time the conductor was satisfied, I was beyond feeling the cold, or much of anything else.

The storm finally let up the second night. The wind was more normal, and the snow seemed to have stopped, though it was still blowing around. After bringing in another day's supply of coal, I volunteered to see if I could shoot something to eat. There was almost nothing left of our box lunches and dried foods.

Hoban also had a rifle, and the two of us went in opposite directions; I walked on my snowshoes to the west, secretly hoping to run into Jim, or even our cabin.

I soon spotted a patch of brush upwind, giving me an excellent hiding place for a clean shot at what looked to be an animal trail, even under all the snow. After a two-day blow, animals would need to find food. I hoped deer would work through the drifts.

Instead, I saw six turkeys coming my way. They were feeding on branches above the snow. I had to remind myself to be patient. When the birds were within ten feet of the target zone, I slowed my breathing and sighted down the gun barrel. I was ready to shoot the first bird when I saw the third and fourth birds were staying side-by-side, so I allowed the first two to walk past my sights. When the two were in right position, I fired, quickly levered in another round and shot at a third bird making the mistake of flying straight away from me, an easy shot, just the way Frank had taught me.

I quickly picked up the three birds, gutted them, and cleaned them before they froze. At the train, we sliced the meat into chunks, with some dropped in boiling water and the rest spread out in the empty car to freeze. The boiled meat had little flavor, but it was nourishing. One woman had a small chunk of salt to add to the water.

David Hoban returned an hour later with two rabbits. The rabbit meat joined the turkey to freeze.

Our rescue train appeared that afternoon, and a crew spent most of two hours digging us out and breaking loose the wheels that were frozen to the rails. They towed the dead engine and our lifeboat toward Mission as I stood next to the tracks, waving goodbye. My plan was to hike through the snow to my former home with no more delay.

77 Light

By the time I arrived at the cabin, night was in control. Two years before, I'd approached from the west; this time it was from the east. I kept to the trees to avoid detection, reaching the tree line close to where Wallwork had tied his horse two years ago; the horse that led me to him. I could almost see it standing there.

Thinking of the horse triggered five flashes of light, without sound.

I did not have to shrug it off and go on with work. There was no need to continue running. This time, I cried for my dead family. I shook. Tears froze, and I cried even more. I leaned against a tree, untied my snowshoes, and slowly slid to the snow. I sat looking away from the cabin, our cabin. I closed my eyes and allowed the darkness and the cold to both numb and calm.

When I finally pulled myself up and looked again at the house nearly lost in the dim light of a new moon, I had a tingling at my neck; something was curious. I studied the scene, waiting for discernment. I thought I must have been overreacting; the only thing wrong was the lack of light in any window, but that was not unheard of. They could have covered the windows against the storm. I listened for any noise and watched for any movement, but there was nothing. The scudding clouds did not help.

Then it came to me: a dark cabin was normal, but a cabin with no fire was not. There was no smoke from the chimney. Had my uncle discovered that I was on the way? Had he made a run for it? Would I have to begin all over?

I quietly chambered a shell in my rifle and slowly circled the edge of the clearing. Next, I rigorously checked all the small outbuildings. I found animals, some dead and some alive, but without feed. I found a wagon and a buggy. What I did not find was any evidence that the people who lived here had left.

I stood for a long time, mulling over what might have happened. It was possible that they'd traveled with someone else. It did not seem likely that they had another wagon, because there were no empty stalls for horses. My experience of two years ago probably clouded my judgment. Nonetheless, my conclusion was that murder had found my aunt and uncle.

I made my way to the cabin with my rifle at the ready, even as I realized the likelihood that a murderer was still inside was nearly zero. I could not let go of the images of those pistol shots. As I stood on the porch and studied the closed door, I half-expected to open it and see my family on the floor.

When I did open the door, I could see nothing in the darkness. I stepped quickly inside and against the wall. I listened for the slightest suggestion of another person in the room, ignoring my over-active heart.

Satisfied I was alone, I pulled the matches from my pocket and separated one from the wax coating. With my right hand trying to keep the rifle ready, I struck the match against the door and held it above my head.

Shocked, I fell back against the wall, dropping the match. I could not have seen them, not two years later. I tried to steady myself by taking several deep breaths and holding them for a while until I was again under control.

Striking a second match, I looked more carefully at the room. In the faint light, I could see two people curled on the floor, not five. I struck another match and looked for a lantern. There was one near the door, but it was dry. I saw the iron stove and went to it. There was no wood, shavings, paper, or anything else flammable.

Burning more matches, I realized there was not a stick of wood in the room: no chairs, no table, no bureau. The only thing left to burn was the clothes they were wearing.

I looked carefully at the faces of the two people but saw only strangers. I sat by them for a time and rehashed all I knew. My uncle had arranged to kill my father as some kind of punishment, and now he was lying frozen on the floor where his brother had died.

I searched again and found a leather pouch containing what appeared to be legal papers. One was a deed to the farm, my farm, in the name of Tomos Lewis Bevans. So, my uncle.

I sat in the dark, leaving the door open for the infinitesimal starlight that filtered through the clouds. For the first time in two years, I had nothing to ponder, no decision to make, no reason not to go my own way. It was over.

But, my family was still dead, even as their true killer lay on the floor and the hired shooter headed for the noose. I was still an orphan. I'd even lost my best friend. How could I go my own way, and what was my way? Ultimately, who was I without family? I had more questions than when I'd started my quest.

I gave up thinking in any ordered sense. I walked outside and searched the area again for something to burn for some light. I found a lantern just inside the door of the barn still containing kerosene. With the light burning, I set about feeding the living animals. The horses had fared the best because they had a substantial building for protection with hay on the floor. They needed water, but they had to make do with snow.

I returned to the porch and scooped snow away so I could sit on my favorite spot with my feet over the edge. I could no longer swing my legs above the ground as I had done ten years ago, but it was still my spot.

An image of Father came suddenly to me. We were in the field when I was eleven. Father had spent much of the morning teaching me to guide the plow while controlling two mules. It had been a cold April day, but my clothes had been soaked with sweat. Father had walked beside me the whole time, giving encouragement and directions. At last, it had clicked for me, and I had smiled at how easy it was.

Father had said, "Now you've got it," and clasped my shoulder, giving me a victory shake. Even now, I could feel the tingle of gratification from that touch. Why had I let so much come between us? Father had been a good man.

The clouds opened a small hole to allow a few seconds of dim light. I saw my footprints in the dark snow, prints stretching from here to New York and back. I could almost hear Father say, as he had next to the plow, "Well done."

As the stars once again disappeared, the tears of joy froze on my cheeks.

The Truth of the Story

1 Coins

Until after WWII, the average height of American men was five feet, six inches. Therefore, Remmy would have been one of the big boys. Today, the average is five feet, ten and one half inches.

One dollar a day was the standard wage from the Civil War to World War II. That is not to say there were no other starting wages for unskilled workers, but it was the most common. Naturally, skilled workers earned more.

Contrary to popular conception, Kansas is not a tabletop. It rises from 679 feet in the southeast to 4039 feet on the western border. True, the slope is often flat, but there are many exceptions. Timber covered the eastern edge of Kansas in 1850. Because the foothills of the Missouri Ozarks extend into Kansas, there are low hills throughout the fifty plus miles of the east. Even today, trees cover the real site of Remmy's fictitious cabin.

2 Run

The events of this chapter begin with history. On March 8, 1886, someone entered the home of the Sell family and brutally murdered the parents and two of their three children. Willy Sell, who was 16, was in the house, but the killer somehow missed him. Willy told the sheriff that he attacked the killer and chased him from the house. The whole community of Erie and the farms around almost immediately concluded that Willy was guilty and tried more than once to lynch him. He was arrested, convicted, and served 21 years in prison on death row before the governor gave him a full pardon. There are many theories about who may have actually committed the crime, but no one else was ever arrested.

A book published in 2014 describes the case in detail. *Thy Brother's Blood* by John Hasty.

3 Hide

Clearly, the most dangerous blizzard in Kansas history blew into the state January 7, 1886, killing some 100 people. The snow and sleet described in the following chapters were reported events. I do not know the extent of rail stoppage in the area of this story. I have probably described the impact more in terms of the middle of the state because I have not found records specific to Neosho County. That, plus we want to read an exciting story of survival.

4 Coyote

Nearly all farms in Eastern Kansas divide the land into smaller plots by leaving rows of trees to protect the fields from damaging winds and large animals. Most farmland west of the Allegany's was divided into sections of 640 acres. Most of Southeast Kansas was further divided into quarter sections by the farmers and was often bought by the quarter, 160 acres. That was enough to support a family of modest size if the land was debt free.

Today, bulldozers have removed many of the hedgerows (called after the European style) to allow farming with large machines. Also today, supporting a family of 6 to 10 without additional income on a farm with fewer than 1,000 acres is difficult.

A coyote might have been out in that blizzard. It had been a long hard winter and the hungry have to hunt. Typically, they would sit out the storm.

The Missouri, Kansas, & Texas Railroad was first nicknamed the MKT, then the KT, and, for more than a century, the Katy

Eastern Red Cedar trees are indigenous to Kansas and often cluster to form tightly packed copse. I have some on my place where lower limbs have not had water touch them in countless years.

5 Cedars

My description of Big Jim is not excessive. The Osage were the NBA of the tribes. They formerly lived in Missouri and Arkansas but the government forced them into South Eastern Kansas in 1825, then to Indian Territory after the new "treaty" of 1870. They established three main communities that grew into Oklahoma City, Tulsa, and Ponca City.

I use the terms jerky and dried meat interchangeably in the story. The difference is significant to us today. Dried meat is that and no more; nothing added. Generally speaking, it is not safe to eat unless it is eaten soon, cooked later, or today, packaged in airtight containers. People typically used salt in the 1880's to cure meat. Jerky has been treated with salt at least and today many other spices. The salt is crucial to long-term preservation. Meat hanging over an open fire as described in this story takes all day to dry, especially in freezing weather. Meanwhile, bacteria will get a foothold and cause problems later.

People in 1886 were used to eating higher bacterium content food, so Remmy could eat it for a few days and not suffer if it were dried quickly enough (in other words, cooked).

6 Jim

Waterproofs in 1886 applied to large cloths and raincoats alike. Hemp was used to make the best canvas of the day. Hemp is naturally water resistant as well as resistant to molds and insects. Today, cotton is usually the choice because it is cheaper and more readily available and is treated to resist all of the above. In 1886, beeswax mixed with oil, turpentine, or kerosene was used to waterproof any fabric. It is likely that Jim would have brought treated lightweight cotton, something easier to carry.

7 Traps

When the Osage lived in the area that became Neosho County, the Jesuit Missionaries led by Fr. Schoenmakers established a church and school for the Osage. That was in 1847. The site was first called Catholic Osage Mission, but as settlers began to move in, the name was changed to Osage Mission, and in 1895, it was changed to the present St. Paul. A school has existed on the same plot of land since 1847, now the public school of St. Paul.

The Osage won the tribal lands lottery. In 1871, Congress was feeling generous and paid the Osage $1.25 per acre instead of the 19¢ most received, a total of over $8.5 million that the tribe left with the US Treasury to draw interest. They also received what turned out to be some of the most valuable lands in what became Oklahoma. They were able to sell land for some of the cities and received money from the large oil discoveries, though not as much for either as they should have gotten.

8 Walnut

Walnut was and is a small town; today 220 people. Every town established in the westward expansion struggled for the key ingredients that would give it a chance to survive. Getting the Katy to build a depot there was big news, but it never became more than a refueling station, so few people had a reason to live there. Santa Fe built a spur line from Iola to Joplin just before this story, but, again, it did little to encourage growth. Both rail lines were torn up in the downsizing of the 1970's.

9 Paint

Red Beard's horse might not qualify as a paint today, but the term was loosely used until modern times. He could as easily have been called a pinto or a bay, or perhaps just a nag.

10 Camp

11 Peaches

12 North

One news item from north central Kansas during the January blizzard described eleven steam engines in tandem being used to clear the line, and they became stuck.

The way car is a railroading term for the caboose.

Many passenger cars were tacked to the rear of freight trains in more rural areas, especially when they were trying to clean up the traffic jam after a storm.

Hepler, Hiattiville, and Walker were all stops on the line to Fort Scott.

The Kansas City, Fort Scott, and Gulf RR was the name for the line in 1886. Though the history of ownership and acquisitions is complex, The Frisco owned them for years, but Burlington Northern-Santa Fe (BNSF) now owns most of Frisco.

13 Woodshed

Fort Scott had two depots in 1886. The one for Katy was at the north edge of town near the old fort and the KC, FS, Gulf was along the east side just a few blocks from National Street, the main street.

The description of trolleys and street lamps is based on a photo of National Street.

Bread in those days contained no perseverative and was baked fresh daily either at home or at a bakery for sale. The loaf was sold whole and un-wrapped and was stale the next day, hence the need for toast. Sliced bread was first sold in 1928.

14 Cook

Most buildings in cities in eastern Kansas in 1886 used a combination of wood and coal. Because coal was more expensive, it was often reserved for overnight use when a couple of big chunks in a damped stove could last ten hours, though not producing a lot of heat. A person would set his feet on the floor of the bedroom as low as the upper thirties after a cold night.

Sausage, generally sold in links, was made by filling the long gut of the pig or other animal and twisting it every few inches. The ground meat was mixed with salt, pepper, garlic, vinegar, and/or several of a thousand other possibilities. With the right blend, the sausage could be stored in a cold room for days uncooked, longer cooked.

Bacon, like bread, came unsliced, though the butcher could slice it. Bacon is pork belly cured with sugar and/or smoke in 1886, though today with chemicals.

15 Clean

16 Jumps

17 Remorse

18 Tales

The Pottawatomie and Kickapoo tribes are the only ones allowed to maintain their reservations in Kansas, probably because they were so small. They are both located north of I-70 about halfway between Topeka and Kansas City. The government pushed the Quapaw tribe out of Arkansas in 1834 to the northeast corner of Indian Territory/Oklahoma.

I used the history of the 7th Indiana Cavalry in this and the following chapters. Brit's descriptions of the battles follow the facts. The 7th website also had a complete roster of soldiers during the war, and I plundered the list for names to use all through this story.

The Union needed so many horses for the cavalry that they contracted with ranchers in the far west to supply them. Most were literally wild mustangs in need of more training.

19 Mine

During the first years of the war, Missouri was the source of constant guerrilla warfare with the move by General Price being the last significant effort to regain the state for the South. Even after Price left, guerrilla tactics continued until the end of the war.

Fort Scott had been decommissioned before the war and reopened during the war. It was mainly a supply base for the western war effort, which included operations along the Mississippi as well as the far-flung encounters farther west where the South was trying to gain access to the California gold.

20 Gargling

Actually, when Grant was appointed by his congressman, his name was inadvertently entered as Ulysses because he went by that, and his mother's maiden name, Simpson, because the congressman thought that was correct. Once at the Point, he either entered under that name or waited another year. His classmates started calling him Uncle Sam, then Sam.

21 Volunteer

Brit described smooth bore muskets and more modern rifles, but left out the muzzle loading rifles. They looked like smooth muskets, but they had groves in the barrel so that the mini ball would spiral and maintain an accurate trajectory. They were not widely used because they took four times as long to load.

22 Stockyards

The Kansas City Stockyards in 1886 were located in Kansas on the west side of the Missouri River and just north of the Kansas River. The yards eventually expanded across the river to Missouri before they closed in 1991.

23 Bread

24 Job

25 Whiskey

The news article on the baseball Cowboys is a direct quote.

26 Change

27 Shock

The January 7 blizzard did kill 100 people and at least 100,000 cattle, still the most deadly in state history.

28 Flowers

The news stories recounted are from papers of the day. However, the construction of the Lincoln Memorial did not begin until Lincoln's birthday, February 12, 1915, and was finished May 30, 1922, at a cost of $3 million.

The Southwest Rail Road Strike of 1886 was nasty and violent. At the time, Jay Gould owned or controlled those three lines and used harsh treatment to increase his revenue to use in other investments. During the strike, the Pinkerton Agency was hired to break the strike, which it did by attacking strikers. The National Guard was called in to assist the Pinkertons until the strikers gave up. We do not know how many people died.

Today the Katy and Missouri Pacific are merged into the Union Pacific, along with several others.

29 Longhorns

30 Special

Zac Sanders was a close friend of Cody and the real foreman of the livestock operations.

A special was a train that did not follow a regular schedule. They generally had to wait for all regular traffic before they could proceed, so they spent time on the sidings waiting for others to pass. Some wealthy individuals who traveled had their own car or cars that could either be attached to an existing train or become a special. They were the jet set of 1886.

The history of type writing machines is long and painful to read, but the first successful one in the US came out in 1873 using the QWERTY keyboard arrangement, the one still used worldwide. They were in common use in offices all over the US.

In the early years, the show hired several translators until they decided that was a waste and hired English speakers only, unless someone was too valuable to pass up.

It is worth noting that most of the whites in the west in 1886 had little trouble working with other racial or national groups. There were many black and Mexican cowboys. Intense hatred and violence tended to spring up along the border with Mexico and in the far west with the Chinese and Japanese. The treatment of the Irish in the East was similar. As civilization tamed the West around the turn of the century, the cultural lines were more clearly and more tightly drawn.

31 Omaha

The Union Stockyards of Omaha did not open until 1883, so were not very large in 1886. By 1900, they surpassed Kansas City in size and volume. The yards closed in 1989. Like Chicago and Kansas City, the meat packing industry no longer needed them.

In his first season of 1883, Cody lost $50,000 and seriously considered giving up. However, he was able to sell half of his business to Nate Salsbury who ran the show and kept the books. Cody was the front man and Nate was the mover and shaker. They made such a great team that Cody alone took home $50,000 in

1884 and never made less until Nate died in 1902. After that, the show quality declined along with income and Cody ended his life in bankruptcy.

32 Chicago

This trip to Chicago is my invention. Most likely the two trains left from either North Platte, Nebraska or Omaha, depending on where the equipment was stored.

Jerry the Moose was a well known and popular attraction to the show. He was really a pet.

Bill Cody in 1886, still had brown hair, but pictures just a few years later show a great deal of white.

The system described of stopping at sunset and sunrise to offload, feed, water and reload stock was always followed throughout the history of the show, and probably by most circuses.

33 Easter

The Adventures of Huckleberry Finn was published in 1884.

The *Voice of the Workers!* was the major socialist paper in Chicago at the time.

The disagreement between Karl Marx and Johann Most is accurate as is the book, *Revolutionary War Science.*

May 1 was celebrated as the day workers were to get the 8-hour day.

34 Workers

The mainline newspapers in Chicago, as well as around the country, always wrote *Albert Parsons and his Negro wife, Lucy*, or some variation to make sure everyone knew about the miscegenation, even if it was legal there. Respectable white women were never referred to by their first names.

There was in fact one meeting that Remmy and JR attended that remained peaceful and another at the McCormick plant where the shootings occurred.

35 Haymarket

This is one of the crucial events in American labor relations. There is a wealth of information about it, but several key questions remain unanswered, notably: who threw the dynamite and, were the people hanged actually guilty of any crimes?

The square was the result of some six streets converging with the decision to leave a large open space for traffic to sort itself out, there being no lanes marked in those days. Instead, it became the exchange site as described in the chapter. The large square no longer exists, but there is a memorial to the event.

The police were there in large numbers, and they all emptied their six-shooters, firing indiscriminately. The shooting was so wild that their brothers in arms shot several policemen.

36 Guilt

37 St. Louis

I never found a conclusive statement that the show used two trains in 1886. They used one engine in 1883, and three by 1890, so I gave them two in 1886. The number of trains depended on how much weight one engine could pull. Most boxcars of the day were either 35 feet or 40 feet. They could hold about 15 baggage horses or 17 riding horses, loaded crossways like the cattle.

Railroads charged a flat fee for 20 cars and a different fee for the next 25, so every circus packed as much as possible onto each railcar. Today, the rail companies charge by the ton.

St. Louis Brown Stockings Baseball Team rented its grounds to the Wild West in 1886.

The show was always set up in a horseshoe fashion with the expensive Red Section at one end and the show entrance at the other. The Blue Section was on both sides. All of the acting and shooting was done close to the Red Section.

38 Rehearsal

Again, I found little detail about how the show was put together in 1886. Most such details come from the later years. But the Wild West was at heart a circus and was put together in the same way. Training the livestock is important for any circus. For the Wild West, getting them used to gunfire was important. A few animals refused to cooperate with guns around, so they were sold. Cody's workers would have worked with the animals over an extended period. Some of the show horses belonging to individuals would have needed the most work in St. Louis.

The cowboys and Indians in the show had to practice controlling all the stock turned loose in the arena. The first row of seats had no wall or railing and animals did run amuck into the stands from time to time.

39 Show

Every show was opened by the Cowboy Band playing the *Star Spangled Banner*, which did not become the national anthem until 1931. The Wild West no doubt helped sell the idea.

Don Viscente Oropeza was chief of the Vaqueros and Joe Esquivel headed all the cowboys and a few women riders. Don Viscente later taught Will Rogers the art of rope twirling. Among the women was Georgia Duffy, who also did rope tricks, Senorita Rosalie, Mollie Moses, and others unnamed. Della Ferrel and Emma Lake Hickock joined the show to go to London. Hickock rode two horses by standing on each saddle. Women rode with split skirts, and were not called cowgirls until 1905.

Cody did spend a couple of days at the St. James Hotel with Mollie Moses. She became enraged with him sometime in August and left the show.

The Wild West, like every other circus, had an advance team who traveled weeks ahead of the show and made all the arrangements. They booked and paid for the site, water, feed for the stock, and food for the crew. They also arranged to have posters and flyers printed with the details and hired people to have them put up or handed out. By the time the show arrived, all they had to do was perform. The time of the parade was posted on the advertisements, and it was generally over the noontime to attract the most people.

Judging from photos of the period, the Wild West created the over-the-top cowboy dress styles that Hollywood took to extremes by the 1950's.

40 Doc

It was typical for a veterinarian to treat humans in the period, especially in a circus.

The Buffalo Bill Historical Center provided the route for 1886 as well as the dates for each stop.

A 4-8-0 engine consisted of four small wheels in the front with eight large drive wheels and no wheels behind them. In the late 1930's, the Union Pacific built the biggest engine called the Big Boy, a 4-8-8-4; sixteen drive wheels.

41 Rain

Bridle Bill was real, as was his broken arm.

Gabriel Dumont was as described, though not the drinking incident of this chapter.

42 Frogs

43 Oakley

I have tried to represent Frank and Annie Butler as fairly as possible. The more I read about her especially, the more impressed I am.

Captain Bogardus was the star, after Cody, in 1885, but he left the show after one season.

44 Kendall

Kendall Green was out in the country in 1886, though only a short walk to the Capitol Building. In 1856, Amos Kendall donated some of his land to create a school for the deaf and blind. The next year he convinced Congress to charter the school as the Columbia Institution for the Instruction of the Deaf and Dumb and the Blind. The first superintendent was Edward Gallaudet. It began as a secondary school that eventually became Gallaudet University. It is still dedicated to teaching the deaf. The school's football team gets the credit for inventing the huddle so that they could all see the play being called and the opposing team could not.

If you check a map of DC in 1886, you will see many differences from today, including railroad tracks between the Capitol and the Washington Monument. The area now taken over by the Lincoln Memorial, Kennedy Center, Tidal Basin and the Jefferson Memorial was mostly swampland.

The Wild West parade went up Pennsylvania Avenue as the Cowboy Band played *Marching Through Georgia.*

45 Surprise

I have Doc treating Remmy with whiskey, but more than likely, he would not have done that. When the US entered the Great War in 1917, most US doctors still did not believe in the germ theory and did not bother to wash their hands as they made rounds, examined patients or performed surgery. Doctors in most of Europe had already made the change. It's not likely any doctor in 1886 would have treated the wound with anything except possibly sulfur powder, if he had it.

The movies have it both right and wrong. Whiskey was used, but only as an anesthesia, a very poor one. It will work as an anapestic, but it does contain particulates that could lead to infection. Using a hot iron to treat the wound, sometimes seen in movies, was done to stop the bleeding. We now know it would also disinfect.

46 Dinner

Annie's description of her time with the Wolves is accurate as she told it.

47 Family

48 Bruised

St. George was the ferry terminal for the island, and a train carried the citizens along the eastern coast of the island to their respective communities. Wiman built a four-mile stretch of track from the terminal to Erastina just for the Wild West.

The Wild West grounds were fully electrified with the powerful arc lamps for the arena.

49 Storm

50 Parade

Annie and the insect bite is a true account. In all her years with Cody, she only missed 3 other days.

The summer show schedule is on record.

Kicking Bear was knocked out as described.

51 Newsboys

The account of the newsboys is true, including Father Drumgoole and the boys from the St. Vincent's Home for newsboys. Cody brought in 1,500 boys, including bootblacks.

While JR is fiction, his account of the orphan train is not. In fact, in the story I had him adopted by a real couple who appeared on a list of people at the last stop of one such train in Kansas. The trains operated from 1853 to 1929, relocating about 200,000 orphaned, abandoned, or homeless children.

52 Angel

In 1886, there were fewer than 300 employees, but they spent about $300 a day on food. Think about it. One dollar a day was enough for a whole family to buy food, clothing, and shelter.

Buck Taylor was the first to be called the King of the Cowboys, and rightly so. He featured in several dime novels as the King of the Cowboys.

There was a battle north of Dodge City with the Northern Cheyenne as described. Their flight to find food in their real homelands is a powerful and sad story.

Cody's description of his speech and his father being stabbed is true as is his becoming a bull-whacker and on to greatness. He earned the *Buffalo* appellation shooting buffalo in Kansas for the crews building the Kansas Pacific Railroad as well as for the army.

53 Sheep-dip

The stories of Cody's drinking are the stuff of legends while being mostly true. It is true that he missed many shows in 1883 because of drink, but Nate Salsbury only agreed to join the show if Cody agreed not to miss shows. Accounts differ on how well Cody managed to control himself. I included one such event, but I have no record of it happening in 1886.

54 Baseball

The National League of Professional Baseball Teams first formed in 1871 and the American League of Professional Baseball Teams first formed as the Western League, a minor league, turning major in 1901. The two merged into Major League Baseball in 1903 and played the first World Series won by the Boston Americans over the Pittsburg Pirates.

The New York Metropolitans formed in 1880 as an independent professional team. In 1886, Erastus Wiman bought the team, hoping it would bring in more business to Staten Island; it did not and he folded the team after the 1887 season.

The American Association formed in 1882 and folded in 1891, the end of the beer and whiskey league. Charlie Comiskey managed several teams until he bought the Western League club in Sioux City and turned it into, some years later, the Chicago White Sox. He was a driving force behind the formation of the American League in 1901.

The descriptions of St. George and the baseball field are accurate as far as they go.

While the Wild West game and its players are fiction, the description of the pitching box is accurate. The raised mound developed around the turn of the century.

The description of the hurricane season in 1886 is from the record books. The seven that struck the US remains the record according to the National Hurricane Center. In addition, the decade of the 1880s had the most hurricanes strike the US in any decade up to 2010.

55 Doubt

Colt made the first double action pistol in the US in 1877. They made the Army and Navy versions in 1882, which is more likely the style Red Beard would have used. Before double action, the user had to retract the hammer before every shot, so the double added speed. Moreover, they were considerably more expensive in the mid-80's.

56 Sand

The fight between Annie and Lillian began as soon as Lillian joined the show at Erastina. For some reason, Cody sided with Lillian while they were in London in 1887, so Annie left the show at the end of the London stay. She did not return to the Wild West until Lillian left in 1889. While Annie never said anything in public ("I do not wish to talk about that girl" is all that has been recorded), it was at Erastina that she shaved 6 years off her age to compete with the 15-year-old Lillian. Lillian stayed in show business a few years, going through several marriages and affairs while eating herself out of show business.

Beaches were a big attraction for New Yorkers on Staten Island.

57 Moody

The Charlestown earthquake is today estimated to have been a 7.0 magnitude and was felt well beyond NYC.

Moody was little known outside Chicago until he did a three-year preaching tour of the British Isles starting in 1872. When his ship arrived in NYC Americans thronged to hear him. By 1886, he was at the height of his popularity.

He was self-taught and began his work during the Civil War with the YMCA. In his early years, he was a hell-fire preacher, saying that God hated sinners. That changed the first time he heard Henry Moorhouse preach on John 3:16...seven days in a row.

58 Geronimo

The basic facts are as reported in this chapter. His real name was Goyathlay ("one who yawns"). After the Mexican army had killed his family, he and about 200 warriors spent years killing the army. When the US took over the territory and broke all its promises, he began attacking again, this time the US. He earned his nickname from the Mexicans who feared him and often called on St. Jerome to protect them. It is Jerónimo in Spanish. At least that is one story regarding the famous name.

The army took Geronimo by train to Fort Pickens and then to Fort Sill where he lived the rest of his days under guard. Except in 1904, he was allowed, under guard, to be one of the displays at the St. Louis World's Fair at the age of 85.

I found no record that Cody tried to recruit him for the show.

Sitting Bull toured with the Wild West in 1885.

The story told by American Horse is copied from http://snowwowl.com/nativeleaders/americanhorse.html

an excellent site. American Horse (Wasechun Tashunka) was chief of a band of the Oglala Sioux. He kept his people out of war. As a young man, he did fight several battles against the army, even killing an officer with his war club.

59 Coppers

I have used the term *copper* throughout because it was common in that period, but unlike England where it was almost exclusive, in the US, many other terms were used in the 1880's. I also put these six coppers in blue suits like the NYC police of the period. I have no picture or reference to the uniforms of the Richmond County sheriff's department of the day, but I like the image of the Keystone Cops chasing the two men.

Bill Sweaney did direct the Cowboy Band from the beginning in 1883 to the end in 1913.

60 Garden

This first version of The Garden at Madison Square (now Madison Park) was a mess not fit for much of anything except a circus. PT Barnum leased the Garden, and he either used it or rented it for eleven years. That structure was torn replaced in 1890. The first formal name appears to be The Garden, but it also seems to have been called by several names, including Madison Square Garden. The current Garden (#4) is nearly ten blocks north along Broadway (built on top of the old Penn Station with active rail lines underneath), but still carries the Madison name.

Before Barnum and Bailey merged their circuses, Barnum and others worked together at different times. The Adam Foropaugh Circus was one of the biggest in the 1880's. The two cooperated in 1886 because the Garden could house both and their shows complemented each other more than competed.

The last show at Erastina was September 30, and they did have to wait for the Garden, but I don't know how long.

61 Celebration

The National League ended the season in this order: Chicago White Stockings 90-34; Detroit Wolverines 87-36; New York Giants 75-44; Philadelphia Quakers 71-43; Boston Beaneaters 56-61; St. Louis Maroons 43-79; Kansas City Cowboys 30-91; Washington Nationals 28-92.

The Chicago White Stockings began in 1870, changed their name to the Colts, then the Cubs. They missed two years after the Chicago fire of 1871. The Giants survive today having begun life as The Gothams in 1883, and then moving to San Francisco in 1958. The Philadelphia Quakers also began in 1883. They were nicknamed the Phillies that year and officially changed to that Phillies in 1890. The Boston Beaneaters started as the Boston Red Stockings before the National League formed and included them as charter members. They changed the name that year but kept the color red. They went through several name changes until they settled on Boston Braves. They moved to Milwaukee and then Atlanta as the Braves. The St. Louis Maroons became the Indonapiolas Hoosiers the next year and folded in 1889. The Washington Nationals also died in 1889. The Kansas City Cowboys closed in 1886.

The World Championship Series occurred as described. The American Association was not the same as the American League nor was the World Championship the same as the World Series. In 1901, The American League became an equal of the National League and the first World Series was played in 1903. There is a debate about the oldest surviving team in baseball. Choose between Chicago Cubs or Atlanta Braves. Contrary to logic, the White Sox was a new team in 1901 and the Chicago White Stockings was renamed the Chicago Cubs in 1906. Confused? That's baseball. Even more confusing, the White Sox were originally named The Chicago White Stockings, but the newly named Chicago Cubs would not allow the American League entry to use the word *Chicago* as part of their name.

The dedication of the Statue of Liberty was a massive event. The parade through NYC did experience the first recorded ticker tape celebration. Cody did rent the *Staten Island Ferryboat* for his crew.

62 Indoor

I do not know for sure how the animals were transported to the Garden, but it is likely they were loaded on the boxcars at Erastina to ride all the way to the Garden.

The Forepaugh Circus left the tents at the Garden for the winter, with Cody paying rent.

The Dead Rabbits and Bowery Boys did rule much of NYC in the mid-1800's. The Whyos mostly replaced them. The Bowery Boys are not to be confused with the comic movies of the 1950's.

Mike McGiloin did hang for murder, and had been the leader of the Whyos.

63 Newspapers

Steele Mackaye wrote the four act entertainment and Cody added the short fifth act. Jerry did go off script and did kick an Indian into the seats, most likely the $12 box seats.

The million customers at Staten Island and million at the Garden are the numbers of record.

I did not find any details on room and board for the stars and crew. They may have maintained the show kitchen at the Garden and probably the concessions for the customers as well. I decided to put them in hotels and apartments for lack of information.

All of the newspapers listed were published then and dozens more besides.

The second Croton Aqueduct was as described. It stood where the New York Public Library, with its lions, is now. Bits and pieces of the aqueduct system can be seen today all around NYC and points north.

Grand Central has changed since 1886, but it is still in the same location.

64 Sick

65 Memories

66 Beecher

The story of the revolution in Hawaii and deposing King Kalakaua is substantially correct. Missionaries were at the heart of it for financial reasons.

Henry Ward Beecher was one of the tireless champions of the underdogs in America. His sister was Harriet Beecher Stowe. The quotes in this chapter are his.

The apple incident with Jerry and the sleigh did happen and did cost $5. Remember, that was a week's income in those days, though not for Annie.

The cost of the show is well documented in later years, but the incomplete records of 1883-87 make the $7,000 number only a little suspect. It is in line with later records. Also, the cost at Staten Island was probably different from the cost at the Garden, which had to be rented. It is known that attendance was significantly reduced around Christmas to the end of the run. Twelve dollar box seats could be had for a dollar in those weeks.

67 Dawes

The death of sixteen buffalo with no other animals affected has never been explained.

The information and quotes about the Dawes Act is accurate. Remmy sides with the Indians in the whole affair, as do I. The result was the sale of some 66 million acres to whites. But the law had many aspects to it and some websites provide more detail. When oil was discovered in abundance on Indian lands in Oklahoma (statehood 1907, no longer IT) other laws were developed to rake off most of the money from the oil *owned* by Indians.

Chief Jack Red Cloud was with the show, but I do not know much about him.

68 Closed

February 22 was the last show in New York before the London trip. The Wild West did sail on the *State of Nebraska.*

The items about Beecher came from news reports regarding his death.

Cody was generous in gift giving, much like Elvis and other stars of today.

69 Wrestling

Dwight Lyman Moody remained at home all summer in 1887 hosting the Northfield Conferences. He rarely traveled in the summer, preferring to remain at his home in Northfield, Massachusetts. However, I wanted him to add his message for Remmy, so I created a fiction. Moody was 50 that year.

Moody was a powerful speaker, which was necessary in the days without microphones and amplifiers. He was willing to talk with people, but refused to allow compliments about himself. He always turned away when that happened.

To get a sense of the importance of DL Moody in 1887, consider the importance of Billy Graham in 1987.

Sankey was 46 that year.

Ira Sankey singing The Ninety and Nine the historic 1898 recording of his most popular song.

https://www.youtube.com/watch?v=ACqeqjLRCCo

Do note that Moody's words in the story came from me and not from his sermons, though I doubt that he would disagree too much.

There were a number of different types of paper currency in the period; the two gold-backs mentioned are unusual and rare today.

70 Congregational

The Coates House and Opera House were located at 10th and Broadway.

Rev. Henry Hopkins, Doctor of Divinity, was the minister of the Congregational Church that year.

71 Follow

Louis Lingg did blow himself up and we still do not know who supplied the dynamite. The rest is a direct quote.

72 Arrest

73 Hopkins

74 Why?

75 Plan

I was lucky enough to eat at the Harvey House in Union Station in Kansas City before it closed. I am sure it would have looked different in 1888.

76 Stranded

The first of two massive blizzards in 1888 is often called the Children's Blizzard because it struck Nebraska after sunrise January 12. The children went to school in 50° weather, so they wore lightweight winter clothes. The storm struck with a combination of below zero temps (as low as -40°, a 90° drop) and winds over sixty miles an hour. That makes for a wind chill of -91°. Hundreds of people froze and hundreds more suffered frostbite. One of the country schools had the roof blown off, but Minnie Freeman managed to lead all her students to safety. The storm came out of Alberta with the front itself traveling one hundred miles an hour. The forward movement of the storm slowed but still crossed Nebraska and Kansas in one day.

The storm killed most of the remaining cattle in the northern plains, many having already died in the 1886 blizzard and the 1887 drought. The Blizzard of '88 finally put an end to the open range system everywhere but Texas as cattlemen put up fences and mowed hay to story for winter feeding. Modern cowboys spend their time mending fences and putting up hay.

To fit the story, I have pushed the facts somewhat. Mostly, the storm had lost much of its punch by the time it hit Neosho County, though the extreme temperature drop was still a killer and there was plenty of snow.

The other 1888 blizzard struck the Northeast March 11-14, hitting NYC the hardest with drifts as high as fifty feet. As a result of the storm, the city decided to move electrical power and the train system underground.

77 Light

Having used the case of the Sell family murders to begin this book, I have ended it with another true event in Neosho County; an all-too-familiar account of a couple caught is a blizzard without enough fuel to survive. They were discovered frozen in their cabin, having burned all the wooden items in the house, hoping to outlast the storm.

Chapter one of *Brotherly Love*, the sequel to *Dark Snow.*

Standing on the porch of what had once been my home, I watched the eastern sky lighten with the approaching sun. Behind me were the frozen bodies of my aunt and uncle, the man who had killed my family and tried to kill me. The two-year quest to find him was complete, but I sensed another odyssey ahead.

The drifting clouds separated at the horizon, allowing a burst of red sunlight to filter through the denuded trees and paint the deep snow a soft pink. With that beautiful reminder of my lost home, I turned away to begin a new life.

Having discovered two people dead at the hands of the Blizzard of '88, I should have gone to Erie to tell the sheriff, but I walked the opposite direction, to Mission and the cabin of my friend, Jim Bighorse. I would not face the sheriff who'd posted my name as the murderer of my family. I sent him a telegram regarding my discovery. He would have to come to me if he needed more from me.

Yet, I could not avoid Erie altogether. The court decided that my uncle obtained the farm by illegal means—namely murdering my family—and that I was the rightful heir to the property. While I did not disagree with the decision, I had no interest in keeping the farm. I arranged to sell it to a neighbor, and entered the courthouse to have the transaction properly registered. The result was a windfall of $480, blood money to my mind.

It belonged to my parents, because the farm was theirs. I could in no way consider using it myself. If I spent it on myself, I would become like the killer. I knew it was irrational, but the feeling was too strong to ignore. Still, what to do with it?

Many ideas came to mind, but the only one I was comfortable with was some kind of memorial to my family.

Not a stone with their name, but rather some worthwhile program, something like the Mission where Osage children could learn to read and write. I would have given it to the school, but Jim told me they planned to close it in a few years because it was too far away from the homes of the Osage, now that they lived in Indian Territory.

An idea surfaced as I considered some other option. My parent's lives before the time of my birth did not exist for me; why not track down their families and get to know my parents before there was a me? Days later, it was the only idea still standing, so I puzzled out a way to make it happen.

When I said I knew nothing of my parent's early life, I was not understating the case. I had a vague notion that they might have come west from Pennsylvania, and that was it. I know I was born in a wagon west of St. Louis, but my only memories were of the farm and a couple of miles around it.

Where to start?

I did have a letter, which proved to be the key to unlocking the mystery, a mystery way beyond my parents' stories. The letter was an introduction to any agents of the Pinkerton's National Detective Agency, written by Tom Gibson, former Pinkerton and current head of security for Buffalo Bill's Wild West. Having spent most of a year with Cody, Annie Oakley, and all the other great people of that show, they helped prepare me to face the daunting task of finding the murderer of my family. Tom, who had helped keep me alive through the several attempts on my life, had told me he thought I had the makings of a detective. At the time, I'd simply smiled and thanked him. Now I knew he might be right.

By the middle of March, all the paperwork was completed; a $480 cashier's check was in my hand as was a train ticket to Kansas City. If there was no Pinkerton office there, I knew the headquarters was in Chicago. One way or another, I would first become a Pinkerton and then use that knowledge to find my parents. I did not know that I would not find the parents I expected.

Mike Lawrence is a retired history teacher and lifelong Kansan. He lives with his wife in Neosho County where the story begins. Three of his four children live in Kansas City and one in Chicago. When he is not writing his books, including *Brotherly Love*, the sequel to *Dark Snow*, or his blog—mikhaeltheteacher.com— he takes trips to Haiti, rebuilds houses, and tries to harvest a garden before the deer to eat it.

www.ingramcontent.com/pod-product-compliance
Lightning Source LLC
LaVergne TN
LVHW010602100826
845148LV00014B/2810

* 9 7 8 0 6 9 2 6 1 5 4 2 3 *